CRITICS AR
KATHLEE
CALAM

GHOULS JUST WANT TO HAVE FUN

"An enjoyable, easygoing mystery... A slight touch of the paranormal gives this title a nice twist."

—*...iews*

"[A] hilariously funny story with a hint of suspense and my favorite heroine, Tressa "Calamity" Jayne Turner doing what she does best.... Get ready for a roaring good time when you open up *Ghouls Just Want to Have Fun*."

—*Romance Reviews Today*

CALAMITY JAYNE RIDES AGAIN

"With potential wacky disasters lurking around every corner, Bacus takes readers on a madcap journey through Tressa's world of zany characters and intrigue... A cute comedy infused with a light mystery in a fun, small-town setting, this novel is enjoyable."

—*RT BOOKreviews*

CALAMITY JAYNE

"Bacus's riotous romantic suspense debut offers plenty of small-town charm and oddball characters... Filled with dumb-blonde jokes, nonstop action and rapid-fire banter, this is a perfect read for chick-lit fans who enjoy a dash of mystery."

—*Publishers Weekly*

"Frothy and fun..."

—*RT BOOKreviews*

"Making her entrance into the world of romance with a story full of mishaps, danger, and well-crafted characters, Kathleen Bacus does a superb job with *Calamity Jayne*. This reviewer can't wait for more..."

—*Romance Reviews Today*

THE FINAL QUESTION

Townsend waved a hand in my face. "Spare me. I've heard all about the Carson College crime wave, your journalism project, your tanking grades, the tailing of a registered sex offender. It's always something with you, Tressa. A body in a trunk. A psycho clown. A reclusive writer. A campus criminal. I feel powerless to protect you."

He made it sound as if I'd gone out and campaigned to be in the wrong place at the wrong time.

"We've got a big problem here, Calamity," he said.

"We do?" I asked.

Townsend put a hand on each of my shoulders and took another look at my lips before his gaze switched to meet mine. "I think I may be falling in love with you, Tressa Jayne Turner," he said. "The problem? I'm not sure I want to."

CALAMITY JAYNE
GOES TO COLLEGE

KATHLEEN BACUS

LOVE SPELL NEW YORK CITY

For Katie, my first
reader this time around. Thanks,
sweetie! You did a bang-up job.
And for Nick, who, along with
Tressa Jayne, headed off to
college—we miss you, bud.

LOVE SPELL®

April 2007

Published by

Dorchester Publishing Co., Inc.
200 Madison Avenue
New York, NY 10016

ISBN-10: 0-505-52701-4
ISBN-13: 978-0-505-52701-1

The name "Love Spell" and its logo are trademarks of Dorchester Publishing Co., Inc.

Printed in the United States of America.

Visit us on the web at www.dorchesterpub.com.

CALAMITY
JAYNE
GOES TO COLLEGE

CHAPTER 1

Rick and Tressa are sitting in Catholic school. Tressa is sleeping and the teacher, realizing this, asks her a question: "Tressa, who created Heaven and Earth?" Rick sees Tressa is sleeping and, meaning to help out, quickly pokes her with a sharp pencil.

"Jesus Christ Almighty!" exclaims Tressa.

"Correct," says the teacher, surprised.

The next day, the same incident occurs and the same question comes up. "Who created Heaven and Earth?" asks the teacher.

Tressa—again sleeping—is poked by Rick's pencil. "Jesus Christ Almighty!" she exclaims.

"Correct again," says the disgruntled teacher.

The next day, for a third time, the teacher sees Tressa snoozing. She decides to trick Tressa and asks a different question: "What did Eve say to Adam after their fifteenth child?"

Tressa, poked by Rick's pencil once again, this time

screams, "If you stick that thing in me one more time, I am going to crack it in half!"

Hi. My name is Tressa Jayne Turner. I should tell you up front that I never attended Catholic school. (The "Rick" I referred to, however, did—and does—exist. And the name has not been changed to protect the innocent.) I'm a dubious poster child for public school education. I should also admit here that I probably would have benefited from attending a school where you wore uniforms and the educators were allowed to rap your knuckles with a ruler and slap you upside the head just to make sure you were paying attention. I slept through more high school credits than my gramma does TV newscasts. Not that that's something I like to crow about, but there you have it. You get the point: School and I weren't what you'd call simpatico.

It wasn't that I hated school exactly. I just didn't like the early class times, the course material, the administration, some of the faculty members, and all those really silly rules. You know, like no dodge ball at recess. They even outlawed Red Rover, Red Rover because Dorky Donnie Douglas got clotheslined during one session and bruised his windpipe!

In junior high, there were all those lovely little after-school detentions if you were tardy. I got to know the janitors real well. And in high school? Well, they had no sense of humor at all when it came to being late for class. It was like baseball: Three strikes and "YOUR-RRE OUT!"

Then there was that ridiculous rule about bringing food into the classroom. What a joke! Like some pathetic prohibition was going to stop me from sneaking in contraband Twinkies and candy bars? It was a no-brainer to get around. They don't make that handy dandy pouch in the front of a hoodie for nothing, right?

Last but not least, there was that pesky bit about staying awake in class. It got to the point where teachers requested I bring disinfectant spray so I could de-drool and sanitize the desktops at the end of each period. Sigh.

Yes, I was the kind of student whose parents got real used to seeing the notation STUDENT NEEDS TO APPLY HIM/HERSELF on report cards. Guess they didn't have a drop-down selection with STUDENT DOESN'T GIVE A RIP on those computerized reports, huh?

Despite my difficulties, I did manage to avoid total, abject humiliation, and received my high school diploma along with my classmates by means of some summer school sessions and a mother who threatened to take away my livestock if I didn't graduate on time. Talk about your motivation! I ended up with a GPA and class ranking that, while they didn't result in colleges beating a path to my door begging me to attend their fine institutions, did get me a lot of attention from recruiters for the various branches of the armed services. I considered a stint in the military for a bit . . . until I got a look at the shoes they have to wear. And camouflage is so not my color.

I live in small-town Iowa—just FYI, we grow corn and soybeans here, folks, not spuds—and I've achieved some level of . . . shall we say "notoriety" in the last several months—purely by accident and happenstance, you understand. You see, stuff has a way of happening to me. A lot of stuff. I have the nickname to prove it. Thanks to a certain Department of Natural Resources officer who has invested an inordinate amount of time and energy messing with my head—

okay, and at times my body, too—I was dubbed "Calamity Jayne" at about the same time I was learning how *not* to ride a bike—feet on handlebars and hands on pedals is not so safe, I found out—and discovering that not only was skirt-wearing not recommended when playing on the swing set, but-skirt-wearing in general was something to be avoided at all costs. Especially when one was a bit of a tomboy, loved to ride horses and climb trees and romp with puppy dogs. (Okay, so I still love to do all those things. What can I say? I'm a free spirit.)

By the time I was in second grade, my mother had given up on outfitting me in anything with a frill, ruffle, or bow, except for on Sundays when I was forced to wear my "girl clothes" to go and sleep in church. (I gladly left all "little princess" trappings to my younger sister, Taylor. She looked the part. She still does, as a matter of fact.) To be honest, on Sundays I generally ended up looking like Little Orphan Annie playing dress-up after her dog, Sandy, took her for a run though a thicket.

Your basic "girlie girl" I wasn't. While cowboy boots may be a great fashion accessory when you're twenty-three, an almost rodeo queen, and finally (I hope!) coming into your own, wearing boots with shorts and skirts in elementary school was just looking for trouble. As if I ever needed to look.

My time in middle school was no less bumpy, but luckily I found sports—or they found me—and that kept me operating just well enough to avoid the ineligible list. Most of the time. It was in middle school that I also learned I perform better at individual sports. (Something about getting along well with others.)

By high school I had adopted a bit of a rebel-without-a-cause identity—developed in response to chronic harassment from that certain rangerly friend of my brother who went on to become too good-looking for my own good, an ever-growing series of misadventures, and a reputation for being a bit of a nonconformist . . . as well as someone to avoid during an electrical storm. Or at weddings. (I'll explain the latter later.)

From then on there seemed to be no turning back. I was a hormone-driven, harmlessly rebellious, cock-eyed cowgirl with a turbocharged motor mouth. And believe me, I wasn't afraid to use it. With a superjock older brother and a beautiful brainiac younger sister, I found comfort and safety in mediocrity. And the mouthiness, you're wondering? I'm blaming that one on genetics, folks. My gramma is known as Hellion Hannah, if that helps explain things.

Truth be told, I saw myself as a kinder, gentler—and female—version of James Dean. Oh, I have a soft, gooey center, but I just wasn't comfortable showing it all that often. For me, showing feelings was like being caught with your pants down. You know, uncomfortably exposed. At a distinct disadvantage. I am slowly learning how to embrace the inner me and to pursue my destiny in a confident, mature manner. Dr. Phil and Oprah have counseled me during this ongoing process, so I have high hopes that I will figure it all out before I have to sign up for Social Security benefits or croak, whichever comes first. But with my history, which includes matching wits with murderers, playing hide-and-seek on a carnival midway with psycho dunk tank clowns, and pursuing reclusive authors in houses only Norman Bates could love, I'm not bettin' the farm on makin' it to retirement age. Still, one has to plan ahead.

This financial planning was what compelled me to drop in to college for the fourth time after three previously unsuccessful attempts to expand my cranium tanked big time. To be fair, I do have to add that at the time of those earlier collegiate experiences, I was still searching for that inner self I mentioned earlier. My niche. You know, what I wanted to be when I grew up.

Through the process of elimination I had discovered what I *wasn't* supposed to do with my life: One, veterinary medicine. (I just can't inflict hurt on an animal even in the name of healing.) Two, psychology. While I'm totally into Dr. Phil, I discovered I don't have the stomach to sit and wait for anyone's response to the question "Tell me how that makes you feel." Blech. I'm thinkin' I'm more of a "Suck it up, Nancy," kind of therapist. As you might have gathered, I don't deal comfortably with emotions. Or mushy love stuff. Oh, or diets. Sigh.

There was also my short-lived stint as a massage therapist. Unfortunately, the reality of rubbing oil on some stranger's naked body for a living grossed me out more than I anticipated. Ah, she has intimacy issues, you're thinking. I see you watch Dr. Phil, too. Good for you.

With a string of dead-end jobs behind me—well, maybe not exactly behind me yet, but I have high hopes—I finally found a vocation where I could utilize my skills. Okay, so maybe being a Nosy Nellie type isn't exactly a job skill you can include on a résumé, but it does come in handy as a newspaper reporter. Which was what I became. Well, at least part of the time. Off and on. Now and then. I'd been rehired for the third time at the *Grandville Gazette*, my hometown newspaper—the only hometown newspaper—less than a year earlier when I'd been a key figure in a homegrown whodunit. My writing skills were adequate and, for once, being a magnet for chaos was a point in my favor. Like, who knew?

Stan Rodgers, my boss at the *Gazette*, and I had discussed compensation issues last fall after I'd sniffed out the goods on a famous chiller/thriller author who'd turned Houdini. Stan had agreed to give me a raise and benefits if I got some college journalism courses under my belt. He'd even offered to pick up half the cost of tuition after I threatened to proffer my nose for news to his closest competitor and biggest rival, the *New Holland News*. I jumped at the chance.

I enrolled at Carson College in nearby Des Moines for the spring term, taking Basic Reporting Principles and Investigative Journalism. Despite the lure of higher pay and the perk of health insurance bennies, I discovered it wasn't any easier this time around. It was high school all over again, with one notable difference: This time I was paying for it. Kinda. Sort of.

It was the same old, same old:

Tressa struggling to get to class on time.

"Tressa?"

Tressa struggling to stay awake in class.

"Tressa?"

Tressa struggling to get her homework done.

"Tressa!"

I blinked and looked up from my spiral notebook to find my fellow students staring at me, along with Professor Stokes, who, I gotta tell you, looks way too much like Saddam Hussein for my peace of mind.

"Present," I responded, no clue what the journalism

instructor wanted since I'd been spacing off for the last ten minutes.

The classroom snickered.

"I was inquiring as to what you've decided on as the topic for your investigative report," the professor said. "As you no doubt recall, this paper will serve as a huge part of your final grade, so it's extremely important to pick something that you can sink your teeth into." He took a long look at the candy wrappers on my desk. "Journalistically speaking, of course," he added.

Oh, buddy, Tressa Jayne was not going to earn her little gold star for the day. I'd completely forgotten today was the day we were scheduled to get our topics approved by Saddam—uh—Stokes. I didn't have clue one what to suggest as a topic for investigation. All of my previous journalistic coups had basically found me, not the other way around. And somehow I didn't think a piece on how long the new gaucho pants trend would last or a debate of the state guidelines pertaining to the handling and application of livestock manure in an environmentally friendly way constituted the hard-hitting, gritty investigative report the good professor had in mind.

"Uh, well, you know . . . actually I've already kind of, like, done this assignment," I told the man standing at the podium and looking at me as if I were an infidel. (Which I suppose is always possible. I'm not quite sure of the meaning of that word, but it seems to get thrown around a lot lately.) "After all," I continued, "I did break the Elizabeth Courtney Howard story."

The professor gave me a hard look. "Yesterday's news, Miss Turner," he responded. "We don't recycle old headlines for final grades here at Carson. We require current, topical events. You know. *New* news."

I wondered who the "we" was that he was talking about, but decided it was safer not to ask.

"Yes, Professor," I said, sensing a promised brand-spanking-new office desk and ergonomically designed leather chair slipping away from me. "But, you see, I have this best friend who is getting married this coming Saturday and I'm her maid of honor. She went with dusty blue and peach for her colors," I felt compelled to add for some strange reason. My friend, Kari, had selected peach for my dress. With the holiday weight I'd packed on, I'd sure look ripe for the picking. I just prayed there wasn't any kneeling involved or I'd split my peel. "As the maid of honor, I've had to do some heavy-duty hand-holding and snot wiping to get my friend to this point. You all know how emotional brides can be."

Emotional? Try mercurial. The same woman who could handle a roomful of middle school students without breaking a sweat had become apoplectic when she discovered the mints were not a perfect match to the flowers and napkins.

"Not to mention the best man is the same grooms-man who gave me an extreme wedgie at my brother's wedding," I told the class. "And I dropped a little smokie dripping with barbecue sauce down the front of my dress. I ended up with all side poses in the wedding pictures, and believe me, it's harder to hold in your gut through a marathon photo session than you'd—"

"Thank you for sharing, Miss Turner," Professor Stokes said with a tight smile, "but unless you're planning an article on prenuptial stress or how to remove cocktail wiener stains or wedgies, we're still waiting for your topic selection."

The class roared with laughter. Who knew Saddam had a sense of humor?

I quickly typed out up a short throw-me-a-line-I'm-going-under-Lord plea for inspiration, hit my send-to-Heaven key, and fidgeted a second while waiting for a response.

"Miss Turner?"

Heaven's server must have been down because I wasn't receiving any divine reply.

"Uh, you said we needed to tell you today, right?" I stalled.

"That's correct."

"Technically, 'today' ends at eleven fifty-nine and fifty-nine seconds or thereabouts, right?"

The professor hesitated. "I suppose that's technically correct," he agreed.

"So, technically, I have until midnight tonight to get the proposal to you? Right?"

I was really grasping at straws. The chances that I would miraculously find a newsworthy story to investigate by that evening were roughly the same as me being able to get into the bridesmaid gown I'd already had let out twice (please don't snitch on me to Kari) without requiring me to wear an all-over elastic undergarment to flatten the fat. Have I mentioned that weddings give me a great deal of anxiety? When I'm anxious, I eat. A lot. Okay, so I eat a lot when I'm not anxious, too. Still, about the dress alteration? It's our little secret. Okay?

"And you think the additional"—the professor looked at his watch—"fourteen hours will give you sufficient time to select your topic?" he asked.

I nodded. "I'm almost sure," I said. "In fact, I guarantee you I'll e-mail it to you before the stroke of midnight," I told him. Or Tressa Jayne Turner would turn back into a minimum wage worker with no bennies and a shoe itch she could never scratch.

Professor Stokes removed his glasses and rubbed his forehead. Why do people do that around me so frequently?

"Very well, Miss Turner," he acquiesced. "By the stroke of midnight it is. However, if I don't receive your topic choice, I'll have no alternative but to drop your project a full grade."

I gulped. I was hovering around a C– right now. Holding down several jobs, taking care of a small herd of horseflesh and two yellow labs who love to romp and play, keeping tabs on a seventy-year-old grandmother who had taken up residence with me to escape her "captors," as well as reassuring a best friend in the throes of prewedding mania had a tendency to cut into one's study time.

"Roger that," I said. "Midnight it is," I added, sensing the amused smirks of my classmates. Good thing I'd had some experience with this sort of thing or it could really have affected my self-esteem. Instead I gave them all a wide-eyed *I'm blonde and I'm proud* look and batted my mascaraed eyelashes. "Isn't he just the sweetest thing?" I said, gathering up my books. "And I'm going to just knock his argyle socks off with my final article," I told the other students. "Just blow him away."

The bell sounded, signaling the end of class. Whew. Dodged that bullet. For now. I started to gather up my books.

"Tick-tick, Turner. Hear that?"

"Huh?" I looked up to see fellow student and teacher's pet Ramona Quimby—I mean, Ramona Drake—standing beside my desk. I *so* have a problem with perky brunettes. Especially ones who put other people down to make themselves feel superior. Ramona first came to my attention when she pointed out during class, quite unnecessarily I might add, that I snored like a fat old woman with sleep apnea. Since then, I've made it a point to keep my distance. Not that I'm intimidated by her, you understand, I just don't want to get on Professor Stokes's bad side any more than I already am by taking my dog-grooming tools to the rottweiler Romana.

"Tick-tick. Time is ticking away. Tressa, Tressa, Tressa—you can admit it. For all your PR, you really are scratching at thin air, aren't you, you poor dear?" Ramona gave me a look designed to appear sympathetic but wasn't. "I'm working up a piece on teenaged prostitution rings at our truck stops and what drives these young girls to that life," she told me. "If you like, maybe I could help you out. You know, suggest something suitable. Hmmm. Let's see. How about an insider's look at the ice cream business? You know. Hard-packed versus soft-serve. Pros and cons?" She laughed and punched my arm.

Ho-ho. Whaddaya know? We had a regular Sandra Bernhardt here.

One of my three current jobs was working at my uncle Frank's Dairee Freeze business. It was in this capacity, hawking ice cream confections at the state fair in August, that I set out to nail a soft-serve saboteur, and in the process met a really dishy state trooper who actually liked me for me. I'm still trying to figure out what's wrong with that picture.

"Or maybe you could conduct an in-depth study of what exactly goes into a hot dog?" Ramona continued. "I hear it can be pretty disgusting. And there's always another 'unsafe at any speed' spin off. You know, a look at junk cars motoring down our state's highways and byways." She paused and put an apologetic hand to her mouth. "Oh, you don't still drive that infamous white Plymouth, do you? The one we read about in the papers last summer ad nauseum?

I did and she knew it.

"I carpool with friends," I told her, which was also true. I shared rides from Grandville with my cousin Frankie, who had enrolled in criminal justice courses after he'd had a date with destiny last summer and decided that a career in law enforcement was where it was at. He'd also decided he was in love with a five-foot-five-inch barrel with legs, his father's soft-serve competitor, Dixie Daggett. Dixie had taken together-ness one step further, registering for classes in criminal justice right along with her fiancé. We usually picked Dixie up from the Daggett digs in Des Moines and hauled her—uh, sorry, this sounds like transporting livestock, but if you knew Dixie—to classes at Carson, which translated into a very long car ride several times a week for Tressa.

Dixie and I didn't exactly jibe. We're like oil and vinegar. Insects and Deet. Nair and hair. Dixie and I are attempting to overcome our mutual hostility for Frankie's sake, so give us an A for effort. Though, maybe an A is stretching it. After all, just this morning Dixie informed me my hair looked like a small critter had crawled into it and made a nest, and urged me to pull it back in a ponytail so she wouldn't have to look at it all the way to Des Moines afraid that something would crawl back out again. I requested she do the same with her own hair—on her arms. Sigh. Old habits die hard, folks.

"Oh? You have friends? That go to school *here*, I mean?" Ramona asked.

I nodded. "My cousin is taking courses in criminal justice. He plans to go into law enforcement," I told her with a take-that-toots tilt of my nose.

"Uh, is there something wrong with your neck?" Ramona asked.

Note to Tressa: Nuke the nose move. It's not workin' for you, girl.

"Speaking of Frankie, I'm sure he's out there cooling his heels waiting for me," I told her. "And I wouldn't like to keep a future officer of the law waiting," I added.

"Is he that tall, gangly guy with all those sharp, bony edges?" Ramona asked. "Don't they have a weight requirement for peace officers?"

God, I hoped not, or Frankie would never meet the minimum. I frowned. I also wondered if they had a separate height/weight chart for barrels.

"Frankie's tougher than he looks. He played a pivotal role in exposing a criminal element at the state fair," I bragged. "And he was dressed as a chicken at the time," I added.

Ramona blinked. A lot. That's another response I receive more often than I'd like.

"Well, good luck finding your article, Tressa. Toodle-loo!" She waved and bounced out of the lecture hall.

I followed at a safe distance, not trusting myself within yanking distance of her shiny, silky hair, or to resist the temptation to draw a pitchfork on her white Aéropostale hoodie with my black permanent marker.

I waited until Ramona was out of sight before I proceeded to the parking lot and my old white Plymouth Reliant. We shared quite a history, this ol' car and me. We'd been through some twists and turns but always managed to stay on course. Which is not to say that I didn't secretly yearn for a shiny red sports car with leather interior and a bitchin' sound system.

I jumped in the Reliant and pulled my sweatshirt up around my shoulders. March had come in like an albino lion, dropping a foot of snow on grass that was just starting to green up. Over the last couple of weeks we'd lost the snow, but the days were still chilly and damp. I was hoping for a warm-up in time for next week's spring break. I wanted to spend some quality time with my critters and lie outside in the sun and pretend I was snoozing on a white sand beach somewhere in the Caribbean, Orlando Bloom tickling my nose with one of those tiny umbrellas you find in exotic fruity drinks.

I heard voices behind me, prepared to look in the rearview mirror, then remembered it had fallen off months ago—which in turn made me recall Ramona's "unsafe cars" article suggestion. I bit my tongue to keep from letting fly with a really bad word. I yanked my key out of my pocket, and jabbed it in the ignition, turning the car on just as the passenger-side door flew open.

"You aren't gonna freakin' believe this!" Frankie said, folding his long limbs into the front seat of the Plymouth. His fiancée levered her girth into the back.

"What? Has Dixie the Destructor finally found a depilatory that works?" I asked, still ticked at his fiancée's earlier disdain for my coiffeur. Is it my fault I have hair that thinks kink is an actual salon style?

"I was thinking maybe you'd found a miracle comb that actually makes it through that mane of yours without getting lost," she said. "You have horses. Ever consider using their curry comb?"

"You ever consider using their fly repellent? It's called Wipe, and is available at fine veterinary clinics everywhere," I remarked. "It works wonders keeping flies away."

"I'm sure you know from personal experience," Dixie replied.

"Would you two just button it? This is really intriguing stuff. We've got one hell of a crime spree going on right here on campus," Frankie announced, removing his glasses when they began to fog up.

"What are you talking about, Frankie?" I asked. "What crime spree?"

"Where have you been all term?" he asked. I flinched.

"Uh, who have you been talking to?" I responded. "Ramona the Woofer?"

Frankie gave me a funny look.

"Haven't you heard about the rash of crimes that have been committed on campus?" Frankie went on. "Vandalism. Malicious mischief. Break-ins. Thefts!"

Okay, so maybe I had caught some shut-eye off and on and had missed these events. I was way overextended. I shrugged. "So? It's a college campus, Frankie. There's bound to be crime. That's what they have those campus police people for. You know, the ones who should be catching criminals but aren't allowed to carry revolvers and instead waste their time writing parking tickets." And I had a decent collection to prove it.

"Ah, but this is no regular crime spree," Frankie added. I could tell by the tiny bubble of saliva collecting at the corner of his mouth that Frankie's juices were flowing.

"What do you mean?" I asked.

"What he means, Blondie, is that every time our criminal law professor introduces a new crime and highlights the elements of that offense, that same crime is committed that very night—right here on the hallowed grounds of Carson College," Dixie explained.

I grabbed my rearview mirror from the floor of my car and held it up, catching Dixie's reflection in the clouded glass. And I didn't even wince. "Are you serious?" I asked. I looked over at Frankie. "Is she serious?" I asked him.

He nodded. "That's the way it looks—at least to Dixie and me. I don't think anyone else has made the connection, though. We kind of stumbled on it ourselves after we heard about the mugging last night."

"Mugging?" I grabbed Frankie's arm. "Crime spree! Ohmigawd! Frankie! Do you know what this means?" I asked.

"That by day this campus harbors a mild-mannered, book-bag-carrying college student, but by night a psycho serial stalker wanders in search of his next victim?"

I beamed. "Exactly," I said. "Oh, Frankie!" I reached across to give my confused cousin a big bear hug. "You've made me so happy!"

CHAPTER 2

I turned to share my enthusiasm with Dixie, realized what I was about to do, and settled for flashing her a thumbs-up.

"You are so weird," she said and shook her head.

I drove the three of us to the student union for a bite to eat, wanting to hear more about Frankie's class and why he and Unibrow thought there was a connection between recent crimes on campus and his instructor's lesson plans. And there was the added bonus that Frankie had arranged to meet my most favorite policeman in the entire world, Trooper P.D. Dawkins, there to discuss the upcoming screening process for candidates applying for the next Public Safety Academy.

How should I describe Patrick Dawkins? The first things I noticed were his amazing blue eyes. Clear, bright, and glorious as an Iowa lake in midsummer, they flashed like reflected sunlight when he laughed. What's that? You don't believe it was his eyes that first caught my attention? Okay, so I'll admit that his rather striking rear end wasn't exactly lost on me, either. But seriously, by far the most attractive quality about Patrick Dawkins was his natural inclination to accept me for who I was—and this right smack dab in the middle of one fine, sticky fair mess, I'll have you know. Up to that point, all the people in my life had been after me to change. To figure out what I wanted to do with myself. To stop acting one way and to start acting another. To get a job and keep it longer than a pair of shoes. Demands, demands. P.D. never once judged, second-guessed, or criticized me. He just plain liked me. For me. And that, I found, was very much of a turn-on.

"So what time did Patrick say he was going to meet you here?" I asked Frankie as I sat down at a table and tore into the Italian sub sandwich I'd bought.

"He said he'd ten-twenty-five me here at eleven hundred hours," Frankie replied.

I raised an eyebrow. "Good to know," I said through a mouthful of salami, Italian ham, and cheese. Shhh. Remember. What Kari doesn't know won't hurt me. "So, tell me again why you two think the on-campus criminal activity is linked to your Criminal Law course."

Frankie took a bite of his chicken salad croissant—he was in training for the physical agility and endurance portion of the academy application process—and wiped light mayo from his mouth with a napkin.

"We started out the term covering simple misdemeanors like littering, vandalism, trespass, et cetera, and then moved to serious and aggravated. Then we moved to the different classes of felonies and crimes that fell into each of those categories. It wasn't until today, when we learned that Friday night one of our classmates was assaulted, that we realized we'd gone over the elements of assault Friday in class. At first we thought it was just a coincidence, but then we got to backtracking and matching up crimes and lectures and dates, and a pattern emerged."

"By pattern you mean that the criminal acts committed here at Carson College this term were included in your professor's lectures? Are you *sure*?"

"As near as we can tell," Dixie said, taking a big bite out of her slice of pepperoni pizza. "It's been like this freaky crime wave predictor," she said.

"Or producer," I suggested. "Who is the professor?" I asked.

"Billings," Dixie said. "Barbara Billings."

I stopped chewing. "Isn't that the name of Beaver Cleaver's mom?" I asked.

Dixie shook her head. "That's Barbara Billings*ley,*" she said with a disgusted look. "This is Barbara Billings, and she used to be a Des Moines police officer back in the early eighties when women were first being recruited for law enforcement. You should hear some of the stories she tells. She took a hell of a lot of heat being one of the first women to break into the good ol' boys club. Not everyone agreed with affirmative action back then or thought women could hack it as uniformed peace officers."

I nodded, impressed. "I get it. Law enforcement's equivalent of Chris Columbus, Ferdinand Marcos, Lewis and Clark," I noted.

"That's Ferdinand Magellan, Einstein," Dixie the stickler for details snapped.

I shrugged. "Whatever. Just think of all the girl-sized

shiny black patent leather footsteps that followed after her. Now, there's a story for you," I said, thinking this could be the subject of a future article. "I'll need to speak with Professor Billings, of course."

Frankie's head jerked up. "What? Why?"

"Because I need to ask her some questions, silly," I said. "From what you've just told me, it's likely that the person who is committing these crimes is one of your classmates. How else would he or she know what crimes were discussed in class each day?" I reasoned. "So that should narrow our suspect field a bit," I said, then paused. "Just how many other students are in your Criminal Law course, anyway?" I asked.

Frankie's shoulders sagged. "Thirty-two," he said.

"Thirty-two! You gotta be freakin' kiddin' me!"

He shook his head. "It's a growing field. There are more jobs in law enforcement post Nine-Eleven," he said. "Homeland Security. Airport security. People like this kind of work. Good job security and excellent bennies."

Rub it in, Frankie. Rub it in.

"But, thirty-two! How are we going to zero in on a handful of suspects from that large a pool?" I asked. "Unless you've got some ideas of your own from sitting in class with them since the beginning of the term," I suggested.

"Well, if it isn't the notorious Calamity Jayne and her scholastic sidekicks!" I felt a hand on my shoulder and turned to see those beautiful baby blues I mentioned earlier smiling down at me. I blinked. A woman could drown in those depths. Happily. "Are we keeping the peace or disturbing it today?" Trooper Dawkins asked, pulling out the chair next to me and taking a seat.

"Now that you're here, what choice do we have but

to abide by the law?" I asked, coming up for air. "You're packin'." I pointed to his gun—a state-issued Smith & Wesson .44 auto. One learns these things when you hang out with the coppers. "And as for keeping the peace—well maybe you can help us out on that one, Super Trooper Dawkins," I added, batting my eyelashes over my own set of baby blues.

His eyebrows disappeared under the brim of his dark brown Smokey hat. "Are things going to get messy again, Calamity?" he asked.

I wrinkled my nose. "Only as messy as a piece of cake, Officer Dawkins," I responded, raising my little finger. "Pinky swear."

I explained the situation to Patrick, with added emphasis on how I was trying to resuscitate grades that were on their last legs (poor babies) and how busy I'd been with news, nuptials, new roomies, bosses, brides, and beasties. By the time I got to the end of my explanation, the trooper's eyes were beginning to glaze over. Then again, it could have been allergies.

"And you think there's a chance that the person committing these crimes is sitting in class right alongside you, taking notes on the finer points of criminal pathology?" he asked Frankie and Dixie.

"It sure looks that way," my cousin said.

"And you don't think anyone else has made the connection?" Patrick asked. "Campus police? Fellow students? The professor himself?"

"Herself," I inserted. "Professor Billings. Barbara Billings. Not Billingsley as in Beaver Cleaver's mom," I clarified.

Dawkins raised an eyebrow. "I know Barb."

I raised an eyebrow of my own. "Oh? 'Barb,' is it now?" I said.

Dawkins nodded. "As a matter of fact, I received some instruction from her myself."

"Law enforcement related, I trust," I said.

Patrick grinned. "Professor Billings is just slightly younger than my mother. What do you think?"

I batted my eyes some more. "What? You've never heard of a May/December romance?"

"Certainly," he said. "And maybe I'll even consider it—when I'm the December, that is," he added with a yummy grin.

"Uh, could we curtail this so-called flirting that is activating my gag reflex and get back to the business at hand?" Dixie injected. She aimed a sour look in my direction.

"Curtail?" I said. "Now, there's a post-secondary word if I ever heard one."

"Curtail. To curb. Inhibit. Rein in," Dixie offered. "As in 'rein in your mouth!' "

Ouch. Unibrow was on a roll.

"I'm pure impressed by yer gel's edgycation, young feller," I informed Frankie with a slap on his shoulder. "Us hillbilly types don't cotton to book learnin' much, but we's shore do like the sound of them thar big words comin' out of the pie holes of edgycated folks like yore sweetie pie over yonder. Do some more, lil' lady," I said. "Purty please."

"Screw you, Turner," Dixie growled. "And the hay-seed wagon you rode in on."

I shook my head. Some folks have no sense of humor. I turned my attention back to Patrick, who was much easier on the ol' retinas anyway.

"What we figure is there's a good chance the person committing these crimes has a rap sheet," I told the trooper.

"A criminal history," Frankie corrected.

"Whatever," I said. "So, you state poe-lice types have access to computerized databases that check for"—I gave Frankie a dark look before proceeding—"criminal histories, right?"

"Of course," Dawkins replied. "NCIC. CODIS. VI-CAP—"

"Yeah, yeah, okay, good, we get the point, Mr. Acronym," I said. "What we really need is a way to run these students through the system. You know. To find out if any of them have a record. You could do that, couldn't you, Trooper Dawkins?" I shifted my body in his direction, put my elbow on the table to rest my chin in my hand, and batted my eyes. "For me," I added. "After all we've been through, for old times' sake, because you like me for me—"

"Oh Gawd, I've died and gone straight to cliché hell," Dixie moaned.

What a coincidence. I was wishing her to perdition at that very moment.

Patrick removed his hat and ran his hand through his dark blond hair. It fell back neatly into place. So not fair.

"I have a dispatcher friend," he said, obviously having to take some time to think things through. Of course, I couldn't blame the poor dear for proceeding with extreme caution. First the fair fiasco and now this.

"I'm sure you do," I told him with a wicked leer.

He grinned. "We'd need dates of birth. How many are we talking about?" he finally asked. "Ten? Fifteen at the most?"

I looked at Frankie and he looked at me.

"Thirty-two," my cousin said.

"Thirty-two!" The trooper let out a whistle like I do

when I'm calling my horses into the barn for grub. "That's impossible. No way would I be able to slip that many requests for criminal histories under the radar," he told us. "I'd be called in and, if I was lucky, all I'd receive is an ass chewing."

Which, of course, made me think about the trooper's backside and how it wouldn't be so bad to nibble on. Okay, okay, so I'm in really bad shape here. I'm a regular sex camel—the two-humped variety, since I'm female. I've gone without sex longer than most camels go without water on their treks across the Sahara.

"Now, maybe if you could whittle it down to ten or under, I might be able to help you out," he said.

I looked at him. "How are we supposed to do that?" I asked.

He shrugged. "Process of elimination," he said. "You know, a little covert observation. Keep an eye on the other students in the class. Note any suspicious behavior. Interact with these individuals. Casually. You know—coffee or drinks after class. Get them to talk, open up. See if any of your fellow wannabe peace officers act hinky."

"Hinky?" Dixie asked.

"Hinky. Acting in a manner that draws suspicion. Abnormal. Strange. Unusual," I supplied with a proud smile.

Dixie shook her head. "Oh. *Hinky,*" she said. "As in, 'hinky'—see Tressa Turner.'"

Oh, Dixie was just a barrel of fun. Literally.

"So, say we finger ten or so suspects. How do we get their dates of birth?" Frankie asked.

"Well, you can figure an approximate age just by looking at a person. Observe what they wear, what music they listen to. Heck, even check out My Space. You'd be amazed at what you can find out online. If you get together for coffee, you can always talk about horoscopes and zodiacal signs, historical events, culture, anything to narrow it down to an approximate date," Patrick suggested. "It's not so crucial if they have an uncommon name, like Engelbert Humperdinck—"

"Engelbert who?" I asked.

"Humperdinck. A singer. Had some hits. The women loved him," Patrick said.

"They did?" I asked. He nodded.

"Mr. Romance," he elaborated before continuing. "But if you're dealing with a name like Smith or Jones, you're gonna need more concrete data to pin it down," he said. "And you can probably start off by eliminating most of the female students and focusing more on their male counterparts."

"What! Why?" Both Dixie and I jumped on Dawkins like my pooches on Purina.

"What? You don't think girls can commit murder and mayhem just as well as guys?" Dixie asked, and from the way it came out, I was glad she'd said it instead of me.

"Whoa. Slow down. No offense, ladies," Patrick said, putting his hands out in a don't-shoot position. "But given the nature of the crimes we're dealing with, and what Frankie said about the little description victims provided, it seems more likely that we're dealing with a guy. But if it makes you feel any better, ladies, you'll be happy to know that I'm an equal opportunity law enforcer. I'll keep an open mind," he advised with a wink. "Of course, it goes without saying that if you do this 'covert research,' you need to operate in pairs," he told us. "You're looking for someone with a criminal agenda here. Don't ever forget that."

I felt some of my appetite shrivel at Dawkins's advisory. In my excitement over finding a compelling topic to investigate, I'd neglected to consider there might actually be an element of danger. Silly me.

"There's one of our classmates now," Frankie said, keeping his eyes averted from the person in question so as not to attract attention. "And he seems to be watching us rather closely."

"Where? Where?" I said, craning my neck to look around.

"Oh, good grief," Dixie snorted. "Did you miss the word 'covert' in Dawkins's presentation just now? You might as well slap a big sign on your forehead that says 'I've got my beady eyes on you!'" she said.

I slouched down in my chair, feeling somewhat chastened. I was still new to all this espionage-type stuff. To make matters more difficult, I was pretty much a what-you-see-is-what-you-get kind of girl. And let's face it. I'd never been very good at watching my p's and q's—whatever that entails.

"At the table. Near the condiments," Frankie said, keeping his eyes on the people at our table. "His name is Trevor Childers. He's wearing a brown bomber jacket, khaki-colored baggy carpenters, and an orange-and-tan-striped shirt.

I ran a hand down the back of Frankie's head, trying to discover the eyes there. "How'd you do that?" I asked.

Frankie shrugged. "It's a gift," he said. "Besides, I noticed what he was wearing in class earlier today. A very tasteful, well-coordinated, and accessorized ensemble."

It was Dawkins who winced this time, and I figured

he'd never heard a prospective cop talk like that. He was probably hoping for something more along the lines of: *"There was just something about the dirtbag that got this copper's radar hummin' like a son of a bitch."*

Or maybe not.

"What should we do?" I asked Dawkins. "Go over and ask him his zodiac sign?"

"Yeah, you do that, Turner," Dixie said. "The rest of us could use a good laugh."

"Got a mirror?" I asked. "That's quicker."

"He's pretty much a loner in class," Frankie went on. "Rarely talks or interacts with anyone. Seldom adds to the discussion. Just sits and takes notes."

Personally, I didn't think this qualified as particularly suspicious. After all, it was almost a carbon copy of what I did in class most days. Minus the notes. And my little catnaps, of course.

"Don't a lot of serial stalkers and killers keep to themselves?" Frankie asked Patrick. "You know. Antisocial. Emotionally shuttered. Incapable of real human connection and attachment?"

I stared at Frankie. "Have you been reading about Ted Bundy again?" I asked.

"FBI psychological profiling," he answered. I frowned.

About that time Trooper Dawkins's radio squawked, and he pressed the microphone clipped to his shoulder tab and responded.

"I've got to go," he said, picking his hat up and putting it on his head, then securing the back strap. "Ten fifty P.D."

"Motor vehicle accident. Property damage," Dixie and Frankie translated in unison. I looked at them.

With these two around, I'd never need to memorize ten codes.

"Frankie, I'll give you a call and we'll get together to head out to the academy obstacle course. I'll put you two through your paces," he said. "We'll have you lean and mean by the time the selection process rolls around."

My ears perked up. "Obstacle course?" I questioned. "Sweet!" This sounded entertaining. Especially the part where I got to watch Dixie crawl under barbed-wire fences—uh, make that *roll* under barbed-wire fences—and scale tall walls in a single bound.

"Bring her along," Dawkins said, motioning to me. "We'll see what the cowgirl's made of."

"Bullshit," Dixie suggested with a laugh. I flipped her off under the table.

"Later," Dawkins said, then did that trademark pole-up-the-back trooper walk across the student union and out the front door.

"He's leaving!" Frankie exclaimed.

"Yeah? So? He got a call, Brainiac. A ten-something or other. And just when I thought you were so observant," I told Frankie.

"No! *He's* leaving!" He pointed to his sharply attired classmate across the way. "We should follow him," my cousin suggested. "See where he's going. We have to start somewhere."

"Uh, isn't it going to look really suspicious if the three of us follow him?" I asked.

"Remember what Dawkins said. We shouldn't spy solo."

"But don't you two have class shortly?" I asked.

Frankie looked at his watch. "Damn. You're right."

I gathered my stuff. "Let me take a whack at him," I

said. "It's broad daylight. What could happen? All the bad stuff happens at night, right? Besides, I've got my cell phone and I can call for help if I need to."

"I dunno . . ." Frankie said. "It's not SOP. Whaddaya think, Dix?" He turned to his "little" woman.

She gave me a tight-lipped smile. It was more of a sneer, really. "Like Calamity here said, what could happen?" she echoed.

"I'll meet you back here at two sharp," I suggested.

"You hope," Dixie said with a fiendish look.

I hurried out, finding myself wishing I hadn't been quite so quick in my offer to follow contestant number one in this serial stalker version of campus Jeopardy. Alex Trebek, I wasn't.

I waited until Trevor Childers had reached the corner of the student union and followed in lukewarm pursuit. A light drizzle began to fall from low, gray clouds. I pulled my sweatshirt hood up to keep my hair from becoming a sodden mess rather than just your basic frizzy mess, and kept a prudent distance. Yes, I can do prudent. Sometimes.

We headed south across the campus at a brisk pace. I was glad I had chosen to wear my Nike cross-trainers that morning. Not that I actually do any cross-training—or any training of any kind for that matter—but at least I look like I do. And someday, I will. Really.

We approached a rather new-looking building, long and modern, like a medical or dental clinic. Frankie's "loner" moved around to the back and down a short flight of stairs. I peeked over the railing to watch him descend before I followed. He approached a door on the side, hidden underneath a small parking ramp. I slipped to the corner of the building, concealed myself behind a large potted shrub, and looked on as the guy slipped a card into a slot beside the door and waited for the buzzer. He entered just as I hoofed it to the door. Whipping a plastic card out of my pocket, I flashed it at him, along with a "thanks, pal" smile of camaraderie and gratitude. The guy gave me a curious look but didn't perform a closer inspection of the card in my hand. Good thing, as it was a punch card for a free sub sandwich and complimentary fountain drink.

I pretended to go down a different hall, stopped, then popped my head back around the corner to see which direction Childers was headed. He took a hallway to the right and I backtracked on tiptoe to peek down it. A door somewhere down that long, long hallway, which brought to mind an industrially austere hospital corridor, clicked shut.

I headed down the hall, noting the numerous closed doors, many with designations like Exam Room A or B, Storage, Records. Some had nothing at all.

It was like *Let's Make A Deal*. Pick a door, Tressa. Any door.

I moseyed down the hallway and started with door number one, which was labeled a storage room. It was locked. I continued. Since I really, really wanted an A in Investigative Reporting, I decided I'd go with Exam Room A next. But I'd knock, too—just in case some poor soul had her heels propped in a set of stirrups with some white-coated doctor-type between her legs. Ugh.

I rapped on the door, prepared to issue my *"I was looking for my grandmother, I am* soo *sorry"* excuse to go along with my mortified apologies to all concerned, but received zero response. No doors flew open. No irritated nurses chided me. Nothing. I took a deep breath and turned the handle and opened the door. The light was off so I slipped in before I turned the switch on. When I turned around, I was surprised to see the room was starker than the hallways.

Large and spacious, the room was absent of any touches of warmth and color. Not only was there no tile on the floor, but it looked almost like bare concrete, treated with a high-quality concrete sealer. I looked at the shiny examination table, totally stripped of pad, cover, or sheet, and frowned. The place looked like the kind of clinic where you'd find Dr. Death and his patients. Or Dr. Frankenstein. I sniffed. The place even had a fusty smell.

I checked out the ceiling and squinted at the industrial-strength light fixtures with high-wattage output. *The better to see you with, my dear,* I thought. Frankly, I couldn't imagine any patient voluntarily stretching out on this shiny, hard, stainless steel examination table waiting for Dr. Coldfingers to declare, "Just relax. You may feel a bit of pressure here."

I picked up a box of what looked like paper hair nets and made a face. Next to it was a box that looked like those funny little elastic slippers surgeons use to cover their shoes in the operating room or nurses stick on patients before a medical procedure. I looked around some more, opening a couple of the cupboards for curiosity's sake. Strange. For a doctor's office, you'd expect to find items relating to patient care. You know, those wide Popsicle sticks. Those long Q-tips they swab the back of your throat with for strep that make you gag big time. Gauze pads. Thermometers. Lubricating gel. That grotesque, cold, metallic speculum thingy. Eeeow!

What kind of doctor's office was this?

I prepared to open the door and leave when I noticed a white jacket hanging on a hook on the back. I looked around the room—like I do in the kitchen when I'm about to sneak in and slice off a hunk of frozen cookie dough from my folks' freezer—and pulled the white coat from the hook and slipped it on, curious as to how doctorish I'd look dressed in it. Okay, let's be honest here. Haven't *you* always wondered what you would look like as a doctor or surgeon? And how many of you gals have never taken a pillow and stuck it under your shirt to see how you would look eight months pregnant? And I am so not believing you've never pilfered those purple latex gloves and taken a few home to blow up and entertain yourself with later. Hmm. I thought as much.

I grabbed one of the paper hair nets and, dropping my hood, stuck one on my flyaway (fly-far-far-away) hair. It took some doing to get my abundant mane stuck up under the net, but I managed. I bent over and pulled the slippers on over my Nikes, slipped my hands into a pair of purple latex gloves, and looked at my reflection in a mirror on the wall. I gasped, startled. My massive hair made my head look the size of a classroom globe. Or an alien's cranium. I looked about as medically savvy as Dr Pepper.

I flipped off the light and prepared to proceed to door number two. Maybe this was a veterinary clinic, I considered, thinking that could explain the lack of amenities. It could be one of those on-campus teaching facilities where veterinary science students received their hands-on-critter experience. Maybe instead of Dr. Death, we were talkin' Dr. Doolittle here. The possibility made me feel ever so much better.

I straightened my white coat, opened the door, and

stepped back out into the hall—and ran smack dab into another white-jacketed individual. She slapped a pair of really freaky-looking goggles in my hand as she passed.

"It's about time. Emmy's waiting on you, and you know how she gets when she has to wait," the other person said. "We've got two up and two in the queue. I'm heading to lunch."

I felt my breath hitch in my throat and managed to mumble something like "Gotcha, enjoy your lunch," then saluted her retreating back with the goggles.

Emmy?

Curious about who Emmy was and what she had four deep in the queue—hey, I warned you I was nosy—I headed down the hall toward a room with wide hospital doors with horizontal handles. I shoved the door inward, intending only to take a peek for curiosity's sake and then hightail it out of there, but I was hailed the second I poked my nose in the door.

"Get over here and help me!" a woman across the room, presumably Emmy and clad in aqua scrubs covered by what looked like a paper apron, called out. "Where are your scrubs? Never mind. I need you to hold this open while I get a picture."

The room was so bright I almost needed sunglasses to avoid squinting, and was expansive with windows that traveled its length. Long, deep stainless steel sinks ran along the middle of the room, perpendicular to off-white walls. Fluorescent light fixtures were in place over the sinks, and more heavy-duty lighting was installed at pivotal points in the ceiling.

"Well? What are you waiting for?"

The threads of a smell I'd gotten an unfortunate whiff of not so many months back made its way up my nostrils and I started to become uneasy. I took a hesitant step forward.

"Some time today would be nice," the woman at the shiny stainless table said, and I blinked when I saw she was standing over what looked like a naked patient, bottoms up.

I averted my eyes, and on legs that now seemed as sturdy as paper clips, I slowly made my way in her direction. My breathing was hurried and heavy. By the time I got to her, my goggles were all fogged up. Both inside and out.

"Here," she said. "Hold these flaps back while I shoot a couple pictures."

She motioned for me to take the place of her hands, and I squinted through my goggles so I could see where she was directing. And so totally wished I hadn't. I found myself staring down into the bloody red, wide-open skull of a human being, holding back flaps of scalp with stainless steel tongs similar to the ones I use to pick up the crab rangoon and vegetable lo-mein at the China buffet back home.

"Hold it. Hold it. Right there!" *Snap*. The camera flashed. "And one more. That's it. Perfect!" Another flash. "Super! It's a wrap!"

I looked down at what once upon a time was the epicenter of some poor soul's nervous system, and felt the makings of my recent meal burn the back of my throat, as it made its way up the down staircase.

I dropped the tongs inside the gaping cranium, slapped a purple-gloved hand to my mouth, threw a salute to Emmy, and flew toward the door. The last thing I saw before I exited was a big sign on the wall that read SCRUBS, GOWNS, AND APPLICABLE ACCESSORIES REQUIRED IN AUTOPSY ROOM AT ALL TIMES.

I bolted for the nearest exit. I ended up yanking off my hair net and releasing my stomach contents into it, my flight surely setting the standard for the shortest medical career on record.

Dr. Ditz, I presume?

CHAPTER 3

The trip home was somewhat subdued—mainly because I was still feeling weak and pukey from my short stint as Igor to "Emmy's" Dr. Frankenstein. My cousin was behind the wheel and I was trying to come to terms with the reality of walking into the Iowa State medical examiner's office, suiting up and marching smack dab into the middle of an autopsy. *With two on deck and two in the queue,* I reminded myself with a shiver.

"So, Trevor Childers works at the morgue?" Frankie said. "Huh. Guess that explains why he isn't too talkative. It's not as if he has anyone to converse with at his workplace," he added with a smile. I winced.

"You hope." Dixie rose from the backseat like a lunatic in a bad horror flick. "Bwahhaha!" she said.

"Very funny," I snapped. "You two wouldn't find it so humorous if you were the ones holding back a bloody scalp so the M.E. could photograph the rather prominent dent in some poor guy's skull," I said. "Not exactly my idea of a Kodak moment," I told them.

"And you really saw the dude all laid out and cut open?" Frankie asked.

I shook my head. "Just the head," I replied. "Well, what there was left of his head, that is. But it was more than enough for me and my Italian sub—which, by the way, I will never ever be able to eat again for as long as I live, thank you very much."

"I guess we can probably cross Childers off our list of possible perps," Frankie said. "If he works at the M.E.'s office, he had to pass a thorough background screening, plus a polygraph examination."

I stared at Frankie. "How do you know all this stuff?" I asked.

"*I* do my homework," he said.

Personally, I didn't want to think about homework, but there was still the issue of e-mailing my topic to the good professor before midnight. Plus I needed to start organizing my notes on the story and figure out our next move.

I grabbed Frankie's laptop—a wireless with all the bells and whistles—and started it up, sending an e-mail to Stokes and one to my boss, Stan, to let him know that I might be on to something we could run with in the *Gazette*. Double duty and all that.

"Is there any way you can get a list of all the students in your class?" I asked. "So we have someplace to start?"

"It's a done deal," Dixie said, and I turned to stare at her.

"How so?"

"Professor Billings has us sign in when we enter the

lecture hall," Dixie explained. "She's a stickler for attendance. She's got extra rosters stuck below the top ones to cover the entire term. I just slipped back into the classroom after lunch and pilfered one. Nothing to it."

I'd forgotten how conniving and underhanded Dixie could be. As a general rule, these dubious talents were locked, loaded, and aimed straight in my direction. Being in the backfield rather than the receiving end of her skullduggery was a totally unfamiliar—and surreal—experience to say the least. I hadn't decided yet if I liked it.

"Okay, so we take the list, split it up, and see what we can come up with by Googling the names. Who knows? We might luck out and get a break," I said. "Someone who jumps out at us as a prime suspect."

"What time should we meet to head back to the campus?" Frankie asked. "We have to make sure we're back on the scene before dark."

I looked over at him. "What do you mean, 'on the scene'? My night class isn't till Thursday night," I reminded him.

"Yes, but our next crime is scheduled to go down this evening," he said. "And if we happen to catch the perpetrator in the act, just think of the story that would make—not to mention the grade," he added.

I eyeballed Frankie. Where had he learned the art of manipulation?

Oh, yeah. From me.

"It wouldn't hurt your chances of cinching a spot in the next academy either," I reminded him.

He shrugged. "Everybody wins," he said.

"So, just what is the crime of the day?" I asked, not really wanting to know but figuring I'd better ask.

"A heaping helping of hit-and-run, with a vehicular manslaughter chaser," Dixie recited.

"You're kidding," I said.

"Think we need some extra help?" Dixie asked.

"I think we need freakin' Robo Cop."

We dropped Dixie off at the Daggett digs in Des Moines and headed for Grandville. Once I left Frankie at Uncle Frank's and Aunt Reggie's—yes, he still lives at home, but I'm in no position to criticize—I stopped off at the *Gazette* to touch base with Stan.

Stan Rodgers could almost be a twin to that guy who used to be on *NYPD Blue*. No, not the cute one; the roly-poly bald one with thinning hair and a gruff attitude. Stan is fond of wearing those goofy half-glasses. You know, the ones that can't decide if they want to be glasses or a lorgnette when they grow up. He has a habit of peering over the top of them that really gets on my nerves. Probably because he's usually chewing a piece of my hide when he's doing it.

"So, how's school going?" he asked. "What can I expect to see when I get a peek at your final grades?"

"Whiteout?" I suggested.

"That bad?" he asked. I shrugged.

"It's hard keeping all the balls in the air, Stan," I complained. "Real hard."

"Try doin' it when you're fifty, overweight, with a bum knee and two kids in college."

I shook my head. "No, thanks. I think I'll stick with my two hairy hounds," I told him. "I can't even afford obedience school for then. Anything you want me to jump on before I head home to work on my big journalism final?" I asked. "I've already thought of a title," I added. " 'Crime by the Books: Campus Crime Wave

Linked to Professor's Lecture Series.' Whaddaya think? Pretty catchy, huh?"

"Sure. If the story pans out," Stan said, sticking an unlit cigar in his mouth. I've never seen Stan light up. He basically chews the thing to death. Not a pretty sight.

"What do you mean?"

"Just that. In this business you never know when a story will take off like a red-hot rocket on the Fourth of July or fizzle like a defective sparkler," he said.

"Hey. Haven't I always delivered?" I asked, not particularly thrilled with the references to fire and fizzle considering I might be tracking a freelance criminal.

"Yeah," Stan said. "COD."

I shook my head. "COD?"

"Corpse on delivery," he told me and chuckled. Frankly, I saw little humor in it.

"Hardy-har-har," I said. "But you'll be singing a different tune when I come home with a big fat A on my final and another story of crime and punishment to grace the pages of your newspaper."

Stan grunted. "In the meantime, Ms. Pulitzer, run over to the courthouse and pick up the arrest reports from the sheriff's office and Clerk of Court filings, would you?" he ordered.

"Sure, boss. Anything you say."

I stood in the doorway of Stan's office and looked across the room at my tiny little table, sad, straight-back chair and ancient computer, then shut my eyes and rubbed both temples, emitting a low hum.

"Uh, was there something else, Turner?" Stan asked.

"It's a technique I saw on one of those late night motivational shows. 'If you visualize it, you can realize it,' they say. So I'm visualizing my new office furniture and laptop computer," I told him. "High-back leather chair. Nice, big oak desk. Top-of-the-line laptop notebook with mobile technology." I shut my eyes again. "Just about there. Yes. Yes. I can see it!"

"Can you also see me docking your pay for wasting my time?" Stan asked. " 'Cause I seem to recall giving you a job to do."

Phhft! My office furniture fantasy disappeared faster than M&M's from Stan's candy dish when he's not around. (Hello. It's chocolate!)

I grabbed my backpack and hauled my cookies down the block and across the street to the Knox County Courthouse. A three-story baby-poo shade of brick, the courthouse got a face-lift several years ago that had included new windows and a roof. The century-old jail was still down in the bowels of the square structure. When I was a child it gave me the willies to walk by those bottom windows and see the bars on them. All right, so maybe they still do give me cause for pause at the ripe old age of practically twenty-four—my birthday being a week off. April 1. Yes, as in April Fools' Day. No smart-mouthed remarks, people. Like most blonde jokes, I've heard 'em all.

I entered the courthouse and headed first upstairs to the Clerk of Court's office, putting off the visit to the sheriff's for as long as I could. I have a complicated relationship with the current sheriff. I came to know him pretty well last summer when I was trying to convince local law enforcement there was murder afoot in our little hamlet, and the cops, now-Sheriff Samuels among them, took me about as seriously as bridegrooms take wedding planning.

Besides, this gave me a chance to drop by and see my sister-in-law, Kimmie, who works in the treasurer's office at the county courthouse. Kimmie is married to my older and only brother, Craig. They met when Craig was delivering vehicle titles to the courthouse one day. Craig is a salesman for a local car dealer. I'm sure you can imagine the heat I take from him for driving a car that needs to be crushed. I'm used to his abuse. He and his best bud from grade school, Rick Townsend—or Ranger Rick as I like to call him—along with some other carefully crafted, made-for-the-occasion monikers such as Bass Buster, Carp Cop, the Poacher Patrol, Rickie Raccoon, and the Don Juan of the DNR to name a few—have hassled, harped on, heckled, and humiliated me (and there was that time they hog-tied me, but I don't like to go there) so long and so often I need a scientific calculator to keep track.

I was what you would call "ambivalent" when it came to Ranger Rick. Dark brown hair and warm maple syrup eyes, the guy is tanned and fit and oh so easy on the peepers. And he knows it. He can also be a bossy arrogant know-it-all with a tendency to irritate to such a degree that one will be found in the pharmacy aisle with the Preparation H and Tuck's Pads seeking blessed cooling relief. It was Rick Townsend who saddled me with the colorful "Calamity Jayne" monitor that is harder to shuck than the husks of roasting corn ears when you're wearing mittens.

Lately the good ranger had been giving me some not-so-subtle signs that he was ready to move our volatile relationship to a whole new level. While the idea of volatility as it pertains to passion in a relationship is, I admit, something that has definite appeal (as does the ranger in question—on occasion) I was somewhat concerned that the mixing of such unpredictable and dissimilar components could generate a combo so combustible and potentially explosive that the Haz Mat crews would have to be put on standby.

And there were also other questions that probably needed answers before I considered giving my heart—or other crucial body parts—to someone else for safekeeping. Like, what the heck is romantic love, anyway? I love my family and friends. And my critters. But what does the let-me-put-my-tongue-down-your-throat-and-see-you-naked kind of love really look like? Feel like? How will I know when I'm in it, and can I expect it to last forever? Can *anyone* expect love like that to last forever anymore? Okay. I hear you. Pull out the fiddle and rosin up the bow, 'cause that sounds like the words to a country-western ballad. Am I right?

Still, on the subject of everlasting love, I really had to ask myself, was I even ready for that kind of love? I'd only just begun to discover a direction for my life, plotted a course, however elementary, and ever-so-slowly started to take kindergarten steps in that direction. Was I ready to share my life's highways and byways—not to mention detours, roadblocks, and potholes—with another person?

With all the uncertainty tied to my love life, the question that plagued me the most, the one that really needed an urgent answer, was also the one most prone to cause compulsive nail-biting and obsessive appearance anxiety: Was I really ready to show my naked body—wibbly-wobbly bits and all—to someone who wasn't a medical professional and paid to look at it? That, my dears, was really the question. The idea of exposing my healthy, homegrown, raised-on-country-sunshine-and-toned-on-the-back-of-a-horse hips and thighs to a guy who makes Hugh Jackman look old, wizened, and out of shape, frankly made me more than a little phobic.

As a result, much to my gammy's dismay (she had the hots for Townsend's granddad, Joe) I wasn't falling into the sack without the proper protection. Uh, I'm talking coronary care here. I wanted to make certain both the timing and the man were right for longer than a roll or two in the hay, regardless of how rock-my-world glorious the rolls might be.

"Hey, Kimmie!" I greeted my sister-in-law, an extremely pretty girl with dark blond hair and brown eyes. Kimmie always looks so fresh and energetic. Her makeup is always just-so (except when my brother is being an insensitive dorf-wad and she cries and her mascara runs) and she has the best fashion sense of anyone I know, which I totally envy. I can't wear a pair of socks the same color.

I stopped at her counter and leaned my elbows on the varnished wood. "How's it going? Any news from the baby beat?" I asked.

Kimmie had been trying to convince my brother, Craig, that he was ready for fatherhood. So far, with minimal success. The two had been married for going on four years now and Kimmie wanted a baby. Craig still wanted to sit in a straw-covered boat and take pot-shots at Daffy Duck and crawl on his belly in a cold, wet cornfield to carry out sneak attacks on goosey, goosey gander. And all, I might add, with the undermining assistance of a certain "fishy and foul" officer.

"Your brother is slowly coming around," she said with a glint in her eyes and a set to her mouth I hadn't seen before.

I raised an eyebrow. "I'm intrigued. Please explain."

"Well, let's just say I decided that a period of abstinence might give us both some clarity on the situation," she said.

Both my eyebrows were elevated, along with my interest. "Abstinence? Isn't sex not only recommended for conception but kind of, like, required?" I asked.

"It is. But unlike some of those conniving women you see on daytime TV, I'm not about to get myself pregnant and then hope the daft fellow comes around. So I'm planning to give him a little shove in the right direction."

I wrinkled my brow. "By withholding sex?"

"Just temporarily. I'm calling it a cooling-off period. You know, time to reassess our priorities, set common life goals, and establish a timetable for meeting same."

I scratched my forehead. "Priorities. Goals. Timetables. You make it sound like a business plan," I observed.

"It *is* a business plan," Kimmie maintained. "Serious business. It's a plan for a lifetime."

"But where does that leave romance? Passion?"

She stared at me. "Have you met your brother? His idea of setting the mood is cutting his toenails and trimming his nose hair. After which, I'm expected to be ready and waiting and panting to have him."

I made a face. By comparison, Mrs. Doubtfire's "Brace Yourself, Effie" was a real turn-on.

"Do you think this is the best way to handle Craig?" I asked. "He's kind of stubborn. He can dig his heels in pretty deep," I said, thinking that was one thing my brother and I had in common.

"So can I," Kimmie said with a tilt to her chin that

left me in no doubt that she'd ride this particular pony to the end. To her, the stakes were that high.

I sighed. It looked like Craig and I had one more thing besides mule-headedness in common. And, while I wanted to be an aunt almost as much as I wanted to be skinny, debt-free, and able to groom my hair without breaking comb teeth off right and left, we sex camels had to stick together.

I said good-bye to Kimmie, telling her I'd see her the following evening at Kari's bachelorette party. With my being maid of honor, it fell to me to plan the event. Which meant, of course, that absolutely nothing had been done. I was hoping Kari would be content to tip back a few with several girlfriends and maybe dance a final two-step with a cute cowboy at my favorite country-western hangout in Des Moines. (Okay, I hear you city girls going "Eeeww!" Tell me you didn't think the cowboys in *Brokeback Mountain* were hunka-riffic. Okay, so apparently they were also gay, but I betcha they knew how to show you a good time on the dance floor. And sometimes, that's all a girl wants. Isn't that so, ladies? I know what you're thinking, "So says the sex camel," right? You guys.)

I grabbed the court filings from the clerk's office and headed back downstairs to the main level where the sheriff's office was located. There I took time to pop a quarter into the dispenser and snare a handful of peanuts to satisfy an urge for something crunchy and salty, then I made my way to the glass double doors that housed the offices of the county's chief law enforcement agency.

The communications center is located across the hall. Most of the time I like to pick up the sheriff's re-

ports after hours so as to avoid any unpleasantness
and misunderstandings that might have resulted from
past encounters with the fuzz—uh, law enforcement
personnel—and between you and me, I'd called the
new sheriff by so many different—okay, and
unflattering—names, I'm afraid one of them will pop
out of my mouth whenever I chance upon him.

Imagine this scenario: "Good afternoon, Miss
Turner. And what brings you to the courthouse on this
fine spring day?"

"Just picking up traffic and court filings, Deputy
Doughboy—Dawgface—Dickless—Dorf-wad." Or, my
personal favorite, "Deputy Dickhead." And those, my
friends, are just off the top of my head. Of course, now
that Samuels has been elevated to sheriff I've had to
come up with new material. Let's see. There's Sheriff
Sitsalot, Sheriff Shitsalot, Sheriff Sourpuss, and Sheriff Saggy Britches. Now you can see why I prefer to do
a Santa number on this one and make my stops only at
night.

I was about to open the door into the sheriff's office
when; "Well, good afternoon, Miss Turner. What
brings you to the courthouse today? You finally planning to pay those parking tickets?"

I turned. Deputy Di—Sheriff Sits—damn—Sheriff
Doug Samuels stood across from me, Ranger Rick
Townsend flanking him. Next to the stout, stocky, no-
necked Samuels, the DNR officer looked tall, broad,
and more tempting than a platter of brownies, frosted
and without nuts.

"Why, you're well versed in the law, Dep—Sheriff
Samuels," I said. "You know I have to pay my tickets
before I renew my registration on my birthday," I told

him. "But that's still almost a week away. Plus I think I get a thirty-day grace period beyond that. Right?"

He shrugged. "Just makin' small talk, Turner," he said. "Jeesch."

Like there was anything small about him.

"That's right. You have a birthday coming up," Townsend remarked. "Twenty-four, isn't it?"

I nodded. "But who's counting?" I asked.

"So, you never did say why you're here," the suspicious sheriff followed up. I frowned. Just because there were occasions in the past where my presence at the courthouse meant murder and mischief didn't mean there wasn't a completely innocent reason for me to be here now. Which, of course, there was.

I flashed the court papers at him. "Errand-girl duties," I explained. "I'm here to pick up the weekly court, traffic, and arrest info. I was just on my way into your office to grab them," I said.

"I'll get them!"

Both Townsend and I stared at the uncharacteristically helpful sheriff, who happily took my arm and steered me to the opposite end of the hallway, far away from his offices. "You just stay here and visit with Townsend and I'll go get those for you right now. Save you some steps," Samuels said.

He hurried away, and I glared at his big, tan-uniformed back.

"That really was uncalled for," I complained. "Almost like he didn't want me within spitting distance of his precious office. Didn't even want me to step a foot in there." I stopped. "He's definitely hiding something," I said.

Townsend laughed. "You been reading Dan Brown

again?" he asked with a grin. "Not everything is a conspiracy, Tressa," he said. "I think Doug still has bad dreams about what prompted your past visits to this office."

"And *I* don't?" I exclaimed. "I still make the sign of the cross when I have to open a trunk, and I'm not even Catholic!" I said.

"I haven't seen you around much," Townsend remarked, capturing my eyes in a "what gives?" look.

"I've been busy," I said, shuffling my feet. "You know. Stuff. But I still live at the same address and I haven't changed my phone number," I told him. "Or entered the federal witness protection program."

"Ditto," Townsend said. "How's life as a college coed—the second time around?" he asked. It was actually the fourth time, but I wasn't about to correct him. "Strange, you dropping in to college at the same time your sister dropped out," he added.

"Yes, isn't it?" I said. I'd gotten so used to being the dumb sister that I had to admit the reversal of fortune between Taylor and me was one I rather enjoyed. Of course, I was keeping my current GPA pretty close to my vest to maintain the illusion of academic success, but with the project I had planned, I'd be back in the respectable range by the end of the trimester and would shout it from the barn roof.

"So, classes are going well?"

"Definitely," I responded. The classes were going well. It was me that was the problem.

"I hear from Brian that Kari is a little bit stressed out getting ready for the wedding," he said.

I nodded. "I think that's probably pretty typical," I said. "Brides have a lot going on. How is the groom holding up?" I asked.

"Like a rock," Townsend said.

Of course he was. All the groom had to do was show up. It was the bride and her family who did all the heavy lifting.

"How nice for him," I said. "I suppose as best man you're planning the traditional raunchy bachelor party. Women get stuck sipping punch with old ladies with blue hair who fall asleep during lame games, and guys get to sow their last wild oats with strippers, beer, cigars, and lap dances." I cocked my head to one side and tapped my cheek. "What's wrong with this picture?"

Townsend put an arm on the wall behind me and moved closer, our bodies almost touching.

"You sound like you have inside knowledge of what goes on at bachelor parties," he said. "By the way, did you know they used to be called stag parties? In Australia they're called 'buck nights.'"

I felt my eyebrows rise along with my body heat. "So named, no doubt, for the amount of rutting that goes on," I said, feeling a wee short of breath.

"Naturally," Townsend agreed. "Or so I've heard."

I snorted. "Yeah, right. You possess no inside knowledge of what goes on at buck nights and stag parties."

"Brides have their night out, too, now," Townsend said, taking a nicely shaped hand and tucking a length of loose hair behind my ear.

"Yeah. Hen night. You guys get a big macho rutting stag of a party and what do women get? A bunch of clucking ol' biddies. I'm crying fowl!" I said.

Townsend laughed. "Some of those parties can get a little wild," he said.

"They can?" I asked, dubious. "How so?"

"A lot of women hire male dancers—strippers—to

perform for the bride," he said. "Or they go to a strip club."

"They do?" Hmmm. Maybe hen parties were more than they were cracked up to be.

Townsend looked down at me. "You're not getting any ideas, are you, Calamity?" he asked. "Because Brian's a little nervous about you being in charge of the night's activities as it is."

I frowned. "Oh? He is, is he?" I said. "I get it. What's good for Bambi isn't good for Faline," I said.

Townsend frowned. "Who the hell is Faline?" he asked.

I tapped my toe. "Bambi's childhood friend and future mate," I informed him. "Didn't you ever see the movie?"

He gave me an evil grin. "I couldn't handle the part where the hunters shot Bambi's mother," he said.

Yeah, right. Truth be told, her head was probably on Townsend's wall.

"Well, all I know is that I intend to make Kari's Doe Party a night to remember," I said. "A blow for equal rights."

Sheriff Surly appeared, and he stuck a stack of papers between Townsend and me. "Here's your paperwork," he said. "Nice doin' business with you. Now, I know you have to run."

I gave the sheriff an aggravated look and grabbed the papers. "Stags," I hissed. As I exited the courthouse, the scent of Townsend clung to my clothes.

CHAPTER 4

"You're going back to Des Moines tonight? Mighta let me know ahead of time. I put on a chicken." My gramma slammed the pots and pans around in the kitchen like an aggrieved spouse.

"What kind of chicken?" I asked.

"The only kind I make. Baked. I got a couple of them stuffed chicken breasts from the Meat Market and I brushed 'em with butter and sprinkled on some seasonings."

Seemed harmless enough. My gramma and I are not known for our culinary competence, but we both have major, long-term attachments to our Slo Cookers and microwaves.

Gramma had moved back into her double-wide mobile home—and, consequently, in with me—last autumn after "breaking out" of the "penal institution" run by my mother, Warden Jean Turner. Too many falls and near misses had forced Gramma to move in with my folks several years before. Since I was still living at home (I know, how pathetic is that?) we'd traded spaces. I took the double-wide and she took my bedroom. And the living room. And the kitchen. And the dining room.

I had hoped the lure of a toasty, crackling fire in the fireplace would entice Gramma to return to hearth and home—my folks' hearth and home—when winter set in, but instead she'd settled in for a long winter's nap with me, and cranked the thermostat up to eighty. That first morning I'd awoken to sheets and undies so wet you could wring water out of them. I'd thought I was already experiencing night sweats. As a result, I was for the first time sleeping with my window open in the dead of winter and shucking my jammies at bedtime in favor of a tank top and undies. I just couldn't bring myself to sleep "nekked" as my gramma likes to say. One of us was more than enough.

"Uh, sides?" I asked, the lure of food getting me back on topic.

"Broccoli and cheese sauce—one of them microwave cook-in-the-bag numbers—and garlic bread."

"I don't have to leave for a while yet," I waffled, zeroing in on the garlic bread reference. "And I wouldn't feel right if I didn't eat after all the work you've gone to," I told her.

"Oh, you got something in the mail from that college," Gram said, setting the broccoli on the table while I removed the chicken from the oven. It smelled surprisingly good.

"College?"

"Could be a bill. You get a lot of them."

I sighed. Sad, but true.

It turned out to be a notice of a substandard grade

report for a D+ I was currently carrying in Investigative Journalism. At a C, my Principles of Reporting grade wasn't all that much better.

This cinched it. I desperately needed to bring home an outstanding grade on my project to salvage my GPA and dreams of financial success. Plus there was that office furniture and computer upgrade to consider.

"I saw Manny in town today," Gram said between the forkfuls of chicken and stuffing she was shoveling into her mouth. "He had a message for you."

I stopped chewing. I'd been trying to avoid Manny Dishman-DeMarco—de-whatever the heck he was calling himself these days. Manny had been of assistance to me some months back, but had a disturbing habit of popping back into my life when I least expected it. Built like a Rock—literally a younger, stronger, sexier version of the pro wrestler turned Scorpion King—Manny was your classic bad boy, with all that those sinful, but seductive danger-ahead signs implied.

I'd agreed to do a teensy-weensy favor for Manny when we'd both thought his poor, sick Aunt Mo was on her deathbed. I'd signed on to pose as his girlfriend/fiancée so the ol' gal could drift off into the hereafter comforted that the boy she'd raised from a pup and loved like her own had found his soul mate. At the time, Manny had slipped a ring on my finger the size of one of those Ring Pops, and I'd expected my performance to be limited to a onetime, one-act play. However, Aunt Mo had surprised us both by not only weathering her medical crisis but, now, with her nephew being engaged and all, she was determined to hang around for the nuptials and for dandling baby versions of little Manny/Tressa on her knee.

I'd managed to keep news of this engagement under

wraps. Aunt Mo had left Grandville for her customary southern migration to warmer climes last fall, and Manny assured me by the time she returned, he'd have broken the news to her that we had mutually decided to go our separate ways.

"Uh, what was the message?" I asked my grandma.

"Let's see. How did he put it again? Oh yes. 'Manny's aunt Mo not in the know,'" she said.

I frowned.

"Are you sure that's what he said?" I asked. Manny is a man of few words. Plus he has this weird habit of referring to himself in third person. You know. Manny likes. Manny wants. Manny gets. Gulp.

"Not like a person's apt to get something like that wrong," Gram responded. "Mind translating?"

I chewed my meat with less enthusiasm. "It means your granddaughter is about to be *so* screwed," I replied.

"Oh, Tressa! I'm so happy!" Gram exclaimed. She put her fork down. "Wait a minute. Is Ranger Rick the lucky stud muffin, or is Manny? I admit I never thought of you with Manny before, but come to think of it, he's no slouch. A little too dark and mysterious for my taste, and big as a mountain, but I'm thinkin' that means he's loaded for bear!"

"Gram! I'm not talking about 'screwed' in the sexual sense," I said, scandalized, and Gram shook her head and picked up her fork again.

"I mighta known," she complained. "So what are you talkin' about? What's this 'Aunt Mo not in the know' all about?"

The last thing I wanted to do was explain to Gram the whole situation. When it comes to spreading the word, she makes the Internet seem like the pony express.

"Uh, I've just been helping Manny with a little ongoing secret surprise for his aunt is all," I told her. "And he was just letting me know that she wasn't, uh, privy to our, uh, project yet," I said.

"So what's that got to do with you being screwed?" she asked.

My gammy gets a hold of something, you need wire cutters to disengage her.

"I just don't have the, uh, time right now to devote to the project," I explained, thinking I mainly didn't have the stamina to pretend to be Manny's best girl. I'd bestowed a kiss on him several months back as part of the faux engagement—and because he'd done something unexpectedly touching for me. Okay, so it probably involved some questionable tactics, but still, it's the thought that counts, right? That unexpected act—and the kiss that followed—had affected me more than I'd bargained on. Manny DeMarco/Dishman was one supersized complication I didn't need in my life right now. Probably ever.

"I was attracted to a bad boy once," Gram remarked. "Johnny Devlin. Wore white T-shirts with his smokes folded up in one sleeve, cigarette stuck behind his ear. Greased-back hair and denim jeans that rode low on lean hips. I knew he was trouble from the moment I saw him."

"How, Gram? How?" I asked, thinking this was a talent that had bypassed me, but one that could come in very handy indeed.

"How? Why, he had it tattooed on his right bicep—T-R-O-U-B-L-E."

"Good catch, Gram," I said. Checking the time I added, "I've got to head out. Just leave the dishes in the sink and I'll tend to them when I get home," I told her, feeling guilty that she'd made the meal and was now stuck with the cleanup.

"Not to worry. Joe's coming over and he'll help," she said. "You know, it's kind of nice having a man around the house again. 'Course, your Paw Paw Will, God rest his soul, used to have his nose in the newspaper most of the time. Still, it's nice to have someone around to share things with."

"I know, Gram," I said, reaching down to give her a kiss on one dry, perfumed cheek. I just wished she'd have picked someone other than Ranger Rick's grandpappy.

"I shouldn't be too late," I told her.

"If the trailer's rockin' don't come knockin'," she warned with a wink.

I shook my head. The image she'd brought to mind was only marginally more appealing than that of the naked dead guy with the dented skull I'd seen earlier that day. If the trailer was rockin,' later tonight, this little horse soldier was gonna be in full retreat.

Frankie picked me up some twenty minutes later. He was driving his uncle Frank's Suburban, which gets about three yards to the gallon. Uncle Frank's a big guy and he likes his transportation substantial and roomy.

"Where's *your* car?" I asked.

"Repair shop," he said. I nodded, familiar with the concept.

"So, what exactly is the plan?" I asked. "Shouldn't we alert the campus police to the situation? Make them aware of the possibility that they have some psycho nut job acting out Iowa Criminal Code 101 on the Carson College campus?"

He looked at me. "Sure. We could do that. But what

evidence do we really have beyond our own speculation? You think the campus cops are gonna buy in to
our theory? Just remember how hard it was to get
highly credentialed law enforcement officials to take
you seriously when you told them your 'there's a murderer right here in good ol' Grandville' story. As I recall, you said they looked at you like you'd just told
them you'd found Elvis in the trunk of your car."

I hated to admit it, but Frankie did have a point. I'd
had about as much credibility with the cops as Dusty
Cadwallader did, who regularly calls in reports of
UFOs in the night sky and strange lights in the woods
just beyond his house. The cops had even taken wa-
gers on when I'd next find myself in hot water with local officials, the fiends.

"Plus these campus cops probably don't have the
level of expertise your county and state officers have.
Getting them to believe our 'crimes and how to commit them' scenario may be more difficult than it was
getting the local yokels to take you seriously." Huh. In
his quest for his destiny, Frankie was becoming an insensitive doofus.

"So we just conduct campus surveillance and hope
we luck out?" I asked. "I dunno, Frankie. I'd feel better if we gave the campus police a chance to at least
consider what we have to say," I told him. I'd still get
my story, but at less personal risk to various body
parts. Mucho appealing.

Frankie shrugged. "It's not like I can stop you," he
said.

"Good." I smiled. "We're in agreement, then. First,
we fill in campus police so they can issue a red alert to
the student body. Then we convince them to let us patrol with their units. Then we'll be there for the big

takedown." I had it all worked out. We'd let the campus cops conduct the risky business, and I'd be there to grab the story, make the grade, and get the glory.

Worked for me.

By the time we picked Dixie up at her apartment, it was nearly eight and beginning to get dark.

She opened the front car door, saw me, shut it, and climbed into the back. We headed for campus.

"Have I got news for you!" she said, sliding across the seat to poke her head up between Frankie and me in the front.

"You're running away to join the circus?" I guessed. "Dixie Daggett, the human cannonball! Your parents must be so proud."

"Funny. Leno should be, like, so worried," she replied. "As a matter of fact, I was going through my list of classmates and got a hit on one!"

I turned to look at her. I'd totally forgotten about my own list. Some investigative reporter.

"Are you kidding?" Frankie almost ran off the road. "We need details!"

"When I Googled Keith Gardner, he came up on the Iowa Sex Offender Registry!" she said with a "top that, Tressa" look.

I thought about it and shrugged. I had nothing.

"A sex offender? That's fantastic news!" Frankie said. "Way to go, Dix!" He reached over and high-fived Dixie, and I stared at them both. Something was seriously wrong with a relationship where the couple got their jollies by discovering a sexual deviant in their midst.

"Sexual misconduct with a person under the age of consent," Dixie told us.

"That could mean anything from weenie waving to actual physical contact," Frankie said.

I raised an eyebrow. "Weenie waving?"

"Indecent exposure," Dixie offered.

I winced. "So, what does this Keith look like?" I asked.

"So glad you asked," Dixie said. With a great deal of fanfare and flourish, she presented a color printout of a mug shot. "Keith Gardner: twenty years of age, five feet ten, brown hair, brown eyes. I made copies for each of us."

"Smart thinkin', babe," Frankie said, casting a lovesick look at his girlfriend.

Damn. This *was* impressive. And I didn't like it one danged bit.

"How about you, Turner? You get anything on that list I gave you?"

Did grease spots from potato chips count?

"I'm working on it," I told her. "I had some stuff to do for Stan. Majorly important journalistic-type stuff," I added.

"That's funny. Rick Townsend stopped by the Dairee Freeze and told Taylor you were chewing on peanuts and playing errand girl for Stan earlier," Frankie said.

Nice.

"Rick Townsend has lost his grip on reality, the poor demented fellow," I said.

"Well, I came up high and dry," Frankie went on. "Nothing but some high school sports and activities on my list. So I'm still thinking our best bet is to cruise the campus and keep our eyes open for anything out of the ordinary. You girls will have to pair up. I'll go it solo."

"Uh, wait a minute. Aren't you forgetting something?" I said. "Patrick made it very clear we should be with someone else at all times. I don't think you should be running off by your lonesome," I told him.

"I'm a big boy. I can take care of myself," he said. This coming from a guy whose mother still fed him Jell-O, tea, and toast when he was sick, and who was allergic to so many things that he carried a three-pack of epipens. "Besides, I'll be in the Suburban, driving around."

"Oh? And what will we be doing?" I asked.

"Jogging, of course," he said. "It's the perfect cover. Lots of people jog around campus at night."

Yeah? Well, lots of people didn't include this here little filly. I was built for speed, not endurance. Luckily, Dixie spoke up first, saving me from having to defend my sad, sedentary lifestyle.

"You want us to jog around campus?" she asked.

"Well, you do need to be getting in shape for the academy," he said. "They run three times a day, you know."

Three times a day? If I was lucky, I'd run three times all last year—and two of those times I'd run from people who were no longer among the living and couldn't even chase me.

"I am *not* about to run around campus at night at the same time I'm trying to keep an eye out for a psychopathic criminal bent on mayhem," Dixie said.

"The Destructor's right," I said, thinking that was probably the first and last time those words would ever spring from my lips. "What if we spot the culprit in the act and we're so worn out from running that we're too pooped to pursue him and too winded to call for help?"

"Yeah, what about that?" Dixie asked.

"Oh, all right. Power-walk for crying out loud."

I looked over at Frankie. "You have got to be kidding," I said. "You mean, go out there and walk like one of those spastic automatons who march and swing their arms like soldiers in the robot army? No friggin' way. We'd draw way more attention than we want given the circumstances."

Frankie put a hand through his hair. I was glad to see that it stuck up like my own did. Ah, family ties.

"All right, all right. Jeez. Then just walk. But step out so that it looks like you're out here to walk, not snoop. We don't want to be too obvious."

"I still don't know why I get stuck with her," Dixie pointed to me. "Why can't she drive the Suburban and you and I do the walking?"

"Because my dad threatened me within an inch of my life if I let her behind the wheel," he said.

Tsk-tsk. Would Uncle Frank ever let bygones be bygones? After all, the Dairee Freeze looked ever so much better after the remodeling project. Honest.

"Dixie could drive the Suburban and you could walk with me," I suggested. Frankie shook his head.

"What would she do if she came upon the bad guy?"

"Scare him off?" I suggested with a snort.

"No. I don't feel comfortable with either of you on your own." Frankie pulled up in front of the campus security office. "Why don't you let me handle the security people?" he said, looking at me, not Dixie. "After all, I'm enrolled in Criminal Justice courses and looking to go to the DPS Academy next year. That ought to gain me a little credibility."

I felt my lip curl. "Be my guest, Mr. Big Shot," I said.

"I'll just catch a few z's waiting for you to impress the fuzz with your credentials." I was finding this new take-charge Frankie as annoying as old lady stockings on my shower rod.

"You comin', Dix?" my cousin asked when he realized the slight to his sweetie.

"Naw. You go on. I'd better keep an eye on Ms. Calamity here," she said. I became slightly nauseated when Frankie leaned back to give Dixie a quick kiss.

"Do you two mind?" I said. "Jeesch."

Frankie exited the vehicle and entered the security office, and I searched through the CD case for a decent tune. Uncle Frank's taste ran to songs from the fifties and sixties, with an eclectic mix that included Buddy Holly, The Beach Boys, Chicago, and some classic country legends like Johnny Cash, Alabama, and The Oak Ridge Boys. While I was cool with these oldies but goodies, I found I wasn't in the mood for any of them. I slid behind the wheel, turned the key to accessory, and switched on the radio. A caller was whining about her mother-in-law's meddling, and Dr. Laura was chewing her a new one for not letting her children see their grandmother. How depressing.

"Here." Dixie handed me a CD. It was Carly Simon's Greatest Hits. I was pleasantly surprised. I'm always in the mood for Carly. Isn't everyone?

"Cool," I said, sticking the CD in and sitting back to wait for Carly to work her magic.

We took turns selecting songs. I started with "Anticipation." Dixie picked "Haven't Got Time for the Pain." I went with "You're So Vain" next. Dixie countered with "Legend in Your Own Time." At "Mockingbird," we'd started to sing along, and by the time we got to "Let the River Run," we were belting it out right along with Carly.

" 'Let the river run—!' " I was really getting into it when Dixie reached up and cut the music.

"Uh, what's the problem?" I asked.

"Besides that caterwauling? Look!" Dixie pointed to a parking lot adjacent to where we sat in the suburban.

"What?" I looked around.

"Not what! Who. It's Keith Gardner!"

"Keith Gardner, the weenie waver?"

"One and the same. What do we do?"

I watched Gardner get in an older model, dark blue pickup and back out. "We follow," I said, starting the SUV. I put it in reverse and backed out.

"But the Suburban! Your uncle Frank! Frankie!"

"It's okay," I reassured her. "I've had experience tailing a suspect before."

"In a thirty-thousand-dollar automobile?"

I blanched. My first home probably wouldn't cost that much. "Would you rather drive?" I asked. I swung out of the lot and slid in behind Gardner's pickup, staying three car lengths back.

"What will Frankie think when he comes out to find you've taken off with the Suburban?"

I picked up on the *you* part right away.

"I'll tell him you made me do it, of course," I told her. "After all, it was you who pointed Keith out. I was perfectly content with my Carly sing-along till you sounded the perv alarm."

"We seriously can't get a scratch on this car," Dixie said. "Seriously, Turner. Frank would never forgive me. And he'd never let Frankie hear the end of it. As it is, he's none too thrilled with the prospect of a Daggett becoming his daughter-in-law. Wrecking his Suburban would be the kiss of death to him ever welcoming me into his family."

I reached into my backpack for my digital camera and pulled it out.

"What are you doing?" Dixie asked as the Suburban made contact with the gravel shoulder and she fell to the side.

I turned the camera on, waited for the green light to appear, and pointed it in her direction.

"I'm recording this moment for posterity," I said. Pressing the button I added, "The first documented occasion of Dixie the Destructor sniveling and whining like a little girl. Well, except for that time you were drunk as a skunk, but we won't go there. Smile!" I snapped a picture.

"Why am I not surprised at your insensitivity?" she asked as we continued our leisurely pursuit. "And you're hardly an expert on relationships. Frankie tells me you haven't had a real date in over a year."

I looked over at her. "Why, that little pipsqueak! Did he also tell you I had to swear an oath to Lacey Simon that Taylor would tutor her in Algebra Two if she went to the senior prom with Frankie? Or that I used to catch him practicing how to kiss in the mirror at the Dairee Freeze? By the way, he doesn't still do that, does he?" I asked. "Or how about the fact that the guy is twenty-five and you're the first girl he's ever brought home to meet his parents?"

Dixie looked over at me. "I am?" she asked, and I could swear her eyes were beginning to water. "Honest?"

Great. First a whiney Dixie Daggett and now? Now

I was looking at a barrel about to runneth over with teardrops. Big ones. How do you spell "hormonal"?

I shrugged. "My point is, if I've being going through a bit of a dry spell in the romance department, my dear cousin, by contrast, pitched a freakin' tent in the Sahara for most of his life," I said.

"Until I came along," Dixie said. The dreamy look on her face made me want to whack her one. "Where's Keith going, do ya think?" she asked, as we both watched the taillights ahead of us.

"I dunno. The crimes we're dealing with pertain to automobiles, right?" I said. "So, if the pattern holds true and if Mr. Gardner is our guy, then he should try to do something vehicular."

"Holy shit! I knew it. We're gonna crash Frank's SUV," she said.

"Relax. We're only going twenty miles per hour. What could happen?" I assured her.

"That's what you said before you found yourself elbow deep in some dead guy's brain," Dixie reminded me. I shuddered. I'd been trying to get that picture of the morgue out of my head, but thanks to Unibrow it was back, playing front and center on the big screen of my subconscious. In living color. Or maybe not. Thanks, Dix.

The truck in front of us suddenly sped up and took a fast left.

"What now?" I said.

"He's speeding up!"

"Oh, really? Ya think?" I shook my head and increased my speed proportionately.

"Uh, what are you doing?"

"I guess you could say we're in pursuit," I said.

"Oh no, we're not!" she snapped.

"Oh yes, we are," I said.

"Shit!"

"Nice language," I commented, keeping my attention on the truck in front of us. "Do you talk like that around Uncle Frank?" I asked. " 'Cause I'm pretty sure that might be one reason he hasn't welcomed you with open arms. Not everyone likes the idea of a gal who swears like a truck driver raising his grandkids. I can see it now. Everyone in eager anticipation of Baby Barlowe's first word. Cameras at the ready to record the joyous event. And out of the mouth of Baby Barlowe comes . . . 'Shit!' Yep, one for the DVD collection for sure."

"Well, according to your brother, your first word was 'poo,' so you don't have much room to talk," Dixie countered.

"Oh? Didn't you know? My brother, the poor, sick, delusional dear, was sent away as a child for a rather long stay in a mental hospital. He wasn't around much when we were growing up," I lied. "Besides, if I did say 'poo'—and I'm not saying I did—it was because my favorite teddy toy was Winnie the Pooh, so that's the 'Pooh' I was talking about."

The dark truck in front of us had really picked up the pace. I responded appropriately.

"Wow, this vehicle of Uncle Frank's really has some torque to it," I said as I tromped the accelerator. Keith Gardner's truck ran a stop sign ahead and pulled out onto the county road that ran adjacent to the college. "Lots of power under the hood," I noted as I made one of those rolling stops that always made my driver's ed instructor grab the dashboard and stomp on the extra brake pedal. I tromped on the gas and left behind a teensy bit of rubber as I made the turn a wee bit too fast.

"Holy shit!" I heard again from the backseat, and out of the corner of my eye saw Dixie roll from one end of the Suburban to the other.

"I guess I should have suggested you buckle up," I said, trying unsuccessfully to find her reflection in the mirror. "But, like, who knew?"

The vehicle in front of us increased both its speed and its lead.

"He's made us," I told the Humpty Dumptyette in the backseat attempting to right herself. "And he's trying his best to lose us." I floored the Suburban and continued the chase. The Suburban was soon going eighty-five, but it felt like nothing at all. What a sweet ride. My Plymouth would have been losing crucial component parts like doors and quarter panels and hubcaps if by some fluke I ever managed to get it going this fast.

We came to a sudden curve in the road and the pickup's brakelights were a warning beacon for me to slow down before I entered the curve. And I did. Just not enough to prevent Dixie from spinning out of control again. She flew from one side of the car to the other, across the flat interior where the seat back would have been had it not been folded down for easy transport of buns and other Dairee Freeze food items. She rolled across the interior of the vehicle again once I'd negotiated the curve.

"Sorry!" I said, taking a quick look into the rearview mirror and seeing only her behind.

Keith suddenly veered off to the left and onto a gravel road.

I prepared to follow.

"Oh no, you don't!" Dixie said, trying to gain a handhold on the back of the driver seat. "You are not going to take this vehicle on a high-speed chase down a dark gravel road you've never been on in your life!" she said, and somehow managed to haul her body over the back and into the front seat beside me. "The madness ends here," she said. "Back off, sister, or I pick up the phone and call your uncle Frank," she added, holding up Frankie's cell phone. "Just ease off the accelerator and nobody gets hurt. Do it!"

I saw the taillights of Keith's pickup grow dimmer and dimmer, and I turned onto the gravel road, slowing my speed somewhat.

"Oh, for heaven's sake, it's just a bunch of itty-bitty rocks," I said. "This is a Chevy truck. You know. Built tough."

"That's Ford tough, you maniac!" she said. "Now slow down or I make the call," she threatened holding out the phone.

"Jeesch. Excuse me for wanting to catch the bad guy," I growled, no longer even able to follow the dust trail of the long-gone Chevy. I peered out at the dark road.

"Look out!"

I saw the big, butt-ugly, had-no-business-being-in-the-center-of-the-road opossum a tenth of a second before I slammed on the brakes and we went careening sideways down the gravel road. Someone screamed, but I wasn't exactly equipped at the moment to figure out who it was. For all I knew, it coulda been the possum. I turned the wheel in the direction of the skid and let off the brakes. We flew past the fat opossum—one at least twice the size of my gramma's spoiled, chubby cat, Hermione—narrowly missing the nocturnal creature. I saw the glare of the headlights reflected in his dark eyes as we veered past him and headed for a rather deep ditch.

"Turn! Turn!" Dixie yelled, and she grabbed the steering wheel. If too many cooks spoiled the stew, you can imagine what too many drivers did to a sideways slide down a dark gravel road. Uh, and no cracks about women drivers, you hear?

"Get your hands off the wheel!" I yelled, wishing Dixie was still rolling about in the backseat. "I've got it! I've got it! Let go!"

The Suburban's tires bit into the gravel, sending it spitting out in all directions. I winced when I heard a rock fly up and ding the doors, but I had my hands full trying to avoid the opposite dark ditch.

"I got it. I got it!" I repeated, just as the multiton SUV lurched to a screaming stop.

Dixie managed to extricate her body from where it was wedged between the door and the floor and pulled herself onto the seat.

"I told you I had it," I said, all of a sudden feeling very shaky. I saw Dixie's hands reach out for me— well, for my neck anyway—and I scrambled up and out of the car and out of her range. "We'd better assess the situation before we decide on a course of action." I said, leaning back in to turn the four-way flashers on.

"Just let me know when we can squeeze in a few minutes for me to put a hurt on you, would you?" Dixie said, slowly getting out of the vehicle.

I decided it would be safer for the both of us if I kept my distance, and I walked the length of the Suburban, checking out the sides and back. When I saw how close to going into the ditch—and possibly into a rollover—we'd been, I wiped a hand over my eyes. Talk about too close for comfort.

I breathed a sigh of relief that nothing on the vehicle appeared to be damaged. Nothing except an even more strained relationship with Frankie's fiancée, that is. We'd be a ton of fun at family reunions.

I walked along the sides of the dusty automobile several more times for good measure and finally smiled. "Not a scratch on it," I pronounced. "Some dust and dirt is all. Nothing that a run through a car wash won't remedy."

"I thought you were banned from all the car washes in Knox County," Dixie said, looking a bit better now that it appeared she wouldn't have to explain a crumpled fender or sprung chassis to her future father-in-law.

"Ah, but we're not in Knox County anymore," I pointed out.

"No, but it felt like I was in a freakin' cyclone back there for a while," Dixie said. "Your driving is worse than an amusement park ride. No wonder your car looks like it's been used as a bumper car and has been around the block a time or two. And with you, a block is an eternity. I was rolling around back there and shooting off the sides of the car like a pinball!"

The image brought a smile to my lips, but I quickly covered it with a cough. No sense provoking the little pinball any further.

"Sorry," I said again. "But you know if you'd been wearing your shoulder harness none of that would have happened. Good safety tip to remember in the future," I added.

"Why, you—"

"Oh, would you look at the time! We'd better get back to Frankie. He'll just be worried sick about his little Dixie bear," I said, and heard the far-from-cuddly coed snarl. I shrugged.

Headlights appeared over the hill about a mile and a half down the road. We watched as the vehicle suddenly slowed and stopped.

"Maybe it's a cop," Dixie said.

I shook my head. "I don't think so. Not many doughnut shops on gravel roads," I said.

"Farmer?"

"Could be. Looks like a pickup."

"Could be Keith Gardner's pickup."

The vehicle slowly began to drive toward us. I was suddenly reminded of that movie *Christine*, with the out-of-control psycho car.

I joined Dixie near the front of the Suburban and we squinted at the car in the distance as it approached, still maintaining a low speed.

"I don't like this," Dixie said, and for the second time that night I found myself agreeing with her. It had to be a record.

"It is kind of odd—in a Stephen King kind of way," I added.

In the time it took me to finish that sentence, the vehicle, now less than a half mile away, suddenly accelerated. I could hear the rapid revving of the engine and the spinning tires attempting to gain traction on the loose gravel as the car bore down on us. The headlights suddenly went off, but I could still hear the motor gaining power and speed. I caught a flash of moonlight on the hood of the car as it barreled down on us, and a sudden short flash of light from inside the vehicle.

"Son of a—jump!" I screamed, grabbing the barrel-like girl beside me. She was seemingly nailed to the road, but I used one of those body-jarring moves football defenders use to illegally take receivers out of a play—and hopefully out of the game. I thrust my arms out at waist level and shoved Dixie as hard as I could in the direction of the ditch, hurling myself headfirst behind her just as the car screamed by. The sound of metal scratching metal accompanied my less than graceful dive into the depths of the ditch.

I lay there a few minutes, taking stock, recalling another time I'd taken refuge in a dark, water-filled ditch and how that had all turned out. It was not a comforting walk down memory lane.

I remained prone, listening to the sound of my own harsh alto breathing in discordant cadence with Dixie's bass breaths.

"You all right?" I asked after a few minutes.

"I'll live," Dixie replied. "I have to. 'Cause as soon as I feel up to it, I am so gonna put a hurt on you," she told me.

I grunted. "Take a number," I said.

CHAPTER 5

Once we dragged ourselves out of the weeds and pulled ourselves together, we met up again at the front of Uncle Frank's Suburban. The other vehicle was gone.

"So, what did you see?" I asked Dixie. "It was Keith Gardner, wasn't it? Did you happen to get the plate number of the truck?"

"Uh, let's see," Dixie said. "I have this monstrous truck accelerating straight for me, do I take the time to record a plate number? Hell, no, I didn't see the plate. What about you?"

I shook my head. I had just learned what they meant by the term "paralyzed by fear." It sucked.

"I'm pretty sure it was Keith Gardner, though," I said. "Too coincidental not to be. We'd just followed him onto this road. He was driving a dark blue pickup. And, like you said, the truck was heading straight for you, not me. He'd do that, you being in his class and all." For once I was content to be left out.

"That makes me feel so much better," Dixie said.

"Ohmigosh! Do you know what this means? We've just experienced the next 'by-the-book' crime!" I told Dixie. "Hit-and-run! With attempted vehicular homicide thrown in as an added bonus."

"You can quit making me feel better any time, Turner," Dixie said.

I nodded. "Okay. Then you can check out Frank's vehicle," I told her, motioning toward the passenger side of the car. "After all, you're gonna be one of the family."

"What? No way! You're already one of the family, so you do it," she said. "Besides, after this little demolition derby, the chances I'll become a Barlowe any time soon have probably bit the dust as well."

I sighed. "Fine," I said. "I'll do it."

I rotated my head to crack the tension from my neck and straightened my spine. I took a deep breath. Suck it up, Tressa. You can do this, I told myself. Besides. How bad could it be?

Bad, I decided. Very bad, I revised as I stepped around the front of the truck and discovered the passenger-side rearview mirror was missing and a long, nasty scratch ran the distance of the passenger door.

"Bastard!" I hissed as I bent over to pick up the busted part. I looked at my reflection in the cracked mirror, wondering if it was a vision of the Tressa to come when Uncle Frank was through with her.

We'd just decided to stay put and call the police to report the hit-and-run when Frankie's phone started chirping from the front seat of the Suburban.

"Get it!" I said when Dixie made no move to answer.

"Forget it. What if it's Frank? Or Frankie? Or my dad? No way."

I grabbed the phone and checked the incoming number but it was no help.

"H'lo?" I said.

"What's going on? Where the hell are you and where the hell is my dad's Suburban?" It was Frankie.

"Aren't you going to ask about your fiancée?" I asked. "Don't you want to talk to Dixie?"

Dixie made a slashing motion around the area of her neck and then pointed to mine.

"What is going on, Tressa? Where are you?"

"Uh, are you still at the Campus Security office?" I asked, prolonging the inevitable due to sheer cowardice.

"Where else would I be? You have my vehicle."

"Yeah, about that, Frankie . . . ," I started. "Could you have security contact the state police"—I *so* had a better track record with the state than the county—"and tell them there is a report of a ten-fifty p.d. about two miles east of Highway 69 on the second—or is it the third—gravel north of Carver College Road?"

I held the phone away from my ear to protect my auditory nerve from damage resulting from the shrieks and screams coming from the cell phone. I held it out to Dixie.

"He wants to speak to you," I said.

Eventually a squad car pulled up to our location. By this time I'd gotten real used to hearing "I knew it, I knew it," complete with knuckle-cracking and murderous looks intended to intimidate aimed in my direction by Dixie the disgruntled. When I spotted the light brown patrol car and recognized the badge number inside the cute little red stars, my lower lip began to tremble.

Patrick stepped out of the cruiser and headed in my direction and I found myself walking right into his arms. They closed around me.

"Frankie called," he said. "He took a chance I was still on duty. I was just heading home when I got his call."

I sniffled, my nose at badge level.

"I can explain everything," I said.

Patrick gave my back a rub. "Don't worry. I'm sure you'll have ample opportunity to explain your actions," he said.

And, as luck would have it, I'd had lots of experience doing just that. Sigh.

Frankie arrived at the scene a few minutes later. I bit my lip when he ran first not to his bountiful betrothed, but to his borrowed bucket of bolts. From Dixie's unhappy expression, Frankie's misplaced priorities weren't lost on her either.

I almost teared up again when I saw that familiar, somewhat dazed, hangdog look on Frankie's face as he held the Suburban's mashed mirror in his hands and stared at his distorted reflection in the cracked glass. I felt like something left on my cowboy boot after a walk through the barnyard after a rain.

I walked over and gently pried the mirror from his impossibly tight grip and handed it to the trooper, who then put it out of sight.

"I know this looks bad, Frankie," I said, "but it's really only the mirror and the one door that's dinged. And see!" I opened the damaged door and closed it, then opened it again. "It works just fine. And there is a silver lining, you know. We've nabbed the campus criminal! We know who it is! So when they arrest him for the dirty deeds on campus, they'll charge him with hit-and-run and Uncle Frank will be able to get him to pay for damages!" I tend to chatter when I'm nervous. Or when I'm trying to make myself feel better. Sometimes it takes a lot of words to accomplish that.

I saw a muscle bunch in Frankie's cheek and, although it was hard to tell in the limited light, his face appeared to take on a rather sickly shade of gray, his eyes as big as our ancient librarian's behind her pop-bottle-bottom glasses. A woman so blind she never noticed patrons visiting inappropriate sites on the library computers. Or dropping bits of chocolate-flavored Ex-Lax in poor little Hamlet the Hamster's cage. Or leaving snarky notes in all the how-to sex manuals for horny library patrons to discover. (Hey, it's not as if there was a heckuva lot for kids to do in good ol' Grandville, USA, folks. And back then I was easily bored. And hated being stuck at the library. And I wasn't the mature, thoughtful, considerate young woman I am today. Uh, I heard that snickering. Don't make me come over there.)

"Uh, Frankie? Bud? You okay?" I asked.

Frankie's shoulders began to jerk up and down. He suddenly let out a long, loud gasp and clutched his chest.

"Frankie!" Dixie yelled and grabbed his hand. "Frankie, what's wrong?"

His breaths now came in shallow, rapid bursts of air, kind of like you find in childbirth classes. "He's having a seizure!" Dixie screamed, and Frankie's eyes, if possible, grew even bigger.

"No! He's hyperventilating!" Patrick said.

I'd seen enough shows on TV to know just what to do. I pushed Frankie into the front seat of the Suburban and shoved his head between his knees.

"Breathe. Breathe," I coached. "That's it. Nice and easy."

"Here." Patrick had left and returned with an empty McDonald's sack. It smelled of a Big Mac and fries. Ah, a man after my own heart. "Put it over his nose and mouth so he can breathe into it."

I yanked Frankie back to a sitting position.

"Slow now, Frankie," Patrick urged. "Nice and slow."

"Is he all right?"

A woman had joined us at the Suburban. Really tall and broad-shouldered with short dark hair, she dwarfed poor Dixie by a good half foot. I looked down to see if she was wearing three-inch heels—I always check out the shoes—and was surprised to find what looked like pricey Manolo Blahniks two-inch tan suede bow pumps on her feet. (I go online sometimes to drool and dream.)

"Professor Billings?" Dixie greeted the newcomer. "What are you doing here?"

I took a closer look at the fashionable newcomer. So this was the professor whose lesson plan was being used as a blueprint for the campus crime wave.

"Barb." Patrick nodded at the professor.

"Hello, Dixie. Patrick." She acknowledged the greetings. "Is he going to be all right?" She motioned at Frankie, who was still holding the Mickey D's bag to his nose and mouth. When he saw his professor, he dropped the bag and looked up with one of those guilty faces you expect to find on a high school kid who's just been caught smoking on school grounds. Uh, or so I've heard.

"I'm fine," Frankie said, his dilated pupils saying otherwise. "I just got a little light-headed there. I didn't eat much supper and I'm a tad hypoglycemic."

I looked at Frankie with admiration. That was a pretty good recovery considering it was on the fly and all. I'd have to remember that one. Except I wasn't hypoglycemic. And I rarely ate too little at mealtimes.

"What happened here?" Professor Billings asked.

"One of your students nearly had two one-of-a-kind human hood ornaments, that's what," I told her.

"Who are you and what on earth are you talking about?" the professor asked, giving me the same once-over I'd given her earlier.

"I'm Tressa Turner. I'm an investigative reporter." Okay, okay. So I gave myself a little promotion there. I was earnestly trying to follow the tenets of that motivational infomercial I mentioned earlier. You remember. If you perceive it, you can achieve it. Unfortunately, the infomercial host didn't quite cover how you got other people to believe it. "What I'm talking about is Keith Gardner and his no-budget production of *Denting Ms. Dixie*, and how he almost plowed the two of us over," I told her.

"Keith Gardner?" She shook her head. "I don't understand."

Poor woman. One couldn't really blame her. After all, she probably only held a master's degree. Or two.

"Join the club," Frankie said, giving me an aggrieved look.

"I promise we're going to get to the bottom of this," Patrick said, bringing out the legal pad much as he had the first time we met. Ah, memories. "Okay, ladies," Patrick said. "Let's start from the top."

We filled the handsome trooper in on the events leading up to the hit-and-run, including Keith's criminal record, our suspicions, the short pursuit that I refused to characterize as a chase, and the fact that the

driver of the vehicle had deliberately aimed for us—
and the Suburban—and fled the scene.

"Did you get a look at the driver? Plate number?"
Patrick asked.

I looked at Dixie. "I was too busy pushing *that* out
of the path of the oncoming vehicle," I said, pointing
to Dixie's ample behind. "It kinda filled my field of vision, you know."

Frankie got out of the car. His gait was unsteady as he
moved over to me. "You mean you saved Dixie's life?"
he asked. I blinked. I'd never stopped to think about it in
those terms, but now? Now that Frankie had introduced
the possibility of real honest-to-goodness heroism on my
part—well, contrary to what you may have been led to
believe, my mama didn't raise no dummies, and I
planned to milk this particular cow till its teats fell off.

"Well, I suppose you could say that," I said, trying
not to sound too eager to take credit for said heroic
feat. "But I didn't do anything that any other loving,
caring, supportive, potential family member wouldn't
have done."

A loud snort could be heard from the direction of
Frankie's apparently less than grateful fiancée.

"You seem to forget if you had followed my advice, I
wouldn't have been out here in the boonies in the path
of that maniac in the first place," she pointed out.

"Yes, but we wouldn't have been any closer to finding out who is terrorizing your classmates and campus
either," I responded. "I'm sure you've heard of 'the
greater good,' Dixie, and it's just your recent brush
with death, which was narrowly averted by my swift
actions and quick reflexes, that is clouding your as-
sessment of the situation right now. I, like, so totally
understand," I assured her.

All of a sudden I felt like I was in a remake of the horror flick *A Howling in the Woods*, as Dixie let out this shrill from-yer-gut growl and went for my throat. Patrick and Frankie restrained her before I had to put the hurt on. Lucky for her.

Once Dixie calmed down, Patrick returned to his patrol car to run Keith Gardner through the system. I decided to accompany him rather than risk further incidents with Dixie.

I sat in the front seat of Patrick's cruiser while he fiddled on his computer.

"Your car smells much better than the other patrol cars I've been in," I told him. "Knox County's cars smell like dirty sweat socks and stale coffee. What do you use this for?" I asked, reaching out to pick up a stopwatch and click it on.

"Speed enforcement," he said, and took it from me and put it back where I'd found it. "I time speeders through predetermined and measured speed zones. Like the airplanes do, only from the ground."

"Sweet," I said. "What about this?" I picked up a plastic case and opened it. There was an assortment of instruments like compasses and protractors and little plastic stencil thingies. I took the metal compass out and snapped it open and closed a couple of times.

"Technical accident investigation," he explained, and took the math tool from me, replaced it, and stuck the case in the backseat.

"Interesting," I said. I flipped his passenger-side visor down and found myself staring at a picture of the handsome trooper at the fairgrounds with his arm around a very attractive blonde.

I looked at the trooper. "Care to explain this?" I said, holding out the picture to the trooper.

He looked at the snapshot, paused for a fraction of a second, and shrugged. "It's a photo," he said.

I frowned. "I know it's a photo, but what's it doing here?"

He shrugged again. "I don't know. I just stuck it up there. Why? Is it a big deal?" he asked.

It was—because the blonde in the photo was me. And when you carried pictures of people with you to work, it meant something. I swallowed, and was pretty sure Patrick could hear it from the other side of the car.

"No big deal," I said. I seemed to be fibbing a lot lately. "It's cool. Good times," I added, tapping the picture. "Good times."

"I need your driver's license, Tressa," Patrick said.

I looked over at him.

"What! Why? I wasn't driving at the time. The car was stationary—and the four-way directional hazards lights were not only functional, but actually flashing," I told him.

"I need it for the report," he said.

"Couldn't you just use Dixie's?" I asked. "After all, she's going to be one of the family."

"Tressa, your license, please," Patrick insisted.

I fumbled around for the license. "This won't go on my record or anything, will it?" I asked. " 'Cause I'm thinkin' that wouldn't be fair. I was parked at the time. It would be like charging a cow that got out of the pen and plowed over by Farmer Jones with a moo-ving violation," I said with a grin. "Not that I'm calling Dixie a cow, you understand," I added.

Patrick took my license and wrote down the information.

"You know, when I gave you tips on narrowing the field of suspects, I didn't exactly mean for you to chase one down a dark, gravel road, Tressa. You two could have been killed."

I nodded. That possibility hadn't escaped me.

"Bingo," Patrick said and clicked his computer. "Looks like you may be right. Keith Gardner lives right down this road about two miles or so," he said. "And he has a dark blue Ford pickup registered to him. From the paint that was left behind on the Suburban, I'd say Mr. Gardner's going to have a lot of explaining to do. I'll call for backup and we'll go pay him a visit."

"Oh, Patrick! This is going to be so cool! I'll be at an actual police interrogation—someone else's for a change! Are you going to read his Miranda rights to him and everything?" I felt around in my bag for my camera.

"Uh, sorry, Tressa, but you'll have to sit this one out," he said. "I can't take a civilian along without permission," he told me.

"Civilian? I cracked this campus caper for you. Now I have to sit on the sidelines and watch you big-shot, strutting troopers waltz in and take all the credit?"

Patrick smiled and reached out to pat my hand. "Good. I'm glad you understand how it works."

I wrinkled my nose. Just when I thought Patrick was different from all the others.

"You can wait at the campus security office and as soon as I know anything, I'll contact you there," he promised. "It's the best I can do, Tressa," he said, and I nodded. It was better than leaving me out of the loop altogether.

Thirty minutes later, Frankie, Dixie, Professor Billings, the campus security chief named Hector, and I sat in a small conference room in the security office awaiting word from the authorities.

The vending machine left much to be desired in the way of snack items, but I consoled myself with a Coke and M&M's.

"My dad is gonna be so pissed," Frankie said, not for the first time.

"Relax, you don't want to have to breathe in a paper bag again, do you?" I said. "Besides, everything will work out. Insurance is a lovely thing."

"What if the dirt bag doesn't have any?" Frankie asked. "What then?"

I shook my head. I wasn't about to borrow trouble when I had enough right here to focus on.

"You never did say how you came to be out there tonight, Professor Billings," I said, thinking it was odd that she was still hanging around.

"I received a call from Campus Security and they requested I come down to their office. They told me about Frankie's theory relating to the crimes on campus and a link to my lectures, and wanted me to come to their office to discuss it," she said. "I had to admit, I thought it was pretty far-fetched when I first heard it."

"And now?" I asked.

She shrugged. "I was a cop for over fifteen years and I'd thought I'd seen about everything. I always try to keep an open mind," she said. "I know firsthand how many kooks there are out there. But the idea that someone would take a course in criminal law and use it to terrorize this campus and their classmates? Well, that's a first," she admitted. "And a bit of a stretch, even for this ex-cop."

"But Keith Gardner is a student of yours. Isn't that right? And he does have a criminal record. Right?" I said. "So what is a guy with that kind of background doing taking courses in criminal justice?" I asked, baffled.

"Keith Gardner's case is a classic example of what's wrong with our laws relating to sexual abuse and the sex offender statutes. We clump all these offenders together like they're all birds of a feather. And they're not," Billings said. "Keith got involved with a fifteen-year-old girl. He had no idea she was that young at the time. She was a willing participant in the relationship until her mother found out, and then the young lady turned on Keith. He was charged with sexual abuse of a minor under the age of consent, and he's now branded a sex offender with very little distinction between him and Lester the Molester who rapes five-year-old girls or Merv the Perv who sodomizes young boys. There's no sense of equity under the law as it stands. Everyone is painted with the same broad brush and it's just not right. It serves no one's interest, least of all society's."

Wow. Open can. Find worms. I am so a pro at this.

"But why criminal justice?" Frankie asked. "With his background, no way would he be hired in law enforcement," he pointed out.

"Quite correct," Billings agreed. "But Keith works for an attorney—his attorney as a matter of fact, and a friend of mine—doing odd jobs on various cases for him. Keith is good with computers and does research and gathers information on individual cases for his employer. He wants to become a full-fledged legal assistant so he can earn a decent living and he's taking courses to facilitate that goal."

"Aren't there, like, restrictions on where sex offenders can live and work and stuff?" I asked, thinking this had been in the news a lot lately. "Some two-thousand-foot rule or something?"

Billings nodded. "That's why he lives in the county. He has a small home he rents. He takes care of the owner's cattle and gets a break on the rent."

She knew an awful lot about this particular student, I thought.

"I just can't believe you're right about Keith," she went on. "Things have been going so well for him. Why would he throw it all away by running you two over?"

"Maybe there's some underlying physiological or psychological issue that is causing this behavior," Frankie said.

"Or, here's a novel thought. Maybe he's just a really evil dude who gets his jollies by committing crimes and terrorizing innocent people," I suggested.

"Sociopathic personality disorder, also known as antisocial personality disorder," Frankie supplied.

I stared at him. "Bud, you need to get out more," I said.

The door opened.

"Barbara, I got your call. What's going on?"

The newest addition to our odd collection of crime fighters was a fellow I judged to be somewhere in his mid-thirties, with prematurely graying temples and a nicely trimmed beard. Black glasses rode low on his nose—not by design, but by neglect. He finally reached out to nudge them back up to the bridge of his nose.

"Sherman. It's really the most bizarre thing," Professor Billings said, standing to greet him. "This is Professor Sherman T. Danbury," she told us, "a colleague of mine in the Criminal Justice Department," she said. "You know Frankie and Dixie," she said. "This is Frankie's cousin, Tressa Turner," she said, motioning at me. "I called Professor Danbury after I received the call from campus security," she explained. "I thought maybe he could shed some light on the situation as he has had many of the same students."

"Tressa Turner?" Sherman Danbury looked at me. "Wasn't that the name of the girl who discovered the murderous misdeeds in Knox County last year? And I seem to remember something about the state fair this past summer."

Great. My reputation preceded me yet again. I shoved a hand his direction. "Tressa Jayne Turner. Finder of stiffs and magnet for psychos. Nice to meet you," I said. He raised a brow, but took my hand. His handshake was weaker than an old lady's who suffered from acute arthritis. Bleah.

"So, tell me again what's going on, Barbara." Professor Danbury turned back to Professor Billings and she quickly explained.

I watched for Danbury's reaction. He seemed as surprised—and dubious—as his colleague.

"I still don't buy the theory that someone in my class is committing all these crimes," Billings went on. She turned to address the security officer present. "How do you know that they are even connected, Hector? Do we have witnesses who can say for certain that the assailant is one and the same?" He shook his head.

"No connection so far, Professor Billings," Hector said. "But that may change tonight, with Keith Gardner," he added.

"I guess we wait, then," she said, excusing herself to step outside and light up. Professor Danbury followed her out.

As neither Dixie nor Frankie was in the mood for conversation and none of us smoked, we waited, a silent, somber trio.

The news, when it came, was mixed at best. I had hoped for an immediate arrest of a suspect—not only to mitigate my damaged relationship with Uncle Frank, but to give me what I needed to write my article.

The good news? The police had located Keith Gardner's pickup truck in a ditch a mile from his home. It showed unmistakable evidence of being the vehicle that had almost run us down and plowed into the Suburban.

The bad news? When the police got to Gardner's residence, he was sitting in front of the television watching reruns of *M*A*S*H* and appeared genuinely shocked that his pickup was not in his driveway and that it had been used in a hit-and-run earlier that evening. When questioned, Gardner admitted he'd been out when he was supposed to have been home and had gotten spooked thinking he was about to get caught. He'd kicked up his speed in order to get home. He also admitted to having beer in the vehicle with him, something else that could violate the terms of his release, landing him back in the slammer.

Gardner vehemently denied any involvement in the criminal activity that currently plagued the Carson College campus, and, for now at least, the investigation was ongoing.

Campus Security, along with the State Patrol and County Sheriff's office, would work the case jointly. They would be in contact with Gardner's employer and probation officer and let them know what was going on. Meanwhile, while the evidence against Gardner was considerable, the cops weren't ready to make an arrest just yet.

"Well, that's that," Professor Billings said and got to her feet. "I have early classes tomorrow. See you two then," she told Dixie and Frankie.

"Uh, for curiosity's sake, what does your lecture cover tomorrow?" I asked Billings as she prepared to leave.

The cop-cum-professor stopped at the door and turned. She looked at me.

"Rape. Sexual assault," she said.

I winced. No woman would be safe on the Carson College campus the next night. And I got the kick-in-the-gut feeling no one was going to do a diddly-squattin' thing about it.

CHAPTER 6

I woke up the next morning with a splitting headache that had almost nothing to do with the fallout from Uncle Frank when he saw the condition of his Suburban. I'd felt I owed it to Uncle Frank—and Frankie—to be there when he was told, and to divert as much of the heat off Frankie and onto me. I didn't have to live and work with Uncle Frank day in, day out like Frankie did (picture me here on my knees giving thanks) and I didn't want Frankie's situation with his parents to be strained just because I was a bit, uh, overzealous in my efforts to get to the bottom of the case of the campus criminal.

Unfortunately, like Dixie, Uncle Frank also failed to be impressed by my "for the greater good" logic, and he'd proceeded to terminate my employment at the Dairee Freeze, declaring I was persona non gratis. Once I got some time to Google that particular phrase, I'd decide how upset to be.

I padded out of my bedroom and down the hall to the kitchen around 6:00 a.m. wearing nothing but an *it was a dark and stormy night* Snoopy T-shirt and red bikinis and walked right into Ranger Rick Townsend.

"Oommphf!"

His chest was a rock-solid wall of khaki. I brushed my tangled hair out of my half-opened eyes and, in the bright light, squinted up at him. The look on his face opened my eyes the rest of the way. Last night's news couldn't have traveled this fast. Could it?

"To what do I owe the pleasure of this early morning visit?" I asked. Somehow I didn't think it was to catch a peek at what I looked like in the mornings when I first crawled out of bed. Frankly, most mornings it's hard to tell where the unmade bed ends and I begin. "Was there a report of a confused crane or a pelican gone postal in the area? A raccoon requiring relocation? Or are you out in our neck of the woods recruiting more stags for Brian's bachelor buck party?" I asked.

"I saw your uncle Frank at Hazel's this morning," he stated, folding his arms across his chest.

Nice.

I frowned. "How did you get in here again?" I asked, folding my arms across my chest for entirely different reasons. It was chilly in the double-wide and Townsend's nearness always wreaks havoc with my nerve endings. The last thing I wanted right now was perky, puckered nipples. I'm guessing that may be one of the few times you'll ever hear me say that.

"Your grandmother was on her way to your folks' house," he explained. "She let me in."

"Was she clothed?" I asked him. My gammy likes to sleep "as God intended"—well, except for heavy, wool socks, that is. I'm thinking if God intended my gammy to sleep nekked, He needs a long vacation.

Townsend gave me a queer look. Queer as in strange or weird, you understand. Ranger Rick Townsend is definitely a manly man.

"Of course she was clothed. I get the feeling you're trying to distract me from the point of my visit," he said. "And it's not going to work."

I walked past him and into the kitchen, pulling my T-shirt down over my butt to cover my panties as I walked away. "And what was the point of your visit again?" I asked as I took a cup and poured myself a generous amount of coffee. I raised the cup in Townsend's direction. "Coffee?"

He shook his head. "Damn it, Tressa," he said, covering the distance from the door to where I stood by the kitchen sink in record time. He took the cup from me and set it down and grabbed my elbows. "What in God's name is wrong with you? Why in the hell do you keep putting yourself at risk? Do you have a death wish or something?"

I stared at him. Ranger Rick had gotten upset with me in the past, primarily because I'd put his grandfather, Joltin' Joe Townsend, in jeopardy. Quite by accident, I remind you. But I'd never seem him quite as upset as he was at this moment, his tanned face flushed red and his neck a mass of bulging veins that looked about ready to pop. His outburst unnerved me. Confused me.

"Answer me!" he said, and I felt his fingers dig into my arms.

"What was the question again?" I asked, finding myself oddly reluctant to find out exactly what was really behind his anger.

Townsend gave my arms one more squeeze, then let go and ran a hand through his hair.

"I don't know if I'm the man for the job here, Tressa," he said, and I blinked. I hadn't known I was hiring.

"What do you mean?" I asked. "What job?"

"Protecting you from yourself," he said.

He got my attention with that remark.

"That's a little over the top, don't you think?" I asked. "What's to say I need protection at all?"

"The mirrorless, dented side of Frank's Suburban, for one thing," he pointed out. "Your skinned knees for another."

I looked down at my scratched, scabbed-over knees.

"I can explain—" I began my mantra again.

Townsend waved a hand in my face. "Spare me. I've heard all about the Carson College crime wave, your journalism project, your tanking grade, the tailing of a registered sex offender. It's always something with you, Tressa. A body in a trunk. A psycho clown. A reclusive writer. A campus criminal. I feel powerless to protect you."

He made it sound as if I'd gone out and campaigned to be in the wrong place at the wrong time.

"I wasn't aware your duties with the Department of Natural Resources extended to providing personal bodyguard services to blondes with death wishes, Mr. Ranger, sir," I said.

"Just one particular blonde with a death wish," he said, and I could swear his voice grew huskier.

Just when I was prepared to rip into the guy like my gramma does macaroons fresh from the oven, he goes and says something totally unexpected.

"What blonde would that be?" I heard myself say, wishing I'd at least had time to wash my face and swish some Scope around in my mouth. "Cute cowgirl type? About five feet seven? Curly locks? On the lippy side?" I asked, detecting the pathetically hopeful edge to my tone.

Townsend moved closer and looked down at my mouth.

"Definitely on the lippy side," he said, not taking his eyes off those lippy lips.

I stared up at him.

He bent down and pressed his lips to mine and, morning breath or not, I didn't resist. I found myself leaning into his arms, leading with my chin as I so often do. He deepened the kiss and I opened willingly for him. His tongue was hotter than those cinnamon toothpicks I used to smuggle into class and suck on. I gasped as his hand slid to the front of my nightshirt and underneath, his palm flat against my abdomen. I sucked in my gut. (Oh, get real. Tell me you don't suck it in for all you're worth when a gorgeous guy is caressing your tummy.)

I slid my arms around his waist and pulled him closer, careful not to break a kiss that generated so much heat I waited for the smoke detectors to go off. I moaned into Townsend's mouth when his hand moved upward to cover a very needy breast.

"You're wearing too many clothes," Townsend said, breaking the kiss and resting his forehead against mine.

"I was just thinking I wasn't wearing enough," I told him.

He groaned and removed his hand from under my T-shirt. "We've got a big problem here, Tressa," he said, giving me one more quick kiss before he stepped back.

"We do?" I said.

Townsend let out a long, shaky breath. "We do," he said.

"And what is this big problem?" I asked, hoping to God he wasn't talking about erectile dysfunction.

Townsend put a hand on each of my shoulders and took another look at my lips before his gaze switched to meet my anxious gaze. "I think I may be falling in love with you, Tressa Jayne Turner," Townsend said. "The problem? I'm not sure I want to. I'm not sure at all."

I met his gaze directly, hoping the effect of his words wasn't readily apparent in my expression. I'm a lousy poker player. I wear my emotions on my face like a painted-up circus clown.

I felt my lip tremble like it had last night, but this time I wasn't sure if it was due to fear or hurt. I heard the front door open and shut as my grandma returned to the house.

"Did Rick get a hold of you?" she called out.

We broke contact just as Gram entered the kitchen.

I looked at Townsend. "Ten-four, Gram," I called out. "He got hold of me," I said, watching as Townsend backed away.

And then some.

After Townsend left, I shuffled off to my bedroom, feeling pitiful and forlorn and wishing I could just crawl back in bed, cover my head, and let the world turn without me one day. Since I had a class at eight and that night I had to throw a heck of a hen party for Kari, I recognized I didn't have that luxury.

I trudged to the bathroom and took a quick shower, dressed in jeans, a white Carson College T-shirt and gray hoodie, and went to touch base with Gram. She was in the living room sipping a cup of coffee and nibbling a blueberry bagel with cream cheese. I hoped to heck she hadn't noticed I'd switched the real thing with the one-third-less-fat variety. I like to do my part for my gammy's heart health.

The TV was on and a skinny lady in a pink leotard was sitting in a straight-backed chair doing butt clenches. It looked seriously messed up.

"I'm going to be shoving off, Gram," I said. "What are your plans for today?" I asked, sitting on the arm of the couch. Sometimes that question isn't as innocent as it sounds.

"Joe and I have plans," she said. Joe was Joe Townsend, Gramma's contemporary and sometimes cohort in chaos, and grandfather to Ranger Rick Townsend. He had serious crime-fighting fantasies and had played The Green Hornet (I had no clue what a green insect had to do with crime fighting at the time) to my Catwoman-gone-straight (rrreeeaaarrr!) back when the Grandville body count was rising faster than my credit card balance at a horse tack auction. Plans with Joltin' Joe could mean anything from an evening at bingo to sitting outside the East End Tavern with night-vision goggles waiting to see who left with whom.

"What sort of plans?" I asked, uneasy.

"Oh, this and that," she said, rather more vague than usual. "We might go up to the malls in Des Moines. I still need to get a dress for Kari's wedding. You keep promising to take me, but I don't see any action. And I'm not wearin' something I've already been seen in. Abby Winegardner would be the first to point it out, the ol' bitch."

Abby Winegardner lived around the corner from Joe and kept him in a supply of tasty homemade treats, much to my gammy's displeasure. Joe has quite the sweet tooth, which endears him to me. If you're going to eat naughty, it's nice to have company.

"I told you I would take you when I had some spare time, Gram," I said. "It's just been crazy lately."

She snorted. "Chasing a rapist cross-country in your uncle's truck and getting canned kind of crazy? I didn't know there was so much excitement on campus. Maybe I should sign up for a class. Joe and I were watching TV the other night and they had a news story about a bunch of old people—much older than we are—heading back to college in droves. Something about keeping their brains from turning to mush by learning new stuff. Joe e-mailed for a catalog of classes and we're going to look it over. Wouldn't that be something, Tressa? First roommates and now college chums!" she said, and I hoped that sudden buzzing in my head didn't mean something was about to blow.

"Where did you hear about last night?" I asked. "And who told you Uncle Frank fired me?"

"Taylor mentioned it when I went over to get some cream cheese," she said. "Ours tasted spoiled."

I winced. Busted.

And, just great, Taylor the tattler had spilled the beans. No doubt she was glad for my goof-up. It took the attention off her and her rather surprising exodus from academia. With Taylor working the Freeze more and more, it wasn't as if I racked up all that many hours. Still, the free food I consumed as additional compensation would be missed—by my palate and pocketbook if not by my hips and thighs.

"I gotta hit it, Gram," I said. "I'll call you later," I gave her a kiss on the cheek. "Have a good day."

"You too, dear. By the way, you wouldn't mind if I hit

Frank up for a job, would you?" she asked as I prepared to leave. "After all, we should keep it in the family."

Initially I planned to dissuade her in the gentle, soothing way I have, but when I thought about how Uncle Frank had dismissed me last night as if I were yesterday's French fries (Uncle Frank recycles the onion rings but don't tell anyone—I'm saving this information to hold over his head) I decided maybe having Hellion Hannah as hired help was exactly what the soft-serve king needed.

"Knock yourself out, Gram," I said. "You have my blessing."

She smiled and patted my hand. "You're a good girl, Tressa," she said. "Don't have a clue what to do with good-looking men, but you're a good girl."

I sighed. Yeah. I was a regular Liza Doolittle, I was.

I hurried next door to my folks' house to mitigate the damage made by my little lapse of judgment the night before. I was sure that once I'd left Uncle Frank's the first person my aunt Reggie had called was her sister. My mom. Aunt Reggie and my mother are close. Plus they're a lot alike. Both are pragmatic and serious. My mom is a certified public accountant with a bookkeeping service and an office in her basement. For most of the year she's cool, calm, and collected. During tax season, however, she's a little scary to be around. Fortunately, she stays secluded in the basement for long periods of time only to emerge around April 16 looking like a movie poster model for the thriller *It Came from the Basement*. Her sis—and my aunt Reggie—is the brains behind Uncle Frank's soft-serve businesses. He's the muscle.

I entered through the patio door off the dining room, which is right next to the kitchen. My folks have one of those old-fashioned bars between the kitchen and the dining area where you can pass the bowls and platters of food through. I appreciate this, as it speeds up the meal prep time—and cleanup afterward.

"H'lo!" I called out as I walked into the kitchen and opened the refrigerator door to check out the leftovers situation. I removed the foil off a glass pie pan and discovered leftover hamburger pie. Yum! I missed my mom's cooking. I nuked a sizeable portion in the microwave and was sitting at the dining room table when Taylor walked in.

"Oh. I didn't know you were here," she said, all dressed up in a black and white running suit. "Care to join me in a short run?" she asked. I frowned. Here I was eating beef, cheese, and some decadent mystery sauce for breakfast and Taylor the Toned seriously thought I was up for a run down a quiet country road? She don't know me very well, do she?

"I'd love to," I fibbed, shoveling in another mouthful. "But I have a class this morning. Maybe some other time." Like, when the Vikings won a Super Bowl. And when our gramma finally made nice with Abigail Winegardner. "Where's Mom?" I asked.

"Working," Taylor replied, hovering in the doorway for a second before she approached the table and sat down across from me. "I heard about your close call last night," she said. "And about Uncle Frank's Suburban."

I really started shoving the food in, figuring there was a good chance I'd lose my appetite shortly and wanting to get a jump on that. "Yeah, it was quite the deal," I said, not sure what to say.

"Did Uncle Frank really fire you from the Freeze?" she asked. Taylor had surprised everyone by announcing she was taking a semester off from college to sort out some career issues before she invested more time and money. A psychology major, she was currently working full-time for Uncle Frank at the Dairee Freeze and had convinced Uncle Frank and Aunt Reggie to leave her in charge more and more. She actually seemed to enjoy puttering around the Freeze, and had implemented some innovations and suggested improvements to Uncle Frank that would increase efficiency, as well as the bottom line. Since Uncle Frank is as tight as my peach maid-of-honor dress, (shhh! It's our little secret, remember?) it suited him fine and dandy.

I shrugged. "Yeah. So? Big deal. It was time for me to move on," I said, unwilling to acknowledge the hurt I felt at having been sacked. I'd been fired before. Okay, multiple times. But I'd worked for Uncle Frank since I was fifteen and the Dairee Freeze had been a big part of my life for a very long time. The idea that I might not be welcome there left me feeling somewhat adrift. Plus there was all that lost free food to think about.

"You really do have a knack for finding trouble, Tressa," Taylor said, and I looked up. Hello. I didn't find trouble. It found me.

"Everyone has their gift," I snarked. "Guess that's mine."

"You do understand that you put not only yourself at risk, but others as well," she went on. "And eventually you're going to tempt fate once too often and either you or someone you care about is going to end up getting hurt," she said. "Have you thought about that?"

Following a vehicle at nine o'clock at night hadn't seemed all that risky to me. And who could have anticipated the driver would turn Speed Racer on us?

"Contrary to what you may think, little sister, I don't run ads in the *Gazette* looking for trouble," I told her, finishing my cheesy pie and standing to take the plate to the kitchen.

"Oh, really?" Taylor asked. "Then why does some lady named Mo think you're about to marry her nephew?" she asked. I dropped my plate. Good thing it was from my gammy's ancient melamine set and virtually unbreakable.

I turned. "Uh, what?"

"Some lady came into the Freeze yesterday looking for you," Taylor said, standing and coming over to me. "She said she'd just gotten back in the state after wintering in Arizona and couldn't wait to see you. She said you were engaged to her nephew, Manny, and she wanted to hear all about the wedding plans. Of course, I'm sure you have a perfectly good explanation for why this nice lady thinks there are wedding bells in your near future. It's all a great big misunderstanding, right?" She crossed her arms.

I bent over and picked up my plate and fork, rinsed them in the sink, and put them in the dishwasher.

"So? What's the real story here, ace cub reporter?" Taylor continued, one foot tapping in time with my increased pulse rate.

"Would you believe I was doing a good deed for a friend?" I asked. "Well, not actually a friend. More like an acquaintance. A casual acquaintance. Not even a casual acquaintance, really. Almost a business acquaintance." I was into full Tressa nervous chatter now. Not a good sign.

"And Manny DeMarco is this acquaintance?" Taylor asked with an upward lift to her eyebrow.

I grabbed a glass and poured some water. "He could

be," I said, not even sure that was his real name. He'd used several since I first came to meet him. I took a sip of the water.

"Isn't he the guy you bailed out of jail last summer?" she asked.

"He could be." I took another sip of water. He'd actually been known as Manny Dishman back then.

"The same Manny that Joe Townsend hit with pepper spray?"

"He could be." Then again, it might've been mace.

"And he thinks you're engaged to him?" she asked.

"Of course not," I told her, draining the water and adding the glass to the dishwasher tray. "Just his aunt Mo," I said. "Oh, and his cousin Mick. And maybe Mick's girlfriend. But that's it. Honest."

Taylor dropped onto one of the bar stools at the dining room counter. "I know I'm going to regret asking this, but how in the world did you get yourself engaged to a guy you barely know who has had brushes with the law and whose name you're not even sure of?" she asked.

I washed my hands and wiped them on a kitchen towel. "You'll understand completely when I explain," I promised. "And you'll see what a kind, noble, compassionate soul your older sister is," I told her. She gave me an I-doubt-that look.

"Go on," she said.

"Manny's aunt Mo raised him. She thinks of him as her own child. He is very devoted to her. Last summer she had a health crisis and it was almost certain she wouldn't recover. Manny knew how important it was to her that he find his life partner, so he wanted to give her this final gift before she drifted off to the hereafter. So he asked me to pose as his fiancée for his aunt Mo on her deathbed. I didn't see how it could be harmful to grant an old woman's deathbed wish, so I agreed," I told Taylor. "But what happens? Aunt Mo goes and has this shocky cardiac episode and it jolts her heart back in rhythm and, voila! She lives! And I get royally screwed big time."

Taylor gave me an odd look.

"Uh, I didn't mean that the way it sounded," I said. "I didn't want Aunt Mo to croak or anything. But now I'm left having to break up with a faux fiancé without sending a nice old woman back into another cardiac crisis." Usually when you verbalized a dilemma, it sounded less daunting and problematic than you anticipated. In this case, with the personalities involved, it sounded like a job for a trained hostage negotiator. Or maybe Dr. Phil. Unfortunately, I couldn't quite see Manny, me, and Mo sitting on Dr. Phil and spilling our guts.

"Does Rick know?" Taylor asked, and I shot her a you-wouldn't look.

"Uh, no. Like I said, it was a one-act, single-performance play that was supposed to close once Aunt Mo left this world with a happy, contented smile on her face," I said. "The spoiler was that she—through no fault of her own, of course—survived. And since she was way down in Arizona . . . well, that 'out of sight, out of mind' thing kinda kicked in and I didn't think much about it. I guess I thought Manny would find an opportunity to break the news of our breakup to her," I said, wondering for the first time why he hadn't done just that. While I knew I was a bit of a blond bombshell—hey, cut it out, I can hear you snickering—I didn't think that the one kiss I'd given Manny had affected him so much so that he'd fallen for me and was secretly pining away. Still, why hadn't he handled the situation before now?

"Well, apparently your fake fiancé hasn't terminated your invented engagement yet," Taylor said. "And if I were you, I'd make sure it was a done deal before Rick hears about it. If you care about what he thinks, that is," she added.

I looked at her through the opening above the counter. Not so long ago I'd wondered if Taylor harbored some tender feelings for the great-looking ranger. Townsend had convinced me they were merely good friends. I hadn't thought to wonder if my little sister held the same view.

"I know where I stand with Townsend," I told Taylor, which did little to relieve my anxiety. After all, Rick was straddling the fence with his feelings for me more capably than a six-foot, four-inch, bowlegged cowpoke. Somehow I got the idea that me being intermittently engaged to someone who addressed him as "Rick the Dick" on a regular basis would likely not do much to dissuade him from the idea that falling in love with me was comparable to signing on as one of Captain Jack Sparrow's crew. Arrgh, matey!

"And you don't think he'll have a problem with you hiring yourself out as an all-occasion girlfriend to a guy who has body tattoos that frighten young children?" she asked. "They have a name for that kind of business, Tressa. I think it's called an escort service," she said.

The thought of anyone hiring me as an escort—unless it was to a dude ranch or on a trail ride—was beyond ludicrous.

"No money changed hands," I reminded her, and

then wondered if it would have been better had I charged a fee.

"And Townsend?"

"What Townsend doesn't know won't hurt him," I said. Hmm. I was using that phrase a heck of a lot as of late. "And, like I said, I just need to figure out how to break the engagement without breaking an old woman's heart in the process—maybe fatally," I added and winced. I had gotten myself into another fine mess, hadn't I?

Taylor stood up. She shook her head. "Your life reads like a really seriously messed up soap opera written by the creators of *The Simpsons*," she said, pulling her long, shiny dark hair back into a ponytail and securing it with a black scrunchy in a single, smooth motion. Not one clump of hair stuck out anywhere on her head. That's just not right. "I hope you know what you're do-ing," she added. "Because it sounds as if there are a lot of people who could be affected by your actions."

I nodded. Sometimes it was hell being the center of so many people's universe. Yeah, yeah. I know. She's a legend in her own mind, right? Can't you tell by now when I'm kidding? Jeesch.

"And what about Uncle Frank?" Taylor went on. "How are you going to handle that situation?" she asked.

Until Uncle Frank cooled down a bit and could ar-ticulate his feelings without clenched fists and spittle flying from his lips, I decided discretion *was* the better part of valor and planned to keep my distance.

"We'll eventually sort things out," I told Taylor. "Until then, you could do me a big favor," I added.

She looked at me. "And what is that?"

"Bring me home a doggy bag now and then?" I said hopefully.

Taylor shook her head. "I should've guessed," she said, zipping up her jacket and leaving.

I shrugged. You can't blame a junk food addict for trying.

CHAPTER 7

I headed for Des Moines, but not before I reminded Taylor about Kari's hen night festivities that evening—not that I really wanted Taylor to attend, you understand. How can I put this nicely? Taylor can be a bit of a party pooper at times. However, she's known Kari for as long as I have. Kari hung out at our house so much she kept pyjamas, toothbrush, and a change of clothes there. So basically, I had little choice in the matter. Besides, I'd never hear the end of it from my mother if I kept the little princess out of the loop.

I loitered outside Professor Billings's classroom waiting for Frankie and Dixie once my eight o'clock class was over. I was a little nervous about how Frankie would treat me after yesterday's unfortunate incident. I'd always felt a certain sympathy with Frankie who, until recently, had been a walking and talking poster child for Losers Anonymous.

I'd been waiting fifteen minutes when students began to file out of a nearby classroom. I watched and looked on as Professor Billings's associate from the night before, fellow professor Sherman T. Danbury, brought up the rear. I grinned like a goofy adolescent when I realized what the good professor's initials spelled out: STD. What were his parents thinking?

Since I had a few minutes to spare, I figured I might as well see what, if anything, Professor STD brought to the table. Besides a hilarious monogram.

"Well, hello, Professor Danbury," I said, approaching him with a hand out. "Tressa Turner. We met last night at the Campus Security office."

He looked at my hand, his brows almost meeting in the middle of his head before he took my hand in the limp-wristed handshake that was so memorable from the night before.

"Of course. Hello again, Miss Turner," he said, quickly withdrawing his hand. Mine came away moist with his perspiration. Gross.

"Eventful night last night, huh?" I asked. "I understand Professor Billings shared our little crime-by-curriculum theory with you. So, what's your take on it? Do you think we're on the right track or, like your colleague, Dr. Billings, do you feel it's mere coincidence? Anybody you know here on campus besides Keith Gardner who might have the pathology to be capable of this type of activity?" I asked him. Once I finally get someone's undivided attention, I have the tendency to bludgeon them with babble.

"I haven't made a judgment one way or the other on possible motives, if any, that are driving these crimes. I just want to see them stop," Professor STD stated.

"I understand. It can't be easy to think someone who has taken up space in your classroom and listened to your lectures day in and day out is meticulously plotting to pull off a crime right under your nose," I said. I hadn't intended for it to come out sounding quite so insulting, but realized that was the end result when Danbury's face and ears turned dark red.

"It wouldn't be an ideal situation," the professor admitted.

"So, is there someone you've taught whom you could see committing these crimes?"

The professor shook his head. "How does one really get to know an individual in the span of an hour or so once a day for twelve weeks, when you have a classroom of them? It's just not that simple," he said.

I nodded. What did I really know about Professor Stokes, and what did he know about me? Other than the fact that I liked candy and coffee, required a lot of sleep, and sometimes acted like I should be standing in the corner of the classroom, with a pointed hat on my head, staring at the wall.

"How long have you taught here, Professor Danbury?" I asked.

"Five years," he replied.

"So, you're pretty well set, then," I said. "Don't university professors usually get tenure after five years or so?" I knew about tenure from Kari, who railed about how many of her tenured professors at college no longer even taught classes, but nontenured, low-wage, low-benefit adjunct profs taught those classes on a contract basis. Kari said with the bucks she was spending to attend college she at least ought to have her classes taught by the real thing.

The professor's face grew redder than mine does when I put on a Tae Bo tape and try to keep pace with the instructor. Professor STD's hand shook as he put his fingers to the nosepiece of his glasses to shove them back on his nose.

"Have you been talking to someone?" he asked. "Because I don't appreciate people poking their noses into something that is of a private, personal, and purely professional nature," he said.

Hello. What do you know? Chalk one up for Tressa Jayne Turner, who'd just struck a nerve without even trying. Which wasn't all that unusual for me, I suppose.

Hmm. Let's see. Now, how to capitalize?

"Well, one has to wonder if there could be a connection," I said, no clue what I was suggesting, but figuring it was generic enough for the professor to take any way he liked. "I imagine there were hard feelings. Disappointment. Anger. Betrayal even."

"What did they expect? That I'd jump for joy when I was denied tenure by the committee?" he said. "And over what was at worst an isolated, understandable indiscretion?" He seemed to realize he was disclosing way more than he'd intended—and to a member of the hated press corps to boot. He straightened his spine. "I fail to see what this has to do with the rash of crimes here on campus."

I gave him a wide-eyed look. "Probably nothing," I said. "When we find out who is responsible, I guess we'll know for sure," I added.

Professor Danbury gave me a considering look and then turned on his heel and left, leaving me to wonder what isolated indiscretion had torpedoed his bid for tenure. Of course, nosy person that I was, I intended to find out.

I waited another five minutes or so before Frankie's class was dismissed and students began to file out. I watched closely to see if Keith Gardner was among them, but didn't spot him.

Frankie and Dixie were the last out of the classroom. I grabbed Frankie's elbow as he walked past me, and he squealed and jumped.

"Hey, take it easy, Frankie," I said. "You're way too tense, bud."

"Don't sneak up on me like that!" Frankie looked around. "It's embarrassing," he said.

I blinked. "How was I to know you'd leap around like a loopy ballet dancer just because someone touched your arm? Take a chill pill, Frankie," I said. "H'lo, Dixie," I greeted his girlfriend. To say she stared daggers at me was as much of an understatement as me saying, *I like beef.* "So, how did class go? Did Billings go ahead and stay on point with the next crime?" I asked.

Frankie nodded. "She was a rock," he said. "No stepping down or backing off. She was in your face, I double-dog-dare you to use this lecture as a crime primer, bring-it-on-punk kind of righteous indignation," he said.

"I thought she didn't buy into our theory," I said. "Wouldn't she be business as usual if that were the case, too?" I asked.

Frankie thought about it for a second. "Oh yeah," he said.

"Still, if the perp was sitting there, going ahead with the next lecture could be interpreted as throwing down the gauntlet, couldn't it?" Dixie asked.

With a psycho nutcase? It was anyone's guess.

"So, if our theory is right, we're looking at a sex-based crime next," I said, and we all noticeably sobered.

The very idea that some woman could be attacked and cruelly violated on the Carson College campus that very night made my bowels clench. "Do you think we could persuade Campus Security to issue a warning to female students and beef up their patrols tonight?" I asked.

"It's worth a try," Frankie said.

"You'd better approach them," I told Frankie. "After last night, I'm thinking you'd be received more . . . cordially than I would," I said, not thrilled to admit it, but there it was.

"I can give it a try," Frankie said. "Maybe I'll get a hold of Patrick and see if he'd be willing to back me up. A request from the state police to ratchet up Campus Security would probably receive more action on the part of security than a suggestion from a lowly wannabe criminal justice major." I wondered what happened to Frankie's puffed-up persona of yesterday. It had probably taken a beating along with Uncle Frank's Chevy SUV, I decided.

"I've got a lead to follow that requires me to touch base with Professor Billings again," I said and saw Frankie's nostrils flare.

"What lead?" Frankie asked.

"I'll explain later," I told him. "You need to get on the security angle pronto."

"Dixie's going with you," Frankie said.

"What!" Both Dixie and I responded with equal levels of enthusiasm.

"To keep Tressa from getting into more trouble," Frankie elaborated.

"I don't need a babysitter," I told my cousin, raising my chin. "All I'm going to do is talk," I said.

"Yeah. And last night all you were gonna do was sit

in the Suburban and wait in the parking lot for me," he said. "You're taking Dixie."

I gave in to the inevitable. I'd take the keg with legs. Only because I knew I could outrun her if I had to.

We backtracked into the classroom Dixie had just exited only to find the professor had somehow slipped past us.

"We could check out her office," Dixie suggested.

I nodded. "Great idea. Where is it?"

Dixie got this I-know-something-you-won't-like grin on her face.

"You're already familiar with the location. Her office is in the same building as the medical examiner's office," Dixie said, and I could feel my sphincters pucker.

"The M.E.'s office?"

Dixie nodded. "The college ran out of room in Proctor Hall several years ago so they arranged to lease some offices for the criminal justice program from the Department of Health. It seemed appropriate to share digs, given the fact that some of the forensic classes are held in labs in the same building."

I felt a gurgle of indigestion ripple through my belly. I'd had an up-close and personal look-see at Dr. Frankenstein's laboratory the day before. I wasn't sure my constitution was ready for a sequel—in this case *The Bride of Frankenstein*, featuring Dixie in the role of the barrel-chested bride, of course.

"Is something wrong, Miss Lane?" Dixie asked. I frowned.

"Huh?"

"Lane. You do envision yourself as a sort of modern day Lois Lane, don't you?" she asked. "You know. The fearless and intrepid female reporter who will stop at nothing to get the story? Of course, in your case, it's more Lois Lane meets Betty Boop. Or Laverne and Shirley. So, how badly do you want to speak with Professor Billings?"

I thought about it. How badly *did* I want this story? Enough to step foot inside a place where the clients have had more recent stitching than my maid-of-honor gown? Where you get a lovely toe tag when you check in—and a tiny slab of real estate six feet under when you check out?

I rubbed my temple. Making the grade shouldn't be this hard.

"Why, you're not scared, are you, Turner?" Dixie probed.

Unibrow had me in checkmate and she knew it. I'd sooner admit I was a straight-ticket-voting Democrat than admit I was chicken. Well, almost.

"What's to be afraid of?" I asked. "It's daylight. We're working as a team. I have my running shoes on this morning." No matter that I'd never actually run in them, I was still confident they could carry me away from trouble faster than Dixie's tree stumps could carry her. And though it would grieve me sorely to choose between getting the story to the masses and leaving Dixie the Destructor behind, there was still that greater-good angle to consider.

"Then let's go," Dixie said. "And en route you can fill me in on just what you hope to learn from Professor Billings, and why you think she can help."

Talk about bossy. Anyone care to bet on who'd be wearing the pants in Frankie's family? Come on, folks, place those bets! It was probably a good thing odds were heavily in Dixie's favor here, though. I couldn't imagine for one minute Dixie Daggett in a skirt . . . and didn't want to.

We made our way across campus and I related my conversation with Professor Danbury (pointing out his unfortunate initials with an admittedly adolescent snort) and said it appeared there was more to the professor than met the eye.

"Tenure can be denied for a variety of reasons based on the institution," Dixie explained. "Usually the professor's record in various areas such as teaching and service is evaluated. At research-intensive universities a professor's record in research and snaring research grants is also considered. Often a review committee made up of department faculty members makes the final decision to award tenure, but ultimately the university president makes the final call."

I looked at Dixie. "How do you know this stuff?" I asked.

She shrugged. "I watch a lot of *Jeopardy*," she said.

"So a professor would have to be deemed deficient in one of those areas to be denied tenure?" I asked.

"There's also moral grounds for being denied," Dixie added. "Maybe he slept with a student."

I thought about that a second. STD didn't look like any campus Casanova I'd seen. Of course, I hadn't really seen all that many, so what did I know?

We arrived at the M.E.'s building and located the Criminal Justice annex portion. I relaxed when I realized that although the two were in the same building, they had separate entrances and were in different parts of the facility.

"So, what floor is Billings on?" I asked.

"Downstairs," Dixie said.

"Uh, as in the basement?" I asked.

"Hey, beggars can't be choosers," she said. "The Criminal Justice Department was fortunate enough to get any office space on campus," she pointed out.

We opted to take the elevator since we'd already gotten our exercise by hoofing it across campus.

"Which way?" I asked when the elevator door opened.

"Left, I think," Dixie said. "I've only been here once."

We stepped out of the elevator into the poorly lit hallway. The college certainly saved on its light bill down here.

We headed down the hall to our left and I noted the office door of Professor Danbury as we passed. It was closed, but a cardboard clock on it indicated he would be back in his office at two thirty. We moved on down the hall and located Professor Billing's office two doors down. The door was ajar, which I took to mean the professor was inside.

"Hello," I said, reaching out to push the door open. "Professor Billings? It's Tressa Turner from the *Gazette*." Dixie gave me a sharp jab in the ribs and I continued. "And Dixie Daggett from the *Daily Destructor*." Another jab in my ribs. Not everyone appreciates my humor.

The professor didn't call out to me, but I swore I heard paper rustling inside the office so I opened the door and stepped in, Dixie on my heels.

"Professor?"

The light was off and the basement windows provided very little in the way of illumination this time of day. I shook off a sudden sense of claustrophobia and was about to switch on the light when a dark figure popped out from behind the desk and ran past me, *barrel*ing right into Dixie. (Sorry, I just couldn't resist.) Whoever said weebles wobble but they won't fall down was just plain wrong. Dixie went down like one of those inflatable punching clowns with the big red nose and stupid expression but with insufficient air to pop back up again.

"Who was that?" Dixie yelled.

I didn't take time to answer. I figured we'd interrupted a burglary in progress, and while this wasn't the scoop a campus stalker was, chasing down a burglar would still make a pretty nifty article for my reporting assignment. I pivoted and ran out into the hall and the chase was on. I caught a look at the tail of a white lab coat as it disappeared around the corner at the far end of the hall.

I was gasping for air before I'd run fifty feet. I really needed to go on a diet and exercise routine. I rounded the corner and caught a glimpse of a black heel as it turned yet another corner. By this time I could pick up the harsh rasp of heavy breathing. Jeez. I was worse off than I thought. I sounded like a wheezing old geezer.

"Which way?" I heard, and realized the loud, raspy wheezing didn't come from me, after all, but from Dixie, who had somehow managed to pick herself up and put herself back together without the assistance of all the king's horses and all the king's men. She was breathing down my neck. Well, midback, at least.

"Down the hall and to the right," I huffed.

"Ten-four," she said, and a blast of hot air hit me again.

I looked at Dixie. "You've been eating chocolate," I

accused. I hit on the scent of chocolate like trained cadaver dogs do decomposing flesh. Uh, forgive the taste-
less simile there, folks. My bad.

"So what? Is there a law prohibiting chocolate con-
sumption I don't know about?" Dixie asked as we ran
down yet another hallway.

"You could have shared," I puffed. "That would
have been the polite thing to do."

"You could have listened to me last night and stayed
put. That would have been the smart thing to do," she
countered.

We ran down another hallway, and I heard the click
of a key-carded door. "Quick, the stairs!" I said, and
ran to the heavy door.

I reached it a second before it clicked shut. It
opened to a staircase, and I hurried over and looked
down, remembered we were in the basement, then
peered up the stairway to find our fleeing fella. I
caught sight of him in the staircase a floor above.

"There he is!" I shouted, and started up the stairs after him. I could hear Dixie's heavy footsteps hitting the
steps behind me. *Tromp, tromp.* Who's walking across
my bridge?

We ran up two short flights of stairs and through
another heavy door and into another long hallway. A
familiar sensation of déjà vu came over me. You
know. Been there. Done that. Don't want to do it
again.

I stood in the hallway and listened. All I could hear
was the incredibly loud sound of heavy breathing. In
stereo.

Down the hall a door shut. I looked at Dixie to see if
she appeared nervous at all. She didn't. Damn it. Just
winded. We moved slowly down the hall and toward

the door that had just clicked shut. A sheet of paper was on the floor outside. I stopped to scoop it up and handed it to Dixie. I put a hand out to open the door. I turned the handle and it moved easily. I opened the door and we walked in.

It was a small room, almost like an outer office. It contained a desk and chair, a storage closet, and very little else. A second door was located at the back of the room. I walked over to it, turned the handle, and opened it with a kick of my foot and a bellowed "aaggh!" for effect.

The door hit the wall, flew back and struck my kneecap.

"Son of a Buick for Chrysler's sake," I said, rubbing my knee bone. I'm trying really hard to clean up my language. One of many little self-improvement pledges.

I shoved the door with an open palm and moved into the dark room and looked around.

"What is this place?" Dixie asked, joining me.

"The door!" I yelled, way too little and way too late. It clicked shut on us just as I reached it. I tried to open it, but it was locked.

"Great," I said. "Just great. 'Take Dixie with you,' Frankie said. 'She'll keep you out of trouble,' Frankie said. And look who gets us locked in God knows where," I complained.

"You were in the lead," Dixie said. "You were the one who chose to come in here in the first place, so how is it my fault we're locked in here?"

"Because you were bringing up the rear. Everyone knows the rear is responsible for the exit strategy," I pointed out.

"I see what you mean. Like Bush being responsible for our Iraq exit strategy," she observed.

I shook my head. Only a lib could think of gaining political advantage at a time like this.

I tried the door again just to make sure it was really locked and started to beat on it with an open palm.

"H'lo! Anybody out there? We're locked in. Hello!"

Dixie looked at me. "That door has to be at least three inches thick," she said. "Plus there's that other room before you even get to the hallway. I'm not sure anyone can hear us yell."

"Good point," I said, reaching in my book bag for my cell phone. "I'll just ring up Frankie and he can come and get us," I said and hit the speed dial. A phone began to ring and I frowned. Dixie gave me a strangled look and reached in the pocket of her pants and drew out Frankie's phone and silenced it.

"What are you doing with Frankie's cell phone?" I asked.

"He wanted me to take it just in case you pulled me into another one of your escapades," she said. "Which, of course, you have."

"Uh, Frankie forced me to bring you along," I reminded her. "And you were the one who let the door shut on us."

"And you were the one who took off running after the guy in the first place. Face it, Turner, your record with chases sucks. Give it up," Dixie said.

"Well, that's gratitude for you," I groused, grabbing Frankie's cell and punching in P.D. Dawkins's number. It went to his voice mail. I considered leaving a message, but it would take way too long to explain.

"Grateful? What the hell do I have to be grateful for?" Dixie asked. "I was almost run over last night, and today I'm locked in some antiseptic hole with you.

Gratitude is not the emotion that comes to mind at the moment."

I shook my head. Everyone was so touchy these days. I found the light switch and flipped it on.

Dixie and I stared across the room at the shiny, stainless steel doors that lined the opposite wall. Approximately three feet by three in measurement, a dozen of them, six on top and six on the bottom.

We looked at each other.

"No friggin' way," Dixie said.

I moved over to the far wall and put a palm on the front of one of the shiny doors.

"Cold," I said.

"No friggin' way!" Dixie said again.

I removed my hand and could see the impression of my palm quickly fade.

"Way," I said.

Dixie joined me near the rows of doors. She put a hand up to grasp the handle of the nearest.

"What the hell are you doing?" I asked.

"Do you think I'm going to let an opportunity like this go by without at least taking a peek inside?" she asked.

"But it's so . . . so . . . wrong!" I told her.

"Merely professional curiosity," Dixie said.

"Oh? How's that? Are you changing your major to mortuary science with a minor in cadaver cosmetology?" I asked.

"Funny," Dixie said, and grabbed the handle of the first drawer.

"I so don't like this," I told her. "Have you considered the possibility that the guy we were chasing managed to get in here with enough time to crawl into one of these cold compartments and, at this very moment, is hiding in one of them?" I asked, hoping to dissuade the little bulldog from sticking her chased-a-braking-car-too-close nose into places it didn't belong, then realizing what I'd just suggested about the burglar could actually be true.

Gee, I'm way sharper than you thought I was.

I saw from Dixie's reaction that she hadn't considered such a possibility. I watched as she appraised the row of doors.

"I suppose you do have a point," Dixie said, backing off.

"Still, we probably need to be sure," I said, and Dixie looked at me, her eyes suddenly showing a lot of white.

"Oh, so now you think we *ought* to check it out, huh?" she said. "What happened to 'boo-hoo, it's so wrong? Bad, bad, Dixie'?" she asked.

"That was before. This is now. Besides, if we were to apprehend a perp in a morgue cooler, think of the ensuing publicity. It could really jazz up your résumé," I told her. "You remember. In the interest of professional curiosity and all that."

"I'm gonna regret this, aren't I?" Dixie said.

"There's only one way to be sure," I replied. "And everyone knows fear of the unknown is always so much worse than fear of the known."

We looked around for instruments that we could use to defend ourselves, if necessary. The pickings were slim. Dixie selected a large pair of scissors. I armed myself with the two-hole, heavy-duty punch. We started at one end, taking turns opening the doors. The first three units were empty, thank goodness. Four through eight held various deceased persons in various stages of "decomp"—or so Dixie called it. Compartment nine held the fellow with the skull fracture photo op from the day before. Poor guy. He didn't look much better right side up. We stood outside the final and last compartment.

"My turn to open the door," I told Dixie, thinking I didn't want to be the one to have to bludgeon the guy with a two-hole puncher if he was in there.

"I don't think so," Dixie said. "You started with door number one, so it would be my turn to open, yours to attack."

I squinted at her. "Are you sure?" I asked. "Because I distinctly remember it was my turn to open and yours to defend," I said.

"Nice try, Turner," Dixie said, and put a hand on the last and final door. "We go on three."

"Is that on three or after three?" I asked.

"On three!" Dixie yelled.

"Gotcha," I said, feeling very much like I might wet my pants at any given moment, and for sure would if that door opened and something was squirming around inside.

"One," Dixie counted. "Two. Three!"

Dixie yanked the door open.

"Aaaaaggghhh!" I took a savage swing downward with the paper punch. I felt the punch smack a soft object, and as the hole punch moved downward, the shiny steel slab reverberated with the clash of metal striking metal. The only person I could have hit with that resulting sound was Dorothy's Tin Man.

I opened my eyes to see what I'd made contact with and found myself staring at what used to be a foot-long, paper-wrapped, tuna salad submarine sandwich and a slightly dented Tupperware container shaped like a wedge of pie.

I looked at Dixie. Her arms were crossed and she was tapping her foot.

Extra, extra! Read all about it! Dixie the Destructor and Calamity Jayne Turner just tag-teamed someone's lunch.

CHAPTER 8

"I cannot believe you!" Frankie hissed across the table at me while we sat in the security office waiting for Hector, head of security, to rejoin us. "Didn't last night teach you anything?" he asked.

Yeah. His fiancée had a really low center of gravity.

The owner of the tuna sandwich had discovered his demolished lunch—and us—and had immediately notified Campus Security, who had escorted us to their office where Frankie was waiting.

Once we'd explained why we'd given chase and how, as a result, we'd gotten locked in the morgue, Hector dispatched security personnel to Professor Billings's office and had contacted Professor Billings to meet the officers there to try and figure out what, if anything, had been taken.

I remembered the sheet of paper that I'd picked up and handed to Dixie while giving chase.

"Do you still have that paper I gave you?" I asked her.

Dixie looked through her bag and pulled out a crumpled sheet. "This is it," she said, putting it down on the table and smoothing it out. We peered at it.

"What is it?" I asked.

"Looks kind of like a lesson plan," Frankie said. "For Professor Billings's class. It appears to be an outline of what we are scheduled to cover for the remainder of the week," he said.

I looked up at him. "What would a burglar want with this?" I asked.

"Maybe he wasn't your average, everyday burglar," Frankie said.

There was such a thing as an average, everyday burglar?

"What do you mean?" I asked.

"What he means, Lois, is that there's a good chance you had us hoofing it after the nutjob who has been terrorizing this campus," Dixie pointed out.

"He does? I did?" I said.

"Could be the unsub thought he needed a little advanced preview of coming attractions so he could do a little precrime production prep work before actually executing the crimes," Frankie suggested.

"The perp stole lecture notes so he could do his homework ahead of time?" I said. "Sounds like an obsessed overachiever to me." Or my sister, Taylor, maybe. "We're dealing with a seriously screwed up individual," I told Dixie and Frankie.

We hung around the Campus Security until Hector let us know that his officers had checked out Professor Billings's office and the only things that appeared to be taken were some personal papers and miscellaneous course materials. We relayed our theory—Frankie's theory—that the burglar and the campus criminal were one and the same, and that he'd wanted a sneak peek in order to plan his crimes ahead of time.

Hector pointed out that we couldn't be certain what the burglar's intent was, reminding us that we'd interrupted the break-in in progress so there was no way of telling what other items might also have been stolen had we not dropped by when we did.

We made one more plea to the security chief for him to issue an alert to coeds and to crank up his patrols and he said he'd think on it. He wasn't convinced there was anything to our theory and didn't want to cause a campus-wide panic if he didn't have clear, convincing proof that there was a link to Professor Billings's curriculum.

He promised he'd confer with Professor Billings and the university president and then consider his options carefully. He also warned us not to indulge in any campus patrols of our own. He'd seen how that played out, he told us, and once was more than enough. He ushered us out of the security building with a bit more enthusiasm than I personally thought the occasion warranted.

"I still need to talk to Professor Billings about her colleague Professor Danbury," I told Frankie, explaining why I wanted to find out more about the untenured prof. "But I have Kari's hen party this evening," I added.

Frankie and Dixie stared at me.

"Hen party? What are you talking about?" Frankie asked.

"The female version of the bachelor party," I explained. "I know. Gag me. I picture a bunch of fat-breasted Hennie Pennies strutting around cackling and clucking and scratching the ground. So not cool. But since Kari doesn't have a sister and I'm her maid of honor, it's my job to throw her a traditional last fling before the final, irrevocable *I do*s"

"What do you have planned?" Frankie asked.

I started to scratch the ground with the toe of my shoe.

"Don't tell me. Let me guess," Dixie said, tapping her chin with a stubby finger. "Absolutely nothing. Am I right?"

"I've been busy," I said. "And it's not as big a deal as all that. Just a few friends getting together for a couple drinks and some laughs. I thought we'd do some club hopping, hit the favorite spots, get some breakfast, and then call it a night."

"Sounds like a real yawner," Dixie said.

"Where will you be starting off at, and what time should Dixie be there?" Frankie asked. "We have night class, but that's done by nine," he said.

"The hell you say!" This invective came from Dixie before I could even get "the" or "hell" out of my mouth. Okay, yes, I know I said I was trying to clean up my language, but I wanted to say something that started with "bull" and ended with—well, you know. See? I'm really trying.

"You *were* planning to include Dixie, weren't you?" Frankie asked me. "After all, she's going to be your cousin-in-law. She's known Kari since she started to work the fair when she was sixteen. And I'm invited to Brian's stag party this evening."

"I don't need you to plead my case, Frankie," Dixie said, shooting a dark look at her boyfriend. "Besides, I don't even want to attend this lame party. And have you forgotten that there's another crime on tap for Carson College this evening, and all we can do is hope that the university powers-that-be will do everything possible to protect their students?"

Both Frankie and I sobered. Dixie was right. We had to keep sight of the big picture. Put petty grievances behind us. Move to a higher level of social consciousness. All for one and one for all. I'd invite Dixie and hope the bartender didn't confuse her with one of his kegs.

I left Frankie and Dixie with a promise to call Frankie's cell phone to let Dixie know where we'd be at nine, and headed back for Grandville. I needed to call and remind Kari's bridesmaids and other friends that we were hanging out that night in honor of our mutual friend who had decided to trade in a footloose lifestyle for a ball-and-chain existence.

It was also, I decided, time for a little personal grooming. I hadn't shaved my legs in way too long—Iowa winters can be brutal and you need all the extra layers you can get—and my feet were probably in worse shape than Fred Flintstone's. I hadn't taken a pumice stone or nail polish to my tootsies since the fair.

I dropped by the *Gazette* to touch base with Stan, but he was out. I followed up on the sticky notes he'd stuck on my desk, and once that was out of the way set about calling the hen brigade to tell them we were meeting up at The Wild Side, one of my favorite country-western hangouts in the capital city. I'm notorious there. I used to hold the girl-riding-mechanical-bull record (gee, that didn't come out as I intended) until some rodeo queen from Omaha bumped me from the top spot. I usually try to dethrone her each time I visit.

I finished up my phone calls, checked the time, and saw it was half past three and well past time for me to refuel this finely tuned, supercharged, superfine body. (Okay, so I thought you were due for a laugh.)

I gathered up my stuff, filed things in the appropriate places, stopped to grab a handful of hugs and kisses from Stan's candy bowl (Shhh! Don't tell!), and left the newspaper office. Destination: Hazel's Hometown Café. Hazel's has been a dining tradition in Grandville for generations. One of those hometown restaurants handed down from one generation to the next, Hazel's features home-cooked meals from the heartland delivered amidst décor with all the ambience of an auto repair shop.

I slid onto a stool at the discolored Formica counter and Hazel's daughter, Donita, had a cup of coffee in front of me before I'd had time to brace my feet on the counter foot rail.

"Thanks, Donny," I said.

"What'll it be, Tressa?" she asked.

I don't require a menu at Hazel's. I've got everything memorized down to the latest price increases.

"Hot beef sandwich, please," I said.

"Full or half order?" she asked, and I raised an eyebrow.

"Sorry I asked," Donita said with a pained look

I sat at the counter going over in my head various outfits I could wear that evening, discarding ones I knew were still waiting to be washed and others that made my butt look larger than life. Maybe I'd even try wearing my hair down that night. Get an industrial-strength tangle tamer and whip it into shape.

The stool next to me creaked—a lot—and I looked to my left to find Manny DeMarco-Dishman occupying the seat. I cast a worried glance at the chair, which looked way too flimsy to hold even one of Manny's butt cheeks.

"Uh, hey, Manny," I said. "What's new?"

He took my arm. "Manny needs a booth," he said, pulling me off the stool and over into the corner. I waved at Donnie and pointed at the booth. Her mouth flew open, but she nodded.

I slid in on one side of the booth. Manny slid in opposite me, shoving the table in my direction to give him enough clearance. Manny's enormous. All muscle. No love handles. One of those persons whose body fat doesn't even register. You know. The people that give the rest of us a bad rep and make us feel like Jabba the Hutt.

"I haven't seen much of you lately," I told Manny. "What have you been up to?"

He picked up a pink packet of Sweet N Low. "Been out of town," he said. "Just got back."

I nodded. Good. He could inform his aunt that we'd parted ways. Amicably, of course.

"I heard your aunt Mo was back in town," I said, and Manny looked up at me.

"Barbie's seen Aunt Mo?" I'd been Barbie to Manny since I first bailed him out of the Knox County Jail where he was cooling his heels after a little fracas at the local bowling alley, Thunder Rolls.

I shook my head. "My sister, Taylor, said she stopped by the Dairee Freeze yesterday looking for me," I informed him. "She, uh, seemed to, uh, think that the two of us were, uh, still engaged," I said. "But now that you're back in town and she's back in town and all, you can break the news of the breakup of our fantasy engagement to her. Right?"

I waited for Manny to agree, but he just sat there

twirling the pink fake sugar packet in his large, dark fingers.

"About that, Barbie," Manny began, and I started to get a really bad feeling.

"Yeah?"

"Gonna need more time," he said.

Manny is a man of few words.

"How much time does Manny need?" I asked, feeling my anxiety level rise faster than the dew point in Iowa in late summer.

"Till Aunt Mo settles back in," he said. "She had another episode. Needs time to recover. Then Manny'll tell her. Does Barbie still have the ring?"

Barbie nodded.

"Yes, but I can't very well wear it," I told him. "How would I explain it to my family?"

"Here." Manny produced a fine silver chain. "Put the ring on this. Wear it around your neck under your shirt. Barbie sees Aunt Mo, Barbie can slip it on."

I hesitated. "I'm not sure this is a good idea," I told him. "Are you sure Aunt Mo's heart isn't up to a teeny-tiny shock? After all, it's just an engagement. And not even a real one at that."

"Doc says her heart can't stand the strain of another shock right now," Manny told me. "Manny needs to prepare her. Smooth the way. So Aunt Mo won't go into defib."

He put the chain in my hand and closed my fingers over it. His gaze locked with mine and I was struck by how dark his eyes were.

"Thanks, Tressa," he said, squeezing my fingers together with two big hands. He got up and was gone as quickly as he'd come.

I felt a sudden thickness in my throat. Ohmigawd, he'd called me Tressa. Major gulp moment.

I'd decided to wear a pair of boot-cut black Levi's with a pink rhinestone belt and a white long-sleeved, button-down shirt for the clucky clatch. I'd had to settle for my black Durango harness boots since my hot-pink Tony Llamas were nowhere to be found.

I sat at a big table in the corner of the The Wild Side and listened to Kari's other friends and bridesmaids giggle and prattle on about wedding gift nightmares, favorite honeymoon spots, and wedding night antics. Two of Kari's bridesmaids were already married and the other one was set to march down the aisle in late fall. I sighed. It was official. I was now what my gammy was fond of calling a "third big toe." You know. In the way. A bit of a nuisance. Not quite sure what to do with it.

Taylor had already been discovered by a cute cowboy who had just finished veterinarian school and was employed by Heartland Racetrack and Casino as one of their three full-time vets. And me? I'd been nursing the same Coke for so long it was warm as horse whiz. As hostess, I was also a designated driver, so I was alcohol-free for the evening.

I'd left a voice mail on Frankie's cell phone for Dixie to let her know where we were and that we would be here for some time if she wanted to join us.

I was just about ready to make a trip to the restroom to let my belt out a notch when I noticed a man and woman—definitely not of the spring chicken variety—garbed in gaudy, country-western shirts and blue jeans with huge shiny belt buckles enter the bar.

"Excuse me, ladies," I said to the hens, and hurried to greet the newcomers. "Well, if it isn't Roy Rogers, King of the Cowboys, and Dale Evans, Queen of the West!" I said. "What brings you ramrods to these here parts?" I said. "Are you lost? The Bingo Parlor is three blocks down and two blocks over," I said.

"We're in the right place, girlie," Joe Townsend scolded. "You got a problem with us listening to a tune or two and maybe mixing it up on the dance floor?" he asked.

I did, but clearly it didn't matter.

"How did you know we were here?" I asked.

"I heard you talking about it on the phone," my gammy said.

"I called everyone from work," I told her. Just to keep her from eavesdropping.

"You musta doodled it on a notepad, then."

"I chewed that note up and swallowed it," I said.

"Then again I mighta heard it from Taylor," Gram said, and I turned a dark look on my baby sister.

"Isn't it past your bedtimes?" I asked the couple, glancing back. "Don't your dentures have to soak for at least ten hours?" I asked.

"Funny lady," Joe Townsend said. "You sure you're not in the wrong place? This isn't one of those comedy clubs, you know."

Good thing. The last thing I felt inclined to do was laugh.

"Isn't this the place with the bull you can ride?" Gram asked. " 'Cause that's one thing I've never tried and I'm thinking that time may be running out," she added.

"The bull broke down," I lied. "The last rider weighed three hundred fifty pounds. You should have seen the crucial internal parts start shooting out the bum hole."

"The rider's?" Gram asked with a troubled look on her face.

"The bull's, Gram," I said. "The bull's."

"Well, shoot. I guess we'll just have to wait for another day for that," she said. "I'll have to be content with having a handsome cowboy sashay around the dance floor with me."

"Good luck luring him away from Taylor," I said, gaining a dark look from Joe.

"Let's find a nice secluded table," he suggested, taking my grandma's arm. I looked down at her feet. She had a pair of hot-pink Tony Llamas on. A very familiar pair.

"Nice boots, Gram," I growled. "Was it very taxing or inconvenient for you to have to go into my closet and pick them out?" I asked, my voice thick with sarcasm.

"Oh no, dear," Gram said. "It gave me a chance to try on all your shoes."

I shook my head, excused myself, and headed to the restroom where I could bang my head on the stall wall in relative privacy.

I returned to the table with Kari and her other attendants. Taylor had joined the group. The current topic was which diet plans worked the best (like I wanted to talk about this) and how much weight the bridesmaids had collectively lost so they would look like sticks in the front of the church. As far as I was concerned, I figured it was part of the maid of honor's official duty to look as bad as she possibly could so that the bride would look breathtaking in comparison. Just doin' my part for wedded bliss.

I shook my head and found myself playing with the

delicate silver chain around my neck. When I realized what I was doing, I grabbed the offending hand with my other and yanked it away from the necklace.

"That's a beautiful chain, Tressa," Kari's teacher friend, Courtney, commented a few minutes later. I realized I was clutching Manny's necklace again. "Where did you get it?"

I dropped the chain like it was one of Ranger Rick's reptilian pets.

"It is lovely. Do tell, Tressa," Kari's other bridesmaid, Simone, chimed in.

"Pffftt." I made a raspberry sound. "It's nothing," I said. "Bargain City's luxury jewelry. Twenty bucks tops with my discount," I added.

Kari reached out and lifted the necklace from beneath my blouse. She stared at the sparkling stone that dangled from it. Her eyes grew big as the gem.

"Oh my Gawd!" she said, her mouth flying open. "It's an engagement ring! And it's to die for!" she screamed and hugged me around the neck. "I can't believe it! Why didn't you say anything?" She stopped. Her arms slid from my neck and she looked at me. "Why *didn't* you say anything?" she repeated, her inflection noticeably altered.

"It's not exactly an engagement ring," I said, surprised at how unexpectedly nice it felt to finally be included in the gushing, giggly, girlish goings-on. "It's more like a promise ring, really," I elaborated, seeing a tight frown spread across Taylor's face.

"Whose promise ring?" Kari asked.

"Did I say 'promise ring'?" I asked. "I meant friendship ring."

Kari's eyes grew big. "Ohmigawd, it's Townsend's, isn't it? Rick Townsend gave it to you, didn't he?"

A strangling sound erupted from me and I looked down to see I'd twisted the chain tight around my throat like a noose.

"I'm really not at liberty to say more," I told the gaping gaggle of hens. I'd already said way too much. "I'd appreciate your discretion," I said. And a roll of duct tape to go.

My cell phone began to play "Roll out the Barrel" and I pulled it out, glad for the distraction.

"Tressa Jayne Turner, *Grandville Gazette*," I said. After all, it was the *Gazette*'s cell phone and they were picking up the tab.

"Oh, puh-leaze," I heard on the other end. "Let me pull over a second so I can get out at the side of the road and retch."

"Who is this?" I asked.

"It's Dixie."

"Where are you?" I asked. "Did you get lost, or were you afraid someone might stick a spigot in you?"

"Good one. I take it, then, you're not interested in getting more information for that story of yours," she said.

I stood and moved away from the table.

"Go on," I said.

"A bunch of the guys from Professor Billings's class are going out for a drink at a bar in the county," she said. "They convinced Billings to join them. Apparently she likes fraternizing with students on occasion. You still need to talk to her, right?"

As fate would have it, I did have questions for the ex-cop-turned-collegian.

"So, you up for a little process of elimination?" Dixie asked.

"What does Frankie think?" I said.

"He wasn't there. He ditched the last half of the class to head to Brian's party," she explained.

"Did you try to call him?" I asked, not totally comfortable pairing up with Dixie again without Frankie's okay.

"I have his cell phone," she said. "But I think this will give us a chance to chat with a bunch of the people, and maybe we can whittle our list down to size."

I thought about it. It was a golden opportunity to make a major dent in our investigative reporting. And I had planned to take our little hen party on the road.

"I'm in," I said. "So what's the name of this bar?" I asked.

"It's called Big Burl's," Dixie said.

"Big Burl's?" I winced.

With a name like Big Burl's, my guess was that before the hens went home to roost, more than a few feathers would be ruffled.

Bawk, bawk.

CHAPTER 9

I gathered the chicks together and told them it was time to take our little gaggle on the road. I didn't tell them where we were headed—the name of the place didn't exactly inspire confidence—but, instead, told them Dixie had discovered the place (wicked little Tressa) and it was a surprise, and to follow me.

I got directions from Dixie and told her we'd be heading that way shortly, and asked her to wait in the parking lot for us. With good reason. The last time Dixie ventured into a bar she'd ended up onstage with a microphone in her hand and interesting food combos in her hair. Trooper Dawkins and I had to carry her out of the establishment before the crowd turned violent.

While the girls were using the restroom, I stopped to let Gram and Joe know we were heading out.

"Young folk these days don't have the stamina our generation did, do they, Joe?" Gram said. "When I was your age, Tressa, I could dance till dawn."

"We're not done, Gram. We're just doing a little bar hopping. Checking out other hot spots for fun," I explained.

"Where you off to?" Joe asked. "Another country-western club? Sports bar? Jazz club? Or you plannin' to take in one of those male strip joints? I hear that's a popular activity for brides to do these days."

I could see the whites of my gammy's eyes increase and her nostrils flare in the dim light of the bar.

"It is?" she said, her eyes unnaturally bright. "Male strippers? You gonna go see one of them Chip-and-Dale dancers, Tressa?" she asked, and I got a so-not-sexy picture of two naked little furry rodents grinding and thrusting for all they were worth. Ugh.

"No, Gram," I said. "No male strippers. No Chips. No Dales. Just some harmless clubbing."

"Oh, hi, Hannah! Hi, Joe!" Kari joined me at the seniors' table. "I didn't know you were here. Do you come here often?" she asked.

Joe shook his head. "First time. But we'll be back."

"You two are just the cutest couple," Kari went on, and I suspected the two beers she'd consumed had already gone to her head. "You look so darling in your little costumes," she said. "You should hang with us. We're taking this party on the road, aren't we, Tressa?"

I applied pressure to Kari's instep.

"Uh, you two will be able to find your way home from here, right?" I asked. "And don't make too late a night of it, hear?"

"We're hardly children, Tressa Jayne," Gram scolded. "We should be the ones saying that to you."

"You're right, Gram," I said. "Sorry."

Gram reached out to pat my hand. "Not to worry,

dear. You run along now with your friends and have a good time. We'll head out shortly."

"Let's go, Tressa!" Kari grabbed my arm. "So many bars. So little time. Where are we going again?"

I shoved her out the door.

We pulled out of the parking lot. I was in the lead with my white Plymouth, and Taylor followed in my Paw Paw Will's full-size Buick. The Buick had undergone a makeover after some lowlife had trashed it—unfortunately while in my possession—and my sister had never really forgiven me. I guess I can understand; every time she gets behind the wheel I'm sure she recalls the obscene renderings in red spray paint scrawled across the dashboard the dubious artiste left behind.

I'd jotted down the directions to the bar on a napkin, and we headed north out of Des Moines and into the county. I checked the outside rearview mirror from time to time to make sure Taylor was still with us.

"What's the name of this place?" Kari asked as we passed several shady-looking dives. "Have you been there before?"

"Relax, Kari," I said. "You're gonna love it. Trust me."

We drove north another mile or so when off to the right the world seemed to glow like one of those used car lots with the strings of amber lights blinking off and on. Off and on.

Nah. Couldn't be. I took another look at the napkin directions. Please, God. No.

I took a right turn and there, according to a big, bright, blinkin' sign, was Big Burl's. The sign was shaped like a pair of sexy legs.

"Big Burl's? This is it?" Kari asked.

I shrugged. "Guess so. There's Dixie's car."

"What kind of place is this, anyway?" Courtney spoke up from the backseat. "It looks kind of sleazy."

Sleazy was putting it mildly. The place made The Wild Thing look like Trump Tower.

"Maybe we should take a pass on this place," I said, getting a bad feeling. "There's a really fun group of college hangouts up by Carson College we could check out," I told Kari.

"Are you kidding? When am I ever going to get another opportunity to check out a place called Big Burl's?" the bride-to-be asked. "This is my last hurrah. I'm in," she said.

"Me too," Courtney said. "In the interest of broadening my sphere of knowledge."

I shook my head. She even *sounded* like a teacher. "I'm not sure—"

"I am!" Kari said, and jumped out of the car. I slid across the front seat of the Plymouth and got out after her. (With the driver's door having a tendency to stick, you need the shoulders of a Viking lineman or the Jaws of Life to open it.)

Taylor pulled in beside us, and her passengers got out. They stared at Big Burl's with the same sick fascination that I reserve for the State Fair sideshow that features the dog-faced boy and the bearded lady.

Taylor gave me an "are you nuts?" look, which I ignored.

"It's about time," Dixie said, joining us and staring at the collection of cluckers with me. "You brought *them* with you?" she whispered. "Here?"

"What was I supposed to do with them?" I asked. "Besides, I gave them a chance to bail, but they want to check it out. In the interest of broadening their knowledge base and stepping out of their comfort zone," I explained.

"Then this is the place," Dixie said with a grunt.

We approached the establishment entrance, where we were all carded—well, except for Dixie—and we paid the cover charge and received our sexy leg stamp along with some curious looks from the doorman.

"Cool," Kari said, putting her hand up in front of her face to stare at the stamp on the back of her hand.

We moved into the dark interior of the bar, a tight cluster of precautious poultry—what is the correct name for a group of hens, anyway?—that moved as a single unit. Some funky music played in the background as we made our way past oval tables forming semicircles around a long stage that featured three poles, one center stage with the other two flanking it. Thankfully, no one was currently performing.

Our odd little assortment of stag-ettes received a lot of attention as we made our way to a couple of tables at the far end of the stage and on the middle tier of seating. I'd hoped for a door closer to the exit—and farther from the stage—but Big Burl's was a packed house tonight. Just my luck.

We took our seats, and a waitress who looked like something from the movie *Underworld* came to take our orders.

"I hope you don't mind me asking," she said, "but are you all lost? You're not our usual clientele," she added.

"I'm getting married Saturday," Kari explained, "and this is my last fling as a single woman. So I'm living a little dangerously," she said.

The waitress nodded. "You got that right," she said. We gave her our orders and once we spotted Professor

Billings with a group of her students in the back near the exit, Dixie and I excused ourselves. As we made our way across the smoky bar, it occurred to me somewhat odd that the professor would choose to pass her free time with college students at a strip joint called Big Burl's. Different strokes, I guessed.

We walked up to the group from Carson College.

"Hello, Professor Billings. Hey, guys!" Dixie greeted the group of ten or so—all males, with the exception of the professor.

"Dixie?" Professor Billings seemed surprised to see us.

"You remember Frankie's cousin Tressa," Dixie said, nodding at me. "From the other night."

The professor nodded. "Of course. Hello again, Tressa," she said, putting her hand out. Unlike her colleague's, her handshake was like putting your appendage in a vise grip.

"Hey," I said, resisting the temptation to rub the cramps out of my fingers.

"What brings you ladies to Big Burl's?" she asked. "Can't be the ambience. Or the entertainment." She gave Dixie a second look. "Can it?"

I shook my head. "We just wanted to touch base with you. I'm using the campus crime spree as the topic for my investigative reporting project, and a question or two came up that required some clarification. I was hoping to have a second or two of your time," I told her.

She looked at the other occupants at her table and shrugged. "I suppose I could give you some time. Shall we step outside? I could use a breath of fresh air." She stood and I was again struck by how tall she was. Cop material for sure.

I checked out her outfit: a short denim jacket teamed with a midcalf denim skirt cinched at the waist with a brown leather belt that featured a handmade silver buckle with what looked to me like genuine turquoise. I had relatives near Flagstaff and had spent some time admiring just such craftsmanship at the souvenir shops in Sedona. This buckle was beaucoup bucks.

Dixie stayed behind to write down a list of names of students present just in case something happened on campus that evening. We'd at least be able to account for their whereabouts, possibly eliminating them.

I followed Professor Billings out the door. She towered over me. I looked down at her feet to discover more Blahniks—this time a pair of Italian-made, chocolate leather, two-tone western boots with four-inch heels and a price tag heftier than my tuition bill.

I shook my head to clear it of boot envy. Another couple was just entering Big Burl's as we exited, but Billings's torso blocked them from my view.

"D'ya mind?" Professor Billings asked, holding up a cigarette and lighter once we got outside. I shook my head and she lit up and took a long drag. "So, what's on your mind, Miss Turner?" she asked, which, if one knows me, also knows is one dangerous question to ask. I wished I'd brought a list along.

"A number of things," I said. "First off, I'm curious as to whether you've given any more thought to our theory that the individual who has been committing the campus crimes has been using your classroom instruction as a sort of crime playbook," I said.

She expelled a lungful of smoke in the cool night air. "It just sounds so preposterous," she said. "And what would be the point?"

"Surely with your experience in law enforcement you know that sometimes only the criminal is privy to the point. That the motive is only clear to him," I expanded.

"Or her," Professor Billings said, and I nodded.

"Are there any students in your class that stand out as being somewhat strange? Behaving oddly? You know, where your cop radar begins to hum and ping?" I asked. "Uh—apart from Frankie and Dixie, of course," I added as a second thought.

"I don't really know all that much about many of my students, but, no, no alarm bells go off with the exception, of course, of Keith Gardner, and you already know his history," she said.

"About that," I said. "Have you been in contact with Gardner since the incident the other night?"

She shook her head. "He hasn't been in class. I did call my friend, the attorney who employs him, and he said Keith hadn't been able to get to work as the county impounded his truck. Makes sense."

"I understand you kept to the script, so to speak, and went on with the lecture material as scheduled," I said. "Didn't you consider maybe substituting some crime like littering or public intoxication for sexual assault? You know. Just in case?" I asked. "To buy some time for law enforcement to investigate?"

The professor took a final drag and dropped her ciggy and stepped on it, grinding it out. "I'm employed by the university to present very specific course information to my students and I'm obligated to do that," she said. "These students are paying good money to receive this information. Besides, there's no clear and convincing evidence that my class has anything to do with these crimes at all."

"What about the break-in at your office?" I asked.

"How do you explain that an outline of your upcoming lectures was taken?" I said.

"Ah, but didn't you and Miss Daggett interrupt the crime in progress? So we have no idea of what else may have been taken had the culprit not been caught in the act. Correct?"

She and Hector had obviously been conferring.

"What about you personally?" I said, deciding that I wasn't cut out for pussy-footing. Besides, felines and I have issues. "Is there anyone you can think of who might have it out for you, who might have some reason to want to get back at you and they're using your class, your curriculum, and your students to do it?" I asked.

The professor straightened. "Enemies, you mean?" she said. "I'm an ex-cop. I arrested people for a living. I deprived them of their freedom. My testimony put them behind bars. What do you think?"

"I was thinking of something more . . . recent," I said. "With a colleague maybe?"

Professor Billings pulled a pack of smokes from her pocket, offered the pack to me, and I shook my head. She pulled another cigarette out and lit it.

"Why do I get the feeling you already have someone in mind?" she said.

"It's just something I heard," I replied.

"And what is that?" she asked, a hard edge to her voice.

"I heard that Professor Danbury was denied tenure with the department, and that you were on the committee that made the recommendation to withhold it," I said, making up most of what I'd just shared. In cop talk it's known as playing a hunch. We cowgirl types call it feeding someone a line of horseshit. You take the seed of a story, invent the rest, and proceed to lie through your teeth. They do it on the cop shows all the time to get confessions. And it works.

"You heard, did you now?" Professor Billings responded.

"I also hear that tenure is very coveted and that, once denied, a professor is usually forced to move on down the road," I added. "That would cause hard feelings, wouldn't it?" I asked. "Anger? Maybe even hate? It's not hard to make the leap from that to an act of revenge," I told Billings.

She shook her head and blinked. "You think Sherman Danbury is committing these crimes to get back at me for not recommending him for tenure?" she asked. "That's a bit of a stretch, don't you think?"

I shrugged. "About as much of a stretch as the idea that it is completely coincidental that the campus crimes parrot your lectures," I pointed out.

Billings raised an eyebrow. "I'm sorry. I just can't see Sherman sneaking, stealing, and stalking just to stick it to me. Besides, I thought you'd pegged Keith Gardner as the culprit after the hit-and-run incident the other night. So where does Professor Danbury fit in?" she asked. "Or are you just playing the drive-by media game and stirring the pot to see what rises to the top?"

"I'm investigating every possible avenue," I replied.

"I think you've just hit a dead end, Miss Turner." The professor finished her second cigarette and discarded it in a nearby wastebasket.

Dead end, huh? Story of my life.

"I spent twenty years as a peace officer," Billings went on. "And you expect me to believe I've worked alongside a fellow professor for five years and, with all my expertise, never suspected that colleague was capa-

ble of unspeakable acts against my students?" Billings
shook her head. "I'm sorry, Miss Turner, but I just
can't accept that," she said. She turned to leave. "Now,
if there's nothing else?"

"There is one more thing," I asked. "Why was Danbury denied tenure? Was his classroom instruction in-
ferior? Was he not published enough? Insufficient
student service time? Improper servicing of students?"
I asked.

"I have to hand it to you, Miss Turner," Billings said
with a shake of her head. "You receive high marks for
persistence. Good night," she added, and headed for
the parking lot.

I watched her get in her vehicle and drive away.
Guess I'd spoiled her night out with the boys.

I'd reentered Big Burl's more than ready to gather
my flock and head for the barn when I stopped in my
tracks and stared, my gaze coming to rest on two very
familiar—and very conspicuous—black Stetsons on
two customers at a table well away from the hens.

Why, the duplicitous little bird turds! I'd underestimated Hopalong Cassidy and his comical sidekick,
Hellion Hannah, for the last time. I straightened my
spine. It was time for the last roundup.

I'd just taken a step toward the cockamamie cow-
pokes when a ruckus broke out near the table where
Kari and her friends and attendants were sitting. I
looked up to see a heavy, middle-aged patron pull
himself up onto the stage, shove a scantily clad
dancer aside, and grab hold of the pole nearest our
table.

"This is for the purty blonde who's gettin' married
this weekend," he said, his speech slurred and slow.
"Enjoy!" he said, and I watched as he began to dance

around the pole, sliding it between his legs in a really perverted way.

I looked at the table of hens and had never seen so many mouths fly open at the same time—with the exception of that time when my gammy referred to Abigail Winegardner as "that ol' slut" and was unaware the church choir microphone was on.

I wanted to cover my eyes when the guy reached up and loosened up his black tie and twirled it, then began to unbutton his white shirt. Honest, I really wanted to look away, but it was just like one of those shock scenes in a scary movie where you end up peeking through the fingers over your eyes. You want to look away but, try as you might, you just can't.

The drunk continued to jiggle around the dance pole. He wiggled out of his shirt and tossed it at the table. Dixie caught it and cast a *what do I do?* look at the group, which clearly demonstrated she was out of her element.

Meanwhile, the crowd was getting riled up. The men in the audience who had come to see toned, tanned, busty, naked women were clearly not thrilled with the pasty, sweaty, fleshy white tubbo currently performing an unrehearsed and unpolished pole dance center stage. The dancer began to unzip his dark pants and shimmy out of them. I wanted to scratch my eyes out.

"Get that porker off the stage!" someone yelled.

"Get Big Burl in here!" someone else suggested. "He'll kick his ass!"

"Take it off, take it off, take it all off!" someone yelled and clapped. I recognized my gammy's voice.

The guy disrobed and pranced on the stage, clad only in his black tie, a pair of white briefs, dark socks, and shiny black shoes. The reflection of the lights off all that pale white skin was very nearly blinding. Unfortunately, only very nearly.

More patrons had entered Big Burl's, but my eyes—damn them—remained focused on the stage.

A shrill whistle sounded and I was bettin' it was from Joe, followed by more "Take it off!" from the same general area.

The dancer pulled off his tie, held it overhead, and twirled it like a lasso.

"This is for the little blond bride!" he said, and I looked on in disbelief as he tossed it to Kari.

"Kari?" I heard off to my right, and I turned to see Kari's fiancé, Brian, standing not ten feet away from me. "Kari?" he said again.

"Brian?" I heard Kari say, her voice taking on the shrill tones of a wounded soprano.

"What the hell?" Brian said, just as the dancer turned and flashed a doughy white butt cheek in Kari's direction. Kari's flesh was the color of cement. "You son of a bitch!" Brian snarled.

One minute Brian was at ground level, the next he was onstage with the almost naked male performer getting ready to kick some lily white behind. Screams erupted throughout the bar. Patrons jumped out of their seats and started pushing and yelling at each other. My feet finally remembered how to move, and my first thought was to get my gammy and Joe out of harm's way. I ran over to their table and grabbed both their hands and yanked them out of their chairs.

"We're leaving," I said, pulling them through the mass of bodies and toward the exit. I caught a look at the stage. A huge fellow had a hold of Brian while two skinny but big-breasted dancers looked on.

"That's Big Burl," Gram said.

I made my way through the tangled bodies, stepping over those on the floor and around overturned tables, and was about to sidestep two tall men standing near the front, staring at the melee.

"Hannah?"

"Frankie?"

"Rick?"

"Granddad?"

"Tressa?"

"I can explain!"

The sudden and unmistakable sound of police sirens could be heard above the bump-and-grind music and the grunts, groans, and smacks of a good old-fashioned brawl.

I shoved the old folks at Townsend. "Hurry! Get them out of here!" I yelled.

"But we haven't said good night to Big Burl," Gram complained.

I caught Townsend's eye. He hesitated and then nodded.

"Come on, Hannah. Gramps," he said. "Let's get you to your car."

I watched as Townsend bustled them out the door and turned to gather the hens and get them the hell out of Dodge.

Frankie had located Dixie, and she was trying to explain why she was holding the fat dancer's pants. Kari had joined Brian onstage and was sobbing. Taylor, Simone, and Courtney were nowhere to be seen.

Revolving lights filled the parking lot. I found my feet unable to move, stuck to the gooey, wet floor beneath them. I bit my lip and waited for the cops to storm into the place with their riot helmets and long, black batons and haul this foolish cowgirl's ass to jail.

All of a sudden I was literally picked up and hauled over a strong shoulder like a sack of horse grain and carried behind the bar and out a back door. My mouth popped open and my teeth made painful contact with a muscular back.

The thought occurred to me that I was being either saved or abducted. I started to get really scared when a hand touched my backside.

"Barbie sure knows how to throw a hen party," my rescuer said with a soft spank.

Tressa had been a bad, baadd, baaaddd girl.

CHAPTER 10

I sat across from Manny at an IHOP restaurant, a country omelet, hash browns, and a side of buttermilk cakes in front of me. Manny had ordered a skillet breakfast but had gone with whole wheat pancakes as the healthful alternative of side. I myself had ordered whole wheat cakes once. It was like chewing a potholder.

Manny had hauled me out of Big Burl's, plopped me on the back of his Harley, and we were outta there.

"I am in such trouble," I said, finding the fact that I was now public enemy number one hadn't made even a slight dent in my appetite. What a rip-off. And with Kari's wedding three days away, a heavy breakfast at 1:00 a.m. was probably not a smart choice. Provided there still was a wedding. That thought made me put my fork down and take a breather. "I've done a bad, bad thing," I said.

Manny took a long drink of his orange juice and looked over at me. He took up a good three-quarters of his booth. "Barbie has a nose for finding trouble," he agreed. "Manny likes that in a woman," he added with a sexy wink.

"This is not a joke, Manny!" I said. "For all I know the police have hauled my family and friends to jail, and at this very moment my gammy may be sharing a cell with a whacked-out meth head or a streetwise hooker from down on the block."

Manny shrugged. "That the case, Barbie's gram be havin' the time of her life," he said.

Which was no doubt true. Knowing my gammy, she'd probably demand to be cuffed and stuffed and hauled to the pokey.

"I'm in deep voodoo here, Manny," I said. "Two senior citizens were placed at risk, my sister will never bond with me, and when I left, the couple scheduled to be united in holy matrimony in three days' time were on a strip club stage arguing over a chubby Chippendale wannabe." I sighed. "I am so screwed."

"Big Burl's don't get many bridal parties," Manny admitted.

"And you'd know that how?" I asked.

Manny ignored my question. "How'd you come to pick that bar?"

I explained about the campus crime wave, my deficient grade report, the class assignment, and our theory that the crimes were related to Professor Billings and her class.

"Billings? She a woman?" Manny asked.

"Yeah. Why? Do you know her?"

Manny shook his head. "Know of her."

I sat up in my seat. "Oh? How so?" I asked.

Manny shrugged. "Manny hears a lot of stuff," he said.

Manny always seems to know things. I don't know how; he just does. That fact always made me wonder just how Manny earned a living and how he spent his time.

"What kind of stuff? In regards to Barbara Billings, that is." I put my elbows on the table.

Manny kept chewing his pancake. I should've warned him against the whole wheat kind.

"Spill it, Manny."

Another almost-smile made his lips twitch. Manny had nice lips. I gave my cheek a mental slap. *Focus, Tressa. Focus.*

"Billings was a Des Moines cop. One of the first women cops."

"Tell me something I don't already know," I said.

Manny picked up a napkin and wiped his mouth, then sat back against the booth. "Oh. A challenge. Hmm. Did Barbie know the professor had to either quit or be fired?" he asked.

I stared at him. "Go on," I urged, grabbing a clean napkin from the dispenser and preparing to take notes.

"She had problems with authority," Manny said.

I mulled that over for a second. "She was a cop," I finally said. "How could she have a problem with authority?"

"She didn't like to take orders," he answered.

Ah, something I could relate to.

"So, how did this lead to being asked to resign?" I asked.

"Insubordination," he said. "Multiple counts."

"So she had to resign. Wonder why Dawkins didn't mention that."

"P.D.?"

I looked at Manny. "You know him, too?" I asked.

Manny shrugged. "Maybe. Manny knows a lot of people," he said.

"Uh, I've never asked this before, but what exactly do you do, Manny?" I asked. "You know. As a job. To pay the bills. Bring home the bacon."

Manny smiled. "Manny has several jobs," he said.

"Name one," I challenged.

"Handyman," he replied.

"Name another," I told him.

He raised an eyebrow. "Barbie already forget where nosiness got her?" he asked. I bit my lip.

"Well, excuse me for being harmlessly inquisitive," I said, thinking the less I knew was probably better—at least in Manny's case. "So, the Professor didn't like being bossed around. Who does? Why is that cause for termination?"

"Might have something to do with cussing out the chief when she didn't get promoted to sergeant," he said.

Ouch. Not your smartest career move.

"So she left the force and became a college professor. That's making lemonade out of lemons," I said, very familiar with being handed the fruit if not in producing the resulting beverage.

"Guess it worked out, then," Manny said.

"Do you think we're wrong about the crimes and a link to Billings?" I asked Manny.

"Someone is behind the crimes," Manny said. "Is it the same person? Guess that's the question Barbie needs to answer to make the grade."

"If I survive the fallout from Big Burl's," I said. "You never did say how you came to be there."

Manny drained the last of his juice in one long swallow. I watched his Adam's apple bob up and down with way too much fascination. He ignored my last comment.

"Barbie better get a hard hat," he said instead.

I nodded. A suit of armor was more like it.

Manny delivered me back to my car via his Harley. I was shivering by the time we got there. Thank goodness it wasn't far. As it was, I was almost a Popsicle.

Since I'd left Big Burl's in a bit of a hurry, Manny phoned Burl to get me back in to retrieve my purse. I checked my cell phone as soon as I got in my car. Five voice mails. One each from Frankie, Kari, and Taylor. Two from Townsend.

I checked the messages, relieved that no one needed to be bailed out of the pokey, but not liking Townsend's second, terse "Where the hell are you? Call me!" message.

I checked the time. Almost three. Way too late to call the ranger. He'd be in bed, sound asleep.

My cell phone began to play and I looked at the number. Then again, I could be wrong.

I was tempted to ignore the call, but sucked it up and answered.

"I really can explain," I blurted right off the bat. "You see, I had a tip that someone I needed to interview was going to be at Big Burl's—"

"Where are you?"

I looked at the still-blinking lights on the still-sexy legs on Big Burl's still-surreal sign.

"I'm just leaving Des Moines," I said.

"Where the hell did you disappear to?" Townsend asked. "We were looking for you everywhere."

"A, uh, friend helped me get out the back door," I said. "We went for breakfast."

I was pretty sure the muffled words I heard were of the naughty variety.

"We were worried sick about you, and the whole time you were at Denny's eating breakfast?" Townsend's tone was thick with an "I don't believe I'm hearing this" sentiment.

"No. We were at IHOP," I said, foolish female that I am.

"We? Who is 'we'?"

"My friend," I said, wanting to pull my tongue out and wrap it around my neck.

"What friend?"

"You're cutting out," I said, using my old trick of playing radio static to end a conversation I didn't want to have. "I must be in a hole," I said.

"Turn off the radio, Tressa," Townsend said. "I'm on to you."

Damn clever, cheeky ranger.

My phone began to beep and I saw the low battery indicator flash. *Thank you, God!*

"Listen. You hear that beep? It's my phone battery. I'm losing power," I told him. "Glad everyone is okay. Gotta go before I'm dead," I said and winced. "Heading home. Sleep well. Bye. Bye. Bye." I hit the End button and let out a long sigh. The cowardly lion had nothin' on me.

I decided while I was so close to Carson College, I'd take a quick drive through the campus and drop by the Campus Security office to see if all was quiet. I hoped they'd beefed up patrols and that the string of crimes had been broken.

I drove through the campus slowly, my eyes alert for anything out of the usual. I passed the medical examiner's office just as someone exited. I frowned. What would someone be doing this late? I shrugged. Maybe they had twenty-four hour slice and dice shifts.

I watched the figure, who was dressed in black pants, shoes, and sweatshirt, and when he walked under a nearby streetlight, I recognized Professor STD—uh, Danbury. What on earth could be so important that the professor had to work this late? His pace was hurried as he jogged to a tan sedan and jumped in the passenger side.

I tried to get a glimpse at the driver as they passed, but it was too dark. I felt a certain affinity for the car's owner when I noticed the car was missing a rear hubcap. My car only had one hubcap left. I considered following the professor but thought I'd probably gotten in enough trouble for one day. Instead, I drove to Campus Security headquarters.

The place was lit up like a Christmas tree. Patrick's patrol car was in the parking lot along with a county cruiser. I got a sick feeling in my stomach. And no, it wasn't due to the omelet, hash browns, and cakes, but thanks for asking.

I entered the security office. Patrick was at the front desk. He saw me and walked over, a grave look on his handsome face.

"Oh no," I said.

He nodded. "Campus Security got the report an hour ago," he said.

"Was it—a rape?" I asked, shaken at the thought

that this day's criminal justice lecture had become someone's nightmare.

"Attempted sexual assault," Patrick told me.

My eyes filled with tears. "Oh no," I said again, feeling absolutely no desire to say *I told you so*.

"It gets worse," he said, and I looked up at him. "The victim is Barbara Billings."

Security Chief Hector Maldonado threw me a dark look as he, Patrick, and a Polk County deputy emerged from a room down the hall and assembled at the front desk. I got up from a chair in the waiting area and hurried over to them.

"How is she?" I asked. "Is she hurt?"

Patrick rubbed the back of his neck. "She's roughed up a bit," he said, "but she refuses medical attention. You know how cops are."

I supposed that included ex-cops.

"Did she see her attacker?" I asked.

He shook his head. "She was jumped from behind."

"You said 'attempted sexual assault.' Does that mean it was an unsuccessful attempt?" I asked, hoping for at least a small mercy here.

This time he nodded. "She fought back," he told me. "With her past training, she knew what to do. She said she also screamed bloody murder," he said. "The guy took off."

"And she didn't see him at all?"

He shook his head. "He jumped her as she was unlocking her car door and smacked her head against the car. She's got a good-sized goose egg on her forehead."

I said a sincere thanks that the professor hadn't been seriously injured. I also breathed a sigh of relief. Now that our theory appeared to be confirmed, steps could be taken to prevent further incidents.

"At least maybe this will bring an end to the chronic crime wave this campus has experienced," I commented. "Once the perpetrator sees the increased security on campus and Professor Billings fails to present her lecture material, maybe he'll just call it good."

Patrick picked up his Smokey Bear hat. "Unfortunately, I'm afraid that's not the way it's going to play out," he said.

I raised my eyebrows. "Come again?"

Patrick stuck his hat on his head. "Professor Billings is going to operate business as usual," he said. "She plans to present her lectures as scheduled."

I know my mouth flew open. I couldn't for the life of me stop it. I was stunned. "What?"

" 'The show must go on,' she said," Patrick told me. "Said she wouldn't be intimidated by a two-bit wannabe thug with a criminal agenda."

I looked at Patrick's somber face and took off down the hall in the direction of the room the officers had just vacated. I threw the door open. The professor sat at a table, a cigarette at her lips. She saw me in the doorway.

"Miss Turner, please," Hector said, coming down the hall to me. "Leave Professor Billings alone. She's been through a lot tonight."

"It's okay, Hector," the Professor said, waving him off. "Well, I guess you got your story, Miss Turner," she said. "I suppose you want to interview me." She took a long puff. Her hand shook as she drew the cigarette away and blew smoke into the air.

I approached the table. "Actually, I just wanted to know if you were okay, Professor," I said. "How did this happen?"

She took another hit. "I stopped by my office on the way home from the bar. I'd left my laptop there," she said, motioning at a silver Dell laptop on the table. "It has all my grades backed up, and with that earlier break-in I didn't want to take a chance of losing the data. I was just getting back to the car when I got blindsided. Perp came up from behind me and smacked my head against my car. I dropped my laptop and I went down like a ton of bricks," she told me, rubbing her forehead. She had a humongous lump on her upper forehead. "Pretty hard to swallow for a cop. To let someone get the upper hand like that," she added, shaking her head.

"But Dawkins said you fought him off," I insisted. "And sent him running. That has to feel good. Not every woman would have been able to defend herself after that kind of attack," I said.

She put her cigarette out in an ashtray. The butt joined five others. Nervous smoker.

"I should have seen it coming," Billings said. "I know better than to drop my guard. Especially with all that's going on right now at Carson," she added.

"How did you get him off you?" I asked.

"He was wearing latex gloves, but I managed to get hold of his thumb and I bent it back as far as I could and he finally got off me. I thought I was dead then," she said, "but he surprised the hell out of me by taking off. I was so stunned, I just lay there like a defenseless victim instead of getting up and chasing after him."

"But you were a victim," I pointed out.

"Yes, I know," she said, standing up. She walked over to a bulletin board across the room and tapped a pink flyer advertising the upcoming Carson College drama department's production of *Arsenic and Old Lace* with an afternoon and evening performance on Saturday. I looked down at her feet, admiring the oh-so-fine, two-tone, chocolate-cream leather Manolo Blahnik boots that brought out the little green Tressa in me. You know, the green Tressa who knows she could never in a gazillion years afford a pair of thousand-dollar boots, but can still dream.

"I should have stayed with drama and theater as a career," Professor Billings said, and I joined her at the bulletin board.

"You were an actor?" I asked.

She nodded. "High school and college productions," she said. "As a matter of fact, I was cast as Martha Brewster in the high school performance of *Arsenic and Old Lace*," she admitted; still looking at the poster.

I'd seen the Cary Grant version of the movie several years earlier with Gram. Gram swooned over Cary Grant. Personally, I always thought he talked a little funny.

"But you were one of the first women to join the police force," I said. "And now you're a college professor. I bet your parents are so proud."

Her hand dropped from the bulletin board. "I haven't seen or heard from my mother since I was eleven," she said. "She ran off and left me. I never knew who my father was. A deadbeat, from what my mother said. Before she abandoned me, that is. I was raised by my grandmother Grace," she said.

I felt very thankful that I'd had two parents who'd tried their best to raise me, despite the daunting challenge. "I'm sure your grandmother was very proud," I said.

"She died when I was sixteen." Billings glanced at me. "She drank sometimes. Sometimes a lot. One day she left the stove on, and when I came home from school, she was stone-cold dead in her bed, the house full of gas. I was in foster care for two years and then entered college."

Man alive. With her childhood, it was totally impressive what she had accomplished. I told her so.

"What made you decide on law enforcement?" I asked.

She turned away from the playbill. "I guess I wanted to prove something," she said.

"What?"

"That I could succeed in an area where women weren't welcomed with open arms," she said. "That I could do something few, if any, females before me had done."

"I get it. 'Go where no woman has gone before,'" I said, and she smiled.

"Something like that," she agreed.

"When you were a cop, wasn't your motto something like 'To serve and protect'?" I asked. "And aren't cops supposed to try and prevent crime?"

She nodded. "Of course."

"Then why are you still planning to go on with your lecture tomorrow—today—when you know that you could be putting some innocent person at risk?" I asked. "Isn't that a contradiction?"

She looked at me and seemed to consider my words. "Have you heard the saying 'We don't negotiate with terrorists,' Miss Turner?"

I nodded. I'd seen *Air Force One* a time or two.

"That's where I stand," she said. "That's where I have to stand. I'm not about to give in to some whacked-out miscreant—if that's even what we're dealing with here, that is," she said. "The jury's still out on that one, you know," she added. "It could all still just be a huge coincidence."

"But you don't know that for sure," I said. "Shouldn't you err on the side of caution?"

"You take that first step and permit someone to control your actions through intimidation or manipulation and you're on a very slippery slope. Where will it end? I'm not about to set that precedent at Carson College, Miss Turner," she said. "Or for me. No way. Besides, if your theory about the break-in at my office is right, then the perpetrator already knows what comes next." She rubbed a hand over her forehead. "I need to go. I need to take a long shower, grab a bite to eat, take an aspirin, and lie down to rest for an hour or so before class," she said.

I took a look at her calf-length denim skirt. It was soiled and stained. The shiny silver turquoise belt buckle twinkled at me again.

"I wish you'd reconsider," I told the professor.

"Good night, Miss Turner," she said and left the room.

Good-bye, Ms. CHiPs.

CHAPTER 11

It was after four when Patrick and I walked out of the security office. I was beyond tired. If I didn't get at least a couple of hours' sleep, I'd have to have someone tie me to my chair to keep me upright during class.

We walked across the parking lot to the cars.

"Long day," Patrick said, not bothering to hide his yawn.

I nodded, my own mouth gaping like crazy.

"I don't think it's a good idea for you to be driving as tired as you are, Tressa," Patrick said. "I've investigated a good number of accidents resulting from folks falling asleep at the wheel."

I yawned again. "Not to worry, Officer," I said. "I won't be driving far. I've got a class at eight, so I'm just gonna sack out in the backseat of my car. I'll sleep like a baby," I assured him.

He scratched his chin. I noticed the day's growth of beard. It made him look rugged and down-home good.

"I've got an idea," he said. "I don't live far from here. Why don't you follow me home and you can grab a quick shower and a few winks at my place before you have to be back?" he said.

I blinked, looking carefully at his face to see if I could detect a wink, grin, eyebrow roll, or leer that would suggest undertones of a sexual nature. Frankly, all he looked was beat.

"If you're worried I'll jump your bones, let me remind you that I've been working for going on fifteen hours straight and on about three hours of sleep. All I want is a hot shower and a soft bed."

"If you can't trust Smokey Bear, who can you trust?" I agreed with another loud yawn. "So, lead on, Super Trooper Dawkins."

He wasn't too tired to summon a grin. "Ten-four," he said. "And if you get sleepy while you're driving, just roll your window down, stick your head out, and let the wind smack you in the face. Works for me on the hoot owl shift every time," he said.

I nodded. "Oh? So that story about troopers driving around behind the weigh stations to sleep isn't true?" I asked.

Dawkins gave me a look. "I'm pleading the Fifth," he said.

I think that's what they call a "cop" out.

I followed Patrick to his home, which was in a suburb north of Des Moines. What had started as a bedroom community twenty years ago had grown larger and thrived.

He pulled onto a street in the older section of town and into a neighborhood that featured nice older homes and wonderful, big trees. He drove into the driveway of a charming bungalow with a small bricked front porch and two-car detached garage. He moved the patrol car into the garage and I pulled into the driveway behind him, turned the car off, and laid my head back on the seat.

"Come on, young lady," Dawkins said, reaching out to yank hard on my driver side door and wrench it open. He tugged gently on my arm. "Time for bed."

I groaned and let myself be led into the house.

Dawkins flipped on the inside lights. The home was as cute on the inside as it was the outside. The modest but quaint porch led to a small foyer where an antique table sat. Dawkins peeled off his gun belt and placed it, his hat, and his keys on the table.

Beyond was a small but cozy living room. I followed Dawkins into his kitchen. Bigger than I expected, it was functional and modern with a small center island. I always wanted a kitchen big enough for a center island. Not that I spent that much time cooking, but a center island would make it look like I did.

"Nice," I said as Dawkins opened the ivory fridge and pulled out a carton of cranberry juice. He retrieved two glasses and poured us each one.

"It's good for you," he said when I wrinkled my nose.

I was parched so I took a long drink. It was . . . not terrible.

"You'll probably want to freshen up," he said. "The bathroom is down the hall and to your right," he said. "Towels are in the linen closet in the bathroom. I'll grab one of my football jerseys and you can use that as a nightshirt," he said with a grin.

"Let me guess," I said, putting a hand to my forehead as if I was trying to read my mind. "Green Bay Packers, right?"

"Is there any other football team?" he responded.

Patrick's older brother was an assistant on the Packers' coaching staff.

I downed the rest of the cranberry juice and followed Patrick down the hall.

"I really like your house," I said, stopping to check out the family photos on the wall. "It's got character."

"Thanks. It belonged to a trooper who got promoted to sergeant. I was looking for a place at the time, and when I saw this house, I knew it was the one for me." He paused. "Sometimes you just know," he said, and I got the uncomfortable feeling he wasn't talking about brick and mortar anymore. "Here we go." He flipped on the bathroom light. "I'll just grab that jersey." He hurried down the hall to a room at the end.

I took the opportunity to stick my nose into the adjacent room. It was Patrick's office. A large desk, computer, monitor and printer/scanner/fax/copier, and a tall file cabinet, took up a great deal of space. I padded over to the closet and checked it out. Uniforms, both of the summer and winter variety, hung in the closet along with coats ranging from a winter parka with brown fur to a light jacket. Several pairs of black army boots, box after box of shiny black patent leather shoes, and several pairs of black Nike running shoes sat on the closet floor, lined up just so.

Frames on the wall displayed Patrick D. Dawkins's peace officer credentials, his academy certificates, marksmanship awards, and pictures of Patrick in his uniform.

"Find anything interesting?" Patrick stood in the doorway with a shoulder against the doorjamb. "I forget you're a compulsive snoop," he said, holding out the green and gold jersey.

"Goes with the territory," I told him.

"Your room is next door," he said.

"Thanks, Patrick," I said, and took the shirt. "I'll hurry so you can go next."

"I drew you a bath," Patrick said. "I figured you could use a soak after the day you've had," he said. I thought it was cute when he blushed. "There's a bathroom off the master bedroom," he continued. "I'll just pop in and take a quick shower while you're bathing."

I soaked in the tub, enjoying the pure bliss of the warm water, and didn't realize I'd fallen asleep in the tub until I heard a hard rap on the door.

"You okay in there, Tressa?" Patrick asked through the door.

"Uh, yeah. Just a second," I said, pulling the plug and grabbing a big white bath sheet. "I'll be out in a jif." I quickly dried off, dressed in the football jersey and drawstring boxer shorts Patrick had provided, and gathered up the rest of my clothes and left the bathroom. Dressed in shorts and a white Packers T-shirt, Patrick reached out to take my dirty clothes.

"Here, give me those," he said. "I'll toss 'em in the wash so you'll at least have clean clothes tomorrow. Bad enough you have to wear the same ones. Isn't that like the fashion kiss of death?"

"Either that or it screams, 'Whose bed have your boots been under?'" I said, thinking it might not be all that bad if some folks I could name thought I was getting a little action. "I'm impressed with the service I'm getting here at Smokey's B-and-B," I said. "Clean jammies. Bath drawn. Nice big bath sheets. Laundry service. You're such a good host one would swear you've invited tired, bedraggled young ladies home before," I teased.

"Not as often as you'd think," he said. "Be right back."

I found my way to the living room and took a seat on the smaller portion of the tan sectional and sank down into the soft cushions with a long sigh. The bath had woken me up and I looked at the wide-screen TV across the room thinking it was a safe bet Dawkins had cable. I hadn't been able to afford it but when my gramma moved back into her home, she'd insisted on getting Direct TV.

"I thought you'd be sacked out and snoring away," Patrick said, dropping onto the couch and putting his arms behind his head.

"The bath kinda woke me up," I said, feeling a bit self-conscious lounging around in Dawkins's living room dressed in his shirt and boxers. "How do you know Manny?" I asked out of the blue. I could swear Dawkins tensed.

"Manny? Who's that?" he asked.

"Manny DeMarco. Or Manny Dishman maybe. He likes to use both names," I said.

"What makes you think I know this Manny?" Patrick asked.

"Well, earlier this evening at breakfast we were talking—"

"You and this Manny went to breakfast this morning?"

I nodded. "He kind of helped me out of a tight spot at Big Burl's," I said.

"Big Burl's strip joint? I heard they had to send cars out there for a ten-ten," he said. "What were you doing there?"

I explained what had led me to Big Burl's house of

broads with my little entourage in tow. Patrick just stared at me. "And did you learn anything?"

"I learned never to let Dixie Daggett pick the bar," I said.

"I meant from Billings."

"She wouldn't divulge anything about Professor Danbury," I said. "Being denied tenure seems to be a pretty compelling motive for this crash course in murder and mayhem to me. I thought if I confirmed the tenure angle and was able to find out why it was withheld, that would give me a little insight into Professor STD, to help me figure out if he was campus psycho material."

"I can tell you why Danbury is being denied tenure," Patrick said.

I sat up. "You can?"

He nodded. "And I'm the one responsible."

"You are?"

"I took a class with the professor a couple of years back. He had a habit of being chronically late. Okay. Hungover. One day he was really messed up and I smelled alcohol on his breath. So I reported it. One morning Campus Security showed up out of the blue and made him take a breath test. He tested over .80, which is the legal limit for DUI. He received a written reprimand, a directive to seek treatment, and was put on probation. If he kept his nose clean, he'd be considered for tenure when the time came. Apparently, he didn't and toodle-loo to tenure," he said.

"So, STD's a drinker," I said. "That coupled with a thirst for revenge could definitely fuel some serious payback."

"So you think STD—Professor Danbury—could be staging all these crimes to get back at Billings for denying him tenure?" Dawkins asked. "Mess with her head, maybe?"

I thought about it for a second. Yeah. That's what I was thinking.

"They have a committee that makes a final recommendation. And the president makes the ultimate decision. Why target only Billings?" Patrick asked.

I shrugged. "Maybe he felt she stabbed him in the back, her being a colleague and all." I sat up. "Oh my gosh. I saw him! STD! He was on the campus around the time Billings was attacked," I said, suddenly remembering I'd seen him getting into a car outside the M.E.'s building.

"He was there tonight?" Patrick asked, and I told him what I'd seen.

"We'll follow this up tomorrow," he said. "Make that today."

"So we now have two possible suspects," I said, rubbing my head. "I'm too tired to think this hard," I complained.

"Time for bed, Tressa," Patrick said, and I looked up to find him standing over me. "Let's go."

I stared up at him.

He pulled me to my feet and I tottered for a moment before he steadied me.

"You okay?" he asked.

I frowned. I'd thought only Townsend's nearness could turn my legs to Ramen Noodles. "Sure. Just a little tired."

Patrick tucked a stray curl behind my ear. "I can't imagine why," he said with a smile.

He took my hand and led me to the spare bedroom. "Here you go. I hope you find the accommodations to your liking," he said with a bow. "If there's anything you need, just ring."

"Thank you, kind sir," I said. "I'll be sure to remember you with a big tip when I check out," I told him with a playful smile of my own.

Patrick's eyes turned dark blue. "I'll take that tip now," he said, and dropped his head to take my lips in a soft kiss.

I felt my body lean in to accept the kiss, his lips sweet and strong against mine. Different from Townsend's hot, wet, curl-your-toes kiss, this one promised strength, security, and acceptance. A kiss of possibilities.

I felt the kiss warm as Patrick put his fingers on my head to deepen the contact.

All of a sudden "Roll out the Barrel" began to chime from my purse. I gasped and stepped quickly back.

"My phone!" I said, and ran to get my purse. I shuddered when I saw the incoming number.

"H'lo?" I said.

"Tressa Jayne Turner, where the bloody hell are you?" Ranger Rick yelled.

I considered my options.

"H'lo?" I said. "H'lo? Is anyone there? H'lo?"

Patrick looked at me.

"Good night, Tressa," he said, and went into his room.

I shut the phone off.

And so ended another episode in the continuing saga of Tressa Jayne Turner, College Drop-In. Frankly, I think I'll wait for the movie.

CHAPTER 12

Patrick had placed a travel alarm on the bedside table in the guest room, and I set it for six forty-five. I managed to crawl out of bed around seven to find my clothes, clean and folded, on a chair in the corner. No question, the service was five-star.

I made my way to the bathroom, my eyes cranky, narrow slits until I splashed cold water on my face to wake up. I looked at my hair. It looked like the inspiration for the country nightclub The Wild Side. I grabbed my brush and valiantly tried to tame the beast, gave up, and quickly braided it into a thick, coarse rope.

I tiptoed to Patrick's door, put my ear to the door, and detected the sound of soft snoring, so I scratched out a brief thank-you note and left it on the table propped on his dark brown trooper hat. I exited via the front door, finding the day chilly and dreary. I yearned for the warmth of bright, happy spring sunshine.

I checked my purse to see if I had enough change for a cup of coffee and a doughnut, and after checking the seat cushions and the floor, I managed to come up with enough for a medium coffee and a chocolate frosted donut. I stopped at the first convenience store I came to and hurried in to get a cup of hot brew to keep me semialert during class.

I took the back way to Carson, finding myself on the gravel road where Dixie and I had played dodge-the-pickup-truck several nights earlier. It occurred to me to wonder if Keith Gardner didn't also make a compelling suspect in the attempted sexual assault of the night before. After all, he was a convicted sex offender, knew the victim, and was enrolled in the professor's criminal justice class. That worked out to motive and opportunity, two elements that the crime shows hammered into our heads as being crucial to case-building. Of course, the aforementioned applied to Professor Danbury, too.

My head still hurt this morning. I wished I'd had enough moolah for the jumbo jug of coffee.

I drove slowly past the small brown house I suspected was Keith Gardner's residence. No one was about, but cows congregated in a pen behind the house. The barn looked in better shape than the house. I drove to a lane almost a mile down the road and turned around. As I swung by a second time, someone came out of the house dressed in coveralls. He looked right at me and I recognized his face from the printout Dixie had showed me. It was Keith Gardner.

We made eye contact, and although we were too far apart for me to read his lips, his body language screamed *hostility*. I frowned, confused. I slowed the car a tad bit, thinking maybe I was wrong about the hateful look. Maybe Keith was looking murderous because his assault attempt last night had been unsuccessful. He would have no reason to hate me. The guy didn't even know me.

To my dismayed surprise, Gardner suddenly raised a fist at me, shook it, and began to run across the front yard and toward the car. I hit the accelerator, my bald tires slow to gain traction, and Gardner got way too close for comfort. I finally sped away. Something struck the back of the car and I turned around to see Gardner pick up a second rock and hurl it after me.

My hands had a death grip on the steering wheel and my spit had dried up. I seriously needed to talk to Patrick about what kind of firearm he would recommend for the personal protection of a small-town girl with a big-time penchant for finding trouble. I grimaced. I was sounding more and more like a certain Green Hornet wannabe and his blue-haired partner in crime.

What I really needed was a long vacation.

I drove to the college, parked, and made it to my class with seven-tenths of a second to spare. I really wanted to skip and sneak into Professor Billings's class instead, but with my current grades I didn't dare. Besides, Frankie and Dixie could fill me in later.

I dropped into the nearest seat, threw my book bag on the floor by my feet, and turned to find teacher's pet, Ramona, in the seat next to me. She made a little foo-foo wave.

"Good morning, Tressa," she said, in that bubbly, effervescent, energetic, fakey way that makes you want to punch something. "How are you? You look terrible. Do you want to borrow my concealer?"

Hold me back, Lord. Hold me back.

"Oh. Is your article not going well?" She stopped. "You didn't let the deadline pass without picking a topic, did you?" she asked.

I shook my head. "I came up with a blockbuster article idea—thanks for asking, Quimby," I said with my own version of the wide-eyed gush. "I'm sure Professor Stokes will be very impressed with my final project. By the way, how's that truck-stop-babes story working out for you? Sure gives a whole new meaning to fill-'er-up, doesn't it?" I snorted.

That took the nice right out of Ramona. She picked up her books and moved to a seat across the lecture hall.

I smiled. Mission accomplished.

Professor Stokes entered a minute later, placing his briefcase on the long table at the front of the room. He looked over at me and did a double take.

"Am I correct to assume that the events of last evening account for your bedraggled appearance this morning, Miss Turner?" he said. "Considering your article topic."

I nodded, thinking I must look worse than I thought.

"You will endeavor to stay awake, though, won't you, Miss Turner? We'll be reviewing for Friday's quiz today," he added.

"I'll give it the ol' college try, Professor," I replied.

Great. A quiz. That meant actual studying.

Like I had a choice. Now that I was no longer employed at the Dairee Freeze, I was in serious need of the raise and benefits that would come with collegiate success.

And if Stan reneged? Let's just say, hell hath no fury like a cowgirl who's been sold a blind horse.

I managed to not only remain awake during class but take respectable notes. I hurried out of the classroom to find Dixie and Frankie waiting for me.

"What happened to you last night?" Frankie yelled as soon as he saw me. "Everyone was looking around you for, but it was like you disappeared. We wanted to stay and hunt for you longer, but the cops told us to leave or we'd be arrested and hauled off to jail. Where the devil did you run off to?"

I put a hand out. "Stop right there. I refuse to be yelled at on an empty stomach," I said.

"Isn't that the same outfit you had on last night?" Dixie asked me, and I put my hand up again.

"Ah- ah- ah. I refuse to be interrogated on an empty stomach, either," I said.

Dixie gave me a close look. "Isn't that chocolate on your lip?"

"I also refuse to be accused on a semiempty stomach," I said.

"My, we're touchy this morning," Dixie said, making a hissing cat sound.

"I could use some coffee and a bagel," Frankie admitted.

"And I need to know what went on in Billings's class this morning," I said. "Did she go ahead and teach? What did she say about last night?" I pulled on Frankie's arm. "Coffee. I need more coffee," I said.

Once settled in an Internet coffee shop just off campus with a steaming cup of French vanilla cappuccino with whole milk not skim (compliments of Frankie) in front of me, I briefed the two on the events of the previous evening.

"So Manny DeMarco threw you over his shoulder

like a ripped caveman and rescued you?" Dixie asked, her eyes almost as big as Frankie's.

I nodded. "He carried me out through the back and plopped me on his motorcycle and off we went to IHOP."

"IHOP?" Dixie said, and I remember how that had gone over with Townsend.

"Uh, what I meant to say was, 'off we went, too.' As in t-o-o, and I hoped everyone else got away, also."

Dixie gave me a who-are-you-kiddin' look.

"So, how did you end up back on campus?" Frankie asked.

"I figured while I was out and about, why not do a quick drive-through? Maybe I'd get lucky."

"That'll be the day," Dixie said.

I looked over at her. "Oh really? Then I guess that means I also didn't spend last night at the home of a certain blue-eyed, hunky trooper. So of course there won't be any juicy details to share."

"Get outta here," Dixie said. "No way."

I shrugged. "Whatever you say, Dix. Whatever you say."

Dixie stared at me. "Prove it," she said.

A cell phone dropped on the middle of the table.

"You left your cell phone at my place."

Three pairs of eyes stared at the phone.

"It is your phone, isn't it, Tressa?" Patrick asked, pulling a chair from a nearby table. He had his civvies on and looked a heckuva lot more rested than was right. "You need to charge it one of these days," he said. "No telling what calls you missed."

Frankie and Dixie continued to look at the phone.

"How did you find us?" I asked Patrick.

"I'm a cop. It's what I do," he said. "So, anything new since last night?" he asked.

Dixie finally snapped out of it. "Uh, do you two want some privacy?" she asked.

"He's talking about Professor Billings," I said with a disgusted look at Dixie.

"You were asking about her earlier," Frankie said. "What's the deal?"

Patrick and I filled the collegiate couple in on the attempted assault on Professor Billings and how, unfortunately, she couldn't identify her assailant.

"So that's why she had that knot on her head," Dixie said.

"What knot?" asked Frankie, and I saw Patrick frown.

"The one the size of a Fabergé egg," I said, wondering how on earth Frankie was going to be a cop if he missed details so prominent they were displayed on people's foreheads. "So did she go ahead and lecture?" I asked.

Dixie nodded. "And cool as a cucumber considering what you just told us," she said. "One brave lady."

"Or a very foolish one," I said. "She's playing Russian roulette with the well-being of her students," I pointed out. "What did she cover today? I don't imagine she took my advice and lectured on littering, loitering, and unlawful assembly?" I asked, with a tiny glimmer of hope.

Frankie shook his head. "She covered a virtual smorgasbord of criminal acts. Assault. Aggravated assault. Assault with a deadly weapon. Manslaughter. Pick a crime. Any crime," he said. "You know, maybe we are wrong about this. Maybe it all *is* just a big coincidence. With so many crimes on the menu for to-

GET UP TO
4 FREE BOOKS!

You can have the best romance delivered to your door for less than what you'd pay in a bookstore or online. Sign up for one of our book clubs today, and we'll send you **FREE* BOOKS** just for trying it out...with no obligation to buy, ever!

HISTORICAL ROMANCE BOOK CLUB

Travel from the Scottish Highlands to the American West, the decadent ballrooms of Regency England to Viking ships. Your shipments will include authors such as CONNIE MASON, CASSIE EDWARDS, LYNSAY SANDS, LEIGH GREENWOOD, and many, many more.

LOVE SPELL BOOK CLUB

Bring a little magic into your life with the romances of Love Spell—fun contemporaries, paranormals, time-travels, futuristics, and more. Your shipments will include authors such as KATIE MACALISTER, SUSAN GRANT, NINA BANGS, SANDRA HILL, and more.

As a book club member you also receive the following special benefits:

- **30% OFF all orders through our website & telecenter!**
  (Plus, you still get 1 book FREE for every 5 books you buy!)
- **Exclusive access to special discounts!**
- **Convenient home delivery and 10 days to return any books you don't want to keep.**

There is no minimum number of books to buy, and you may cancel membership at any time. See back to sign up!

*Please include $2.00 for shipping and handling.

YES! ☐

Sign me up for the **Historical Romance Book Club** and send my THREE FREE BOOKS! If I choose to stay in the club, I will pay only $13.50* each month, a savings of $6.47!

YES! ☐

Sign me up for the **Love Spell Book Club** and send my TWO FREE BOOKS! If I choose to stay in the club, I will pay only $8.50* each month, a savings of $5.48!

NAME: _____

ADDRESS: _____

_____

TELEPHONE: _____

E-MAIL: _____

☐ **I WANT TO PAY BY CREDIT CARD.**

☐ VISA ☐ MasterCard ☐ DISCOVER

ACCOUNT #: _____

EXPIRATION DATE: _____

SIGNATURE: _____

Send this card along with $2.00 shipping & handling for each club you wish to join, to:

Romance Book Clubs
1 Mechanic Street
Norwalk, CT 06850-3431

Or fax (must include credit card information!) to: 610.995.9274.
You can also sign up online at www.dorchesterpub.com.

*Plus $2.00 for shipping. Offer open to residents of the U.S. and Canada only. Canadian residents please call 1.800.481.9191 for pricing information.

If under 18, a parent or guardian must sign. Terms, prices and conditions subject to change. Subscription subject to acceptance. Dorchester Publishing reserves the right to reject any order or cancel any subscription.

night, almost any criminal act will fit the pattern. Maybe that's all there is to it. All there ever has been. Coincidence."

I gave Frankie an astonished look. He was backpedaling so fast that he had a hair part down the back of his head.

"Is it mere coincidence that the crimes introduced in a class taught by Professor Barbara Billings are being committed—or, in some fortunate souls' cases, attempted—against students in that class on the very same day they were taught? Is it mere coincidence one of those crimes involved a truck that almost flattened your beloved cousin—oh, uh, and your fiancée, too, of course," I added quickly, "into a fine powder, and the truck is owned by a sex offender who is in the same class, the instructor of which was very nearly sexually assaulted two evenings later? Is it mere coincidence that another professor in the same department who was denied tenure by that very first professor was also seen on campus around the time of the attempted assault? Is it coincidence that Keith Gardner gave me a 'dead meat' glare and ran after my car like a crazed pit bull, baseballing rocks at me as I drove by a couple of hours ago? Is this, ladies and gentlemen of the jury, all mere happenstance?" I asked, thinking I sounded just like those bigshot attorneys on *Law and Order*. Okay, in my case maybe *Law and Order* was reaching. "I think not, ladies and gentlemen. I think someone on this campus is bent on sticking it to Carson College by sticking to Billings's lesson plan."

A lesson plan where the students were sitting ducks.

Frankie looked at Dixie. "What do you think?" he asked.

Dixie looked back at her fiancé. "You weren't out

there, Frankie. You didn't see that truck take aim and floor it right at you. That was no coincidence," she said.

"What's this about you being chased by Keith Gardner?" Patrick asked.

I told Patrick, Frankie, and Dixie about Gardner's bizarre behavior when I'd driven by his house earlier.

"He must have recognized me from the other night," I said. "Or maybe he does that to everyone who drives past."

"The county and I will be having a chat with Mr. Gardner later today," Patrick said. "I'll ask him about it then. In the meantime, are you two up for a workout at the obstacle course in about an hour? I can get you in to run through the paces then."

Frankie and Dixie eagerly nodded.

"You in, Tressa?" Patrick asked.

And miss seeing Dixie crawl on her belly on the cold, wet ground?

"I think I can spare the time," I said. "Besides, I think it would make a great article for the *Gazette*." I put my hand out. "'Togetherness to the Max: Couple trains for Public Safety Nod.' Not bad, huh?" I asked.

"Does she really have to come?" Dixie asked.

"Now, you're not trying to screw with the freedom of the press, are you, Dixie?" I asked.

She shook her head. "I'm trying to screw with *you*," she replied.

I put a hand to my mouth and gasped. "In front of your fiancé?" I said. "And me his cousin? Shameful."

Dixie shook her head again. "Tell me again how we'll hardly ever see your cousin after we're married," she begged Frankie.

I grinned. *Whatever gets you through the day, Dixie. Whatever gets you through the day.*

Patrick quickly briefed us on current security procedures in place at the Iowa National Guard State Area Command Armory facility, Camp Dodge, where the Iowa Law Enforcement Academy was also located. The Department of Public Safety was housed within the ILEA. Since the events of 9/11, security at these installations had understandably been ratcheted up, Patrick reminded us.

"You'll need photo identification to get past the checkpoint at the gate. I'll phone ahead and get your names added to the visitor log at the gate. See you in about an hour," he said and took off.

Once Patrick left, Frankie fixed a questioning eye on me.

"So, just what is going on with you and Dawkins?" he asked.

I thought about it for a second. "I wish I knew, Frankie," I finally said. "I wish I knew."

While we finished our drinks, I borrowed Frankie's phone to check in with Stan and pitch my DPS Academy prep story. He started the conversation much as Townsend had the night before.

"Where the hell are you?" he asked.

I quickly explained that my Carson College crime story was taking me in a totally unexpected direction, but promised that it would be well worth his wait. I also reminded him of my ongoing maid of honor duties that week.

"You need to talk to Lucy," Stan said. "Some lady keeps coming in asking for you. It's getting to be a damned nuisance."

"Lady?" I felt my mouth become dry. "For me?"

"Older woman. Good size. Hair pulled back. Loud. Know her?"

I grimaced. In a manner of speaking.

I assured him I would be in that afternoon and ended the call. Things just kept getting better and better.

We prepared to leave and I searched around for my book bag.

"Did I bring my bag in with me?" I asked.

"I don't think so," Frankie said. "I paid for your drink," he reminded me.

"I probably left it in the car," I said, but when I checked, it wasn't there.

"I was in such a hurry to meet you guys after class, I must've run off and left it in the classroom," I said, silently chewing myself a new one. "I'll have to swing by and get it before I head out to Camp Dodge. It's got my driver's license in it and we need our photo IDs to get in."

"Take Dixie with you," Frankie said. This was getting to be a habit. A bad one.

"Why?" we both asked.

"Until they find out who is responsible for what's going on, I don't want either of you on campus by yourself," Frankie said. "I'll go on out to Camp Dodge, check in at the gate, and tell Dawkins you two will be along." He bent to give Dixie a kiss. I didn't think I'd ever be able to witness their displays of affection without becoming slightly queasy. "See you," he said, ruffling her hair.

Dixie smiled at him as he left, but when she turned her attention to me all traces of affection were gone. Thank goodness.

"You ready to roll?" she asked. I nodded.

"You still have a problem with me where Frankie is concerned, don't you?" She asked on the ride back to

Carson. I looked over at her, surprised. "It's not like you hide it," she continued. "You don't think I'm the right girl for him."

Actually, I didn't think she was the right girl for me. Hey, hold it a second. Don't get any pervy notions here. Give me a chance to explain.

You see, I'd never had a great relationship with Taylor, and ever since Kari met Brian, I could feel her slipping away from me. So, being as close to Frankie as I was, I'd always hoped he'd pick a gal who not only would be right for him, but, in a way, right for me, too. You know, someone who not only shared his interests and passions, but mine as well. Someone who loved horses and dogs. Who adored clothes and was mad about shopping. Someone for whom eating was a pleasure not a curse, and—maybe most importantly—someone who was okay with the fact that she was never ever going to be the one to set the curve.

In other words, someone just like me.

Instead, Frankie had chosen a coarse, cantankerous, mule-stubborn girlfriend with a predilection for pathos and a personality that would make her an ideal mate for Oscar the Grouch.

Okay. So, how to put that diplomatically?

"Can I be frank with you?" I asked. "Uh, not Frank as in Uncle Frank-frank, but as in sincere?"

"I'd prefer it," she said.

"You wouldn't be my first choice," I heard myself saying. I was shocked—okay, and slightly embarrassed—by my honesty.

She sat for a second and said nothing.

"I suspected as much," she finally said. "I appreciate your candor," she added.

I couldn't leave it at that. For some reason I wanted

her to understand where I was coming from. Why I was disappointed in Frankie's choice of mate. Maybe so she wouldn't take it quite so personally.

"It's not really about you," I told her after I'd pulled into a parking space outside the English building. "It's sort of about me," I said slowly. I explained my admittedly selfish hope that I'd personally benefit from Frankie's acquisition of a significant other, and how I'd been disappointed when that hadn't happened.

Dixie turned in the car seat to look directly at me.

"My God! You're lonely!" she exclaimed, and I stared at her.

Lonely? Lonely! Where had this come from? Who had time to be friggin' lonely?

"Are you nuts? What are you talking about?" I asked. "I can assure you I am anything but lonely. In fact, I have been known on occasion to hide out in the barn for extended periods of time just to get away from people," I added.

She continued to study me.

"I think we both know that a person can be lonely in a roomful of people, don't we?" she said.

I thought about it. Was it possible? *Was* I lonely? For as long as I could remember I'd fill my days to the brim with activity after activity, running from one place to another, one job to the next, running, running, running until I fell into bed exhausted only to get up and do the same thing the next day. Was it possible? Could Dixie be right? Had I really been running from loneliness the entire time? The possibility was not a pleasant one, and good-time girl that I was known to be, I rejected it.

"I don't have time to be lonely," I said, and turned

the car off. I tried to open the driver door with a shove from my shoulder, but it wouldn't budge. I looked over at Dixie and she sighed and got out. I slid across the seat and exited from the passenger side.

"I'll be back in a flash," I said, running into the building to retrieve my book bag, hoping and praying it was still there.

I ran into the classroom and over to the desk I'd sat in. My bag was nowhere to be seen.

"Looking for this?" I turned to discover Professor Stokes sitting at the front of the room, holding my bright red book bag.

"That's exactly what I was looking for." I walked over and reached out to take the backpack from him. "Thank you, Professor," I said.

"Do you have a minute, Miss Turner?" he asked, keeping hold of the bag.

"I guess I have a couple of minutes I can spare," I said. "I do have a friend waiting in the car," I added. One could never be too careful these days.

"I must admit when I went through the backpack to see whose it was, I took a peek at some of your article notes," he said. "I'm impressed. You have the makings of a compelling article."

I stared at him. "I do?"

He nodded. "Journalism is an interesting field," he went on. "Certainly a person needs basic technical skills relating to writing, but it takes something more to really shine in this field. It takes guts."

I blinked. "Guts?"

He nodded. "Determination. Tenacity. Resolve. Those qualities are even more vital than being able to construct a grammatically correct sentence. Have you ever wondered why I ride your tail so much in class, Miss Turner?" he asked.

To be honest, I hadn't noticed much difference from my previous classroom experiences. I was used to being chewed out. I shook my head.

"Because I have, at times, seen this dogged persistence, this drive in you, Miss Turner," the professor went on. "On those occasions when you manage to stay awake, that is," he added.

"You have?" I said.

He nodded. "Sometimes what one doesn't have in natural ability, one more than makes up for in sheer obstinacy," he said.

I frowned. Obstinacy?

"Is that like a compliment?" I asked.

Professor Stokes smiled. "It is. Good luck with your story, Tressa," he said, letting go of the backpack.

"Thank you, Professor," I said, feeling tears sting my eyes at the unexpected—and rare—attagirl. Someone in a position to know thought I, Tressa Jayne Turner, had sheer obstinacy. Sweet.

I hurried back to my car. Dixie leaned on the hood, waiting for me.

"I see you found your bag," she said. "You're lucky. My sister put her bag down in the mall to try on shoes the other day and, while her back was turned, some scumbucket ran off with it."

"I didn't know you had a sister," I said. "How come I never met her at the Cluck 'n Chuck or at the fair?"

"Vanessa's a model," she said. "Working around grease makes her break out."

I looked at her. "You have a sister who is a model? As in fashion?"

She nodded. "Hard to believe when you look at me,

right? She got the looks. I got the brains. I'm okay
with that."

I nodded, thinking it was weird we both had beautiful sisters. I didn't want to have anything in common
with Dixie, didn't want to feel a bond. I liked our relationship just as it was: seventy-five percent open hostility, twenty-five percent tolerance.

I caught sight of a man just getting out of a vehicle
across the street.

"There's the morgue worker guy you two Sherlocks
had me tail the day I ended up playing Dr. Quincy,
Medical Examiner," I said, pointing to the dapper fellow walking to the parking lot. "I still owe you for that
one. What was his name again?"

"Trevor Childers," Dixie supplied. "And you survived, so what's the big deal?"

"The big deal is I probably lost ten years off my life,
that's what," I said, looking again at the brown sedan
he'd exited, my eyes widening as I noticed it was missing a rear hubcap. "Wait a minute. That's the same car
Professor Danbury got into early this morning when
Barbara Billings was attacked. What in Heaven's name
would a professor and a student find to do together at
that hour of the night?"

Dixie and I exchanged uneasy glances.

"Care to find out, my dear Watson?" Dixie asked,
with an I-double-dog-dare-ya look.

"Indubitably, Ms. Holmes," I replied. "Lead the way,
good woman."

We headed across the street in Childers's wake,
catching up to him just as he took a seat in a court-
yard by this seriously messed up sculpture thingy that
everyone just calls "the gross statue." If you ever
wanted to arrange to meet someone at Carson Col-

lege, you'd say "I'll meet you at the gross statue" and instantly everyone knew just what you were talking about.

The statue was of this really freaked out naked angel riding a tricycle. The angel's mouth was wide open, as if he was screaming, his eyes wide with surprise. I'd spent more than a few minutes staring at the statue trying to figure out just what the sculptor was trying to say besides "Heh heh, you fools paid two hundred grand for this?"

Trevor pulled a pack of cigarettes from his pocket and lit one up.

I nudged Dixie. "You should approach him. He's in your class. He doesn't know me from dirt," I said.

"What do I say?" she asked.

"Just start with small talk and I'll pipe in when appropriate."

She shook her head and said, "Why do I get so nervous when you begin a sentence with the word 'just'?" But she walked up to her classmate.

"Hi, Trevor," she said. "It's nice to see the sun for a change, isn't it? Feels good. This is Frankie's cousin Tressa." She motioned to me. "She's taking some journalism classes this term."

Childers got a strange look on his face when his eyes came to rest on me. Most of the time when a stranger does this it's because I have some kind of food item on my face or shirtfront. I was pretty sure, though, that this time I wasn't wearing a meal, so there had to be another reason for his adverse reaction. Perhaps a debriefing from his late-night liaison, Sherman Danbury.

"Hey," I said, holding out a hand. "Nice to meet you." He took my hand, his shake firm.

"Hello," he said.

"Lots of excitement on campus this term," I said, not much for chewing the fat when there was red meat to sink my teeth into.

"Excitement?"

"All the crimes that are occurring, and your very own professor the latest target."

He gave me another odd look. "Which professor?" he said, with just a hint of anxiety.

"Professor Billings, of course," I said. "You do know she was attacked last night, right?"

He nodded. "Oh yes. I had heard something to that effect. Sad, these violent times," he added.

"It's not the times that are violent," I pointed out. "It's the people. Have you heard that the cops think someone is using the professor's lecture notes to plot their next crime, and that they are targeting students in the class for their nefarious acts?"

"There has been some talk," he said.

"Do you think it's possible?"

"Anything's possible."

"The question is, why would anyone go to such elaborate lengths to plan and execute such crimes? I'm thinking it would have to be someone with a great deal of pent-up rage or anger, wouldn't you?" I said. "Maybe even someone with a grudge against Professor Billings. Do you know anyone like that, Trevor?"

He occupied himself with his cigarette, much like Billings had done the night before. Sometimes I wished I smoked. You know, you can sit there with a cigarette dangling out of your mouth, looking very pensive and thoughtful while you try to think of what to say next, and no one has to know you really don't have a clue and are just stalling for time.

"Why ask me?" he finally said.

"You work at the M.E.'s office, don't you?" I asked.

"I'm an assistant there," he admitted.

"And you're taking courses in criminal justice," I said.

"I have career ambitions," he agreed.

"So, you have a lot of insight to share, I think."

"Not really."

I took a seat beside him, my back to the gross statue.

"Trevor, I saw you with Professor Danbury last night," I said, and his eyes grew bigger than those bubblegum eyeballs they sell at Halloween.

"What do you mean you saw me?" he asked.

"Last night. Here on campus. Around the time Professor Billings was attacked. I saw Professor Danbury get into your car."

"I think you're mistaken," he said.

"And I suppose that wasn't you Dixie and I chased out of Professor Billings's office and down the corridors of the State Medical Examiner's office the day Professor Billings's office was broken into either," I said, throwing out the possibility once I'd made the connection to Danbury.

"I don't know what you're talking about," Trevor said, and he stood.

"I think you do, Trevor," I pushed. "And I can understand your reluctance to talk about it. Obviously you and Professor Danbury are . . . close, and you don't want to feel like you're narcing him out, but lots of innocent people are being hurt here and it has to stop."

"And you think Sherm has something to do with what's going on here at Carson?" he asked. "You think he was the one who jumped Professor Billings last night?"

I stood.

"How'd you know she was jumped, Trevor?" I asked. "Professor Billings didn't mention a thing about her assault in class this morning, did she, Dixie?" I asked, and Dixie shook her head.

"And I know for certain no one here said anything about her being jumped, so how would you know that, Trevor?" I asked.

He rubbed the back of his neck. "You're wrong about Professor Danbury, you know," he said. "He couldn't do something like that." He hurried to his car.

I thought about how most every other crime had, unfortunately, been successful, but the sexual assault on Professor Billings had not. I thought about Trevor's words: *He couldn't do something like that*. Maybe because his desires lay in another direction? It was something to consider.

Dixie and I were late getting to Camp Dodge, and by the time we'd made it through the various checkpoints and down to the obstacle course, it was almost eleven.

I greeted Patrick with my Lady Di shy look, still kind of ill at ease after our kiss the night before.

"Where the hell have you two been?" Frankie asked. "I was beginning to worry."

Dixie filled the men in on our conversation with Trevor.

"It's still speculation, but it is interesting. And maybe you can use it to lean on Childers," he said, speaking to Patrick. "Maybe pressure him to turn on Danbury—if there's anything there, that is."

Patrick nodded. "It's useful information," he agreed. "Way to go, Starsky and Hutch." He grinned.

"I'm Starsky," I said. "She's Hutch." I pointed at Dixie.

"You can't be Starsky," Dixie objected. "Starsky has dark hair. Hutch is the blond."

"Owen Wilson played Hutch and he has, like, this monstrous nose," I said. "Look. Look at this nose," I continued, turning so the other three could see my profile and pointing at the middle of my face. "Tell me that is even close to an Owen Wilson nose. I may have a butt that is all over the place, but my nose is tiny and cute and adorable."

"Well, you can't be Starsky," Dixie said.

"Why not?"

"You're blond and you're too tall! That's why!

"Ladies, ladies!" Patrick put his hands up. "Let's pretend I said Cagney and Lacey instead of Starsky and Hutch."

"Oh, nice. And I suppose Blondie there gets to be Cagney and I have to be horse-face Lacey," Dixie grumped.

"If the horse face fits, wear it," I said.

"Would you two just can it?" Frankie snapped. "We're here to see if we have the right stuff to be professional law enforcement officers, and you two want to quibble about which of you is going to be which made-up character. Doesn't that sound a bit immature?"

"She started it!" I yelled, pointing at Dixie.

Frankie shook his head. "Carry on, Patrick," he said.

For the first time I noticed what Frankie was wearing. He had on a pair of dark blue, zippered coveralls.

I lowered an eyebrow. "Uh, what are you wearing there, Frankie?" I asked.

"Academy-issued coveralls," Patrick explained. "I

brought one for each of you." He handed both Dixie and me a pair.

"What are these for?" I asked, unfolding mine and holding it out in front of me. "Hey, look! Give me a Captain Kirk mask and I'm Michael Freakin' Myers!"

"Grow up!" Dixie snapped, obviously still bent about the Starsky/Hutch, Cagney/Lacey thing. She unfolded her coveralls and started to climb into them.

"You'd better do some growing of your own if you plan to run in those things," I said, laughing when I saw how far the hems dragged the ground on her.

"At least I can get mine zipped up," she said, watching as I struggled to get the zipper of my coveralls up over my rhinestone belt buckle.

"Patrick must've picked up a small, thinking that was my size, right, Patrick?" I said, giving him a *go along with me or suffer the consequences* look.

"Uh, yeah. Sorry," he said, underwhelming in terms of his conviction.

I finally got cinched in and pulled my camera out of my bag.

"What is that for?" Dixie asked.

"Well, you see, Dixie," I began, "what you do is you look back here, center the object in the rectangle, push the button, and light strikes a digital sensor thingy that has millions of teeny, tiny sensor points called pix—"

"I know how a digital camera works," she said. "What I'm asking is, what do you plan to do with it?"

I looked at her. "Well, you see, Dixie, what I plan to do is look back here, center the object—"

"Oh, for the love of God!"

"Tressa is doing an article for the *Gazette*," Frankie explained. "She thought it might be newsworthy to hometown readers that you and I—boyfriend and girlfriend—I mean girlfriend and boyfriend—are attempting to get into the DPS Academy together."

Dixie nodded slowly. "I see. Tressa thought it would be newsworthy," she repeated. "Did it ever occur to you, Frankie, that maybe she just wants a good laugh at our expense?" she added.

"Dixie! I'm hurt that you can think such a thing! Frankie is my dear cousin. I would never capitalize off his humiliation," I protested.

"But I'm fair game, right?"

"Are we going to do this or not?" Patrick asked.

We made nice and headed to the starting line, and Patrick walked us through the course, starting with a bunch of low ropes zigzagging near the ground.

"Where's the barbed wire?" I asked.

"What barbed wire?" Patrick responded.

"The barbed wire I wanted to see Dixie crawl under."

He grinned. "We use rope."

Rope? How hard could that be?

Patrick demonstrated the proper way of negotiating the first leg of the course without touching the ropes. He dug his elbows in the sand, keeping his tushie low as he pulled himself along the sand like a seal.

Next came the rubber tires, and Patrick quickly showed us his technique for not tripping. Then the monkey bars, which for various reasons I felt sure I could excel at. Then came the rope swing across a water-filled pit, followed by a tall wall with ropes dangling down the side. Dawkins completed the course without breaking a sweat.

"Bravo! Bravo!" I applauded. "Very impressive performance, Super Trooper Dawkins," I said, thinking his bum wasn't bad either. "Really excellent!

"Now, Dixie," I said as we made our way back to the starting line, "if you could just lie down there and dig those elbows in, with your butt down, I think I could get some photos I can work with."

"You first," she said, and I looked at her.

"Huh?"

"Why don't you two race?" Patrick said, and I gave him a *have you lost your mind?* look.

"How can I take pictures if I'm participating?" I said.

Patrick took the camera from me. "I'll take the pictures," he said. "You run the course with Dixie, then I'll run it again with Frankie."

I looked at him. "You're enjoying this, aren't you?"

He gave me a wide-eyed, innocent stare. "Who? Me?" he asked. "Ladies first." He waved his arm.

I took my place at the starting line.

"I want it noted that I'm at a bit of a disadvantage here," I said, pointing down at my harness boots—footwear more designed for the back of a horse or a hardwood country-western dance floor than a race through a tactical course.

"That's what you get for wearing boots so often, Calamity," Dixie said.

I looked over at her and gave her an evil stare meant to psych her out. In return she did the voodoo finger thingy, pointing at me with her fingers and then back at her eyes.

"Okay. When I blow the whistle, take off," Patrick said.

"Here's a kiss for luck, Dix," Frankie said, and he gave his girlfriend a kiss. I made a hacking, gagging sound.

"Here's *your* kiss for luck, Calamity," Patrick said, and I tensed. He brushed a feather-soft kiss on my cheek.

"Thanks," I said. "But this should be a stroll in the park. After all, two of her legs don't equal one of mine."

"I wouldn't get too cocky, Tressa," Patrick warned quietly. "Dixie may be small, but she has the instincts of a feisty little rat terrier."

"In other words, what you're saying is, 'Watch out, she bites!'" I laughed.

Patrick did too. "Something like that."

We took our places, and Dixie and I exchanged final eat-my-dust looks.

Patrick blew the whistle and we were off. I dove headfirst into the sand, getting a mouthful of grit for my effort. I concentrated on digging my elbows in the stuff and keeping my butt down. I'll let you speculate on which task proved easier. I looked over expecting to see Dixie behind me somewhere, but was astonished to find she had taken the lead. Having no legs was a definite advantage in this section of the contest, I decided.

I continued crawling, only to have my ass get hung up in the ropes, and had to backtrack to extricate myself. I emerged from the ropes determined to overtake Dixie on the rubber tires, but instead found my boot heels getting caught on the insides. Dixie had pulled out to a worrisome lead by the time I maneuvered through the stupid rubber.

Once I got to the monkey bars, the competitive nature that had made me so unpopular at team sports kicked into overdrive. I hit those monkey bars flying, feeling a burst of adrenaline that was almost illegal. I was freakin' King Kong! I flew across the bars in record time, picking up precious seconds lost due to my fat arse, and finished the third leg ahead of the Destructor.

We approached the water leg and I grabbed hold of

the rope and leaped on, swinging across. I felt my hands begin to slip a second before I dropped into the cold, disgusting, gross water of the pit.

"Tressa!" I heard Patrick call out, but I ignored him. I floundered for a few seconds before hauling myself out of the water and went back to grab the rope and try again. I saw Dixie clear the water hazard and land safely on the other side. No friggin' way was Dixie the dwarfette going to defeat Tressa Jayne Turner, Rodeo Queen.

Saturated and waterlogged, but bitten by the "can't be a loser" bug, I grabbed hold of the rope and with the cry of a warrior, I hurled myself across.

"Aaaauuughh!"

My soaked boots came to rest on dry land and I ran toward the final obstacle, the "Great Wall," to discover Dixie halfway up and struggling to pull herself over.

I ran at the wall like a crazed person, timed my jump and threw myself at the rope, reaching as high up as I could. I grabbed hold of the thick rope with my right hand and pulled my body up, the pressure on my armpit so excruciating I thought I was going to pull my shoulder out of the socket. I started up the rope, hand over hand, my wet boots slipping and sliding down the side of the wall. Out of the corner of my eye I could see Dixie to my right reaching out to grab the top of the wall. I started moving my feet as quickly as I could, ascending the wall as fast as an eight-legged insect. Look at me, I'm Spider Woman!

Unfortunately, my hand-over-hand performance on the rope hadn't kept pace with my flying spider feet and all of a sudden I found those at a higher elevation than my head. And my hands. The pressure on the wet rope made my hands begin to slide down the rope, and before I could say, "Screw Spider Woman and the web she swung in on," I was hanging upside down from the rope.

"Holy Spider shat!" I yelled, trying desperately to figure out how to right myself. "Hello? Hello? Some assistance would be appreciated!" I yelled.

From my upside-down position I could see Dixie straddling the top of the wall like *she* was the rodeo queen. She raised her hand in the air.

"Woo-hoo!" she yelled. "Wooo-hoo!" I heard clapping and thought it was a rather inappropriate time to celebrate when I was still hanging upside down and slipping more every second.

I heard someone tell me to let go. I looked down. Up. It was Patrick.

"You've got to be kidding," I said. "That's a long way down."

"Take your feet off the wall and let them dangle. Then ease yourself down the rope."

"I'll slide down the rope and get rope burns," I said.

"Let go, then, and I'll catch you."

I shook my head. "You won't be able to catch me. You see, I'm not really a size small."

Patrick had an upside-down grin. "Just do it."

I looked down. I mean up. Oh, forget it.

I felt a tug on the rope. Dixie was at the top of the wall above me. She leaned over the wall.

"Give me your hand," she ordered, and I stared at her.

"Are you insane? You'll let go and drop me on my head!" I accused.

She looked at me. "Hmm. I hadn't thought of that. Thanks." She held out her hand. "Now give me your hand."

I looked at the offered hand up and the alternative—

the hard ground. I grimaced and stuck my hand out and grabbed hold. I was hauled up at least five inches.

"Now grab the rope with that hand and give me your other one," she ordered.

I complied. It wasn't long before my head was back above my feet and I was lifting myself onto the top of the wall.

"Thanks, Dixie," I said, wiping the sweat from my face, with my coveralls sleeve. "That was really nice of you."

"It was nothing," Dixie said with a shrug. "We don't ever have to speak of it again," she added.

I looked at her. "That's amazingly nice of you, Dixie," I said. "What can I do to repay you?"

She looked at me. "Help me get the fuck down.

Dixie and I watched as Frankie and Patrick took their turn at the obstacle course. Patrick had finished, joined us, and polished off a power drink while Frankie was still trying to make it up the wall. He'd gotten tied up in the rope obstacle, tripped up in the tire obstacle, gotten three blisters from the monkey bars, water-logged in the water obstacle, and was now making his seventh run at the fence. And he'd only had to stop and suck on his inhaler twice. It was not a pretty sight.

"He's not gonna make it, is he?" I asked Patrick as we watched Frankie's long legs, slip, slide, and then dangle along the rope.

"It doesn't look good," he said.

"Do me a favor," I asked Dawkins. "Don't tell him yet. Let him live the dream for a while longer."

Patrick nodded. "Done," he said.

CHAPTER 14

Once we'd finished the obstacle debacle, I left Frankie and Dixie reflecting on what they had each collectively learned, and headed for Grandville. I wasn't sure what my obstacle course article would say, but the photos would grab lots of attention, especially the ones of me in my humiliating worm-on-a-hook pose.

My clothes were damp, but thanks to the coveralls the scum and algae hadn't gotten to them. My first order of business was to check in on the welfare of the bride-to-be—if she was still a bride-to-be, that is. And still on speaking terms with me.

Kari had taken a few days off from teaching to get ready for the wedding. The honeymoon would take place over spring break. I drove straight to her apartment. She opened the door when I knocked, saw me, and promptly shut the door in my face.

I knocked again. "Kari! Open up! Please?"

I waited. "Come on, Kari. At least give me a chance to explain."

She finally opened the door. She stood there with her arms folded and raised one eyebrow.

"You have two minutes," she said, and I winced. I couldn't get my name out in that amount of time.

"At least let me come in," I said. When she didn't comply I added, "Okay, whatever, if you don't care that your neighbors hear all the gory details about our evening at Big Burl's strip club, I don't mind."

She reached out and hauled me into her apartment.

"Okay. Two minutes. Starting now," she said, looking at her watch.

"Listen, Kari, I'm really sorry about what happened," I said. "I had no idea what kind of establishment Big Burl's was. And I did suggest we leave and go elsewhere if you'll recall. It's just that I've been trying really, really hard to do really, really good in college, and with the jobs and critters and Gram and stuff, I really, really need a great grade on my journalism project. That's why we went to Big Burl's. I was trying to get information from a source." I was thinking I sounded very journalistic.

She looked at me. "I have never seen Brian so upset," she said. "When he leaped onstage like that, I thought 'this fat guy's given his first and last performance.'"

"Thank God," I said. "Er, Brian wasn't arrested, was he?"

She shook her head. "As a matter of fact, Big Burl was so grateful to Brian for putting the fear of God into Tubbo T. Twinkletoes and hauling his blinding white bulk offstage that he offered to donate entertainment for the wedding reception," she said.

"I trust you declined," I replied.

"Of course. Brian accepted a couple of free kegs of beer instead," she said.

"So the wedding is still on?" I asked with more than a little relief.

"As far as I'm concerned," she said. "But not without a lot of drama and angst. Brian was just so shocked at finding me there," she added.

"Well, I'm sure you were equally shocked to see him," I replied. "What were he and the rat pack doing there anyway?"

Kari got this weird look on her face. She looked at me for a minute or two and suddenly dropped into a chair across from me.

"Oh my gosh. In all the excitement and the mortification of being discovered there, I totally forgot to ask what brought *him* to that raunchy strip club," she said. Her look turned scary. It was like my mother's, when people bring in cocktail napkins with writing on them and want to use them as receipts for business expenses.

"I think my future husband has a little explaining of his own to do," she declared.

I winced. What was good for the hen, it appeared, was about to be good for the rooster. Cocka-freakin'-doodle-doo.

I left Kari after making three very foolish promises. One, to be able to fit into my maid of honor dress. Two, to make it to the church on time. Three, to "abjure" the cocktail weenies. Now that Kari is a language arts teacher she loves to use big words. I thought the first two promises would probably be easier to keep than the third. I can't help it. Give me a little smokie on a toothpick dipped in barbecue sauce and I go wild.

From Kari's I headed over to the newspaper office to touch base with Stan, and then I planned to go straight home, shower, work on my article and go to bed.

I checked out the notes on my table—I refuse to call that piece of furniture a "desk"—and did quick follow-ups on various items. I wrote up a short article and caption to go with the pictures from the obstacle course and ran up front to pick up my messages. Two were from Aunt Mo, asking me to give her a call. Crap. I was just about to sneak out the back door when Stan called my name.

I sighed and headed to his office.

"You lost?" he said. " 'Cause that's got to be the reason you're here. Not the fact that I allegedly employ you," he added. "You write something up on Mr. and Mrs. Smith yet?"

I grinned. "Yes, sir! Written and filed, sir!" I said, snapping to attention.

"And this investigative article of yours? How's it coming along?"

"Super dooper. I think we're really on to something there. The story has something for everyone. Sex. Revenge. Violence. A human interest angle. All the makings of a thriller, complete with a compelling cast of characters," I told him.

"This isn't a screenplay, Turner," he pointed out. "Stick to reporting the facts. Let the readers decide how they want to see things."

"Got it," I said. "Just the facts, ma'am."

Raised voices from out front got my attention, and I looked up to see Manny's aunt Mo standing out at the front counter.

I surveyed the distance to the back door and, calculating that I'd never make it without being seen, I sprinted behind Stan's desk, shoved his chair to the side, and dove beneath the massive piece of furniture.

"What the hell?" Stan said just seconds before a loud bang sounded, signaling his door had been opened with some force.

"I tried to stop her!" Lucy, the *Gazette* receptionist-secretary-bookkeeper-cashier, apologized. She'd had to recite these words a time or two to Stan where I was concerned not all that long ago. Stan glanced down at me with a puzzled look on his face.

"I demand service!" I heard Aunt Mo declare, followed by a smack on the desktop.

"What can I help you with today—Mrs. Dishman, isn't it?" I heard Stan say, his right knee uncomfortably close to my nose.

"Same thing as yesterday and the day before," she said. "I'm here to see Tressa Turner. She works here. Right?"

"Rumor has it," I heard Stan say, and I resisted the temptation to pinch his fleshy calf.

"Rumor has it? That's good. Every time I drop by, she's out," Aunt Mo replied. "Which desk is hers?" she asked, and Stan pointed out my little corner of *Gazette* real estate.

"Over there."

"That little table? It looks like something you'd find at Goodwill. Or in preschool. And that computer belongs in a museum." Ah, bless you, Aunt Mo.

"You're welcome to leave a message," Stan said.

"I've already left two," she complained. "She never called me back. I'm beginnin' to think she's avoiding me."

"I know the feeling. Perhaps if you tell me what you want with Miss Turner, I can pass it along when

I see her and urge her to get in touch with you," Stan the Stickinsky said. I reached over and untied his shoelaces.

"You tell Tressa she needs to get a hold of me so we can talk about the wedding," she said.

"Wedding? What wedding?" Stan asked.

I wanted to bang my head on the desk but couldn't risk revealing myself.

"Her wedding. *Their* wedding," Aunt Mo said.

"Whose?" Stan asked, clearly confused.

"Tressa and Manny's."

"Manny?"

"My nephew, Manny. Manny DeMarco."

"Your nephew is Manny DeMarco?"

"That's right. Sweet, sweet boy."

"And Tressa Turner is engaged to your nephew, Manny DeMarco?"

"Came as a shock to me, too," she said. "I think it was one of those hurry-up deals," she said.

I could only imagine what Stan must be thinking.

"Tressa Turner and Manny DeMarco," Stan said, and I could picture him chewing the heck out of his cigar. "Interesting."

"They got engaged just before I left for Arizona," Aunt Mo said. "I got a trailer down near Scottsdale and winter there every year," she added. "Iowa winters got to be too much for me. I have a heart condition, you know. I've been trying to hook up with Tressa ever since I got back but I just keep missin' her. We've got plans to make," she said.

My plan was to get the heck out of this invented engagement, hopefully without eliminating poor ol' Aunt Mo in the process.

"I apologize, Mrs. Dishman, that an employee of

mine has been so rude and neglectful," Stan said. "I'll personally make sure she gets in touch," he added.

I tied his shoelaces together.

"Thank you, Mr. Rodgers. Thank you."

Chair wheels squeaked and rolled as Stan got to his feet. "Believe me, it was my pleasure, Mrs. Dishman," he said and took a step back. He got a funny look on his face when the other foot wouldn't follow and he fell back into his chair. I covered my mouth with both hands to stifle the giggles. "Uh, thanks again for coming in," he said. "And congratulations to the happy couple!" he yelled.

I waited until I heard the little bell over the front door chime before I crawled out from under the desk. "That was close," I said. "Thanks for not ratting me out, boss."

"What the hell else could I do?" he snarled. "How in God's name would I explain you being underneath my desk? And I'd just as soon Manny DeMarco not get the idea that there's any office hanky panky going on between his fiancée and her boss." He held his bound feet out in my direction. "Do you mind?" he snapped, and I quickly unfastened and then retied his shoes.

"Sorry about that," I said.

"Prewedding nerves, I suppose," he guessed, and I shook my head.

"Pre-breakup jitters," I corrected, and explained the fairy-tale engagement to Stan. "In other words, a good deed gone *sooo* bad," I summed up.

"A recurring theme," Stan observed. I sighed.

"I'm just going to am-scray now. And remember," I told him with a finger to my lips, "I was never here."

I slipped out, but not before I heard "Good ol' Calamity," followed by a hearty chuckle.

Damn.

I was puppy-dog tired by the time I drove into my— uh, our family—driveway. I'd picked up a pizza with the works from Thunder Rolls, our local bowling alley. Thunder Rolls has the absolute best pizza in a three-county radius. I was looking forward to a hot slice and a cold beer and the opportunity to put my feet up and watch mindless, brain-numbing television.

I also had chores to do and pooches to pamper. I decided to do the chores first so I could spend the remainder of the night relaxing.

I entered the house, hounded by the optimistic noses of Butch and Sundance. The house was dark. I switched the light on and called out to Gram but no one yelled back. I put the pizza on the kitchen table and ran back outdoors and called my little herd into the barn for chow, fed them and visited a wee bit, then clowned around with the doggies in the barnyard till dusk. By this time I was so hungry their Mighty Meal began to sound good, so I made my way back to the house. Joe's car was in the driveway. Just what I needed.

I filled the dog bowls and headed to the house, as much drool falling from my lips as from my two pets', thinking about the pizza and beer waiting for me.

The house was still dark when I entered. I walked into the living room.

"Luuucy, I'm hoooome!" I called out as I flipped on the light. There on the couch, wrapped in a passionate embrace, were my gammy and Joe Townsend.

"Eeewww!" rushed out of me involuntarily. My appetite shriveled. The two slowly broke apart.

"Hello, dear," my grandma greeted me. No embarrassed, awkward moments here. At least, not on my gammy's part.

"Hey," I responded, thinking there was a good possibility I might be scarred for life by what I'd just witnessed. "Glad to see your party crashing and near incarceration the other night didn't wear you out too much."

"On the contrary," Joe said. "We were still rarin' to go when Rick hauled us out of there. By the way, where did you run off to?"

"I was cowering behind the bar," I lied.

"Rick was fit to be tied when you disappeared. He almost got himself arrested when he refused to leave."

My appetite shrank even more. "He did?"

"He thought you might be in danger. Someone swore they'd seen you carried out the back by a big bear. Guess they had too much to drink, huh?" Joe said. From the speculative glint in his eyes, it was clear Joe thought there was more to this story than I was sharing.

I'd never tell.

"So, I guess he was pretty angry," I said.

"It was kind of hard to tell," Gramma replied.

I had to ask. "Oh? How come?"

"He didn't say a civil word all the way home."

I frowned at Gram. "I thought you had Joe's car," I said. "Why'd Rick drive you home?"

"He didn't want me to drive all that way at night, so he had one of his buddies take his pickup," Joe explained.

"So . . . he wasn't chatty. That could just mean he was tired, not ticked."

"We didn't say he didn't speak. We said he wasn't civil. He sure had enough to say, but it was all in the form of expletives, if you get my drift. And when he wasn't swearing, he was calling your cell every two minutes," Joe said. "Ended up sacking out on your sofa all night."

This was worse than I thought.

"It was hard to watch," Gram said. "That poor young man. Pacing the floor in the dark waiting for you. Checking his watch. Dialing your number. And what do you do? You don't call. You don't answer your phone. You don't come home at all." She paused. "And now you show up today in the same clothes you had on yesterday," she said. "All I can think of to say at a time like this is, 'Details, Tressa! Details!'"

I shook my head. "Not on an empty stomach, I don't," I said, going to take a quick shower and change out of clothes I never wanted to see again.

When I returned to the kitchen, Joe and Gram were at the table snarfing my pizza.

"Hey!" I said. "That's my supper!"

"But it's a large," Joe declared.

I gave him a hard stare. "And your point is?"

He seemed to think better of what he'd originally planned to say. "Good choice," he said instead.

I went to the refrigerator to grab a light beer. Secured to the refrigerator by a magnet for prescription calcium supplements was the fair photo of Patrick and me I'd discovered in his patrol car.

"Where did this come from?" I asked.

"The pharmacist gave it to me when I refilled my prescription," Gram said.

"Not the magnet," I said. "This picture." I tapped the snapshot.

"Oh, that. I found it on the floor of your room," she said.

I turned to look at her. "What were you doing in my room?"

"I was returning your pink boots. By the way, if you're looking for your tan Dingo slouch boots, I have them," she warned me.

Nice.

I opened the fridge, grabbed my beer, and sat down at the table. I put a slice of pizza on a paper plate. "I must've forgotten to put the photo back on Dawkins's patrol car visor, and instead dropped it into my book bag."

"P.D. Dawkins carries a picture of you in his squad car?" Joe asked, giving me a sharp look.

"Not anymore," I said with a forced laugh. How do I get myself in these fixes?

We ate in silence for several minutes. Frankly, that's as long as either my grandma or I can last.

"So, are you two getting serious?" I asked.

Gram looked up at me. "About what?" she asked.

I blinked. "Each other, of course," I said. "From that little demonstration I walked in on, it looks like things are heating up. I hope you're using protection." I snorted.

"Isn't this bass-ackwards? Shouldn't I be saying that to you instead?" Gram asked. I sobered, suddenly sorry I brought it up.

We continued eating until one last triangle of pizza remained. All three of us stared at the solitary slice, and at each other in turn. It felt like the three of us were in some high-stakes poker game. I saw Gram's fingers twitch. I could tell she wanted the pizza. Bad.

I looked past Gram's left shoulder.

"Ranger Rick?" I blurted. "My God! You're naked!"

Gram's head whirled around so quickly I could feel a breeze on my face. I took advantage of the opportunity and snatched the slice from under her nose.

Once Gram discovered no sexy nude ranger behind her, she stood, harrumphed, and left the room.

"Sneaky girl," Joe said with a grin. "But I would love to see your face if my grandson *did* happen to walk into your kitchen wearing nothing but a smile," he said.

"Not gonna happen." I laughed, shaking my head to clear it of the tantalizing image.

"Oh yeah? Why?"

"I very much doubt if Ranger Rick Townsend walked into my kitchen buck naked that you would be there to witness it," I told Joe. At least I hoped the heck not.

"I don't know. I could go back out and shuck my clothes and come in again," I heard from the doorway. Looking up I saw Rick Townsend standing just inside my kitchen. (Uh, our kitchen.) His dark eyes skewered me like a cherry tomato on a shish kebab.

"Well, hello there, Rick." Joe got up to greet his grandson. "How'd you get in?"

"Hi, Pops," he said, his eyes slowly leaving me to greet his granddad. "Hannah was on the front porch when I drove up. Did one of the mutts have an accident?" he asked. "Because she was muttering something to the dogs about dirty tricks when I walked up."

Joe gave me a curt look. "I'd better get out there and cajole her back inside before she contracts pneumonia."

"Grab a jacket in case she gets stubborn," I told him.

I held out the much desired slice of pizza to Rick, a sort of peace offering. "Last piece. Going, going, gone," I warned.

"Not hungry," he said, taking the seat Joe had vacated. Townsend was wearing blue jeans, a Hawkeyes football T-shirt, and a brown bomber jacket. He looked like he'd just stepped out of the shower. And smelled like it. I resisted the temptation to reach over and sniff his neck. I am, like, so needy. "We have some catching up to do," he went on.

I let the pizza drop to my plate. I wasn't sure how much I was willing to share with Townsend. How much was safe.

"It's this college journalism paper," I told him. "It's snowballed into this really exciting but kind of scary assignment that is shooting off in all directions. And the stakes are high here. My future career aspirations could hinge on how well I perform on this task." I was proud. I sounded like I had my head screwed on straight for a change. Now, that was scary.

"Frankie and Dixie filled me in on the story you're chasing," he said. "All the usual suspects," he added with a disgusted shake of his head.

"What does that mean?" I asked.

"Let's see. We've got multiple crimes including but not limited to hit-and-run, assault, burglary. We have multiple suspects, including as I understand it a registered sex offender. We have possibly targeted hits focusing on students in a specific college class. And we have two sidekicks who want to make a big splash in the law enforcement community," Townsend said. "How am I doing so far?"

I cocked a noncommittal eyebrow. "Go on," I said.

"It's like a remake of a bad movie," he said. "The

Keystone Kop Campus Caper, maybe. Tressa, they have professionals who investigate this kind of thing for a living," he said. "They don't need to rely on rank amateurs."

"Rank?"

"As in complete or absolute," he clarified. "Not smelly."

I nodded. "Glad you cleared that up, Mr. Ranger, sir," I said. "I might have taken oh-fense if you'd implied I oh-fended. And the authorities are on it. I'm merely observing and recording."

Townsend shook his head at my defense. "Observing means look but don't touch, Tressa," he said, clearly getting frustrated. "My point is that you seem to always be in the middle of some drama—and recently those are dangerous dramas. And the evidence seems to indicate that you put yourself there deliberately."

"We're back to the death-wish blonde again," I said. "You forget that an investigative reporter, by definition, has to investigate," I pointed out.

"Some reporters let others investigate and then they report," he argued.

"I'm not 'some' reporters," I told him. "I'm trying to learn a marketable skill here. Isn't that what you've been hounding me to do since high school?"

Townsend looked at me. "Oh, I see. I made you put yourself in danger because I thought it was time you grew up and got a decent job? That's a stretch even for you."

I downed the rest of my beer and pulled a face at the lukewarm contents. I gathered up the pizza box and carried it to the counter.

"You didn't come home last night," he said, and I paused in the act of annihilating the cardboard.

"I know. I'm sorry I worried everyone," I said. "Things happened. Time just got away from me. Thanks for seeing that Gram and Joe got home okay. I appreciate it."

I began to shred the box again, but Townsend's hands stilled mine.

"I was damned near sick with worry," he said, and I looked up at him.

"Huh?"

"When no one could reach you. I don't like feeling that way," he said.

"I'm sorry," I said again, unsure of what to say, what he expected me to say.

"So, where were you? You mentioned a friend you went to eat with. Did you spend the night with your friend?"

I shook my head. "No. I ate breakfast before I took a drive through the campus and discovered there had been another attack," I said. "And by the time Patrick and I left the security office it was nearly four."

"Patrick? You mean Dawkins was there?"

I nodded. "He's helping out on the investigation. The State Department of Health has a building on campus, and that's why the state is involved," I explained. "Plus, you recall, there was the hit-and-run."

"How could I forget?" he said.

"So, it didn't make sense to drive home just to turn around and drive back up to class in a couple of hours, and the way my grades are, I can't afford to miss any more classes, anyway."

"So where did you stay?" he asked. "You didn't stay with Dixie."

I could've slapped myself. Why hadn't I thought of that?

"You know how it is with Dixie and me. We usually require a third party to referee," I said, skirting his real question.

"Where did you stay, then?" he asked, more doggedly determined than my gammy when she's trying to find out what everyone got her for Christmas.

I debated lying, telling him I slept in my car, but deception didn't come easy for me. And for some reason I could never bring myself to lie to Rick Townsend. Oh, I could deny I ate three powdered sugar crème flips at one sitting or that I snuck the dogs into the city pool one night, but I could never seem to lie about the big things. The things one thinks really matter.

I was just about to tell him the truth when the phone rang.

I went to answer it.

It was Patrick.

"Hi, Tressa. I just wanted to call and make sure you were okay," he said.

I looked over at Townsend, who had moved to stand beside the refrigerator.

"I'm fine. Thanks."

"I just got a call from Hector," Patrick went on.

"Hector Moldonado?" I asked.

"How many Hectors do you know, Tressa?" he said. "Anyway, he just wanted to let me know that they were being dispatched to a report of a possible shooting," he added.

"Oh my God. Do they know who the victim is? Is it someone in Billings's class? Is it Billings?"

"I don't have any more details yet, but I just wanted to see if you were all right and let you know that the pattern continues. I've got to go. I'll be in touch."

He ended the call and I stood for a second recognizing that there was no satisfaction in having our theory confirmed. Someone else had been hurt. Maybe even killed.

I suddenly felt in the mood for a big, tight warm hug from a certain ranger, and I turned only to find Townsend was no longer in the kitchen.

"Townsend?"

I walked over to where he'd been standing and caught the scent of his cologne. I looked up and right into the smiling faces of Patrick and me.

I ran through the living room and out the front door just in time to see the taillights of Townsend's candy-apple-red 4×4 disappear into the foggy night.

I settled for warm hugs from two slightly damp but very affectionate beasties. A girl's best friend is her doggies.

CHAPTER 15

I awoke to someone rummaging through my closet, a maroon-covered fanny the first thing I saw when I opened my eyes the next morning.

"Why are these boots damp?" Gram asked, picking up the boots I'd worn to wade through the water hazard at the obstacle course. "I wanted to wear them today."

I rubbed the sleep out of my eyes and sat up. "What time is it?"

"Half past six," she said. "Where's that pair of short black boots?"

"They're around here somewhere," I said. "Why?"

"Never mind. We'll be doing quite a bit of walking. I better wear my New Balance."

I brushed the hair out of my face. "What do you mean we'll be doing a lot of walking? Where will 'we' be walking?"

"You did promise to take me shopping for a dress to

wear to Kari's wedding," she reminded me. "I have a hair appointment tomorrow, so today is the day."

I groaned and dropped to my bed and put my arm over my eyes.

"Don't you have an extra backpack somewhere?" Gram asked.

"Why do you need a backpack?" I grunted, sitting up again.

"Well, I will be on the Carson College campus, and I don't want to stick out like a sore thumb."

"And how will a backpack prevent that?" I asked.

"I'll look like I have a reason to be there. Like I'm taking classes."

I smiled. It was kind of sweet really.

"We'll just hit that new mall on the west side," she went on. "It has the hippest stores. And lunch is on me. I thought maybe that cheesecake place."

"Godiva chocolate cheesecake," I whispered. My mouth began to water.

"Or that Tiara-miss-you cheesecake," Gram said.

"That's Tira-misu, Gram. And you win," I added. "But we'll have to boogie. You can't hit every mall in Polk County and try on every dress you take a fancy to. I have to get you home and then get back for my night class this evening."

"Then you'd better get up and moving," she said.

"I have a few more minutes before I need to get up." I yawned. "We won't have to leave for about an hour."

Gram turned to look at me. "Oh, by the way, you had a phone call yesterday. With all the brouhaha last night, I forgot to tell you."

"Who was it?"

"It was that 'Mo' person. Said she was trying to get in touch with you. She asked for directions out here. I think she planned to stop by this morning," Gram announced.

I flew off the mattress like I'd discovered bedbugs. "Be ready to leave in fifteen minutes!" I yelled.

"What about that backpack?" she asked.

"Hall closet," I told her, grabbing underwear, jeans, T-shirt and a red hoodie, and flying into the bathroom.

I took a quick shower, swiped a razor over my legs, and was out, dried, and dressed in seven minutes. I pulled my wet hair back and hurriedly braided it, then applied my makeup with a swift hand. At seven sharp, I was out in the driveway honking for Gram, checking behind me every ten seconds. Gram finally walked to the car, the black backpack over her bent shoulders.

"What do you have in that backpack?" I asked. "It looks heavy."

"Well, I had to have a binder and some writing utensils, didn't I?" she said. "What kind of college student would I be without pencils and paper?"

I started the car and we headed off to the big city.

"I could do with a sausage biscuit," Gram said.

"We'll stop and get one as soon as we're out of Knox County," I said.

"What's up? How come you're in such a hurry to get out of town?" she asked.

"Hurry? What says I'm in a hurry?" I tried to look innocent.

"That trooper car with the spinning top lights that's behind us," Gram said, and I checked the outside mirror.

I cursed.

"Tressa," Gram scolded. "I thought Oprah had cleaned up your act."

I had taken a pledge to cut out swearing some time

back when Oprah did a show on getting rid of those bad habits. I'd done a decent job under some pretty tense situations. But revolving lights in my mirror? Now, that was what they called adequate provocation. I pulled over to the side of the road, and the patrol car pulled in behind me.

"I don't suppose you could hold this up while the officer is talking?" I asked, showing her the rearview mirror that had fallen off the front windshield.

Gram gave it a dubious look. "I know how you like to talk. I don't think I can hold it up that long, Tressa," she said. "But I can try."

"That's all right, Gram," I said. "Maybe he won't notice it."

I watched a tan trooper leg appear in my side mirror. Soon the trooper was heading in my direction. I cranked my window down.

"Morning, Officer," I greeted the policeman.

"Morning, Miss Turner," the trooper said, and I did a double take, sticking my head out the narrow opening to gawk up at the officer. He looked vaguely familiar.

"You are Tressa Turner, correct?" the trooper asked.

I nodded. "How did you know?"

"Well, besides your vehicle registration, I remember you from the Iowa State Fair," he said, bending down, eyes moving across the seat of my car, narrowing, and then moving back to me.

"I remember," I said, thinking for once I'd lucked out. "You were partnered with Patrick Dawkins."

"That's right. I'm Devin Harris." Another quick glance shot over to Gram for a brief moment. Cops had to keep their eyes moving, it appeared.

"I wasn't speeding, was I, Trooper Harris?" I asked.

"The reason I stopped you this morning, Miss

Turner, is that I have an urgent message for you from Trooper Dawkins." The trooper frowned down at me, and handed over a sheet of paper. I looked away to scan the message.

"How did you track me down?" I asked.

"I was on my way to headquarters and Dawkins had dispatch contact me to call in. Dawkins called dispatch, and they patched him through. He asked me to get a message to you as he couldn't get you at home or on your cell. He provided your probable route of travel and your departure time. And the vehicle description, of course. It sounds like they had a break in your hit-and-run case," Trooper Harris said. "Hope things go well."

The trooper gave one last, long look at Gram. "Uh, be careful when you pull out," he cautioned.

I wiped the sweat that had pooled on my upper lip during the encounter. "I will absolutely do that, Officer. And thank you. Thank you very much!"

The trooper hesitated for a second as if to say more but decided against it, straightened, and walked back to the patrol car. I let out a long sigh of relief. The trooper pulled out first and sped past us.

"Well, I guess that worked like a charm," Gram said while I read Patrick's message through a second time.

"Uh, what worked?" I asked, looking over at her. She was in the process of buttoning a blouse that was unbuttoned almost to her belly button.

"*What did you do*?" I enunciated.

"Just a little diversion," she said. "Ain't no man alive that don't appreciate a little bit of cleavage," she said. "You ought to try it sometime, Tressa. I'll have you know that trooper didn't look once at the mirror," she said.

I could believe that.

"Uh, Gram, there's something I think you should know," I said.

"What's that, dear?"

"That trooper . . . was a woman," I said.

Gram's fingers slowed as they finished buttoning her blouse. "Are you sure?"

I nodded. "Pretty."

She was quiet for a minute.

"This don't make me a lesbian, does it?" she asked, and I fought to hide my grin.

"I don't think so, Gram," I said.

"One of them bisexuals?" she asked.

"Probably not," I told her.

"It'll still be something to talk about," she decided. "Won't it?" She turned a hopeful eye in my direction.

"You'll have the tongues waggin' at the senior center for weeks," I assured her.

She smiled. "Won't I, though?"

At Carson College, the campus was abuzz with talk of the shooting the night before. While the incident hadn't actually occurred on campus, but rather on a bike path between the campus and an apartment complex not far from the school, it was still too close for comfort. And for coincidence. TV satellite vans from the metro news stations as well as news radio were on campus and asking questions.

I didn't care how this coverage might impact my article. I just wanted public awareness of the problem so citizens and students could adequately protect themselves.

Gram insisted on sitting in on my journalism class. She behaved herself—mostly because I'd bribed her with a latte and a jumbo cinnamon roll from the coffee shop off-campus. I had to hand it to Gram; she took copious notes. All I had to do was sit and pretend I was listening. Which wasn't that hard to do since my mind was busy trying to nail the campus criminal before he made his next move.

Patrick's message was encouraging. Preliminary tests on Keith Gardner's pickup truck indicated that his truck was, indeed, the vehicle that had hit Uncle Frank's Suburban and nearly made roadkill of Dixie and me. Although Gardner still denied he was the person behind the wheel, the fact that Dixie and I had followed him from the campus and the incident had taken place minutes later left little doubt of his guilt. And if he was the hit-and-run driver, it was a safe bet he was also responsible for the rash of other criminal acts committed on campus. Court documents were being drawn up, Patrick's note had said, and an arrest would likely be made that day in the hit-and-run case.

I made a mental note to let Uncle Frank know what was going on. I'd need to find out if Gardner carried insurance on his truck, too. I sure hoped so. For my sake.

Class was dismissed and Gram excused herself to use the facilities before we headed to the mall. I fidgeted outside in the lobby and wondered how Frankie was dealing with his substandard performance on the obstacle course. He'd finally discovered what he wanted to do with his life only to come up lacking. I knew exactly how he felt.

"I want a word with you, Miss Turner." I was jolted out of my sympathy pangs by Sherman "STD" Danbury. His expression indicated he wanted more than a word.

"What a coincidence," I said, thinking that this guy was still a viable suspect—at least in my book—and I wasn't about to let the opportunity to probe a little deeper into his possible motive for professitorial pay-back pass without getting my feelers out and poking around. "I have some questions for you as well."

His eyes shut to mere slits.

"I understand you were harassing a student of mine the other day," he said. "Making all kinds of wild accusations, speculating on things that aren't any of your business or germane to the incidents you claim to be investigating. I want it to stop. Or I will have no other choice than to report you for disciplinary action."

Uh-huh. Like I'd never heard this from a teacher before.

"Ever heard of the First Amendment, Professor?" I asked. "Freedom of speech. Freedom of the press. Either of these ring a bell?"

"Just what is it you hope to gain by your prying, Miss Turner? More sensational headlines? Your face on the front page? An impressive byline?" the professor probed with a rather unattractive sneer.

"How about truth, justice, and the good ol' American way?" I asked. He stared at me.

"This isn't comic book fiction, Miss Turner. This is real life. Real people's lives you are screwing with," he said.

"Real people are being more than screwed with, Professor," I shot back. "People are being robbed, beaten, assaulted, almost run down, and now shot at. I have to question why you fail to see the greater harm here. Is it because, when it comes to motives, you are at the head of the class, Professor? That if anyone has a reason to get back at Professor Billings, it's you? After all, she was responsible for you not being offered tenure. At least in your eyes. It probably had nothing whatsoever to do with the fact that you showed up late to lectures hungover and reeking of alcohol. Right? Or that you may be involved in an improper relationship with a student? It has nothing to do with either of those things, right? It's all someone else's fault. Someone else is to blame. Frankly, Professor, that's what we cowgirl types call a load of horseshit. And we shovel enough of it to know it when we see it."

Danbury looked flustered. "You can't think I had anything to do with what happened to Barbara Billings," he said. "That I am responsible for what's been going on here at Carson. That's absurd."

"About as absurd as fraternizing with a student at three in the morning—and on a school night at that," I said. "Tsk-tsk."

The professor's face was now approximately the same color as my gammy's maroon polyester slacks.

"Trevor Childers doesn't know anything. Stay away from him," he said. "Or I will see that you are one sorry little snoop." He turned on his heel and left.

Yeah, right. Like I was gonna be scared off by a guy with a Michael Jackson handshake.

"Who was that pencil-neck?" Gram asked, joining me. "He important to know?"

I shook my head.

"Only in his own mind, Gram," I said. "Only in his own mind.

We arrived at the mall close to eleven and decided to eat first—just in case we ran out of time. We do have our priorities. I kept telling myself that I needed to eat either the chocolate cheesecake or the Tons of Fun burger (with fries) but not both, as Kari's wedding was just two days off. However, given Gram was picking up the tab—almost as rare an occurrence as a solar eclipse—I gave myself permission to eat hearty.

We left the restaurant an hour later, stuffed to the gills.

"I should never have ordered the fries," I said, letting my belt out two notches as we walked through the mall. "My gut feels like it's about to explode."

"It was probably the double patties, double cheese, triple bun, and top-secret sauce on that Tons of Fun burger," Gram said. "You really should've had a salad, dear. You promised Kari you'd fit into that dress. When's the last time you had it on?"

I looked at her. "I tried it on the other day," I said, telling one of those harmless little lies I've alluded to before. The ones that hurt no one by the telling but can hurt me big time if I don't.

"You get it zipped up?"

"Uh, it's a little hard to do by myself with the zipper in back," I said. "But with a little help, I should manage fine."

"You better get a body wax. That way you'll have a fightin' chance of sliding into it. Less friction," she said. I grimaced.

Two hours and three stores later, I was glad I'd braided my hair, or I'd have pulled out a significant chunk. As I feared, Gram had insisted on trying on evening gowns that were more appropriate for Paris Hilton than a woman "of a certain age."

We were now in the dressing room of J.C. Penney's and Gram had already been through the "fun and flirty" department and was currently trying on a halter dress that needed Cher's shoulders rather than saggy ones to work.

"Gram, you're not the mother of the bride," I reminded her. "Nor are you the entertainment. You just need a simple yet elegant dress."

She looked at me. "I did see me a beaded jacket dress out there. It had one of them flowing hems. Comes in purple and navy," she said. "You think I could carry off all that purple without looking like that big, dumb dinosaur?"

"It's a tough call. Not everyone could pull it off," I told her. "It would take someone who is comfortable in her own skin. Who isn't afraid to attract some attention," I added.

She nodded. "It would take a very confident woman, wouldn't it?" she agreed, almost to herself, handing me the black halter dress. "That's the wrong size, anyway. I need a petite."

She threw her clothes back on. "I'll just go get that jacket dress to try on. And I also saw a long jacket dress in periwinkle blue that looked bitchin'," she said and I winced. "Stay here and hold the dressing room for me, won't you, dear?" She disappeared through the curtain.

I took a seat to wait and stared at the black halter dress in my hands. I checked the size out. If I sucked in my gut, I should be able to squeeze into it.

I shrugged, shucked my clothes, and shimmied into the black dress. When I got it fastened—and finally maneuvered one boob to each side of the low-cut gown—I turned to look at myself. Wow. Not bad. Not exactly Cher—my shoulders were more along the lines of a beach volleyball player's than a svelte rock star–type's—but not bad all things considered. I started to remove the dress, heard the rustle of the curtain, and braced myself to see what treasures Gram had discovered, only to find myself staring at a guy who looked a heck of a lot like the one Patrick had told me was about to be arrested for hit-and-run—and who was also our most promising suspect in the series of campus crimes.

Keith Gardner had a crazed look about him, like a tiger about to be captured. Or maybe a felon about to be sent back to the slammer for a very, very long time.

I stared at him, certain I had the same look on my face you get when you don't get the restroom door locked and someone walks in on you while you're on the stool. You just kinda sit there and stare, too stunned to react. I'm thinking that's also what happens when you're in the fitting room of a mall department store minding your own business and a psychopathic registered sex offender suddenly walks in on you. You should be screaming bloody murder, but all you can do is gape.

Gardner advanced on me, his face dark with rage.

"What the fuck are you trying to do to me?" he asked, and I still couldn't make my mouth work. I know, I know. Hard to believe, isn't it? "What have I ever done to you that you want to ruin my life?" he asked.

Duh. Do the words "attempted vehicular homicide" mean anything to you?

"I have been struggling to get my life back, turn things around and have a chance at a decent future, and what happens? Some dumb-ass blonde accuses me of trying to run her down in a goddamned hit-and-run. What the fuck is your problem?" he yelled. "Why do you want to destroy me?"

The dumb-ass blonde reference helped me regain my powers of speech. And indignation.

"Listen, buster, don't try to pull the blonde card here," I said, wagging a finger at him. "My being blond doesn't have a diddly-squattin' thing to do with the fact that your pickup almost ran my friend and me over the other night. Well, she's not exactly a friend, really—more like a forced relation." I shook my head to get back on point. "Not to mention the fact that you plowed into my uncle Frank's 2003 Suburban, costing me a full-time, part-time job plus all the Slurpees, beef burgers, nachos, chili dogs, tacos, and ice cream I could eat for free. So step off, asshole, before this gets ugly!"

Gardner retreated a step. He probably got a good look at my shoulders and decided it was safer. He was probably right.

"I wasn't there!" he insisted.

"What do you mean?" I asked. "Forensic tests prove it was your truck. And it was you we followed off campus. You who drove like a NASCAR wannabe. You who came back to finish us off," I pointed out. "Now, maybe you were too drunk to remember it or maybe you are regretting it, but the fact remains that your pickup was there. And I have the skinned knees, pissed-off uncle, and one less income to prove it!"

Okay, so I can react rather violently when economically and physically threatened—not to mention being denied free junk food.

"What do you mean, 'I came back'?" Gardner asked.

"Huh?" I looked at him.

"You said I came back to finish you off. What did you mean?"

I gave him another look. "I'm not sure I should divulge information in an active, ongoing investigation," I said.

"You fond of that old lady you came in with?" he asked. I flinched.

"Not especially," I lied.

He shrugged. "Fine. Have it your way," he said, and turned to leave.

"Wait!" I said. "Can't you recognize a joke? I was just trying to lighten the mood, you know. Interject a little levity."

"There's nothing funny about being wrongly accused of a crime," Gardner said.

"Right," I asked. "What did you want to know again?"

The guy shook his head. "You said something about me coming back," he said, clearly exasperated.

"Oh, right. Yeah. That's what you did. You went down the road and we—what do they call it? Terminated our pursuit—and about ten minutes later you came back and almost collected two DNR doe tags on my friend and me."

"Ten minutes later? Why would I wait ten minutes later to come back and nail you?" he asked.

I thought about it. "I dunno. Why would you?"

"I didn't!" he yelled. "That's why! I got home, unloaded the pickup, went into the house, and took a shower. I didn't even know the pickup was gone till the cops showed up."

"How could someone take your truck?"

He ran a hand through his hair. "I leave the key in it. I live out in the boonies. It's an old truck. I always leave the key in the ashtray."

"So you expect me to believe that in a ten-minute span of time somebody stole your pickup and tried to run us down, but you have no idea who or why?" I asked. It sounded pretty lame to me. Still, I had asked folks to believe that there was a body in the trunk of my car and a hit man was out to get me, so in the larger scheme of things, Gardner's story wasn't all that unbelievable. I wasn't sure the authorities would agree, however.

"I have no control over what you believe," Gardner said. "But it's the truth."

I stared at him, my BS detector stuck on *inconclusive*. The guy seemed sincere enough, but something told me Frankie would say sociopaths are damned good liars.

"Maybe you could take a polygraph," I suggested. "That might help."

"What would help is if you would change your story," he said. "Say it wasn't me behind the wheel."

"But I couldn't see who was behind the wheel," I said. "It was dark. Except for a tiny flash of light."

"It wasn't me," he said. He took a step in my direction. "You've got to tell them it wasn't me!" he said.

I felt cornered; the dressing room was a rabbit trap and I was Thumper.

I was finally ready to scream like a little girl when the curtains parted and my gammy stood there, curtains in one hand, hanger items in the other.

"I don't think men are allowed in here," she said, giving Keith Gardner an intent look. "Kinda young for you, ain't he?" she asked me.

I hurried over to Gram and shoved her out into the dressing room corridor and back into the store. Gardner gave me a chilling look, raised his hand as if to grab me, but thought better of it and ran out of the dressing room and out of the store.

"Well, how do you like that?" she said with a sniff. "Didn't even introduce himself."

I looked at the direction Gardner had run. "He did to me, Gram," I said. "He did to me."

"You gonna take that dress?" she asked, gesturing to the garment I wore.

I shook my head.

"Good thing," she said. "You don't have enough to fill out that top. Talk about your peep shows."

I followed Gram into the dressing room and changed out of the black dress and back into my street clothes. Twenty minutes later Gram had narrowed her choices down to two beaded jackets: the purple with a short jacket and a periwinkle blue with a longer, flowing jacket and tiered hem.

I pointed out the periwinkle was a perfect match with her hair.

"I'll take it," she said.

Score one for the dumb blonde.

At the checkout I noticed another item in her hand. I motioned to it.

"What is that?" I asked. The thing looked like a device of torture.

"It's a body slimmer," Gram said. "To suck everything in and pull it up."

"Sounds like the stuff they use to repair hernias," I said with a snort.

"It's for you," she said.

I stopped laughing. "Come again?"

"For you to wear under the maid of honor dress," she elaborated. "No offense, dear, but after seeing you put away that lunch, I thought we'd better have a little backup plan—just in case."

I looked at the constricting article of intimate apparel. Visions of cocktail weenies, wedding cake, butter mints, and peanuts traveled through my head. And ice-cold beer. Lots of ice-cold beer. I looked at the slimmer again and calculated how long it would take me to get it slid down over my thighs each time I had to use the restroom.

I gave it a failing grade.

"Just put the body slimmer down and step away from the register and no one will get hurt, Hellion Hannah," I told my grandma.

She looked at me for a second and then complied. Still, give my gammy an A for effort.

CHAPTER 16

Gram and I got back in town around four. I couldn't believe I'd have to turn around and head back to Carson in two hours for my night class. I seriously considered skipping, but really wanted to find out the latest on the campus shooting. All I'd been able to learn from the news reports was that a cyclist had been shot and that the injuries did not appear to be life-threatening. No names had been released.

I also wanted to inform Patrick about my run-in with Keith Gardner in the J.C. Penney's dressing room. I'd leave out the part where I was wearing the peeka-boo halter dress, I decided. I wanted to know, too, if the cops had arrested Gardner yet.

I'd thought about Gardner all the way home while Gram snored in the seat next to me and, once we'd reached our destination, denied she'd slept at all. Lathering up in the shower, I continued to mull over our fitting-room exchange. On the one hand I knew he was a convicted sex offender. That was reason enough to be creeped out at being in a confined space with him. But he'd seemed genuinely outraged that he was being accused, even in the face of compelling forensic evidence and eyewitness accounts. Of course, didn't something like ninety percent of incarcerated individuals swear they were innocent?

So I was back to square one, and feeling like I was running out of time. With the clock ticking down to murder. . . .

I came out of the shower all wrapped up in a big bath sheet to discover a dark-haired, long-limbed, ranger-type asleep on my bed. I stood dripping for a moment and pinched myself—hard—thinking maybe my subconscious had manufactured this intriguing little diorama as compensation for a dry spell in the sex department that had gone on so long I qualified for federal drought aid.

I walked over to the sleeping figure and stared down at him. He looked even more scrum-dilly-icious asleep than he did awake. I bent down to take a closer look. I should have known. Not one damn speck of drool in the corner of his mouth. No snoring. No restless leg syndrome. This was, like, so unfair.

As I bent over the dozing Don Juan of the DNR, a drop of water from my hair fell right in his closed eye. One minute I was on my feet leering down at the safely slumbering Greek god and the next I found myself on top of him, with nothing but a loosely wrapped towel between the ranger and my wet, naked body.

Okay, okay, so this had been part of Tressa's bedroom fantasies, too. Except the Tressa in my fantasy has long, flowing locks of silken hair—of course on my head, you jackasses—a slim, tanned, toned body, dainty soft feet, and an overall complexion that was airbrushed perfection. But other than that, it was me.

"Wanna get lucky?" the now wide-awake ranger asked.

"Uh, ah, whu-huh?" I stammered.

"Easy for you to say," Townsend said, his fantastic whiskey-colored eyes laughing up at me.

Okay, so my fantasy hadn't come with a teleprompter or script—well, apart from the really naughty words I invented Townsend whispering in my ear, that is. (Regrettably for the voyeurs out there, those are of a personal and private nature.) So I was left to wing it. You can see how that worked for me.

"What are you doing here?" I asked. "Other than being an impediment to me getting ready for class."

"Impediment? You use a lot of big words now that you're a reporter, Calamity," he said. "So, I'm an impediment now, am I?" He laughed. "Guess that's an improvement over some of the other names you've called me," he admitted with a crooked grin that was so sexy I wanted to cover his mouth with mine and regret it in the morning.

"You're the only guy I know who thinks being called a hindrance is a promotion," I said.

"And how many guys is that?" Townsend asked, with a serious tilt of his chin upward.

Vixen that I am, I opted to leave the answer to Townsend's imagination.

"So, what are you doing here again?" I asked instead.

"I thought I'd tag along with you to your night class," he said, and I was immediately suspicious. Hey, blame it on the senior citizen I resided with who thinks she's Miss Marple.

"And why on earth would you want to do that?" I

asked. "I'm sure you can think of other more entertaining things to do. Like, clean out your reptile cages.
Or drag my brother away from his wife during her
ovulation cycle. Again. Or help your granddad spy on
his neighbors."

Townsend reached up and pulled the towel off my
head and ran his fingers through my hair. Or, rather,
tried to. They got stuck halfway through. I hadn't de-
tangled yet.

"We could stay in tonight," Townsend said, extricat-
ing his fingers and putting his hands on my bare shoulders instead, lightly caressing flesh that was needier
than a one-legged, homeless hobo. "And make wild
passionate love all night."

I blinked. Had Townsend really said that, or was I
getting bleed-over from Tressa's Bedroom Fantasy
Adventures?

"Ten-nine?" I managed to say—which to those of
you who are ten-code illiterate means *repeat*.

"We could make love," he said. "All through the
night." He gave my shoulders a squeeze to accentuate
the preposition—or more likely—proposition.

"You can't be serious," I said. "My grandmother is in
the other room."

"We'll send her to Pop's."

Townsend must be desperate. He usually wanted me
to enforce a two-thousand-foot rule between the two
seniors.

"I have a night class."

"We'll send Hannah instead. She told me all about
her experience today as a college student. Besides,
from what I hear, she can't hurt your grade. Maybe
she'll raise it." He grinned. "She might even offer to
sleep with your professor."

The mental picture of Gram and Professor Stokes going at it on the same table where the professor kept his dish of butterscotch disks in a tall coffee mug that said *Journalists do it on a tight timetable* was so ridiculous, I began to giggle.

"Is that a 'yes' giggle I hear?" Townsend asked, doing a Groucho Marx eyebrow number.

I sobered. Why shouldn't I? My legs were shaved. I was squeaky clean. Townsend was already in my bed. And I wanted him. *Bad.* Unfortunately, I always kept coming back to that one question: Would he still love me tomorrow?

"Convince me," I heard myself say, although I'd just about already convinced myself.

In a move better suited to a wrestling mat than a bed, Townsend flipped me over onto my back, lock, stock, and bath sheet, and covered me with the hot, lean length of his body. I shivered despite the warmth of him against me.

He bent his head and took my lips in a slow, seductive kiss that sent the chills skedaddling quicker than I could say burn, baby, burn. I moaned like a wanton woman against his mouth.

When his lips began to brand a hot trail across my neck and downward, I arched my back, helpless to fight the flood of conflicting sensations and emotions that always seemed to wash over me where Townsend was concerned.

Hot. Cold. Feverish. Frosty. Bold. Timid. Daring. Scared out of my friggin' gourd.

Sensing my growing anxiety at his growing ardor, Townsend returned his attention to my lips, taking them in a kiss that erased any doubts I had that Townsend wanted to jump my bones. Right now. This very second.

A few more kisses and he would have me.

The ringing of the phone halted our heated embrace. I listened for Gram to call for me. Nothing. I looked at Townsend. He looked at me. I figured my eyes must've said, Go for it. He lowered his head again and had just touched his lips to mine when a loud bang sounded on the door.

"Tressa! That was that Mo lady I told you about. She said to tell you to stay put, she's on her way out," Gram said through the door. "You two all right in there?" she added.

I didn't take time to answer. I gave Townsend a hard shove and he tumbled off the bed. I grabbed for my clothes and hurried to the bathroom and threw on black jeans, a white shirt, and a red sweater vest. I flew out of the bathroom and pulled on a pair of socks and yanked on black high-top Converse canvas shoes.

"Are you going to drive or am I?" I asked, grabbing my purse and backpack. "Forget it. You drive. You have more money for gas," I said.

I left my bedroom and blew my gammy a kiss as I flew past.

"Don't wait up," I told her as I ran for the door.

"Wait! What about Mo?" Gram asked, but I was already out the door and climbing into Townsend's red pickup.

Townsend joined me a couple of minutes later, giving me a superannoyed, superfrustrated look. I couldn't blame the guy. Talk about coitus interruptus.

He started the truck and pulled out of my driveway.

"Your reputation as the rodeo queen of all cowgirls appears to be sadly overrated," he said, shaking his head.

I looked at him. "What do you mean?"

He gave me a sour look. "I gotta tell you, Calamity. That had to be the shortest ride on record," he said; then he gave a wicked, albeit somewhat confused, smile.

Great. Just what I needed. A sexy ranger with a yen for stand-up. Good grief.

At Carson, Townsend opted to hang out at a table in the lobby area while I was at class. Frankly, I have to admit I was conflicted about his insistence on coming with me. On one hand, it meant a lot that he wanted to protect me from a criminal who'd set up shop on the college campus. But that earlier remark about protecting me from myself? Well, let's just say that put a burr under this cowgirl's saddle the size of the stress ball that sat on Stan Rodger's desk at the *Gazette*.

These conflicted emotions pretty much summed up my relationship with Ranger Rick Townsend. His over-the-top sex appeal got every nerve ending in my body humming, yet somehow he also managed to get on my last nerve. He was a man of many talents.

I listened to the assistant professor lecture on Basic Principles of Reporting and took notes like a good little college coed. After class I met briefly with my study group. Each of us was to be assigned a share of our final group project. Surprisingly—or maybe not so surprising—my fellow study group members opted not to give me a piece of the action. I chose to believe they took pity on me (I'd whined about my matrimonial itinerary, my jobs, and my need to focus on my investigative reporting project to avoid failing) rather than assume they thought I was incapable of pulling my own weight. (No smart remarks, now.) Still, I wasn't disappointed when I didn't get an assignment other than bringing treats (translation: bribes) for the class the night we presented, as our fellow classmates would be evaluating our project.

I rejoined Townsend around nine thirty.

"Are you hungry?" I asked him.

He gave me his trademark one-eyebrow-raised look. "What did you have in mind?"

"Something nice and hot," I said, with a look of my own.

"Go on," he said.

"How does hot chocolate and whipped cream strike you?"

"Will one of us be licking it off the other?"

I'm almost certain I blushed.

"Uh, I'm actually talking about hot chocolate from the student union," I said. "And I doubt very much if they permit licking activities like that on the premises."

"What a shame," Townsend said.

We drove to the union and got our drinks. Townsend sat across from me stirring milk into his de-caf coffee with a skinny red and white straw. I found myself watching his long, lean fingers on the straw with more fascination than the occasion warranted.

"So, tell me, Tressa, just how much time have you been spending with Patrick Dawkins?" he asked out of the blue.

It took me a while to drag my attention away from his incredible hands.

"Why do you ask?" I said, sticking my face in my cup and attempting to sip some cocoa out from under the thick layer of foam.

"Curiosity," he said. "He's been in the loop on what's going on up here, so I just wondered how often you see the guy."

I shrugged. "Now and then. Off and on. Here and there," I said, babbling like a fool.

"You sound nervous, T. Flustered," Townsend said. "How come?"

"Flustered? Who's flustered? I'm not flustered," I said. Babble, babble, babble.

He shook his head. "So, if your theory about these crimes is correct, what are we looking at for tonight?" Townsend said, apparently deciding, for now, to drop the subject of P.D. Dawkins.

"Arson, attempted murder, and kidnapping—among other things," I said, suddenly jittery, and not at all due to the chocolate I was sucking down. Sitting around waiting for a serious crime to happen tended to give a person the heebie-jeebies.

"I don't like this, Townsend," I said. "It's like waiting for the executioner to strike. Each time the crime that's attempted—or committed—becomes more serious. More destructive. We've been lucky no one has gotten killed. Yet. That cyclist who got winged was fortunate."

"I doubt he feels that way," Townsend remarked. "What are the campus cops saying?"

"I'm not sure they really believe there's a connection, but they have increased their patrols. And they're discouraging people from going anywhere on campus alone, so that's something. It just doesn't seem like enough," I lamented. "As far as I know, they haven't interviewed hardly anyone from the class—and I know Patrick has passed along what we've learned." I winced, wishing I hadn't mentioned the handsome trooper.

"So, based on what you know, who do you think it is?" Townsend asked me.

I shook my head. "I wish I knew. Keith Gardner has

the pathology and criminal history to follow through with these crimes, and the evidence sure points to him. But Sherman Danbury has the motive and expertise to plan and execute these acts. And there's always the possibility it's someone who's flying way below the radar. That's what's so scary about this kind of criminal, Townsend. I know from experience the bad guy can be right in front of you and you don't have a clue."

"Don't remind me," Townsend said. "Are you ready to go?"

I nodded. I had an early morning quiz and still needed to look over my notes. Gram's notes.

It was almost eleven when we left the student union, our breath visible white clouds as we made our way to Townsend's truck. Shivering, I raised my hood and stuck it over my hair.

Townsend must have noticed, as he put an arm around me to warm me while we walked to the truck. We pulled out and I persuaded Townsend to drive through the campus before we headed for home. We met two different campus security vehicles, and it made me feel a little better that they were taking the situation seriously. We were passing the medical examiner's building when heavy steam caught my attention.

"Stop a second, Townsend," I said, and he pulled over. I rolled my window down and stuck my head out. The smell of smoke met my nostrils. I sniffed again.

"Do you smell smoke?" I asked Townsend.

He opened his door and stuck his head out. At that point an alarm began to go off at the building we were stopped in front of and people began running from the exit.

"Fire!" someone yelled. "Fire!"

"Call 9-1-1!" Townsend shouted, tossing his cell phone at me.

"Where are you going?" I called, punching in 9-1-1, sirens in the distance signaling the authorities were already in the know. I jumped down out of the pickup and followed after Townsend, but couldn't find him. Seven or eight people were standing in the parking lot stamping their feet and rubbing their arms to keep warm.

"Is anybody left in there?" I asked. "Is everyone accounted for?"

"We don't know!" a woman dressed in a white lab coat said. "I think there may still be people in the basement."

"Did you tell that to the good-looking guy just ahead of me?" I asked.

She nodded. "He asked. I thought he was a cop or something. He took my entry card and went in."

I felt a moment of extreme panic. "Give me your card!" I yelled to a guy who stood next to the lab worker.

He stared at me.

"Now!" I ordered. "We're together!"

The guy handed his card over and I ran to the door, jammed the card in, and entered the building. I yelled for Townsend as I ran through the hallways.

I suddenly remembered Trevor Childers worked in the M.E.'s office, and I made my way to that area of the building first but didn't find any smoke or Townsend.

I hurried to the basement of the building where the offices of Billings and Danbury, among others, were located. "Townsend!" I yelled. "Rick!" No response.

I was alarmed when I detected the strong smell of smoke. I hurried to the hallway outside the office area and coughed as the smoke intensified. Noticing a fire extinguisher on the wall, I grabbed it and started down the hall, reading the instructions and praying I could figure out how to operate it.

"Townsend!" I yelled, the smoke getting thicker.

I got to the hallway outside Billings's office and realized the fire was coming from inside. I took a step forward, set the fire extinguisher on the floor to ready it for operation, when, for the second time in almost as many days, I was swept off my feet and settled over a strong shoulder.

"Didn't you hear me tell you to stay put?" I heard, and almost fainted with relief when I recognized Townsend's voice.

"I heard. I just didn't obey," I said. "Uh, you can put me down. I can walk, you know."

"Right. And miss the chance to carry someone from a burning building over my shoulder with impressed taxpayers looking on? Not likely, Calamity," he said. "So just relax and enjoy the ride," he ordered.

I sighed. Now that I knew Townsend was safe, I'd agree to just about anything. Oh, I'd appreciate it if you wouldn't tell him that, however. I've got my reputation to consider.

With a flare for the theatrical I hadn't suspected Townsend capable of, he shoved the exit door open with much fanfare and carted me out to the applause and admiration of the gathered throng. I heard the unmistakable click of cameras and felt the glare of television cameras.

"This is so humiliating," I told Townsend, but figured I owed him his moment of glory. "My ass will be spread all over newspaper and TV by tomorrow," I said.

I could feel Townsend chuckle.

"At least they got your good side," he said.

Nice.

The firemen quickly put the fire out, damage was kept to a minimum, and people began to disperse. The state fire marshal's office had been called in to ascertain the cause of the blaze. Townsend was busy reporting what he'd observed, and he entered the building while speaking to the authorities. I'd grabbed my digital camera and started to snap some pictures for an article when I noticed a familiar figure sitting on the curb. Struck by the sad, lonely pose, I snapped a picture. It was Trevor Childers, and he looked shaken.

"Trevor? Are you okay?" I asked, and when he looked up I noticed his tearstained cheeks. I sat down beside him. "Did you get hurt?" I asked. "Do you need a paramedic?"

He shook his head. "Thanks to your hero over there I'm okay."

"My hero?"

"I was near the basement offices when the alarm went off," he said. "I kind of panicked. Your friend led me out."

"He's a good man in an emergency," I acknowledged. "What were you doing outside Billings's office again?" I asked him, figuring, as upset as he was, he might be more apt to come clean. Near-death experience and all that.

"I was trying to help Sherman out," he said.

"Out of the building?"

Childers shook his head. "Out of tenure hell."

"How?"

"He got a raw deal on that tenure thing. I thought if we got something on Professor Billings, maybe we could get her to change her mind," he said.

"What made you think you could get something on her?"

He shrugged. "Everyone has secrets. It was worth a try. I even thought at one time of claiming she came on to me and threatening to report her if she didn't reconsider on the tenure, but I didn't think I was that good of an actor. For obvious reasons."

"But aren't you and Professor Danbury—uh, doing the same thing?" I asked. "You know. That same prohibition against student/professor, uh, fraternization?"

"Sherman's not my professor. Besides, he's only eight years older than me. And we've been discreet," he added.

Not discreet enough if I'd figured it out.

"Any idea what caused the fire?" I asked. "Or who?"

Trevor shook his head. "But it couldn't be Sherman," he said, tears filling his eyes again. "It couldn't be. He wouldn't do that. Not with me working in the building. He wouldn't."

I handed him a tissue from my purse. "Are you sure, Trevor? Are you really all that sure?"

"Mr. Childers?"

We both looked up to see several Campus Security officers looking down at us.

"We understand you were in the area of the building near where the fire broke out," one said. "We have a few questions for you, sir," the officer said. "If you'd come with us?"

Trevor finished wiping his eyes with the tissue and got to his feet.

"Good luck, Trevor," I told him, thinking he was going to need it.

Townsend and I hung around the Campus Security cop shop waiting for the okay to head home. We'd been waiting for over an hour when Patrick arrived. He shook Townsend's hand and looked at me.

"Are you okay?" he said.

I nodded. "What's going on?"

"So far it appears the fire was intentionally set. Some flammable substance. They're looking into the possibility that it's something from the M.E.'s lab. They probably gained entrance through the service door by the back dock. Someone stuffed something in the door to keep it from latching. No cameras down there unfortunately," he added. "Amateurish job. Professor Billings's office door was doused and set ablaze."

"What about Keith Gardner? Has he been arrested yet? If he's in jail, he couldn't have caused this fire," I said.

Patrick shook his head. "Gardner's in the wind."

"And the professor is clearly a target," I said.

"It appears that way. But getting her to believe that isn't going to be easy," he said. "Even after this."

"You've spoken to her?"

"Just now. Naturally, she's concerned, but she's not willing to back down. It's not who she is, she says," Patrick added.

"But she is the kind of educator who will place not only herself at risk but her students as well," I pointed out. "And all to avoid looking weak and vulnerable. That's totally irresponsible. She's playing chicken with people's lives here!"

Patrick sighed. "I tried to convince her to cancel class tomorrow to give authorities time to investigate and maybe make a break in this case, but she wouldn't go for it. The Campus Security chief is going to make an appeal to the college president to see if he can step in and order her to cancel the class, but he's not hopeful that will happen. These kinds of decisions are, unfortunately, as a rule left to the professor's discretion. I figure it will take an act of God or some kind of unnatural disaster to get Professor Billings to back down."

I pondered his words.

Unnatural disaster, eh? What do you know? My specialty!

CHAPTER 17

Townsend dropped me off at home around one and I didn't even receive so much as a good-night grope. I imagine that was because Townsend suspected I was up to something—okay, okay, so he was right—because he tried everything he could to dissuade me from attending class the next morning. The poor daft fellow even went so far as to offer to buy me breakfast at Hazel's and not make one crack about what I ordered. Nice try, Ranger, but it would take more than hash browns and a double side of bacon to get me to change my plans. Now, maybe if he served them to me in bed, wearing nothing but my gammy's Kiss the Cook apron . . . Hmmmm. I shook my head for fear I'd suggest just that, and shook it again for fear he'd accept.

I spent some time on my schoolwork, working on my campus crime article, my pups running around the kitchen, their toenails clicking on the linoleum as they vied for attention. I grabbed them each a raw hot dog from the fridge (uh, my gammy doesn't have to know everything) and found myself chewing on one as well. I finally fell into bed around two thirty, thinking once Kari was wedded and bedded Saturday, I planned to stay in bed all day Sunday and catch up on my sleep.

I sighed. What a way to spend a birthday.

The next morning I was up early. I'd arranged to pick Frankie up so I could spring my master plan on him. I didn't think he would approve, but it was all I could think of if the professor insisted on going forward with her lecture as planned. I tiptoed out of the house without waking Gram and thought that had to be a good sign.

I picked Frankie up ten minutes later. I'd told him I'd park down the street a piece just to avoid any unpleasantness with Uncle Frank, and from the way Frankie walked to the car—a cross between Shaggy on *Scooby Doo* and one of the walking corpses from *Dawn of the Dead*—it was clear this was one depressed dude. The hour's ride to Carson had just gotten *soooo* much longer.

He slid into the seat beside me. More like slunk.

"Hey, Frankie," I said. "Whazz-up?" I reached out to high-five him but he just looked straight ahead. Uh-oh. Bad sign. I put the car in gear and prepared to pull out.

"I don't even know why I'm going to class this morning," he said. "What's the point? The DPS academy won't accept a guy who can't even beat a girl in an obstacle race," he said.

I put the car back in park. "Whoa there, buckaroo. What do you mean, 'Can't even beat a girl'? That sounds a little male chauvinist oinker to me. I wonder what Dixie would think."

That got Frankie's attention.

"I didn't mean Dixie," he said. "I don't think of her as a girl."

"I'm sure she'll be thrilled to hear that," I told him.

"You don't understand. I poured everything I had into making it in the academy. All my hopes and dreams. Only to discover that my human frailties are going to prevent me from realizing that dream. It's devastating," he said.

"You don't know yet that you won't be accepted," I said, hoping to make him feel better. "They don't even do the physical agility testing for three months. You still have time to get in shape."

"No one has *that* much time," he replied. "You saw me. I made a complete and utter fool of myself. And did you see Patrick's face? He looked like he'd just witnessed a train wreck."

Think Thomas the Tank Engine jumping the track.

"Don't give up, Frankie," I urged. "You never know what might happen. And there are all kinds of jobs in law enforcement where you don't have to be a superhero."

"Yeah right, Super Woman. Name one."

I thought about it. There had to be something.

"What about those CSI guys?" I said. "Forensic technicians and investigators. You don't think they're all really certified peace officers, do you? They just write the shows that way so they can get the story in and use fewer actors. After commercials, they only have like forty minutes to follow the evidence and nab the bad guy, so the CSIs have to do double duty. Personally, I think you'd make an awesome CSI guy—not to mention a really adorable one in those cute lab coats."

Frankie was quiet. "I suppose I could talk to Patrick to see what other opportunities are available. But it wouldn't hurt to ratchet up the training regime. I might still have a shot at the academy if I work at it."

"Attaboy, Frankie," I told him, pulling out again. "You keep that positive attitude."

And he did. Until I told him what I had planned to keep Billings from presenting her last lethal lecture.

He looked at me. "You can't be serious."

I shrugged. "Can you think of another way? Short of kidnapping, that is?"

"Either way, it's a safe bet a law or two will be fractured."

I sighed. "That's why you and Dixie can't be involved. An arrest right now would put the brakes on your law enforcer careers."

"I don't like it," Frankie said. "I don't like it at all."

I wasn't any too thrilled myself.

"Just a word of warning. I go aggravated, bucko, or I don't go at all," I said with a wicked grin.

"Stop the car. I want out," Frankie said.

Dream on, Frankfurter.

I dropped Frankie off at his building, drove to my class, took my quiz (I think I even passed!), and then scrammed, hurrying back to rejoin Frankie.

Dixie met us at class. Her mouth flew open when she learned what I had planned.

"That's your great plan?" she said. "Who helped you come up with it? Inspector Clouseau?"

"That's funny, Dixie," I said. "We're trying to avert a possible murder and you're auditioning for America's Funniest Comic."

"Maybe this won't even be necessary," Frankie said. "Maybe she'll be a no-show."

Yeah, like anything ever went my way.

I stood in the corridor outside Frankie's classroom pacing back and forth, waiting to see if maybe by some miracle the Carson College security professionals had convinced the head honchos at the administration level to put pressure on Billings to cancel her class for that day.

At ten minutes after nine I was breathing much easier. The professor was late for her class. Maybe she had wised up. Five minutes later, Professor Billings strode in, another expensive pair of shoes on her feet—this time a brown-stitched leather pump that tapped out her *once more into the breach* battle cry on the shiny, waxed linoleum.

I stopped her before she got to her classroom.

"Wait, Professor Billings!" I stood between her and her classroom doorway. "Please think carefully about what you're about to do here," I told her. "People's lives and safety hang in the balance. Your own life may be at stake. That has to be more important than proving you won't be the first one to blink."

She gave me a grim look. "We've had this discussion before, Miss Turner," she said. "And nothing has changed. I don't expect you to understand, but I do ask that you not interfere."

"But this is nuts!" I said. "What is it going to hurt to wait a couple days to give the authorities a chance to investigate?"

"Oh, do the authorities have a suspect?" she asked. "A real one?"

I couldn't meet her eyes.

"I didn't think so," she said. "Look, I appreciate your concern, Miss Turner, but I'm a teacher. That's what I do. So I'm going to teach."

"With murder being the lesson learned?" I asked.

I sensed a slight chink in her armor. It was quickly dealt with.

"I'm late for my class, Miss Turner," she said. "If you wouldn't mind?" She motioned for me to step aside.

I considered trying to block the doorway, but figured with her background in law enforcement and her size advantage, she'd dispose of me in short order. I let her pass.

Besides, it wasn't as if I wasn't going to do something I hadn't done before. In, like, grade school.

I strolled over to the fire alarm and pulled it. Then I ran like hell . . . right into the arms of Hector Moldonado, Campus Security chief and so not a current member of the Tressa Jayne Turner fan club.

I frowned as Hector escorted me away from the building. I waited outside for the students to file out, but no one left. Several minutes later I walked over to Hector.

"Why aren't they leaving?" I asked.

He motioned to the microphone attached to his portable radio. "I contacted the office with an all-clear," he said. "They notified the classrooms of the false alarm. Besides, didn't you have a discussion with Professor Billings before you pulled that alarm?"

I nodded.

"I imagine she also realized you pulled the alarm and she threatened to fail any student who left her classroom."

"Can she do that?" I asked.

He shrugged. "What's to stop her?"

And they call blondes dumb.

I broke free of the surprised security officer and ran for the building.

I entered at a gallop and ran full-bore into Billings's classroom, no real clue what I was going to do to cause a classroom commotion. Hard to believe, isn't it? I bet you thought I had a natural gift and didn't have to work at it.

I looked around the classroom and spotted Frankie and I said the first thing that popped into my head. Always a mistake.

"There you are!" I said. "I knew it! You're with *her*!" I pointed to Dixie. "How could you? You knew how I felt," I yelled.

Professor Billings stepped away from the large dry-erase board on the wall behind her.

"What are you doing?" she asked.

I used the line Townsend had used on me. "It's called saving you from yourself," I mumbled. "You can thank me later."

I heard a door shut. Hector had entered the classroom. Crap. My class-stopping performance was about to be cut short. I turned back to my audience.

"I can't believe after all we've been through you'd do this to me!" I wailed.

A skinny kid with black glasses and an overbite raised his hand. "Are you talking to me?" he said.

"Does it look like I'm talking to you?" I asked.

He flinched and lowered his hand and took off his glasses, wiping them on his white shirt. "I'm sorry. My glasses were smudged. I couldn't tell."

"I'm talking to him!" I said, and pointed to Frankie. "The man who broke my heart. Who reached in, grabbed my aorta, and squeezed my heart out like a used-up dishrag," I said, adding a sniffle.

"Huh?" Frankie said.

"Sure, go ahead and make light of it, you hedonistic

heartbreaker," I shouted. "Go ahead and shred my heart like taco cheese through a grater." Okay, so I hadn't put my days at the Dairee Freeze behind me yet. Sniff, sniff. "He'll love you and leave you, too, you know!" I told Dixie.

Suddenly the geekie guy I'd yelled at earlier raised his hand again.

I looked at him. "Uh, yes? Do you have a question?"

He put a finger to the nosepiece of his glasses and pushed them back up on his nose. He peered at me through his still-cloudy lenses. He pointed at Frankie.

"Isn't he your cousin?" he asked.

I blinked. I'd completely forgotten some of the gang knew me from Big Burl's the other night.

"Uh, yeah, that's right," I said, struggling to improvise. "He's my . . . cousin . . . and . . . and—" I looked at Frankie and then over at his fiancée sitting next to him. "He stole *her* away from me!" I screamed, pointing at Dixie.

"What the hell?" Dixie yelled.

"It's true! It's true!" I shouted. "He stole my little Dixie Doodle away from me!"

"That's it!" Professor Billings protested. "I want this individual removed from my class," she told Hector, who was still hovering in the doorway taking in my little impromptu drama. "*Now*, Chief," Billings yelled.

Hector snapped to attention and came after me. I led him on a short slow-speed chase around the classroom trying to use up the final minutes of class time. At last he got me cornered near the back of the room. *Ring you stupid bell, ring!* I chanted, wanting this ring more than the dinner bell at my Uncle Frank's annual hog roast.

"Class, you are dismissed," I heard Professor Billings say with a disgusted tone. Yes!

Everyone gave me strange looks as they filed out of the room. I looked at Hector and smiled. "No harm, no foul?" I suggested.

Hector gave me a disgusted look. "Try 'you have the right to remain silent.'"

"Good advice," I said, and held out my wrists. "I think I'll take it."

CHAPTER 18

Patrick sprang me from the campus equivalent of a holding cell with the promise that if the university chose to file formal charges, I would present myself at the appropriate time. I also got an uncharacteristic butt chewing from Dawkins. It smarted like you-know-what, and got me to thinking maybe he wasn't as accepting of me just the way I was as I'd thought.

"I didn't see an alternative," I told him. "I just wanted to disrupt that lecture."

"You sure did that," Patrick said. "But unfortunately not before she'd covered some of the lecture notes on homicide."

"So it may all have been for naught?" I said.

Patrick shrugged. "I guess we'll find out."

Once I'd been officially released, Frankie and Dixie took off—after more chewing of my butt, especially from Dixie Doodle. Guess she didn't like the idea of being branded Calamity Jayne's little filly. It wasn't as if I was any too crazy about folks thinkin' that the Daggett heifer was the best this cowgirl could lasso either, but I'd been desperate. And desperate times call for desperate measures.

By the time I was a free woman, I was more than ready to head for home. I decided on a quick stop at Burger King first. Being arrested gave one an appetite, I'd discovered. I drove to the nearest drive-through restaurant, and while I waited to place my order, I checked my cell phone, discovered it was still off, and turned it back on to check for messages. The battery blinked to signal it needed a charge. It started to play before I could shut it off.

"H'lo," I said, hoping it wasn't Townsend.

"Tressa? Tressa, where are you?"

I frowned, recognizing the voice—and the incoming number—as belonging to the bride-to-be. "Kari?" My friend sounded more frazzled than ever.

"Yes! Are you still in Des Moines?" Kari asked.

"I was just leaving," I told her, somewhat evasively, thinking surely news of my Tressa monologue hadn't made it back to Grandville already. "Why?"

"You're not going to believe this, but my grandmother's half sister, Great-aunt Trudy, got a wild hare and decided to fly in from Arizona for the wedding. Can you believe it? Eighty-eight years old with a history of coronary artery disease, cardiac episodes, and recurrent respiratory infections and the old lady decides at the last minute to get on a plane all by herself and fly out here! Between the mints being the wrong colors, bridesmaids going on starvation diets, and Brian and me almost breaking up over a place called Big Burl's, I'm about ready to go postal!" She hesitated. "Your dress fits fine, though, right Tressa?"

I winced. Perfectly fine—if it was to be a body stocking.

"Sure. No sweat. Fits like a glove." Like the glove at the O.J. trial, that is. If it doesn't fit, you must acquit. Yikes.

"Well, that's a relief," she said. "I guess I'd better let you go. I have a million and one things left to do."

I frowned at the phone. "Uh, why did you call again, Kari?" I asked, thinking I might've missed something along the way. Yeah. It happens.

"Ohmigosh! I'm a total basket case here! I need you to run to the airport and pick up Aunt Trudy," she said. "Her flight number is 666 and she should be arriving at the airport within the next hour," she said. "We're so far behind with things here that I don't have anyone free to pick her up and deliver her. If I'd known she was coming in advance, I would have added it to the itinerary," she added.

I made a face. You had to have an itinerary to get married? Note to Tressa: *Elope!*

"Hang on," I said, fumbling around for my legal pad and a pen. "Give me her name and the flight info again."

"Her name is Trudy McNamara and she's arriving on flight 666 out of Phoenix."

"Flight 666? Isn't that like a bad omen or something? You know, Satan's lucky numbers?"

"Just pick her up, will you, Tressa? And drop her at my folks' house when you get back in town. She'll probably need to rest."

"What does she look like? So I don't approach someone else's elderly great-aunt and scare the old lady pants off her," I said.

"I haven't seen her in ten years, so how the hell

should I know?" Kari snapped. "She's old, short, and bent over. You figure it out."

Uh-oh. Bridezilla was rearing her scaly head.

"Uh, Kari, at that age they *all* pretty much look that way," I replied. "Some specifics would be nice."

I heard Kari consulting with someone in the background. "She wears a really awful blond wig and carries a cane. She has these black-framed cat's-eye glasses and wears a chain around her neck so she doesn't lose them. But there can't be all that many elderly ladies flying on their own," she pointed out.

"Okay, okay, I'll pick her up for you, but you're gonna owe me big. I'm getting down to the wire here on my journalism project and I need to get moving on it," I told her.

"You didn't wait until the last minute again, did you, Tressa?"

"You know I work better under pressure. And don't you worry about Aunt Trudy. I'll deliver her directly to your doorstep safe and sound, care of Tressa Jayne Turner," I promised.

"At least I don't have to stress about your dress fitting properly," she repeated. "I appreciate your self-control."

"Can I take your order?" the drive-through speaker blared.

"Is that a drive-through speaker, Tressa?" Kari asked. "What are you ordering, Tressa? Tressa?"

I turned the car radio on, twisted the switch to broadcast static, and stuck my cell phone near the car speaker.

"Listen, Kari, my battery's going. I can't hear you, Kari. Chat later! Buh-bye!"

I placed my order, going with a Diet Coke rather

than the real thing—a bone to toss to Kari—along with my chicken strips and fries. I went with the strips and fries as they can be eaten more easily while negotiating the city streets and thoroughfares. Okay, so it's not foolproof easy eating. By the time I got to the airport, I wished I'd worn a black hoodie so the barbecue sauce and ketchup wouldn't show.

I pulled into short-term parking. Before 9/11 there was a chance you could get away with parking at the front doors to run in and pick up your party. Now? No way. Airport security gives you the evil eye as soon as you drive onto airport property, and keeps closer tabs on you than my gammy does on Rick Townsend's granddad Joe.

I parked the car, keeping my driver-side door open a scosh. I wasn't sure Kari's aunt would be okay with me lurching across the seat or crawling in the front from the back. I hurried into the airport, checking the monitors to find that Aunt Trudy's flight had already arrived. I noted the number and hoofed it to the arrival gate. Passengers were beginning to disembark by the time I made it through the security checkpoints. I cooled my heels while I waited for Aunt Trudy to emerge.

It didn't take long. I saw the cane first. She used it like the white stick blind people use and whacked the heel of the guy walking in front of her. He turned around and scowled, but I sensed Aunt Trudy hadn't picked up on it. Especially since she jabbed him in the hiney with her next cane stroke. The fellow hurried his pace to put distance between him and the weapon-wielding senior. I shook my head. By the time I delivered her great-aunt Trudy into Kari's hands, she'd probably owe me her firstborn. From the looks of things, the hour's drive back home could be a bumpy one.

"Mrs. McNamara! Hello! Mrs. McNamara!" I hailed the old woman who wore a bleach-blond wig that looked like it had been pilfered from Dolly Parton. I received no response to my hails. "Aunt Trudy!" I yelled and jumped up and down, finally getting the old girl's attention. I waved to her again and hurried over.

"Welcome to Des Moines!" I greeted her, reaching out to take her small carry-on bag, but she stopped me with a jab to my knee with her cane.

"You've changed," she told me. "Packed on the pounds. And what have you done to your hair?" she asked as I rubbed my knee.

"I'm Tressa Turner," I explained. "I'm a friend of your great-niece, Kari—actually, her maid of honor. She asked me to pick you up and deliver you to her folks' house."

She gave me a long look. "You make it sound as if I'm some parcel to be dropped at the door," she accused. "Fine thing, having a stranger pick me up. Maybe I should just get back on the plane and head home."

I looked at the cane. It sounded like a plan to me.

"Did you want me to check on returning flights?" I asked.

"Here." She reached out and smashed her bag into my midsection. "It's getting heavy. All my medications, you know."

I took the bag from her. "We can collect your other luggage this way." I pointed in the direction of the baggage area. "Then we'll be on our way."

"So you're the maid of honor," she said as we headed from her gate. "You that gel who found the stiffs?"

Some claim to fame, huh?

"Yep. That was me."

"So, people have a way of getting dead around you?"

I shook my head. "The getting was already gotten by the time I found those bodies. I happened along after the fact. Except for the time I was very nearly a murder victim myself. But you don't want to hear about my tale of woe," I said.

"You married?"

I put my hand up to show my ring finger. "Nope."

"I'm not surprised. What man would want a gel who finds corpses?"

I'd wondered that myself a time or two this past year.

We claimed her suitcase and I told her to wait while I ran and got the car out of short-term parking and brought it around front to collect her. I requested she remain close to the door and ready so I wouldn't get hassled by the security officers. I quickly pulled the Plymouth around and waited, but no sign of the old lady. I honked the horn and attracted the attention of several airport security officials. They frowned and I waved.

"Come on, Aunt Trudy. Get you and your crippling cane out here," I mumbled under my breath, smiling at the officer walking in my direction and pointing at the door. "Come on, ol' woman. Shake an arthritic leg."

The officer came over to stand by the front passenger door. I scooted over and rolled the window down. No electric windows for me.

"You can't park here, miss," he said, noting the obvious.

"I know, Officer. I'm just waiting for an elderly lady I'm picking up to get out here. She was just here a second ago. She's like a gazillion years old, is wielding—

er, carrying—this really hard cane, and has on a funky blond wig. Have you seen her?"

"Not that I can recall," he said. "But you'll have to park in short-term parking and go back in to collect her. You can't park here. FAA regulations."

I saw the woman in question appear behind the officer, but unfortunately too late to warn him of the impending assault. I saw the guy flinch and pivot as Aunt Trudy poked him in the back with the cane.

"You may open the door for me, young man," she said, as if she were an actress and he her chauffeur. The officer's ears turned red, but he complied.

"This is the car my great-niece arranged for me to be picked up in?" she asked once she got inside. "Does it actually run? And it smells like stinky feet in here."

"Actually stinky dogs," I told her. "And yes, it does run. On a semiregular basis at least," I added. "It just needs some special attention."

"Hmmpf," Trudy replied, pulling out a glass case and snapping sunglass shades over her lenses.

I pulled out of the airport and headed from Des Moines and for home. At about an hour away from the capital city, Grandville is close enough for residents to get a bit of culture, but not too close to lose our country roots.

Ten minutes into the ride I was ready to conk Great-aunt Trudy on the head with her cane and put her out of my misery. Since the moment she took a seat next to me, I'd been treated to snide comments about my car, my clothes, my hair, my breath, even my shoelaces—cute black-and-white-checkered flag laces designed to go with my black high-top Converse tennies. When the red oil light popped on about fifteen minutes outside

Grandville, I said a naughty word and gained a sharp rib poke from Aunt Trudy's cane in response.

"Watch that mouth!" she said. "And why are we stopping? Are we there?"

I pulled over to the side of the road. "Nothing to worry about," I assured the old woman. "Just some routine maintenance. It'll just take a second and we'll be back on the road in a jiffy."

"We better be. I've got bladder control issues."

I winced. And cane-control issues.

I pulled the hood release, pounded a frustrated shoulder against the door and popped it open, got out of the car and slammed it, then remembered I'd have a heckuva time getting it open again. I cursed. *Whack!* The cane hit the car window, narrowly missing my fingers.

I headed to the trunk, put the key in the lock, and slowly opened the trunk lid. (Since I discovered a body doing a bad impression of a car jack, I have a habit of opening trunks with extreme caution.) Finding only my case of oil, a funnel, and some oily rags, I started to breathe again. I grabbed a couple of plastic bottles of 10W-30 and headed to the front of the car. I raised the hood, located the oil filler hole (I could find it blindfolded), and dumped two quarts in. I have this down to a science by now.

Pound, pound, pound!

I walked around to the passenger side of the car to see Great-aunt Trudy with her cane out the window, rapping on the top of my car. "What's the holdup?" she asked.

"I'm waiting for the oil to seep down into where it's supposed to be so I can check with the dipstick to see if I need to add another quart," I told her.

"Dipstick? You ask me, you're the only dipstick here. How come you didn't check the oil before you came to get me? How come you didn't wash your car and clean it out? How come you didn't fumigate it? You could have a toxic cesspool here."

I felt my ears warm. "Not to worry, Aunt Trudy." I leaned on her car door. "I had the car thoroughly detailed after the body was removed," I assured her.

I noticed her swallow twice in rapid succession and I grinned down at her. That oughta give her something to sink her dental plate into.

I finished up changing my oil, shut the hood, and returned to the car door. I pulled on the driver's door, which of course wouldn't open, and almost swore until I remembered the punishment for said offense was painful.

As I didn't want to ask an eighty-eight-year-old lady who had to use a cane to get out of the car on the bumpy, uneven shoulder, I opted to enter through the backseat, then crawl over into the front and behind the wheel. I got into the backseat, then noticed the old gal up front had her headback against the headrest, apparently catching a few zs. My own gammy can go from conversation to coma quicker than you could say "Time for clean up" after a meal.

I carefully placed my right leg over the seat back, trying to avoid kicking Great-aunt Trudy in the head, then realized I needed to start with my left leg instead. I pulled my right leg back into the backseat and replaced it with my left one, twisting and contorting, huffing and puffing, careful not to wake Kari's cantankerous aunt. If my luck held, Tyrannical Trudy would remain asleep the rest of the way home and it would be a peaceful ride. I managed to get my entire body into the front seat, but ended up wedged behind the wheel of the car. I snuck a peek at the still-sleeping woman, pulled on the door handle, and shoved against it with my shoulder. The door popped open and I fell out on my backside.

I brushed gravel off me and got back behind the wheel. Yes! Aunt Trudy hadn't stirred. I turned the key to start the car and cranked. *Click. Click.* I frowned and tried again. *Click. Click.*

"Shit!" slipped out, and I slapped a hand over my mouth and stole a quick look at Aunt Trudy, who, thank goodness, had slept through my slip. Now what? It was either the starter or the battery. Or maybe both.

I had just pulled out my cell phone to call for assistance—more along the lines of my brother the car dealer than AAA, which I don't have—when I heard a vehicle close by. I used the outside mirror to look back. A Department of Natural Resources state SUV had pulled onto the shoulder behind me. I'd know that vehicle—and the guy behind those dark shades—anywhere. I was really glad to see Ranger Rick. He knew a lot about cars and was cheaper than a hook. I watched his progress up to my door with a normal, healthy woman's natural appreciation for a gorgeous guy in uniform.

He stopped and bent down at my open window. I caught a whiff of his cologne. God, he smelled good. All woodsy and earthy and musky. I caught myself before I drooled.

"Just curious. Have you ever kept track of how many times you've broken down along the side of a road in this car?" Ranger Rick asked. "Because I'm thinking you could qualify for the Guinness Book of World Records here, Calamity," he said.

I shook my head. "No, but I did hold the record for most pounds lost and gained back and lost again—until Oprah edged me out, that is," I said. "It's all good, though. There's still the most-corpses-found competition. And I've been thinking seriously about entering that hot-dog-eating contest. I think I only have to eat fifty-four in twelve minutes to win."

Ranger Rick nodded. "It's always good to have a goal to aspire to," he said. "So, what's up with the old beater?"

"Shh!" I said, putting a finger to my lips. "She'll hear you."

"She? Your car is a she now? And she can hear? Tressa, we need to talk."

Too late I realized he was referring to my Reliant and not the elderly occupant to my right.

"Shh! You'll wake her." I pointed to Aunt Trudy, who was still sound asleep. "And trust me when I say a sleeping Aunt Trudy is vastly preferable to an awake Aunt Trudy any day of the week," I told him.

Ranger Rick took his sunglasses off and stuck them in the tab at the top of his uniform shirt and looked over at my passenger.

"I didn't know you had an Aunt Trudy," Rick said. "Is she the lesbian?"

I shook my head. "That's my aunt Eunice," I informed him. "And this isn't *my* aunt, it's Kari's aunt. Great-aunt, actually. She decided to fly in for the wedding from Phoenix rather unexpectedly, and Kari asked me to pick her up at the airport. But if I'd known how dangerous the transport was going to be, I'd have asked for hazard pay," I complained. "Man, she's brutal!"

Townsend's forehead crinkled as he looked at her. I

felt my fingers twitch to smooth those creases out with a soft caress. Yes, I'm still sex starved. Deal with it.

"Are you sure she's okay?" he asked.

I looked over at her. She hadn't changed any. Still had that cursed cane gripped in her hands at the ready.

"Why? Doesn't she look okay?" I asked.

Townsend raised an eyebrow. "How long has she been asleep?"

I shrugged. "I dunno. Not long enough for me. Like I said, she's brutal, man. Why?"

"She's awful still," he observed.

"So? She's a sound sleeper."

"But her chest should be moving."

I took a closer look at Great-aunt Trudy as Townsend moved around the front of the car to the passenger-side door.

"Mrs. McNamara?" I gave her a little jab in the arm with my index finger. "Aunt Trudy?"

By this time Townsend had opened the door and was crouching down beside the sleeping woman.

"What's her name?" he asked.

"Trudy McNamara," I told him.

He gently prodded her. "Mrs. McNamara?" he coaxed. "Ma'am, are you okay?"

She didn't stir.

"Ma'am?"

I was starting to become concerned and Townsend's gentle car-side manner wasn't helping matters, so I reached out and attempted to pull her precious cane from her hands, thinking that would certainly get a rise out of the old lady. At first the cane wouldn't budge. I gave it another tug. This time not only did the cane move in my direction, so did Aunt Trudy. She flopped to her side on the bench seat like a sack of horse grain when you take a corner too fast. Her head landed in my lap. When her sunglasses popped off and I got a look at her eyes, I knew I was right about flight 666 being bad luck. Apparently, dead right.

Townsend reached in and felt her neck for a pulse.

"Is she . . . okay?" I asked.

Townsend raised both eyebrows this time. "I guess that depends on how she lived her life," he responded.

"You mean she's dead?" I asked, my voice barely a squeak. "Maybe she's just in one of those somnambulant states. You know. Like a deep, deep sleep. Shouldn't we be beating on her chest or blowing in her mouth or something?" I asked, feeling the reality of the situation begin to creep into my consciousness. "Perform CPR?"

"Be my guest, Tressa, but I'd say she was past the point of no return," he told me. "If it's any consolation, however, there was probably nothing you could have done. How old was she, anyway?"

I felt tears begin to pool in my eyes. "A pair of eights," I answered.

"Pretty old to fly across country on your own," he said.

Before I knew she was dead I probably would have made some comment about her flying on her broomstick, but now that she was deceased, she didn't seem so bad.

"What are we going to do?" I asked, disengaging myself from the old woman's body and then realizing I was trapped due to my stuck driver's door. I felt my anxiety level start to rise.

"Uh, Townsend, could you open my door for me?" I asked, pretty sure I was gonna hurl my strips and fries all over the dear, sweet, departed old lady if I didn't get out of the car soon. I already was going to have to try and explain delivering Aunt Trudy COD as Stan called it—Corpse On Delivery. I didn't want the added chore of addressing why dear, departed Aunt Trudy was covered in hurl.

"Just a second," he said. "I'm calling the M.E."

"Seriously, Townsend! I need to get out of the car now!" I was beginning to feel like all the oxygen around me had been sucked up by some invisible force. My heart began to race a mile a minute. I couldn't get my breath. I had to get out of this damned car!

I rolled Great-aunt Trudy's head off my lap and dove out the open driver-side window, headfirst, breaking my fall to the graveled shoulder with my hands. I yelped when the gravel embedded itself into my open palms.

"What the hell are you doing, Tressa?" Townsend asked, coming around the side of the car.

I managed to crawl on my hands and knees to the side of the road and threw up in the ditch.

"Never mind," Townsend said, and I felt his hand light and gentle on the back of my head. I continued to retch. Just the way you want a gorgeous guy to see you. Right, ladies?

One positive thing had come out of this. Those strips and fries would never make it to my hips and thighs. Still, I somehow didn't think that would be enough for Kari. Or her great-aunt Trudy.

CHAPTER 19

I stood outside my open closet door in my bra and panties considering and then discarding one apparel item after another hanging in my closet.

"I can't believe you waited this late to decide what to wear to the rehearsal dinner," my gramma said from her perch on my bed.

"Well, I have been kind of busy, Gram," I told her.

"Yeah. Killing off old ladies," she said. I shuddered.

"Thanks, Gram," I snapped. "I needed that little reminder. So, tell me. What does one wear to the rehearsal and dinner?" I'd tried to delete the details of my brother's wedding from my memory.

"A dress, of course. A nice one. But not too nice. You don't want to piss off the bride by looking better than she does."

I shook my head. Fat chance. Between the extra pounds left over from the holidays, a resolution to diet and exercise that hadn't kicked in yet, and hair that still found a way to frizz despite a jug of gel, it was a safe bet any attention I attracted would be more along the lines of Blackstone's worst-dressed list.

"I don't own all that many dresses, Gram," I said, sorting through more clothes and finding mainly khaki slacks and white T-shirts I wore for my retail sideline at Bargain City, low-waisted slacks for the newspaper, and smocks for the now-gone job at the Dairee Freeze. Quite the designer collection, huh?

"I'm surprised you had un-holey underwear," Gram said. "And that bra? It makes you look like you got no boobies."

"It's a sports bra, Gram. That's the idea. To prevent sagging so I don't end up with nipples pointing the way to my navel."

I noticed my gammy stare down at her own chest.

"You think maybe my boobies could use a push-up bra?" she asked. "When I sleep, they practically disappear underneath my armpits."

I winced. It seemed this particular ship had sailed.

"I think you should go for comfort rather than cleavage, Gram," I told her, just wanting this conversation to end. I checked the time. "Oh Lord, I'm gonna be late and Kari is gonna kill me."

"I have some frocks you could borrow," Gram said. "Course, they'll hang on you in the bosom area. What about Taylor? Shouldn't she have something you could borrow?"

I gave Gram a close look just to make sure she wasn't being comical. Or facetious. Taylor was a good two sizes smaller than I was. Of course, she wasn't addicted to doughnuts and Milky Way Midnight bars and allergic to exercise like I was.

"Taylor's taste is like night and day from mine," I said. "I have a certain style that is unique to me."

"What style is that? The Bargain City Blue Light Special? You need to advertise, girl. Be a little daring. Show a little flesh."

If I had to kneel in that peach frock tomorrow, I'd be showing more than a *little* flesh.

Gram got up from the bed and moved to stand beside me at the closet door. "What about a little black dress?" she asked. "Them's 'all occasion' apparel, 'cause you can wear 'em for all occasions. And with you delivering Kari's great-aunt Trudy in a body bag, I'd say this occasion calls for black. Why, I've worn a black dress to funerals, formals, cocktail parties, even a wedding once."

I turned to look at her. "You wore black to a wedding?"

"The bride was a bitch," she said, sticking her head into my closet. "I know you have to have a little black dress in here somewhere. Everyone has a little black dress." She rummaged about in the closet for a minute before she pulled out a dark garment. "Ha. I knew it. One little black dress."

I winced. "Uh, that's the dress Mom got me to wear to Paw Paw Will's funeral, Gram."

"It is?" She held the short dress out in front of her. "Are you sure?" she asked. "I remember you wearing a long black dress with one of them Chinese mandarin collars."

I raised my eyebrows. "That was Mom."

"Oh," she said. "Well, here you go. Problem solved." She held the sleeveless, short black dress out to me. "It's shorter than I expected. Good for you, girl. I hope you waxed."

I shut my eyes. This was a nightmare.

"I'm not even sure I can get into that dress, Gram," I told her. "It's been years." Years of working at Uncle Frank's, where the food was filling and best of all, free.

"You shoulda let me buy the body slimmer," she said. "But I've got a girdle if you need it. Takes two sizes off your ass." She handed me the dress. "Money-back guarantee. Be right back."

I looked at the little black dress. It was going to be a long night.

It took me forty-five minutes to wiggle into black super-control-top panty hose followed by the little black dress. I marveled at the tummy flattening panel of the hosiery and how it made my gut shrink. Of course, I couldn't take a deep breath, but beauty—or in this case, skinnyness—was pain. My gammy argued—unsuccessfully—when I insisted on searching for a pair of seven-inch Justin Black calfy boots to wear. I told Gram they made a certain statement.

"You're right," she agreed. "They say, look at me, I'm a hick from the sticks."

"I know they're in here somewhere," I said, picking up one pair of shoes after another and tossing them to the other end of the closet floor. "I've hardly worn them since I bought them." I picked up the nearly new Nikes I'd worn the night Dixie and I had been the victims of serious road rage, and swore. The toes of both shoes were scuffed, scratched, and dirty from my headlong dive to safety. And the deadbeat had no insurance.

I finally found my short Justin boots and pulled them out. "Success!" I proclaimed, and hurried to slip them on, took one last look at my face and hair, and headed out the door. And only twenty minutes late.

I could hardly tell I was entering a church sanctuary

for a wedding rehearsal, the tone so funereal when I walked in. From the looks I was getting, it was hard to figure out whether the lukewarm reception was due to the demise of Trudy in transit or bar fight fallout from Big Burl's. Either way, I felt like a PETA activist at the annual Iowa Pork Expo.

Kari noticed me first and threw a quick look in her husband-to-be's direction before she came over to me.

"You're late. I was getting worried," she said. "Cute outfit. Isn't that the dress you wore to your grandfather's funeral?" she added.

"No. I don't believe so," I lied. Jeesch. Had I put on a dress so rarely that when I did people committed the occasion to memory? "I just want to tell you again how sorry I am about your aunt Trudy, Kari. I didn't know her for very long, but the time we spent together was very memorable. She was a sweet, sweet person."

Kari gave me a you-are-so-lying look. "The woman was an ogre," she said. "She liked to kick old dogs and young children. Or maybe that's young dogs and old children."

"Oh, really?" I said with a wide-eyed look. "I never saw that side of her. She was really quite lovely." Kari just frowned. "So, how are things with the groom? Has he forgiven you for the Big Burl's brouhaha yet?"

"Maybe you should be asking if I've forgiven *him* yet," Kari said with a hard glint to her eyes. "Stupid, stupid man. As for you, I'd give my future husband a wide berth."

"Didn't you tell him I was the one who wanted to go somewhere else?" I asked.

Kari took my arm. "I tried to, Tressa. I really did. But he just wouldn't believe me. He kept telling me not to defend you, and he kept going on about how it felt

to see the future mother of his children being sere-
naded by a near-naked Pilsbury doughboy in a seedy
strip club and started getting all apoplectic again, so I
thought it was best to humor him until after the ceremony. Once we're married, I'll make sure to help you
mend some fences," she assured me.

I hoped Kari had plenty of twopenny nails and two-
by-fours lined up.

"Kari, the minister needs a moment of your time."
Kari's mother, Donna, came up and took her arm. Nor-
mally I get a hug from Donna. Today all I got was a
wary nod. "Tressa," she said, and dragged Kari away. I
looked around, wondering how much longer it would
take to get this show on the road and on to Calhoun's
steak house and grill where the rehearsal dinner was to
be held. I was in the mood for a light beer or two and
a nice, thick, juicy rib eye. The bride's family was picking up the tab and I was really hungry.

"Nice dress," I heard in my left ear. Townsend, attired in an orange-and-white-striped polo shirt and
belted khaki pants, appeared beside me. "Didn't you
wear it to Grandpa Will's funeral?" he asked.

"Why is everyone so obsessed with what I wear?" I
said. "Besides, I'm wearing black out of respect for
Great-aunt Trudy."

"And the boots?"

"Out of respect for the hundred bucks I plopped
down for them," I replied. "After all, I need to get
some wear out of them. And shoes don't stay looking
good very long once they're on my feet," I added,
thinking of my poor cross-trainers.

"I seem to remember a certain pair of white sling-
backs that became 'water moccasins' last summer,"
Townsend said.

I sighed, recalling a cross-country trek on shoes with less support than gel inserts.

Frankie, who was an usher, came over to join us.

"Where's Dixie?" I asked. "I noticed it was a full moon. She's not roaming the night in search of innocent victims to quench her bloodlust, is she?" Frankie gave me a disgruntled look.

"She's meeting with her study group tonight," he said.

"Where?"

"Off campus somewhere, I'm pretty sure," he said. "She wouldn't be foolish enough to meet on campus tonight of all nights," he added.

The minister called everyone to their places and I warned Townsend to be on his best behavior or else. I wanted no repeats of the monkey business at my brother's wedding—Townsend being the orangutan in question.

I strolled down the aisle to the music, pretending I was tiny and petite, and concentrated on taking slow, dainty, mincing steps, but from the looks I was getting I guessed I still looked like I had someplace to be and wanted to get there pronto.

I caught Townsend's smile as I took my place on the dais. I sighed. Whoever said the attendants weren't supposed to outshine bride and groom had apparently forgotten to tell Townsend. He made Brian look like a hungover understudy.

Once Kari joined us at the front of the church, I listened to the minister with half an ear, my mind on what might be happening that very night on the campus of Carson College. Professor Billings didn't seem to think she was in any real danger, but in my gut I knew that a murderer in training was on the prowl that night. At least Hector had agreed to double patrols, and Patrick had promised to take several swings through the campus. That was something.

I looked down at my feet and noticed a scuff on my brand-new Justin boot and frowned. How the heck?

"And then I'll say—" the minister was saying.

"Son of a bitch!" I blurted, suddenly receiving a divine communiqué from the Big Guy upstairs. I shoved my pretend bouquet into Kari's hands. "I have to go," I said, running down the stairs at the front of the church. I stopped, turned, ran back up the stairs, and grabbed Townsend's arm. "*We* have to go!" I amended.

"Tressa?" Kari looked bewildered.

"I'll be right on time tomorrow! Early even! Pinky swear!" I told her, holding up my pinky. "But I've really got to go! I'm on a lifesaving mission!"

I pulled Townsend down the carpeted stairs.

"This is highly irregular," the minister said.

"You don't know Tressa," Brian replied.

"What the hell are you doing?" Townsend asked as I dragged him down the center aisle past the pews.

"Hey! Stop swearing! We're in church!" I admonished.

"You just said son of a—"

I reached out and put my fingers on Townsend's sexy lips. "No reason the both of us should burn in hell."

I stopped at the pew in the back where Frankie was sitting. "Come on!" I grabbed his hand and yanked him to his feet. "We've got to get to Carson College ASAP. And we're taking your truck, Townsend," I told him.

"What's going on?" Frankie asked. "What lifesaving mission?"

"Yes, Calamity. Care to enlighten us?" Townsend said.

I kept one hand firmly clamped around both reluctant men's hands and dragged them to the door of the church.

"I know who the Carson College criminal is!" I told them. "And we need to get there before they claim their final victim! Now, who's with me?" I yelled.

"Do we have a choice?" Townsend said. "I'm warning you, if this is another one of your wild-goose chases, Tressa—"

"If I'm wrong, I'll go without chocolate for an entire month!" I blurted.

Townsend looked at me. "Have you forgotten next month is Easter? Chocolate bunnies. Marshmallow rabbits." He paused for effect. "Cadbury Creme eggs."

My absolute, all-time favorite candy. The rat.

"If I'm wrong, I'll gladly give up Cadbury Creme eggs," I told the two. "I'll even go vegetarian for a month of Sundays."

The two men stared at each other.

"My God, she's serious," Frankie said.

Townsend nodded.

I pulled them out of the church and to Townsend's candy-apple Chevy crew cab and I jumped behind the wheel.

"No way," Townsend said, shoving me to the middle. "Nobody drives Big Red but me."

"Big Red? You named your truck?" I asked, as Frankie climbed in the passenger side. "I can't wait till this gets out. Your macho image might take a beatin'," I said.

Townsend looked at me and grinned. "I doubt that. Lots of things come mighty big in Iowa, and we're not too bashful to brag," he said.

I blushed. "You do know the quickest route, right?"

Townsend gave me a "get real" look, started the truck and pulled away from the church.

"Okay, so now that you've dragged us out of the wedding rehearsal and we're all gonna miss a free meal at Calhoun's, please tell us who is responsible for the Carson College capers and why you think that person is the culprit," Frankie said.

I filled them in. When I was done, neither fellow seemed overly impressed.

"That's it?" Townsend said. "That's all you have?"

"That plus a cowgirl's sense of when she's been sold a hayrack full of baled weeds and water grass rather than pure alfalfa," I told the two skeptics. "And I've been around enough manure to know it when I smells it," I added. "So put the pedal to the metal and get Big Red moving. Don't worry about a speeding ticket. Remember, I have contacts in law enforcement."

"How could I forget?" Townsend said. But, much to my delight, he stepped on it.

We were nearing Des Moines when I suggested Frankie call Dixie to let her know what was going on and see if she could meet up with us. That way we could cover more of the sprawling campus. I handed him Townsend's phone.

"That's funny. She doesn't answer," Frankie said. "I'll try her house. Maybe she's home. . . . She's not there?" I heard him ask a moment later. "And her car's not in the garage? Okay, yeah. Thanks, Luther. Yeah. I'll let you know. She's not home," Frankie said, clearly concerned. "So why doesn't she answer her cell phone?"

"Maybe she's out of the car getting gas, or she had the munchies and is in line with a bag of Doritos and a bottle of Coke," I told him, thinking that combo would really hit the spot right now.

"I guess that's possible," Frankie said. "I'll keep trying." He did. With no success.

We pulled onto Carson Drive and into the campus.

"So, what's the plan?" Townsend asked.

"Let's check out the morgue," I said.

Townsend turned to look at me. "You really know how to set the mood, Calamity," he said.

"Wait! Stop!" Frankie slammed a hand on the dashboard. "There's Dixie's car!"

I followed his pointing finger. "Are you sure?" I asked, spotting the car pulled off to the side of the road.

"Of course I'm sure!"

Townsend pulled up to the car and hit it with a spotlight, and I gave him a surprised look.

"Deer hunting," he informed me. "And the occasional moose, of course."

Boys and their toys.

Frankie opened the truck door and hurried up to the vehicle. I followed close behind.

"It's Dixie's car, all right," he said. "This is really strange. Her purse is in here. Along with my cell phone. I don't like this, Tressa. I don't like this at all."

"Maybe she broke down," I suggested. I grabbed the phone. "Let's see who she called and who called her. Maybe that will help us locate her." I began to punch buttons.

"Here. Give me that," Frankie said, grabbing the phone out of my hand. "Her last call was to you."

"What?"

"Have you checked your voice mail messages?"

I grabbed my phone and turned it on. The low battery light was still blinking. I'd forgotten to charge it. I checked my voice mail and, sure enough, there was a new message. It was from Dixie.

"Is this the Tressa Jayne Turner that works for the *Gazette*? The one that kills harmless old ladies with her scary driving? If it is, tell Frankie that my study group has been canceled and I'm going to head home. Have him call me."

"So, what do we do now?" Townsend joined us. "Campus Security is on the way."

"We can't just stand here," Frankie said. "Tonight, murder is on the menu. We need to do something!"

"You two, start at the morgue," I suggested. "Between Townsend's purty face and his official badge, he should be able to get you in there so you can check it out."

Townsend put a hand on my shoulder. "What about you?"

"I'll be fine. I'll lock myself in Dixie's car and wait here for Campus Security. Go on. Go!"

"Call if you need anything," Townsend said. I nodded.

"Roger that, Mr. Ranger, sir," I said, with a goofy salute.

He shook his head, started toward his truck, stopped, then came back and gave me a hard, quick kiss.

"For luck," he said.

I held on to the car to keep from falling over. The man could kiss.

I jumped in Dixie's car, locked all the doors, and waited for the good guys to show up, listening to my phone beep its low battery warning. My stomach growled, and I remembered Dixie holding out on me with the M&M's. I turned on the dash light to see if she had anything stashed away in her car to eat.

I checked the various cubbies in the front seat and all I came up with was those Listerine dissolving strips that are enough to gag a maggot off a gut wagon. One of my uncle Frank's many memorable sayings. I missed them. I missed him.

I'd searched for a moment longer when I picked up a sheet of paper that had fallen to the floor off the front seat. It was one of the flyers the drama department had stuck on the windshields of cars to promote the Saturday night performance of *Arsenic and Old Lace*. I skimmed through it. Then read it a second time.

You've heard of Oprah's lightbulb moments, right? Well, this moment of illumination had all the magnitude of the combined wattage of the lights at Wrigley Field at a night game.

"That's it!" I yelled, and punched Townsend's number, getting that infuriating *no signal* indicator. I searched for the car key and then remembered Frankie had taken Dixie's purse and, along with it, her keys. I sighed. Of our intrepid trio of crime-stoppers, I had to be the closest. I unlocked the car door and climbed out. I started running in the direction of Halliburton Auditorium—so-named for some alumni who had gone on to a measure of fame in the motion picture industry. I tried Townsend's number again. He picked up.

"Townsend, I know where they are!" I said, between sucking in breaths and trying to keep the crotch of my panty hose from sliding down to my knees.

"Tressa?"

"Yes, it's me! I know where they are!"

"You're breaking up! Say again."

"Halliburton Auditorium!" I yelled just as my cell phone died. "Hurry!"

I ran down the darkened streets, not amused to find it was beginning to sleet, freezing rain starting to pelt me. No one was about. I figured they must've listened to the weather guy and had prior knowledge of the ice storm and decided to stay home and off the roads. Good call.

I slipped and slid down the blacktopped streets, one hand on my panty hose and the other carrying my useless phone. The sleet stung as it pinged my cheeks but I kept on running. I saw the auditorium up ahead. It was dark. I ran to the front door and tried it. It was locked. I hoofed it to a side door. Locked, too. I pounded on it and was ready to see if I could throw my cell phone through the window when the door opened and a tiny lady with gray hair and a black overcoat came out.

"Didn't you hear?" she said. "Rehearsal's been canceled due to the weather."

I nodded. "Yes, I know. But you see, I think there may be a would-be murderer lurking in the theater here, and they may or may not have kidnapped a woman and may or may not be about to kill that individual, so I really need to get into this building now," I told her. "You understand. Right?" She stared at me as I squeezed by her in the doorway.

"I'm going to contact security," she said, slipping out the door and into the drizzle.

"Good idea," I said.

I let the door click behind me—in case the post-secondary perp was listening for the last person to leave—then opened it quietly and wedged my useless cell phone in the opening at the bottom so Townsend and Frankie could get in.

I wiped a hand over my wet face and moved quickly down the hallway. I'd only been in the auditorium one time, and that was when I was dating a guy who was starring in the college production of *Grease*. No, he didn't play Danny. Nope. Not Kenickie, either. He was Putzie. 'Nough said.

I thought about how creepy the place looked at night. How it smelled like mothballs. How, if I was right, I was about to match wits with a diabolically clever mind.

And where, within these walls, a murderer might be planning the grand finale.

All I had to do was rewrite the script.

Piece of cake for a smarmy, drive-by media type, right?

And for this cub reporter? One hell of a pop quiz . . . and failure was so not an option.

CHAPTER 20

I tiptoed about fifteen steps down the dark hallway, the sound of ice pellets hitting the roof and windows like the scratches of tons of tiny rodent toenails. I tried several doors, most of which were locked, until I came to one that wasn't. I took a deep breath—well, as deep a breath as you can take when your respiration is constricted by terror and panty hose that could double as a torture device—and ever so quietly opened the door. I was thankful it didn't squeak or creak to announce my presence.

I moved about, the room illuminated only by a lamp from a sewing machine at a table near its center. I looked hurriedly around, deciding I must be in the drama department's costume room. Rack after rack of clothing hung separated by period: Medieval on one rack, poodle skirts and pink jackets on another. Furry animal costumes were on yet another. Hot pants and bell bottoms on still another. Even the American West was represented, and, of course, it was to this rack I gravitated.

I spotted a hot-pink Stetson with an impressive cream and tan feather, and almost stuck it on my head until I realized I'd stick out in the dark like Big Burl's blinking burlesque beacon. Nah, that wouldn't work. I needed something somber, darker, scarier. Something that might give me an edge. Something a bit over the top that might buy me some precious seconds to get the jump on the villain.

I went to the rack that held the grisly costumes. You know. Monsters. Ghouls. Ghosts. I found one that looked like that freaky ghost of Christmases Yet to Be, with the hood that conceals a faceless horror. Now, this, this might just work. I grabbed the hood and began to pull it on my head, thankful I'd given up the attempt to corral my wayward locks and instead fashioned them into a long thick braid. The braid required minimal effort to cram into the hood. Once I managed to get it on, I hurried over to a mirror and almost squealed when I saw how totally terrifying I looked.

I pulled on the long black cloak that went with it, but it was way too long. If I had to run for my life—or Dixie's—I didn't want to trip over the hem. I looked around frantically, knowing I was wasting precious time. Time that Dixie—or some other poor victim— might not have. And then I spotted it. It was a black leather zippered number that looked like something Catwoman might wear. All black leather and sexy. In this I'd be virtually invisible.

I yanked off my dress, flipped my boots off, and stepped into it, sucking in my gut as I moved the zipper carefully up over sensitive areas and tender flesh— a dress rehearsal for tomorrow when I had to squeeze into my bridesmaid gown. As I eased the zipper up, I recalled Gram's waxing comment.

I finally got the zipper secured and let my breath back out. Ah, good, no stitching popped. I stuck my feet into my boots and hurried to find a weapon—or at the very least, a fake one. I found an ample supply of these in the props section, including several revolvers that looked very real and very dangerous.

My hand shook as I picked one up. My eyes strayed to several very mean-looking weapons: knives, swords, and claymores, one of those seriously deranged balls on a chain with those sharp spikes sticking out all over it, plus other devices of death. I figured a ghostly apparition in black leather would go for a more unconventional weapon than a gun and selected a really wicked-looking knife.

As I passed by a prop table, I noticed a timer sitting on it—one of those my middle school teacher used to time how many words a minute we read. (Kari calls the timed readings "dibbles," which always makes me giggle for some reason.) A surprise diversion might come in handy. I set the timer for five minutes, thinking that was all the time Dixie could spare if push came to shove.

This was it. Showtime. A star is born!

I exited the wardrobe room as quietly as one can when encased in five feet of body-hugging leather and, swift and silent as a feline, made my way toward the theater itself. I entered the auditorium from a side door, losing myself among the rows of padded seats and inky shadows.

Crouching in the dark, I waited for a creak, a whisper, even a groan, so I would know my theory was correct. I was beginning to think I'd been totally wrong when I heard the fall of a footstep from the stage. I watched as a solitary light came on. From where I was concealed, I could see that the stage had been turned into the home of the homicidal sisters, Martha and Abby Brewster, complete with the infamous window seat.

I looked on as a figure took center stage. Dressed in a circa-1940s housedress, apron, and white wig complete with a little ol' lady librarian bun, the threatening thespian looked like a close relation of Norman Bates's mother.

The dimly lit stage did not initially reveal the second character, but that was promptly cleared up when Abby/Martha walked over to the window seat and threw it open.

"Forgive the tight squeeze, but your discomfort will be over very soon," the Brewster bee-yatch said, and I added an additional nasty adjective or two in my head.

I hated when I was right. Bad things happened when I was right.

I picked up the sounds of a struggle from the window seat and saw someone manage to sit up and flail about. If Abby/Martha was disturbing, this sight was enough to give you nightmares. It was Dixie. And she was trussed up with so much gray duct tape strung around her that she looked like a beat-up aluminum can. But so not recyclable.

Faint moans and humming noises reached my ears as the pop can tried to communicate with the psycho who wanted to crush her.

"I know. I know. I'm sorry it had to end this way, too," Abigail-Martha said. "But beggars can't be choosers. I really never meant for you to be the final victim, Dixie, but sometimes actors have to improvise.

And the beauty of these crimes is the sheer randomness of them all. I didn't care who the victim du jour was. All that was necessary was a connection to the class. So that gave me a lot of flexibility. Until your little blond reporter friend began to sniff around for a story and, as luck would have it, found one. But, sadly, she didn't fit the victimology, so I couldn't use her. A disappointment, but one must stick to the script, you know."

More protests from Dixie that basically amounted to grunts and groans, and despite her obvious efforts to the contrary, made me feel time was running out.

"I always admired the sisters Brewster," her demented captor went on. "Once they were found out, there was no hand-wringing, no remorse, no apologies. No atonement. I like that in-your-face, just-deal-with-it honesty. Murder was simply what they did when they weren't pouring tea and entertaining visitors. It was who they were. Quite refreshing really. And so it goes with my little play. I call it 'Criminal Acts.' Catchy, huh?"

A pause as the "actor" stared out over the auditorium. "This will become one of those classic whodunits. Years from now people will still be speculating over who the Carson Campus criminal was. Just think, Dixie. On the anniversary of your death for years to come, this case will be resurrected and revisited, looked at and mulled over, reconsidered and reinvestigated. You'll be famous! A celebrity! Posthumously, of course. Still, your memory will live on. That's a positive, isn't it? And I'll sit back and know that I fooled them all. I pulled off the perfect murder. And why, you ask?" The creepy character walked over to Dixie. "You *are* wondering why, aren't you, Dixie? Why all this attention to detail? Why all the meticulous planning and carefully choreographed interactions? The elaborately executed escalation? Well, I suppose I owe you that much. And it's not as if you're going to tell anyone, are you, Dixie? Do you want to know why, Dixie?" Another pause. "Because I can, that's why. Because I can and I want to prove I can." A long sigh followed and I caught the glint of a blade. "And now we find ourselves at the final act."

This was my cue. Dixie's time had run out.

I'm not what most people would call resourceful in a clutch situation. I am, however, creative and impulsive in an over-the-top sort of way. And since we were in a theatrical setting, I decided that my best opportunity to steal the show must, by necessity, include something with a hint of the dramatic. Something larger than life, yet in keeping with the esteemed reputation of the stage, of course.

I crawled toward the area where the light controls were located. I figured my best shot was to either scare the old lady bloomers off Miss Brewster, blind her . . . or both. I managed to reach the control panel and when I took a look at all the knobs and switches, I knew if my cat costume hadn't been quite so tight, I'd be dealing with some serious stomach noises that would probably out me to the enemy. As it was, I simply bit my lip, prayed for supernatural assistance, and hit the first switch my shaking fingers came to. It was a solitary spotlight and it shone directly in the center of the stage where, for most of the monologue, the "star" had stood.

"Who is it? Who's there?" I heard.

I spotted a microphone sticking up out of the console. I searched my brain for something really scary to say, something that would creep out even a psychopathic sociopathic narcissist with dreams of the stage. Something that would make the Carson College criminal think twice about screwing with my final grade.

I took a deep breath and grabbed the mike. "I'm coming for you, Barbara."

The darkened theater grew hushed and eerily silent. I felt like I was in a low-rent mish-mash of *The Phantom of the Opera* and *Shawn of the Dead*.

"Who's there!" came again from stage level.

"Why, Barbara? Why?" I whispered into the microphone, not quite sure where I was headed with this dialogue but feeling the definite magic and lure of the stage.

"Grandmother?"

Grandmother? I blinked, puzzled, but like any good actor went with the moment.

"Yes, Barbara. It's Grandmother," I said with a soothing tone to my voice—in other words, the opposite of my own dear ol' granny. "Grandmother Grace," I added, recalling she'd told me Grandma Grace raised her.

"Why have you come here? Why have you come back?" Barbara Billings asked.

What was I? Psychic Sylvia?

"You know, Barbara," I said into the microphone. "To keep you from doing something you will come to regret."

"But you're dead," Barbara said. "I killed you."

Uh, say what?

Okay, I'll admit there are times I get a wee bit frustrated with Hellion Hannah, but had I ever thought of harming a blue-gray hair on her head? (You can't count the time I accidentally on purpose knocked the winkie off one of her more energetically endowed fertility God statues. That wasn't her. But tell me. How would you like a collection of excited erections decorating your living room?)

Professor Billings's psychopathology read like an M. Night Shyamalan screenplay. No buttered popcorn or Sour Patch Kids during this one, boys and girls.

"Grandmother Grace? Grandmother?"

"I'm here, child. And I've come for you." I was getting close to using up my meager store of dead old lady dialogue. And when you think about me not being able to come up with something to say, well, it's actually quite remarkable.

"Where are we going?" Professor Billings asked.

"To a place where there's no more trouble," I said, borrowing this notable quote from Dorothy Gale. Tell me you could do better.

I decided it was time to make my movie—uh, my move. I started to flip console switches. The entire theater was suddenly filled with tons of dancing lights, as if a gazillion Tinker Bells were frolicking about the room in search of Peter Pan.

"I'm coming for you, Barbara," I said again, and hit the button to start the timer. I crept out from behind the console and slipped across the theater on my hands and knees, shielded by a row of theater seats. I made it to the far aisle and stopped to catch my breath—my tight leather garment constricting lung function—and continued my progress to the front of the auditorium. I crawled across the floor near the front of the stage, no real idea how I planned to disarm the knife-wielding criminal mastermind.

"Grandmother?"

From her voice, I could tell Barbara had moved closer to the edge of the stage. I suddenly recalled an incident from my calamitous childhood that involved Rick Townsend. And no, my story has nothing whatsoever to do with a game of Choo-choo Train or Let's Play Doctor, so get that thought right outta your head, hear?

Rick Townsend was a frequent overnight guest at our house. One particular Friday night, somewhere around Halloween when my parents happened to be working late in the barn and Taylor was at a friend's house for a sleepover (little Miss Popular), I'd decided to watch a monster movie marathon before I went to bed. I was like five at the time. Okay, so I was really seven, but that's not pivotal to the story. Bottom line, folks? Bad idea. Especially with two moronic meatheads in the house. I'd awoken to sounds coming from downstairs.

Picture cute, blond, adorable little Tressa in her Black Stallion pajamas padding down the hall and out of her room to the door at the top of the stairs. Picture precocious little Tressa calling out for big brother Craig but getting no answer. Picture nervous little Tressa reaching out to open the basement door and switching on the light, but it doesn't come on. Picture plucky little Tressa taking a shaky step down the first step and down the second, and on the third step a hand reaches out and grabs Tressa's ankle. Picture poor little Tressa screaming bloody murder and bouncing down the stairs on her butt, squirting pee as she hits each step.

As plans went, it wasn't much, but it did have a track record of limited success—and it was all I had in my bag of tricks.

"Who's out there?" Barbara stepped closer to the edge.

Just a little closer, Professor. Just one more step. I

just prayed Dixie kept still and didn't draw Billings away from the precipice before I had time to spring my trap. Such as it was.

I looked around to see what I could use to lure her closer to the edge, thinking it shouldn't be all that difficult. The loony ex–law enforcer was already way over the edge. And then some.

"Barbara," I whispered. "Barbara." I then followed the whispered entreaty with a soft whimper, hoping I sounded a little like a grieving granny. The stage creaked over my head.

"Where are you?" I heard directly above me.

"Here!" I yelled. "Aaaauuugghhhh!" I surged to my feet and reached out and grabbed Abby/Martha around her skirted legs and yanked as hard as I could in my direction. However, I had underestimated the amount of force required to propel this Punky Brewster over the edge. Rather than tumble off the stage, Barbara buckled at the knees and she went down butt first, hitting the stage hard, her knife flying from her hand and skittering across the ground.

It took a second for me to react. I threw my fake knife on the stage and pulled my torso up and over the edge. I struggled to get my legs to follow, but couldn't bend them due to the tight leather skin I wore. I figured I probably resembled one of Townsend's pet serpents as I slithered my way up. By the time I got to my feet, Professor Billings was sitting there looking at me.

"You're not Grandmother Grace," she said.

"Give the teacher a shiny red apple," I said.

"Who are you?" she asked.

"Why, the Masked Avenger, of course," I said.

"You're Diana Rigg?"

"Huh?" I blinked. Who the heck was Diana Rigg?

Billings spotted my prop knife at her feet and made a grab for it. She struggled to her feet and brandished the knife at me.

We both heard a noise behind us, and a quickly unraveling Dixie had taken the stage. She'd somehow managed to get out of the window seat—I suspect she used the tip me over, pour me out method—and had retrieved her captor's knife and cut the bindings from her hands and feet. She removed the tape from her mouth. I backed toward her, noting the professor's knife in her hand.

"Wrong knife, teach," I said, and Billings looked at the plastic in her hand. She threw it at us. And pulled a gun out of her apron pocket.

"But right gun," Billings said. "Drop the knife, Dixie," she ordered.

"You didn't tell me she had a gun," I said to Dixie.

"Uh, my mouth was taped shut. How could I tell you? Besides, I didn't know," Dixie responded to the criticism.

"Good points," I said. "So, what do you do now, Professor? Your final act has just been rewritten. Your perfect plot now has two very big gaping holes."

Dixie poked me. "Considering she's got a gun pointed at us, I'd stay away from the topic of big, gaping holes," she remarked. I winced.

"Another good point," I said.

"I could shoot one of you and make the other death look like suicide, and that would be the end of it," she said.

My luck to have a psychopathic professor who was a seat of the pants plotter.

"Your suicide scenario has some fatal flaws," I told Professor Billings. "We all three know that no way are we going to go gently into that good night."

"That's right," Dixie added. "And it would be a little difficult explaining why a suicide victim has defensive wounds."

"I'm impressed, Dixie. You *were* paying attention in class," the professor said. "Good for you. But, thanks to your little friend's romantic tragedy the other night, I've been handed a perfect motive for murder/suicide."

"Was my performance that good?" I said. "Sweet."

Dixie gave me a cold look.

"My entire class knows of your volatile relationship," Billings went on. "What did you say again, Dixie? Oh yes: The only thing she could get on an intelligence test was drool. That when she went to apply for a job she had to sing happy birthday to figure out how old she was. That the difference between a smart blonde and Bigfoot is that Bigfoot has been spotted."

I looked at Dixie. "You said those things?"

She shrugged. "Like you haven't said worse."

"Yes, but I say them to your face," I said. "Or what purports to be your face. See? Like that. There's a difference."

"I'll keep that in mind for future reference," she responded.

Billings turned her attention to me. "Tressa Jayne Turner, I presume," she said. "I underestimated you."

"Folks have a tendency to do that," I acknowledged, pulling off my spooky Christmas Future hood now that my cover was blown. Besides, it was hotter than Hades.

"You had me going there," Professor Billings said. "All that 'I'm coming for you, Barbara' bullshit. I wasn't expecting that."

"Gee, I couldn't tell," I said.

"Sarcasm even to the end. I like that."

"And that wasn't bullshit, Barbara," I said. "They are coming for you. The cops. Frankie. The DNR."

"Don't you mean the DCI?" she asked, and I shook my head.

"Department of Natural Resources. They investigate manure spills—among other things."

"Ah, more sarcasm," she said. "I believe I already asked you once to drop the knife, Dixie."

"I think not," Dixie replied.

"I assure you, I can drop the two of you in a heartbeat if you rush me," Billings said. "I used to nail all my firearm qualifications."

"But your nice, pat murder-suicide angle would also be shot to hell," I pointed out. "Not that anyone would buy that lame horse anyway."

It was your basic Mexican standoff—without the Mexicans. The seconds ticked away.

I put a hand out to Abby/Martha's dining room table, and my fingers closed around the sister's delicate teapot. Hardly a weapon of mass destruction. But it was all I had at my fingertips.

"I said drop the knife," Professor Billings said.

"I heard you the first time," Dixie spat, and I thought, under the circumstances, she probably might have chosen a kinder, gentler tone.

"Very bold. Very daring," I said instead.

"Now!" Billings demanded, advancing on us. I sensed she was also past the point of no return.

My fingers tightened on the teapot.

From the back of the university auditorium the timer I'd set began to beep. Billings pivoted in that direction and the gun moved with her. I took advantage of the lapse to smash the teapot down on her hand. The gun went off, the bullet whizzing across the shimmering, disco-dancing Tinker Bell interior of the theater. I grabbed Billing's gun with my left hand and smacked her upside the head with the shiny silver teapot. *Clang.* Dixie, meanwhile, had taken the opportunity to jump on her professor's back and was attempting to get her arm around the woman's neck to choke her.

Boom! I whacked the professor one more time right in the nose and heard a loud crack. She dropped her gun and cradled her cartilage. I kicked her in the knee with my pointed-toe boot and down she went, Dixie straddling her. I plopped my hindquarters on the professor's still flailing legs. The professor wasn't going anywhere.

All of a sudden the twinkling lights shut off and the houselights came up.

"What the hell is going on here?" The tiny lady I'd spoken with earlier now stood at the back of the auditorium; she had returned. Dixie repositioned herself to sit on Professor Billings's squirming shoulders. Billings definitely wasn't going anywhere.

"What are you doing up there?" the woman yelled. I looked at Dixie. She looked at me.

"Would you believe 'all the world's a stage and we're merely players'?" I quoted.

Dixie grunted. "Overactor," she complained.

CHAPTER 21

By the time Campus Security arrived to take charge, Townsend and Frankie had stormed the auditorium and taken charge of our prisoner. Once the authorities took custody of the dazed professor, we sat in front row seats waiting for the police to wrap things up at the scene.

"What took you so long?" I asked.

"We couldn't make out what you were saying when you called," Frankie said.

"So, how did you know to come here?" I asked the slightly tardy duo.

"We stopped by Dixie's car and Townsend saw the play flyer on the front seat. We figured it was a place to start," Frankie said. "I still can't believe it was Professor Billings all the time." He shook his head. "She sure had me fooled," he added, and I felt the old Frankfurter self-doubt creep into his voice.

"She had everyone fooled," I told him. "She acted her part to perfection."

"She didn't fool you," Frankie pointed out. "You figured it out."

"How did you come to suspect the professor anyway?" Dixie asked, sitting next to Frankie as he rubbed her sore wrists with his thumb. How precious.

"It's not something you probably would have noticed, Dixie," I said, letting just a hint of conceit into my voice.

"What does that mean?" she asked.

"Just that you're not the fashion maven I am," I told her. "So this little detail would probably have escaped you. It's nothing to hang your head over."

"What detail?" Dixie demanded.

"Her Manolo Blahniks," I said.

"Her what?"

"I rest my case."

"Oh, for heaven's sake—"

"The shoes!" I exclaimed. "It's always about the shoes!"

Dixie folded her arms across her chest and tapped her foot, apparently still not getting it. And people thought they had to draw pictures for *me*.

"I always notice what people have on their feet," I said. "Always. Especially when someone is wearing a seven-hundred-dollar pair of Manolo Blahniks that I would only be able to afford if I won the Power Ball Lottery or robbed a bank. Billings had them on the night she was attacked. Well, supposedly attacked. I remembered seeing them on her feet at Big Burl's— okay, and drooling over them in a two-size-smaller kind of way—and then at the security office after her attack, I looked at them again. And they looked just the same. No scuffs. No dirt. Nothing. They were pristine. It didn't register then, but when I looked down at my feet at the rehearsal and saw the scuffed toe of my new boot and remembered how my brand-new pair of New Balance sneakers got the toes all scratched up and dirty when I hit the ditch face first, it suddenly occurred to me: If Professor Billings had been facedown on the parking lot or grass like she said she was, the toes of her boots would reflect that. But they were clean as a whistle. It started to make a weird kind of sense. And, of course, once I made the connection to the shoes, there was the silver belt buckle and laptop to consider."

"Belt buckle?" Townsend looked at me. "Laptop? What are you talking about?"

"If Billings fell forward, her turquoise belt buckle would have been dirty or scratched up, too, but it wasn't. And she claimed she'd dropped her laptop when she was attacked from behind, but the case didn't have a scratch on it either. I've seen Frankie's, and as good as he takes care of it, it still has some scratches. If that had been dropped on the cement, it should have shown some signs of outward damage."

Townsend raised an eyebrow. "That's good," he said.

"And then there was the fact that the only crime that wasn't successfully committed was the sexual assault attempt on Billings. At the time of the incident I thought that was due to the fact that she was a former cop and knew how to defend herself, so it didn't raise any flags. But now I know it's because no matter how good an actor you are, it's a bit of a challenge to abuse yourself sexually when there are tests that can be run to verify whether you were sexually assaulted. Billings knew about the tests. That's why she had to report it as an attempt only."

"So, what about the hit-and-run?" Dixie said. "We know it was Keith Gardner driving because we followed him from the campus."

"Yes, but we didn't see who was behind the wheel of the pickup, did we?" I pointed out. "And remember, there was a lapse of ten minutes or so before the pickup came back. Billings was probably sitting on Gardner's place, having decided to use his truck for the hit-and-run. All she had to do was park her car somewhere nearby, watch for Gardner to return home, jump in, and drive away. She almost mows us down, leaves the truck in a ditch, and retrieves her car and drives to the campus. And remember, Billings said she received a phone call from Campus Security? I think her phone ringing in the pickup was that flash of light I saw as the vehicle bore down on us."

"But why pin it on Keith? I thought she was mentoring him," Dixie said.

"What better patsy than a registered sex offender?" I turned to see Patrick Dawkins had joined us. "He was a perfect fall guy if things went south for Billings," Patrick added, removing his trooper hat and leaning back against it. "Is everyone all right?"

Dixie and I nodded.

"So, where does Professor Danbury come in?" Frankie asked. "Was he just another red herring?"

Patrick nodded. "That's right, Frankie. You see, Barbara Billings was smart enough to know that eventually someone would connect the dots and figure out the link to her lectures. As a matter of fact, she counted on it. Therefore, she needed several viable

suspects in addition to the run-of-the-mill kook theory
for authorities to consider, so she served up Gardner
and Danbury. Although I did make that initial com-
plaint against Danbury for drinking, according to Danbury he had joined a twelve-step program and come to
terms with his sexual identity, and he hasn't had a
drink since he was put on notice."

"So, Billings phonied up the tenure paperwork?" I
asked.

Patrick nodded. "And she set the fire outside her
own office to make us think she was a target. And it
worked."

"It's hard to believe someone could be so devious as
to orchestrate this entire production," Frankie said.
"Even down to assaulting herself. My God, she had one
mean goose egg on her forehead. That had to hurt."

"To keep her story as close to the truth as she could,
she probably did get it by hitting her head on the car,"
Patrick guessed. "She just happened to do it to herself.
To corroborate her victim role."

What continued to creep me out was how thoroughly she'd pulled the wool over our collective eyes,
how she'd anticipated each scene so accurately and
prepared for each eventuality so carefully, each part so
well rehearsed as if she'd known what was to come
and had prepared for it. It was utterly chilling.

"One thing is certain," I said, "she'd have made a
heck of an actor. Do you suppose she really killed her
grandmother?" I asked.

Frankie looked at Patrick, who waited for Frankie to
answer.

"You're more of an expert on this stuff than I am,"
Patrick told Frankie.

"Sometimes individuals with psychopathic personality syndrome can start acting out in violent and unsettling ways very early, and their descent into this pattern of behavior may be triggered by a traumatic event in their childhood," my cousin said.

"Like a parent abandoning them?" I suggested, and Frankie nodded.

"As a child she may have felt powerless to control things going on in her life and saw it continuing on forever if things remained status quo," Frankie said.

"So she offed her granny?" I asked.

"Don't get any ideas, Calamity," Townsend remarked, and I gave him a look.

"Maybe she saw that desperate act as gaining back control over her life," Frankie said.

"Or maybe she was just a screwed-up, homicidal adolescent who got tired of Grandma Grace getting drunk as a skunk all the time and decided to do away with her," I proposed.

"I'm confused," Dixie said.

"No shame in that, Dixie," I remarked. "It happens to the best of us at times."

She frowned at me. "Why would she go into law enforcement if she had really done this horrible thing as a child? Isn't that a glaring contradiction?"

Patrick shrugged. "Maybe in some way she wanted to pay for the sins of her past by turning her life into one of service to others. By all accounts, she was basically a good cop."

"Except for that part about taking orders," I added.

Patrick smiled. "Yeah, except for that. I think there was also an element of her wanting to show the 'good ol' boys' that she could do the job just as well as they could. You have to remember, when she joined the department, she took a lot of heat from the boys' club. I think for her it may have been a lifelong battle of good versus evil. Unfortunately, evil eventually won out," he said. "It's a damned shame."

"What do you think will happen to her?" I asked.

Patrick shook his head. "She'll probably be evaluated by some heavy-duty shrinks and they'll decide if she's competent to stand trial," the Super Trooper told us. "Frankly, from what I've heard, my bet is she'll be spending time in a rubber room for the near future. As I said, it's a damned shame. She was brilliant. Apparently psychopathic as well."

"Ah, but brilliantly so," I agreed. "And with a normal healthy woman's appreciation for a to-die-for pair of shoes—which, fortunately for us, proved to be her downfall." I frowned. "Will they let her wear chocolate leather boots in a rubber room?" I asked.

Patrick grinned. "I suspect not."

We ended up being transported to the security office, and gave our statements to DCI agents in separate interviews. I spent my downtime working on my article—for class and publication. I was so gonna get an A+ on this puppy!

By the time we were permitted to leave, it was the morning of Kari's wedding day.

"I'm gonna look like something Gram's cat drug in," I complained once we'd bid good night to Dixie and Patrick. Patrick, I noted, gave me a pat on the shoulder instead of a hug—or anything more—under the watchful eye of Ranger Rick Townsend. I felt like I had an old maid aunt chaperone. "With these black circles under my eyes, I'll probably hiss and shriek at the sight of a cross," I said. "Not a good thing in a church."

"Who's to see?" Frankie remarked. "You'll have

your butt facing most of the people most of the time," he pointed out.

I winced. "That so does not make me feel better," I said. "Have I mentioned I hate weddings?"

"Only ad nauseam," Frankie replied.

"Can you blame me? My track record with things matrimonial aren't good. At Craig's wedding I caught my sleeve on fire at the refreshment table and stunk the place up and dropped barbecue sauce down my front. And this time I've already almost caused the happy couple to break up, delivered a dead wedding guest to Kari's door, run out of her rehearsal night to play pin the tail on the psycho, and now when I show up for her wedding—if I show up—I'll look like I should be laid out beside poor dear feisty old Great-aunt Trudy. I *did* mention that I hate weddings, didn't I?" I said.

"I think I've heard that somewhere before," Townsend said.

I looked at him. "You are going to be on your best behavior this time, aren't you? No idiotic jokes or pranks, right?"

Townsend's eyes grew big. "Who? Me? I'll be a regular Boy Scout," he said.

I scowled at him. "Just make sure you don't work on earning your 'obnoxious jerk' badge, okay?"

Townsend chuckled. "Cheer up, Calamity. You might even enjoy yourself," he said.

I snorted. "I doubt that."

"You never know. You might even end up catching the bridal bouquet, and you know what they say about that. The girl who catches the bridal bouquet becomes the next bride."

I winced, remembering I was kind of already engaged and wanting no part of a bridal bouquet—or anything that went with it. Well, other than terrific wedding night sex maybe.

"When Kari gets ready to toss that puppy, I'm, like, gone," I said.

Townsend gave me a crooked grin. "Guess that leaves the field open to your grandmother," he said.

I shuddered.

I supposed tripping a seventy-year-old woman with osteoporosis was out. Hmmm. Maybe I'd oil my softball glove up and take it along.

"You'll have to shuck the brassiere," Gram said, and I looked at her.

"What?"

"Your bra. You'll have to lose it. This here dress has your basic gauzy yoke. You can't have bra straps showing. You'll look like a joke. People will gawk and stare at you. And more importantly, they won't gawk and stare at the bride, which is who they're supposed to gawk and stare at."

"I can't go without a bra," I insisted. "What if they've got the air conditioner cranked up in the church? I'll get more than gawking and staring if that happens," I advised her.

She considered this. "You're right. Nipples at attention in the sanctuary would make for two definite distractions. And there's the reverend to think of. And there will be children present," she added. "Course, with Joe's grandson being the best man, I'm thinking a couple of twin peaks might just be the ice breaker you two need to heat things up a bit."

My brain froze at all the mixed metaphors. Or is that similes? Oh, who cares?

"I have just the thing!" Gram said, trying unsuccessfully to snap her arthritic fingers. "I saw this on clearance at the mall one day. I just knew someday it would come in handy. You stay there and I'll be right back."

I watched her retreating back with only slightly less anxiety than I reserved for stepping on the scale. Or opening my bank statement.

I shrugged and padded to my chest of drawers and scrounged around for a new pair of flesh-colored, control-top panty hose with built-in tummy flattener, wishing now I hadn't vetoed Gram's body slimmer out of hand. I grabbed a pair and started to pull them on, hopping up and down and attempting to raise the level of the hosiery crotch from just above my knees to something more natural—and comfortable—when Gram returned.

"What," I said, pointing to what appeared to be a boob in each hand, "are those?"

"It's called the Au Naturelle bra," she said. Why wasn't I surprised she owned one?

"They look like nursing pads," I said.

"It's a strapless bra. It's made of the same thing them boob implants are."

I looked at it. "Silicone?" I said. "Where's the rest of it?"

"What do you mean? This is all there is," she said.

I looked at her. "That's it? How does it stay on? Superglue? Velcro? Thumbtacks?"

Gram shook her head. "It's got this here adhesive backing. Gives you lift. And the silicone adds on a full cup-size!"

I took another look at the skin-toned circles. "A cup size?" I asked.

She nodded. "And you could use a little help in that area," she added with a look at my chest.

She had a point.

"I'm not sure . . . ," I said. "What if it comes loose and slides down my dress?"

"It's guaranteed to adhere to your skin," she replied, and the thought of something adhering to my breasts and nipples didn't exactly thrill me. Still, my only other strapless bra was black and would show up like white old lady briefs under white polyester slacks.

"I suppose I don't have a choice," I said. And all it had to do was stay in place long enough to get Kari wedded and pictures taken. And this time, I was staying away from the cocktail weenies.

At least until after the wedding photos were taken.

With Gram's help, we fastened the Au Naturelle contraption to my boobs.

"I'm not sure about this, Gram," I said, looking down at my brand-new, artificially enhanced, freaky-looking bosom. "Do these appear natural?" I said, frowning at my profile in the full-length mirror behind the door. "I wouldn't want to look top-heavy."

"If you don't want 'em, I'll take 'em," she said, and I cast a look at her bustline that also nearly served as a waistline.

"That's okay, Gram. I'll deal," I said.

Standing at the front of the church sometime later—after dealing with strapless cups that were guaranteed to lift, separate, oh, and stay in place, but were already starting to come loose and beginning to migrate to forbidden and unnatural places—I realized I should've let Gram have the pair with my blessing.

I also found myself wishing the good Reverend Browning would speed up the ceremony. In addition to a brassiere that kept peeling away from my body a section at a time, the friggin' crotch of my panty hose had slid down to midthigh level. I stood next to Kari with a dopey, serene smile pasted on my face and all the while my left boob was migrating toward the center of my chest, rapidly creating a "tri-titty" phenomenon that I didn't think would ever catch on. I bit my lip and tried to think of a way to reach down and pull the malfunctioning C-cup out of my dress front. I looked at the two bouquets I held. Okay, it might work. I slowly transferred the flowers to my left hand and slipped Brian's wedding ring—which as maid of honor I was holding for safekeeping—onto my right index finger.

I took a sidelong look at the happy couple. They were making goo-goo eyes at each other and were oblivious of my distressing condition. I checked out the minister. He had his nose in his prayer book or wedding vow book or whatever they call it. This was my chance. Behind the cover of the floral bouquets I'd shoved a hand down the front of my strapless gown and groped my own boobs for a second (how pathetic is that?) when I felt Brian's wedding ring slide off my finger and down-down-down into my décolletage.

"And now for the exchanging of rings," I heard the minister say. I winced.

I caught Townsend staring at me with a wicked, knowing grin on his handsome face. Kari nudged me.

"The ring," she said, putting out her hand.

I gave her an *I am so sorry for what I'm about to do* look and plunged my hand down the front of my dress and felt around for a second before I started to hop up and down. Kari's eyes grew big and wide. The minister pulled his glasses off and looked at me. I kept hopping. My panty hose slid down farther. One-half of my Au

Naturelle brassiere fluttered to the floor and landed between my feet. Two more hops and my panty hose crotch was around my knees. The sound of metal hitting the floor rang out.

I bent over to pick up the shiny gold band from the floor, a look of success at last on my face. I held the ring out in front of me and caught a strange look on the minister's face. Beside me Kari gasped, Brian gaped, and Townsend cleared his throat. He motioned toward my chest. I looked down. My maid of honor bodice had slipped and two "au naturelle" boobs—one size C and one size B—had popped out of my dress and were hanging over the top of my gown.

Red-hot mortification scalded me from head to toe. I wished I could go throw myself into the baptismal behind the altar.

I looked up and met the minister's eye.

Hand on the Bible, folks, I swear I saw him wink.

"Well, as usual you caused quite a stir, Calamity," Townsend observed as we waited for the traditional tossing of the bridal bouquet. We were at the Silver Stone Cultural Center (yes, we do have culture in the sticks), which rented out its huge hall for wedding receptions. I'd shucked my remaining, dangling C cup and had lifted a blue old lady cardigan from the coatrack and slipped it on.

"I do have a reputation to uphold," I told Townsend, tipping a cold bottle of Bud Light to my lips and taking a long swallow.

"I thought Brian was going to keel over," Townsend said, sipping his own beer. "And Reverend Browning—"

I swallowed. "Yes?"

"Let's just say, most of his weddings from now on will seem pretty tame in comparison."

I smiled and spotted Uncle Frank across the room. He raised his glass of beer in my direction and grinned.

"I see all is forgiven between you and your uncle Frank," Townsend observed.

I nodded. "Carson College agreed to cover the costs of repairs on his Suburban," I told Townsend. "Once they learned about the newspaper article I was writing, that is. Guess they wanted to squeeze at least a little good press out of a totally bad situation. So I'm back in Uncle Frank's good graces and back at the Freeze again. If I want."

"You sound like you're not sure about going back," Townsend said.

I shrugged. "Now that Taylor's there, I'm not really needed." I took another long swig of beer.

"There you are, Tressa!" My gammy rushed up to me and grabbed my hand. "Kari is looking all over for you. She's getting ready to toss the bridal bouquet! All us single ladies have to get ready to catch it. I've already rounded up Taylor."

"You better go," Townsend said. "You don't want to miss that."

"Who says?" I said, but allowed myself to be led away. Gram positioned us in prime spots. We waited for the photos to be shot.

"Aren't you warm in that sweater?" Gram asked.

I shrugged. "I don't want to take any chances."

"Kari will go postal if you're wearing that in her reception pictures," she told me.

She had a point. I slipped it off my shoulders and hung it on the back of a nearby chair.

"See what matrimony can do for you?" Gram nudged me. "Kari looks so happy."

I nodded. "She does," I agreed.

"Of course, it could also be the sex," Gram suggested.

"I suppose that's true, too," I admitted.

"You gettin' any ideas?" Gram asked. " 'Cause if you want me to stand down, I will."

I looked at her. "What are you talking about, Gram?"

"Joe asked me to marry him. And I'm thinkin' that if I was to catch Kari's bridal bouquet, that would be like a sign from God that I'm supposed to say yes."

I stared at her. "Joe Townsend asked you to marry him? When?"

Gram looked at me. "Which time?"

"Oh my," I said. "Does Rick know?"

"I don't think it ever came up in a conversation," Gram admitted.

I was pretty sure she was right. If he'd gotten wind of it, Townsend would be running around with patches of hair missing and tearing at his clothing.

"Let's keep it that way for the time being," I suggested.

The party planner stepped up to the microphone and made the customary jokes associated with the tossing of the bouquet. I felt Gram tense next to me.

"Take it easy, Gram. Remember you have brittle bones. I don't want to see you break a hip," I told her.

"It's every woman for herself," she said.

Not a comforting thought.

Kari moved into position. I noticed she made a great point of observing where I was standing. I waved my hands and shook my head at her, praying she'd get the message and send the bouquet in the opposite direction. Hopefully right at Abigail Winegardner.

Kari made a couple of fake tossing motions and the audience began to count.

"One! Two! Three!"

Kari heaved the bouquet. Yep, and right in this cowgirl's direction. I suddenly thought about having Joe Townsend for a step-grandfather and then realized that would make Rick Townsend my cousin by marriage. A kissin' cousin, at that. I winced. I shook my head. I wasn't emotionally prepared to deal with the complications this little blended family could bring.

Gram's sign-from-God remark drifted through my head. "Forgive me, Father, for what I am about to do," I prayed.

The bouquet arced and began to descend right in front of me. I prepared to mow down anyone in my path to possess the posies. It continued on its path right at me. This was gonna be like taking candy from a baby, I decided. I made a wide grab for the bouquet and suddenly felt my back dress zipper spring open and my chest runneth over. I made a frantic attempt to cover up and my gammy reached over and snatched the prophetic petals right out from in front of me.

I turned to see who the smart-ass zipper fiend was. Joe Townsend stood behind me.

"Talk about your wardrobe failures," he said with an evil grin. "Tough break, girlie." He moved to take the bouquet from my grandma. He sniffed it. "Lucky catch, Hannah," he told her, and gave her big kiss.

"I think I'm gonna be sick," I said, and felt strong arms around me.

"I'll hold your head if you hold mine," Townsend said, pulling me close.

"Sounds fair," I agreed, turning so he could zip me back up. I picked up the sweater to put it back on, and Townsend took it from me.

"Nice sweater," he said. "But I think the old lady you lifted it from wants it back." He dropped it onto the chair and ran his hands down my arms. "Nice arms, too," he said.

"Oh, they're nothing special," I remarked, always uncomfortable when talk turned to parts of my body. "I've had them forever."

Townsend smiled. "Speaking of which, I bet you didn't realize that it is after midnight and, therefore, officially your birthday," he said.

"It is?" I grabbed his wrist and looked at his watch. "It is! I'm a year older!" I paused. "I'm a year older," I repeated, not quite sure how I felt about being twenty-four.

"May this humble carp cop be the first to wish you happy birthday, Tressa?" Rick asked, hauling me close to his chest. I knew my strapless was probably gaping open, but since Townsend had already gotten more than an eyeful during the vows I figured, big deal.

"I suppose no harm can come from a simple birthday kiss," I said. "Plant one on me, Mr. Ranger, sir," I said, my teasing words at odds with the breathless quality of my voice and the sudden *thump, thump, thump*ing of my ticker.

"Well, then pucker up, birthday girl, 'cause here it comes," he said. "Happy birthday, Tressa Jayne Turner." He drew my lips to his to give me a long, wild, hotter-than-twenty-four-candles kiss.

I closed my eyes to receive his gift.

"What the hell is goin' on?"

I opened one eye, but didn't break lip contact. My

open eye came to rest on one very large, very menacing, very pissed-off Aunt Mo.

"Aunt Mo?" I said, ending the birthday kiss.

"Don't you 'Aunt Mo' me!"

"What are you doing here?"

"What? You've never seen *Wedding Crashers*? What the hell you doin' lettin' that handsome man kiss you like that?" Aunt Mo said.

"Is there a problem?" Townsend asked the woman.

"I reckon that's up to my nephew, Manny," she said.

Townsend frowned, and I began to back away.

"What does Manny DeMarco have to do with this?" Rick asked.

"I'm thinkin' my nephew might not be too thrilled about his fiancée swapping spit with a nice-looking man like you, especially with her titties hanging out."

Townsend's mouth flew open.

"Fiancée?" he said.

I gulped.

Will Tressa Jayne Turner please report to the principal's office?

Oh, buddy. Circle the wagons. Here we go again.

Get a Clue

SWEEPSTAKES

Do you have what it takes to be an amateur sleuth?

Then put your investigative skills to the test and win a trip for two to a Mystery Destination!

All you need to do is figure out the Mystery Destination (city & country) and enter your answer at www.dorchesterpub.com/mystery by April 30, 2007. You'll find one clue at the end of the following mystery romances:

REMEMBER THE ALIMONY
by Bethany True

KILLER IN HIGH HEELS
by Gemma Halliday

CALAMITY JAYNE GOES TO COLLEGE
by Kathleen Bacus

Clue #3: Known as the "Pearl of the South" and the "Majestic City," this city is known for its tranquil, white-sand beaches and beauty. You'll have plenty of time for relaxing, swimming, and, of course, reading at this hot vacation destination.